D0838991

The Mobster's Daughter

Rachel Scott McDaniel

ALLY PRESS

"Another impressive, immersive novel from Rachel McDaniel! *The Mobster's Daughter* kept me turning the pages until way past my bedtime, only to find the plot tangling even further—in the best possible sense. The final unraveling and conclusion satisfied in every way. Not only does McDaniel create compelling characters and tension against a richly historical backdrop, but she tells the story in prose that sings. Bravo!"

~Jocelyn Green, Christy
Award-winning author of *Shadows of the White City*

"With mobsters and detectives and innocent damsels stuck between the two, *The Mobster's Daughter* is a glittering example of a Roaring '20s historical romance with a sparkle of suspense. Don't miss your chance to burrow into Pittsburgh's Salvastano crime syndicate and uncover if Kate Chamberlin, aka Catarina Salvastano, is as innocent as she seems or maybe it's the handsome Detective Rhett Jennings who's the threat."

~Janyre Tromp,
author of *Shadows in the Mind's Eye*

To my kids, Drew and Meg.

Chase your dreams fiercely.
And know I love you forever.

CHAPTER 1

Snapping wind yanked at the letter in my hand, and my fingers tightened, the crisp edge biting into my palm. The sharp scrawl on the envelope had faded. The ink on the page within had disappeared in worn creases. But I'd committed every word to memory. The vague phrases and lone coin had revealed a crucial message—he needed me.

An ocean had once separated Papa and I, but according to the attendant at the baggage check, the gap had now narrowed to a mere eight blocks. Stomach rolling as if I was still on the S.S. Colombo, I forced myself to walk farther into the bowels of Pittsburgh. My first glimpse of this city had been back at Union Station. The architecture of the railroad depot mirrored my homeland, with its high ceilings and arched entrances, but the more I progressed into this unfamiliar area, the more my wariness rose.

Smokestacks lined the distance. Their blazoned mouths puffed ashen vapors, charring the atmosphere. The buildings diminished in grandeur and increased in decay. Layered with soot, they stood—some leaned—like wounded tin soldiers blackened with gun powder.

After passing several more streets, the stir of people had thinned. Disturbingly so. I glanced at the dulled street sign, my thoughts tangling like the webbing of trolley cables hovering over me. Had the gentleman manning the shoeshine stand advised me to turn right at Wylie Avenue? His Italian accent proved thicker than his earlobes, and—while Madre Chamberlin had instructed that I only speak English in America—I'd succumbed to my native tongue. The man's brows had risen in surprise, but the camaraderie of a shared language had loosened his hardened mouth, and he'd steered me in the right direction. Or so I hoped.

Muscles still aching from the drugs the doctor had forced down me during my challenging time at sea, I trudged forward for the final two blocks. A man hauling wooden crates packed with glass jugs loomed toward me. He sneered, and I jumped out of his way, my elbow skimming the stone wall framing a cigar shop. I scrunched my nose at the grimy residue on my red sweater. Was all of Pittsburgh this neglected? Or only this sad district? I feared the latter. Which only confirmed my mission in coming here. Papa had fallen on hard times.

Papa.

I eyed the letter in my hand. The last one he'd sent. The reason I'd journeyed so far. Papa had been so consistent in his correspondence over the years, almost religiously so. Then to stop writing me altogether? No, something had to be wrong. Papa never missed one month, let alone four in a row. What if he'd had fallen ill? What if...

My vision blurred, the colorless surroundings fading into each other. I had to get to him. Blood pulsing in my ears, I hastened my steps. A few determined blinks cleared my eyes from biting tears. *Papa is okay.* If not, I would've known. One doesn't lose a sliver of its soul without feeling the devastating ache.

Smoke-filled heavens obscured the sun, blocking any light on this cement jungle, forbidding me from judging the time. Was it nearing six in the evening? Seven? And what about my trunks? In my haste, I'd forgotten to ask the baggage attendant if they'd hold my things until tomorrow. Too late to turn back now.

I rounded the corner, the pace of my feet matching that of my heart. Papa had begun each letter—*To my precious Catarina*—but would he even recognize me now? Would he think I resembled Mamma? The earthquake that had ripped through my village had stolen everything in my world. Today, I'd get a piece back.

A dark automobile rattled through the intersection. The driver caught sight of me and slowed the car. My heart punished my ribs, but I kept moving. The car, now rivaling the pace of a garden snail, crept alongside me. I felt the man's unsettling stare but refused to glance over. Thankfully, I only had one more block to Papa.

The car jolted forward, the shriek of tires jarring my bones. Then as forceful as it lurched, the vehicle braked, stopping cold. The man let out a stream of tobacco which landed dangerously close to my shoes. I couldn't help but peer at him. His weathered face framed eyes colder than the breeze rolling off the Atlantic. His lips curled back in a snarl, and he sped off.

I released a shaky breath. What was going on? Were the locals trained to recognize an intruder? Having been raised by missionaries bent on helping the poverty-stricken, I'd been accustomed to the slums. Could navigate without fear through the beggar-burdened streets. But here? Something was noticeably different. An eeriness settled about me, as if the air itself whispered a complaint against my presence.

Could I claim this place as my new home?

My answer came in the form of painted black letters on a slab of wood.

Salvastano Bakery.

Oh, that familiar name. My heart swelled as if filling with a thousand songs, a lively burst of music purposed only for moments like this. I sailed across the street, my oxfords clicking a joyous cadence against the cobblestone. On the other side, my vision registered the storefront as something crunched beneath my feet.

Glass.

The windows of Papa's bakery had been shattered. The shards strewed across the spit-stained walk. The wooden siding pocked with—I gasped—bullet holes? The address my father had faithfully signed on my letters were skewed on the broken entrance door. Why was his bakery destroyed? My eyes narrowed and peered inside the building. Everything was gutted. Hollowed and broken.

Where was Papa?

A low whistle from behind punctured my thoughts, and I spun on my heel. Two men, mouths curled around cigarettes, stood as if they'd been there all day.

"A little late to be traipsing Rumrunners Row, miss." The gentleman's height intimidated me as his gaze roamed from my wool hat to my weakened knees.

Rumrunners Row? I swallowed and inclined my chin despite the unease weighting my gut. "I'm looking for Hugo Salvastano." Aside from a nervous warble, I pronounced the words to perfection, not a hint of my Italian heritage slipping.

"You and about a million others, sweetheart." The other man with floppy hair took a bold step toward me, something glinting in his granite eyes. "Though a pretty young lady like you shouldn't get mixed up with a murderer."

My fingers flew to my breastbone. Wrong move, considering both men's gaze latched onto my chest. I cleared my throat which sounded as if I'd swallowed the chunks of glass beneath me. Maybe they'd heard me wrong. "Hugo. Hugo Salvastano. He's the one I need to see."

Tall Man sucked air through his teeth and sunk onto a mildewed barrel. He patted his thighs as if beckoning me to plop onto his lap. "How about you tell me why you're seeking a coward who plugged his own brothers and then a cop? Sorry to ruin your little plan of *working* your way into his good graces." Smoke billowed from his cigarette, tangling in the shadows. "You're a pretty little thing, but the Salvastano empire is no longer. Big Dante runs the show now."

My breath stabbed my lungs. What was he talking about? Papa *killed* Uncle Lorenzo? Uncle Pedro? That couldn't be right. But then, why had the bakery been destroyed? Why had his letters stopped coming? I eyed the return address on the envelope in my hand, now aware that he'd never shared the location of his home. I'd assumed the building of his bakery was also where he'd lived, like it'd been back in Spirelli. But one glance at the small storefront revealed otherwise.

Oh, Papa, why the secrets?

Was he running from justice? Were these men—whose faces appeared as honest as Mussolini's speeches—actually telling the truth? Fatigue that had lingered at the shores of my soul came flooding in with the force of an ocean. My eyes struggled to control the rush of moisture, losing the battle when a tear spilled down my cheek.

"Look, Benny, you made the dear cry." Floppy Hair's voice dripped with mock compassion. "Big Dante has room enough for everyone, baby. But you have to start at the lower rungs before climbing your way up." His arms stretched forward, reaching, but I jumped back, smacking my foot off a wooden crate.

This Benny person tossed his cigarette on the ground and stood. "We'll be easy with you." His venom-drenched words pulsed dread in my veins. "Honest."

Caging a scream, I sprinted down the sidewalk in the direction from which I came. Heavy footsteps sounded closer and closer. My gaze darted, searching for a shop, any place, I could duck into. All was closed tight for the evening. I wouldn't make it to the station before they reached me. Rounding the corner, I attempted to catch a glimpse of them over my shoulder, but—

Smack.

The impact dipped my hat over my face, but I could still spy the badge.

il Poliziotto.

I'd collided into a policeman. A rather large one. The attackers halted their steps but didn't retreat. My shoulders heaving and breaths cutting, I slid behind the officer's commanding build.

"Are you giving this lady trouble?" The officer's deep voice held an accusing edge, but to me, the tone was as soothing as Mamma's lullaby, a sense of safety unfurling within me.

"Just trying to show her how things are done around here." Floppy Hair taunted. "And you're interrupting."

His back muscles tensed under his navy uniform. "No, I'm taking over."

"This ain't your territory, Jennings." Benny shoved a finger into the policeman's chest. "Remember what Salvastano did to your Pa."

A small gasp escaped my lips, but none of the men took notice. My rescuer grabbed Benny by his collar and shoved him. The man landed hard on his backside.

The officer—Jennings, was it?—took a commanding step toward the ruffians. "I don't take kindly to threats."

Benny skittered to his feet and tugged Floppy Hair's arm. "Big Dante will hear about this. Mark my words." He released a string of cusses as they both darted off.

The officer's gaze followed them down the road until they disappeared. After several pounding heartbeats, his stare shifted to me. "You shouldn't be here."

The need to hide my appearance had me scrambling for the handkerchief in my pocket and pressing it to my face. Here was hoping my hat obscured the rest. There was no telling if any of my features resembled Papa's and I couldn't take the risk. Those men had claimed Papa had killed this man's father? Plus my uncles?

The officer's massive hand cradled my elbow, but I tugged away.

"Let me escort you home." His voice was noticeably gentler than before. "I wouldn't want Big Dante's men getting ahold of you."

I had nowhere to go. Papa was to be my haven. He was to welcome me with an embrace that bridged the seventeen-year span of our separation. He was to smell of Toscano cigars and home.

A sob sank into my bones. I didn't know what world I'd stepped into, but I wanted out. Away from men who accused my Papa of murder. Away from policemen who could discover my identity and haul me away.

I scrambled from the officer and his questioning blue eyes, hoping beyond hope I'd be able to navigate my way to the station. But what then? It wasn't until I reached the third block without stopping that I realized my empty hands.

I'd dropped my handkerchief and . . . Papa's letter.

CHAPTER 2

9 MONTHS LATER

I stepped back from the microphone, famously dubbed by KDKA broadcasters as 'the tomato can' for its tubular appearance and angled away so the world couldn't catch my sigh. My accent had almost slipped on the second verse of the song, winding my nerves tauter than a violin string.

Feeble moments like those were dangerous. If anyone ever found out that the voice radiating from the radio belonged to Catarina Salvastano—that I was actually the mobster's daughter—I would lose everything.

So Catarina Salvastano had been buried in the grimy cracks of Rumrunners Row and Kate Chamberlin had risen in her place. It had taken some adjusting, but the persona was crucial for survival. Kate Chamberlin, my adopted identity since my first evening here, sounded as native to Pittsburgh as Heinz Ketchup. The American missionary family I'd left behind in Italy wouldn't mind if I borrowed their surname.

I ran my index finger along the beige "monk cloth" inside Studio A and waited for the program director's signal. The velvet-blanketed walls from ceiling to floor proved excellent for acoustics, but not so good for the familiar panic snaking across my chest. While the room boasted the radio transmitter, instruments, microphones, chairs, and two fake plants, the ample space lacked what I needed at the moment— an outside view. My eyes slid shut, and I imagined the horizon. A place where I wasn't closed in. Trapped. Picturing the beautiful scope of the vast Spirelli sky dusted with soft pinks and calming blues, my heart relaxed. My breathing evened.

So much for leaving behind my past.

My eyelids opened to catch Mr. Fleck tugging levers and twisting dials on the transmitter box. With a satisfied nod, he gestured a thumbs up, meaning Studio B had overtaken the broadcast.

"Another solid performance, my friend." Peggy set down the xylophone mallet with a beaming grin. "You make performing to the masses look so simple."

I returned her smile with a more delicate one and collected my folder, even though it hadn't contained the necessary song sheet. How could I have mistakenly placed last week's selection into its leather pockets? And today of all days.

"Did you catch Stella's face when you mastered the final section?"

"No." I'd been too focused on not losing my job. I'd been commissioned with the important task of singing *The Town Hall Waltz* in honor of Manchester, England tuning in. My boss, Frank Conrad, had been testing the shortwave transmitter and informed me there'd be extra listening "guests" for today's performance. Good thing I'd taken the time to memorize the song or I'd be making a fool out of myself in two countries. So no, I didn't have cause to throw glances Stella

Kromer's direction. Though I did wonder why the gossip-peddling secretary sat in on my airtime?

"Her face was more sour than drinking a whole can of pickle juice." Peggy's soft laugh tinkled like the chimes she'd played earlier. "One day she'll be sorry for that silly name she calls you."

Killjoy Kate.

Yet not far from the mark. The more stories I'd heard about Papa's dealings the more my soul crumbled to ash. The fire of life extinguished. I had no desire to carry on frivolous conversations, especially on the topics that consumed Stella's attention. *Men and dance halls.* Besides, the less I talked, the better chance I had of disguising my accent. The better chance of no one making the connection between the Salvastano line and myself.

I pressed my lips together. Papa, who always had a ready smile that punctured his cheek with a deep dimple, was the alleged man responsible for fueling all the stills in Pittsburgh. Under the pretense of the bakery, he'd supplied yeast to the bootleggers, had run a notorious speakeasy. A violator of the prohibition. A murderer of the innocent.

I pushed a stray lock behind my ear, wishing I could tame my thoughts just as easily.

I followed Peggy into the room adjoining the studio, filed the music into the tall cabinet, and exited into the hall. My lungs expanded as I peered out the window. The eighth floor of the Westinghouse plant provided a substantial view of East Pittsburgh.

Murky clouds hovered unvarying in their shade. A severe contrast to Spirelli skies, but I remained still—like usual—taking in the expanse. The other buildings utilized by the engineering empire filled my vision. From whooshes and hisses of the generators to piercing steam whistles, this place buzzed with activity. It was the pioneer in technology. But to me, it'd become my convent. My safety. On the fringe of the Steel City, I was tucked far enough away from the tremors of the Salvastano manhunt, but close enough to hear rumors in case Papa was found.

Peggy nudged my shoulder. "I know who you are."

Those five words gripped me by the throat.

"You're not Killjoy Kate. Never will be." She turned serious hazel eyes on me, her voice emphatic. "You're the giving hand that brings an extra lunch for the janitor. The kind face that smiles at me when I hit a clunker on the bells. That gentle voice that sings to orphans on your days off."

Relief spun through me even as suspicion raised my brow.

Peggy's mascara-caked lashes batted sheepishly. "My uncle delivers ice to St. Paul's orphanage. He told me about you."

The gentle man with the wagon and aged mules was her uncle?

Peggy looped her arm through mine. "You don't talk much, but there's more to you than words. You're all goodness."

I offered a tight-lipped smile. If only Peggy knew about the tainted blood coursing my veins. This façade bred enough deception to fill the Allegheny River. The current of my lies threatening to pull me under at any given moment. I glanced at Peggy's innocent face. Could I confide in my friend? Reveal the devastating truth?

No, I couldn't. And for the same reason I had devised the charade in the first place—because of the danger. Not only was the federal bureau after Papa, but so were the opposing crime lords. There was much to fear about those who ran Pittsburgh's underworld. I'd heard too many stories about how mobsters would target the relations of their rivals. I didn't want to imagine what those gangsters would do to me if they discovered who I was.

The less Peggy knew, the safer she'd be.

"And I can see why you do this every day. You're gazing out at your blessings." Peggy motioned to the window. "It's a great reminder to be thankful for where God put us."

My craving for this view wasn't as noble, considering the need had been birthed from tragedy. A time when death had caged me. I stiffened against a chill and clamped my stare on a sparrow in flight. *Oh, to be as free.*

"It's nice to remember, you know? That even on our rough days, we're part of history." Peggy expelled a dreamy sigh. "This radio thing has really taken off. What if we became famous? Wouldn't that be something?"

That would spoil my goal of becoming invisible. "You'd do well in the spotlight." Peggy had a cheery disposition and didn't have a family of murderers. I allowed myself one more glimpse of the outside world before heading toward the cloakroom.

Peggy placed a hand on my elbow. "So I know that it's a gorgeous day to have lunch outside, but…" A conspiratorial smile split her freckled face. "I have it on good authority that the Casino brought back the fig pudding."

Any other day, I would favor the tranquil courtyard by the library over the congested cafeteria. But fig pudding was the food of angels. My stomach rumbled its agreement. "Casino it is."

We strolled the stretch of hallway, Peggy filling my ear with chatter about some handsome gentleman who attended her church.

Harold Arlin stepped in from the stairwell, his youthful face slightly flushed from the multi-floor climb, his arms loaded with folders and papers. "Nice segment today, ladies." His tone rumbled so rich and deep, it was no wonder his audience regarded him as the 'Voice of America'. Harold's gaze bounced between us until settling on me. "I overheard the boss singing your praises in his office to good ole H.P. Davis. How you single-handedly saved the station last week."

A slight smile curved my mouth. Frank never missed an opportunity to brag about me to the vice president of Westinghouse. The man had his doubts when Frank had hired me—upon the insistence of his wife—as Frank's personal secretary without any references. My typing had been adequate, my organizational skills even better, but it wasn't until Frank happened upon me singing at my desk that things had turned in my favor. When I'd admitted I could play piano, too, he'd given me a position as a KDKA musician. "I didn't do much. Just sang a song."

Peggy chuckled, blonde curls dancing on slender shoulders. "Harold, you should know by now that Kate dismisses every compliment thrown at her."

"Doesn't change the truth though." He gave a friendly wink. "She sings much better than Greer Donnelly any day of the week."

I bit back a laugh. Everyone knew Miss Donnelly was one of the most sought out singers in the country, possibly the world. But her popularity instantly declined among Westinghouse workers—especially for Harold—when she hadn't appeared for her interview with him. The place had fallen into chaos. With no one else having anything prepared, I had stepped in.

"Before I forget, this is for you." Harold shuffled the paperwork until he could balance the stack on one hand and offer me an envelope with the other. "It was left in your broadcasting mailbox. Your first fan mail, maybe?" His mouth stretched into his signature grin. "No writing on it. Makes me think your admirer is someone from the inside."

Peggy giggled and my brow scrunched. All I had done was fill in the vacant slot by singing the lullaby Mamma sang over me so many nights. The same gentle melody I'd clung to while trapped under debris those many years ago. The soothing words that'd echoed in my soul my first night in Pittsburgh when I'd returned to the train station only to encounter my boss's wife. I would always be grateful to Flora Conrad for seeing more in me than a sobbing heap on the depot bench.

Peggy peeked over her shoulder at Harold's retreating form into Studio A, and then at the letter. "You know what that is, don't you? I bet you that's from Robert Fuller." She waggled her brows, and heat crept up my neck. "The poor sound man has been making moony eyes at you for weeks. He nearly dropped the microphone stand on my foot last Tuesday when you strode into the room."

"I'm sure he's not interested." I had done my best to make my appearance as unimpressive as possible. As if stepping into the role of Killjoy Kate, I'd routinely dressed in bland, saggy clothes. The rising trend for hairstyle was the bob, chic and just below the chin. I piled my dark locks behind my head in a boring, fat bun. "There's no name on this. It could've been slipped into my box by mistake." I'd never received anything unmarked before. If it was from my KDKA superiors, it would boast the stamped letterhead and not be concealed in a blank envelope.

"Aren't you gonna open it?" Peggy pulled ajar the stairwell door and regarded me with a saucy grin. "If it's not Robert addressing his undying affection for you, I'll buy you fig pudding for a week."

Pulse humming, I broke the envelope's seal. I eased out the paper, but it was blank as well. Odd. I unfolded it, and a card slipped out, falling onto the cement stairwell landing.

I retrieved it and peered at the single marking—a red capitol "S". The top half of the letter morphed into a snake.

Peggy's gasp echoed off the block walls, and she leapt back as if the ink serpent was real. "The Salvastano snake."

Salvastano? I blinked at the card in my hand.

Surely, Papa wouldn't send this. How could he? He didn't even know I was in Pittsburgh.

"Oh dear. Oh dear." Peggy fanned her pale face. "I've heard of it but never seen one with my own eyes."

I placed a hand on Peggy's arm. "What are you talking about?"

"This is known around Pittsburgh as *The S Threat*." Her nervous eyes rounded. "Receiving that card is a death sentence."

CHAPTER 3

If Hugo Salvastano lingered anywhere in the vicinity of the Westinghouse plant, Rhett Jennings would find him. And Lord help Rhett when he did.

Sadly, the fallen crime boss held the advantage. The trolley ride from Rhett's office on Forbes Avenue to East Pittsburgh had taken a punishing hour, granting the fugitive plenty of time for an escape. Rhett had checked the main building and its flanking surroundings, but he hadn't nearly covered the vast perimeter. The plant stood on forty acres with multiple workshops. Hugo could be anywhere, and the longer Rhett sat in the office of Frank Conrad, the narrower his chance of snaring the man who'd murdered his father became.

"I trust I did the right thing." Conrad rested his elbows on his desk and steepled his fingers. Grayed temples gave an air of refinement, while a steely jaw revealed an edge of gruffness. An effective combination for the man overseeing the KDKA station who also served as a chief engineer for the powerhouse corporation. "She wouldn't let me inform the police. So I called you."

She?

Rhett's grip tightened on the arms of his chair, his right thumb pressing into the decorative brass rivet. Why had he been under the impression that the young broadcaster in question had been a man? This could complicate things.

"Your name came up at a party I attended not too long ago. A woman by the name of Ruth Talbert spoke well of your admirable qualities. Said you're the best investigator in all of Pittsburgh."

Rhett hadn't seen Miss Talbert since she ended things with his longtime friend Major Ford, but he was thankful for her praise. "You made the right choice, sir. Not only am I the leading private detective in the area, but I'm dedicated to the Salvastano cases." Since when had he become a blasted salesman? Of his own services nonetheless? He pulled his hat from his head and capped it on his bent knee. "I'm sure you're aware of my personal involvement."

Conrad gave a solemn nod. "Commissioner Jennings was a good man. I'm sorry for your loss."

Rhett swallowed the familiar ache and forced his thoughts on the situation before him. An "S" card. A young woman. And a vile killer who'd seemed to disappear into the haze of oblivion like vapors from the neighboring smokestacks. "May I ask how many people know about this?"

"Not many." Conrad reached for his coffee, the recognizable aroma announcing its contents also included chicory root. "Why?" He took a sip, eyeing Rhett over the mug's ceramic rim.

"If this news gets out, you'll have chaos on your hands." Being supervisor of the most favored news outlet in the region, Conrad would know all too well about the popularity of anything connected to the Salvastano camp. How even the mention of the villain could stir the masses to purchase radios—created by this very plant—in order to learn the latest gossip.

Coincidence?

Rhett shifted in his seat, the holster of his pistol digging into his side. Could this all be a ploy by Westinghouse? A gimmick to fatten their already wealthy pockets? How easy it'd be to attract the public's eye by *uncovering* the latest clue in the Savastano search. By manipulating one of their own broadcasters to play along. No doubt this young woman would be a dozen notches above beautiful and well-groomed for her flicker of time in the spotlight. How far would they go to turn a sale?

Rhett studied the man behind the desk. Conrad's appearance was no-nonsense and stiff, from his starched collar to his perfectly centered tie knot. Even his cuff links were simple but polished. Though just because the chief engineer's exterior was strait-laced by no means meant his inner motives weren't skewed and angled for gluttonous gain. Rhett had seen too much to be fooled. "Do you have a newer kind of radio releasing soon?"

His mouth twitched. "We do actually. The team's been working on a model that increases amplification." He set down his mug and regarded Rhett with an impassive expression. "But I won't distract you with details about something unrelated to your purpose here."

"Are you certain it's *unrelated?*" Granted, he didn't know Conrad well, but he was familiar with the greed that seemed to be the native trait to those dwelling on this charred scrap of land known to outsiders as Pittsburgh. To him, it was nothing but a smoky wasteland. A city that'd become rich during the Great War. Wealth stuffed its soot-crusted borders while the rest had been cheated—robbed of spirit, of life, of everything that'd been held dear. And it hadn't stopped there.

The dark edges of his soul yawned wider, but he refused to feed the emptiness any longer.

"That's quite the question, Detective." Conrad's words yanked Rhett back to the present.

He shrugged. "I didn't achieve anything by taking life at face value." A mutual approach, considering life hadn't given Rhett any slack from day one.

"Me neither." A smile cracked the older man's face as if Rhett had passed an unvoiced challenge. "And to avoid any misunderstanding, I expect the entire investigation to remain a secret."

Ah, maybe this one was honest yet. Though trust was to be earned and not given. "So we're agreed the discovery of the 'S' card won't be featured on your news hour?"

"Keep it all confidential, Jennings."

"Good." Rhett slapped his hat on his head, pushed on the armrests to stand, but froze mid-rise. "Is this broadcaster by some chance married?"

"No."

"Engaged? Or anything of that nature?"

"Not that I know of."

He sunk back onto the chair. "Do you understand *all* the risks that need taken to avoid being exposed?"

Conrad flicked a wary glance at the door behind Rhett as if suspecting someone to intrude on their conversation. "I'll do everything within my power to keep things quiet. You do what it takes to do the same on your end."

Rhett withheld a groan. This case was going to cost him. But if it resulted in Hugo wearing a prison gray uniform and a one-way train ticket out of Pittsburgh tucked into Rhett's vest pocket, then he'd consider the grievances worthwhile.

"Conduct this investigation on your terms, but ..." Conrad's glance flitted to the side wall. Rhett could tell the man wasn't admiring the dulled plaques or framed, fancy-lettered certificates, but rather weighting his words. "I expect you to treat Miss Chamberlin with the respect she deserves."

So Rhett's professional reputation wasn't all this man was aware of. "I was raised to treat everyone with respect." And his parents couldn't be blamed for any of Rhett's wayward decisions. His rebellious blood hadn't come from either of them. He tipped the brim of his hat and stood. "Perhaps I can investigate some more and then chat with the lady."

With a grimace, Conrad looked at his pocket watch and then focused dark eyes on Rhett. "I won't tell you how to do your job, but I suggest talking to Miss Chamberlin first. Seeing that she'll be going home soon and has no idea I called you."

"But you told me—"

"I said she wouldn't let me phone the police. I took it upon myself to contact you."

Couldn't fault the dame for not calling the cops. At one point, the Salvastanos had the majority of the Pittsburgh police department under their dirty thumb. If the officers still bore the grimy residue from the crime family's substantial bribes, then loyalty went to the goons instead of the badge. Which was why Rhett had tossed his own in the garbage, ending his sorry career as a civil servant. "Where is she?"

"KDKA Archives. On the third floor. I sent her there with a sizeable stack of transmitter data to file."

"Alone?"

"She's convinced there's been a mistake. She doesn't think she's in any danger." Deep grooves bracketed his down-turned mouth. "I've heard rumors about the *Salvastano S threat*, but I want to hear it from you. How serious is this?"

"The only time I've ever seen those cards were on dead bodies." His own father's included. "So it's a noted victory Miss Chamberlin is still breathing." A tight band stretched between his shoulder blades. "Now if you'll excuse me, I should locate her." He turned on his heel and strode toward the door.

"Jennings." The older man's voice strained, causing Rhett's hand to pause on the brass knob. "I'll cover every fee. Just keep Kate safe."

Her name was Kate. Kate Chamberlin. He acknowledged Conrad with a dip of his chin and went in search of the woman he was now responsible for keeping alive.

Who'd have thought Rhett's next clue would surface out here? Amidst the bustle of the Westinghouse plant? For over nine months, Hugo Salvastano had been silent. No trace. No evidence of his whereabouts. So why—after lying dormant all this time—would the man emerge from hiding to threaten a KDKA broadcaster? Would her name join the others on that sliver of paper tucked in Rhett's ledger? The Salvastano murder list?

Rhett ground his jaw. Not if he could help it.

Finding his destination proved easier than expected, seeing that it was directly across from the stairway. For being such an expansive building, the archive room seemed the size of a broom closet. Kate Chamberlin—he presumed—was bent over a crate, leafing through the contents within.

Her gaze so absorbed in her work, she didn't notice him standing in the doorway. He took in her dirt-colored dress, which not only faded into the dim surroundings, but hung on her pointed shoulders like it was two sizes too large. Her hair, pulled into a snug bun on the back of her head, would prompt him to question her age if it weren't for its rich dark shade set against a smooth complexion. She slid some papers into the crate, then straightened. She pinned the remaining sheets under her arm and stretched for the box on the top shelf.

Rhett stepped forward. "Can I get that for you?"

She yelped and skittered back. Papers voyaged through the air like tiny white sails, settling around them. Her panicked gaze pierced him, and recognition hit like a smack upside the head.

Those eyes. Brown and scared. He'd glimpsed them before. But from where? "Sorry to startle you, Miss Chamberlin. Your boss told me I'd find you here."

She blinked once. Twice. If her lashes fluttered again, Rhett would offer his handkerchief. No doubt cinders and who knew what else clung to the air. Even now the piercing screech of metal slicing metal from somewhere close by scraped his ears, probably launching more particles into the atmosphere.

"My name's Detective Jennings." He removed his hat and held it over his heart. "Dr. Conrad hired me to investigate what happened today."

Her shoulders spiked with a sharp intake of air.

Interesting. Rhett hadn't expected her to sigh in relief, but he also hadn't anticipated her growing more agitated. Although she'd quite the disturbance to her day with finding the "S" card. And him frightening her probably wasn't the most gallant forms of introductions.

He hazarded another step into the cramped space, shirking to avoid the low-hanging electric lamp, and offered a warm smile which only made her eyes widen. "You seem familiar. Have I had the pleasure of meeting you before today?"

She crouched and scrambled to collect the papers as if any second they'd be carried away by a wind gust. Rhett replaced his hat and joined her, gathering the ones to his right. He extended his meager stack to her. Her hand brushed his, her fingers warm but trembling.

Why so skittish? Conrad had said she wasn't afraid, but her actions declared otherwise. They both straightened.

"Thank you for your concern." Her gaze landed somewhere on his tie. "But this has all been a mistake." She plucked a few papers from the stack and shoved them into the closest box.

He popped a shoulder against the wooden shelving and crossed his arms. "Are you the one who received the S card?"

Her sigh fluttered the lace on her high collar—buttoned so tight around her slender neck it was a wonder if she could get a full breath. "Yes."

"May I see it? Do you have it with you?"

Her chin snapped up, the paperwork forgotten. She opened her mouth, then clamped it shut. A grimace cemented firmly on her full lips, she retrieved a plain, black purse from the table behind her. She fished out the card, and with eyes flooded with uncertainty, handed it to him.

The crimson "S" stained the ivory square, the top portion of the letter fashioned into a snake, complete with beady eyes and a forked tongue. The markings were identical to the cards he'd seen before, to the one he had in his wallet. Rhett and his fellow officers hadn't been able to determine if the victims had received the single letter notes before they'd been murdered or if the cards had been planted on them afterward. If it was the former, his father had never said anything about the threat. If the latter, then it was remarkable Miss Chamberlin still drew air. "Have you received one of these before?"

"No." Her averted eye contact hinted at shyness, but wasn't she a broadcaster? She performed for masses yet shrank in his presence?

Well, there went his thirsty-for-the-spotlight theory. Unless…she excelled in performing and was playing him for a fool. But what would be her motive in that? Questions knotted his brain, making his temple throb against his hatband. *One stride at a time, Jennings.* And the first step would be explaining to her the severity of the card and his plan for keeping things hidden from suspicious eyes. "How did this card get into your possession?"

"It was in my mailbox."

"Only the card? Was there a note with it?"

She shook her head.

"So your name wasn't on it?"

"No. There wasn't any writing at all."

He turned the card over to check her claims.

"See, a mistake. Nothing to fuss over." She turned from him and strained for the crate she'd attempted to retrieve earlier. Her fingertips nudged the edge of the pine container, and it wobbled from the high position. Rhett reached past her, barring the lady between his outstretched arms, and grasped it. The box was light enough for him to raise over her head and step back. Away from her rigid frame and her rose-scented hair. He lowered the crate onto the floor and Miss Chamberlin faced him, her thick-fringed lashes framing wary eyes.

Her hand—which had been clutching the papers to her breastbone—wilted to her side. She took in the visible creases in the once-pristine sheets, and her chin sagged in defeat.

"Maybe ask your boss to invest in a stool."

Her eyes narrowed ever so slightly then eased. "Thank you for your help." Dismissal registered again in her tone.

"Anytime." He smiled, and she answered with a stiff set brow hovering over a cautious glare.

Pressure built in his chest. Was he ready for this? The brilliant strategy he'd devised in Conrad's office now seemed an impossible endeavor—not only would Miss Chamberlin have to cooperate to the fullest, but it now appeared he'd have to coach her if their ploy was to be believable. He probably should inform her of what to expect, and this storage room offered the privacy needed to—

"Now if you'll excuse me. I have to finish this." She blurted, then refaced the tall shelves.

"How about I help?" He stepped beside her and could've sworn he heard a muffled sigh. "We can chat while we work and then I can see you home."

She paled. "Oh, that's not necess—"

"You intrigue me, Miss Chamberlin. But what I find the most interesting is what you're *not* telling me. Like the connection you have with the Salvastano family."

CHAPTER 4

I pulled in a scrape of air and willed my knees not to tremble. All the emotions of my first night in Pittsburgh swarmed my mind with the sting of a host of wasps. *Jennings.* The man in the alley. My rescuer. But he was also the son of the late police commissioner whose blood stained the very hands that had once cradled mine.

Of all the private investigators in the city, why had Frank chosen this one? Had the detective recognized me as I did him?

I stole a glance at the crate to my left. Of course the detective would happen upon me as I was searching retired transcripts of broadcasts about Papa. Guilt finger-poked my heart. I shouldn't be hunting for clues while I was supposed to be filing data, but any information from older interviews and newsbreaks could help me prove my father's innocence. If, indeed, he was.

Thankfully the papers I'd hastily shoved into the box were tucked out of sight. Though I couldn't experience any relief because I faced a bigger problem, and it stood about six-foot-two with a face of a silent film star. "What makes you think I'm connected to the Salvastanos?" I worked to keep my tone even, but my pulse thrummed louder than the area's rolling mills.

"It seems the likely conclusion, given this." Mouth flattened into a thin slash, he raised the card which looked flimsy pinched between his thick fingers.

The "S".

The same initial I'd scripted for the past two decades glared at me, except now it'd been twisted into evil. The serpentine eyes taunted as if it knew my secret. Though someone out there did. Papa? But how? I'd never informed him I was crossing the Atlantic. And I had no success in finding him these past nine months.

My gaze lowered to the remaining papers I clutched, the data sheets listing the locations across the country where my voice had traveled. Had he heard one of my broadcasts? Hope warred with anxiety, tightening my every muscle. But then … even if Papa had listened, how would he recognize me? The last time we'd spoken was on the shores in Naples, when I'd been six and heartbroken.

Sii forte, il mio topo. Be strong, my mouse.

Yet I no longer bore any semblance to his parting words. Time had been both foe and friend—crippling my withered courage while maturing my pitch that had once matched the squeak of a rodent. But if Papa hadn't sent the card, then who? Was another person aware of my identity?

I raised my lashes and almost flinched at the intensity of the detective's questioning stare. How long had it been since he'd spoken? Seconds? Minutes? I focused on my forthcoming words, lest my accent expose me. "I don't understand, Detective. Why would someone threaten me?"

"It's my job to find out." He slid the card into his pocket and locked his gaze on me, his piercing blue eyes the same shade as Spirelli skies. How easy it'd be to gaze into them were they not brimming with suspicion. "I'll need your cooperation. To keep you safe, I need to remain close."

My freehand gripped the wooden shelving. "I-Is that necessary?"

"It is."

How could two tiny words deliver such a massive punch? I dug my fingers into the pine plank, uncaring if splinters poked beneath my nails. I needed to find a way out of this.

If he noticed my hesitation, he didn't acknowledge it. "We need to discuss your role in this investigation. I realize what I'm about to say may be a lot to ask, but there's a risk involved otherwise."

What did he mean? What could he possibly demand from me? Dizziness pressed into my skull.

He took a step toward me, and the room shrank in size, the walls closing in, my chest constricting.

Not now.

Not when I needed to be composed and confident. My childhood phobia had never been charitable, but bullying me twice in one workday? Tremors shot through me, threatening to take me down, meanwhile the detective stood tall and noble like the column of Marcus Aurelius.

What strength I had carried me out the door to the safety of the open hallway. My lungs expanded with a much-needed breath.

Heavy footsteps sounded behind me.

Soon the detective was at my side. "Are you all right, Miss Chamberlin?"

"I dislike … cramped rooms." Which was why I'd always made a point to finish my task as soon as possible and get out of there. Yet today I'd been foolish and lingered longer to scour the transcripts.

He nodded, but his lowered brow displayed his confusion.

Not like I expected him to understand what no one else ever could. Even my guardians had struggled comprehending the trapped feeling that gripped me with the ferocity of a constrictor. At least boas showed mercy in killing their prey. This phobia paralyzed me for the duration of its attack, then embalmed me in shame.

"Now about the Salvastanos." The detective straightened his hat on his head with a determined expression. "If you could tell me why—"

"Oh, Kate?" The grate of Stella's sing-song voice could rival any mechanic's clanking. She emerged from the stairwell with a syrupy smirk. The click of her heels lent a chipper cadence until her gaze landed on the detective, her steps slowing and grin spreading. "Rhett? What are you doing here?"

"Good afternoon, Miss Kromer."

The secretary's tinkling laugh muffled my groan. "I don't remember you being this formal at Johnson's. Say, it's been awhile since I've seen you there."

Johnson's. The popular dance hall on Fifth Avenue.

The detective's sleek pinstriped suit and twinkling eyes complemented Stella's ruby dropped-waist dress and glossy blonde locks, making them a striking pair. Then there was me, with my faded garb and dull…well, everything. I was like the dim void between two glittering stars. Not much to hang a gaze on, but I preferred it that way. Stella could shine as bright as she wanted, while I clung to the shadows.

Stella finally spared me a glance. "I've been sent to relieve you." Her attention drifted back to the detective, her smile as sleek as her red-painted lips. "I'm sure I can take it from here." Her sultry tone revealed her words had nothing to do with filing broadcasting data.

"Excuse me a moment." I stepped back into the archive room and retrieved my bag. Was Detective Jennings serious about walking me home? My ankles threatened to cave. I needed an excuse. One that would deter him and his probing questions. I returned to the hall to find Stella and the detective talking about the recent spells of rain. Maybe my plainness would work in my favor. For who would want to spend time with boring Kate Chamberlin when the exciting Stella Kromer was within reach?

I handed over the wrinkled papers, earning a raised brow from Stella. "I had a small mishap."

Detective Jennings aimed his lopsided smirk at me. "All my fault. I shouldn't have surprised you, Kate."

I couldn't determine what was odder—the fact he'd called me by my first name after such a short acquaintance, or the familiarity in his tone implying we were longtime friends.

"Now that Miss Kromer is here, we should be on our way, sweetheart." The detective's arm curled around my waist, his warm fingers pressing against my side.

My shocked gaze collided with his. No doubt my eyes betrayed my disapproval, but his seemed steady and penetrating as if trying to communicate some hidden message. After a few staccato heartbeats, he released his gentle grip and tossed me a wink.

"Sweetheart?" Stella's reedy voice reminded me of her presence.

Rhett shot Stella an affirming look and then faced me with a suspiciously fond smile. "I know we promised to wait longer before publicly announcing our relationship, but you know I'm not one for playing by the rules." He wove his fingers into mine, and I yanked my hand away, hugging it to my chest.

Had the man gone mad? Or . . . maybe I had. Perhaps my own mind had betrayed me to a point of imagining this bizarre day. Soon I'd awaken to reason—to a place where "S" cards never existed and handsome investigators never invaded my safe haven.

Or not.

Because the detective's spicy cologne teased my senses, proving my current circumstances were depressingly genuine. I had no idea what kind of game he was playing, but I wanted no part of it. There was already enough deception in my life.

"Please don't be cross, Kate." He looked at me with a tenderness that made heat forge up my spine. "Trust me, it's *best* that everyone knows we're a couple."

The shadow of confusion gave way to a sliver of understanding, like light filtering through a crack in a door. Yet I still felt in the dark. Why would this man think it was best to pretend to be my beau? And to ask me to *trust* him when I'd only known him a short while?

I glanced at Stella, whose face was void of color. Skin bunched around her narrowed eyes, her gaze bouncing between us before settling on Detective Jennings. "You?" She sharpened her focus on me. "And her? Are ..."

"Going to be late for our dinner reservations." He finished for her, but I hardly suspected Stella was questioning our impending meal arrangements. But I sure was. Along with everything else.

"Nice seeing you again, Miss Kromer." He tipped his hat to a stunned Stella and placed his hand on my lower back, coaxing me forward.

Despite the numbness coursing through me, I obeyed, if only to leave Stella's scrutiny and demand the detective's explanation.

We passed through the corridor and into the stairwell. I glanced over my shoulder, making certain no one else was near, then faced the man who'd managed to rattle my composure in the course of ten minutes. "What are you doing?"

He shrugged. "Protecting you."

"I don't understand." I pulled in a deep breath and exhaled slow. No matter how my insides quaked, I couldn't get flustered. My accent would surface and then I would be the one having to explain. "You only made things worse. Stella is the biggest gossip."

"Exactly."

Did this man not realize what he'd done? Not only would I have to dodge Stella's interrogations tomorrow but all the people that woman would prattle to. This plant could produce radios and generators in record time, but rumors manufactured just as quickly. There went my prized plan of living unnoticed. "You placed me in the line of fire, is that your idea of protection, Detective?"

"Call me Rhett."

That wasn't an answer. But if he skirted my questions, then that gave me an open invitation to do likewise.

We reached the stairs, and I doubted my rubber legs could manage the three-story descent. I cut a look to the paint-chipped walls. Usually the confined stairways hadn't bothered me, but having fallen prey to two panic attacks, I didn't want to risk a third.

I gripped the railing.

"Wait a moment, Kate. Let's talk here for a second."

"Not now." I hadn't been this weak since my first night in Pittsburgh. I'd survived that, and I would this day as well. With a steadying breath, I made my way down the flights of steps, ignoring the man beside me.

Once on the ground floor, I grasped the brass knob of the exit, but the detective placed a large hand on the door, stilling it. I'd told him I didn't like cramped spaces, and he was keeping me trapped.

Thankfully, there was a modest seating area to my left that boasted a small window. I stole a glance out, gathering scraps of strength.

"Look." He pulled his hand from the door and cupped my shoulder, my cotton sleeve a lousy barrier between me and his touch. "I need to be blunt. I'm going to be around you a lot over the following days. Maybe weeks. Stella knows I'm an investigator. She's sure to ask questions. So I thought it wise to throw her off track by telling her I'm carrying a torch for you."

Carrying a torch? Another American expression I hadn't heard. Though recalling the conversation moments ago, the turn of phrase must mean adoration or something along those lines.

The detective blew out a noisy breath, misreading my confusion. "Do you understand what could happen if word gets out about the "S" card? If the papers got ahold of this?"

I couldn't bear the thought.

"This is the first fresh news about Hugo Salvastano in months." He held my gaze. "They would be all over you like a Doberman on a steak. And just as relentless. They'll follow you, bombard you with questions, and no doubt invent crazy rumors about you."

I winced.

"My thoughts exactly. It wouldn't be pretty. I want to conduct this investigation in peace. And if that means acting as your beau, then so be it." He tacked on a smile, but it wasn't convincing, proving he didn't want to play this ruse any more than I did. "So what will it be, Kate?"

I took in the man before me and glimpsed more than the silvery flecks in his azure gaze. The blues of his eyes were troubled, like a storm over the ocean. My heart squeezed in response.

Could I do this? Assume the role of yet another lie? I faced the same choice presented me nine months ago—adopt the facade or run away? The exact answer came in a lone word—survival. Any limelight on me could attract crime bosses like Big Dante, bootleggers, and any other criminal searching for Papa. I'd don a thousand masks to keep the world from viewing my true face.

He must've detected my wavering, for he offered another smile, a genuine one, but it soon slipped into a grimace. "I should've been more direct with you." His jaw locked tight for a long second as if reluctant to free the words. "Hugo Salvastano, the man I believe gave you that card, is also is suspected of killing … my father."

The caged breath leaked from my lungs. "I'm truly sorry." He couldn't know the depths of my whispered words. Nor the immense truth in them. I'd been handed a rare opportunity to apologize on behalf of my family, one that had wronged his.

Though no words could console the anguish I knew he felt. For I'd experienced that agony. My family had been ripped away in a span of seventy seconds. One buried in Spirelli soil and the other a ghost of what he'd used to be. The Papa I'd known had died that awful day and, if the rumors were true, a monster had assumed his place.

Except for the letters. How could I reason away the kindness and love in the crooked strokes of ink?

"There's never been a more excellent man. If only I could have prevented it." His chin raised, and I saw it—the past tormented him.

Just like it haunted me.

"So you see, this is more than another case. It's personal."

It was more personal than he realized. How would he respond if he knew the truth? That he offered help to, schemed a pretend relationship with, his enemy's daughter.

Though in one conversation he'd managed to target my weakness—compassion. The irksome sensitivity of my heart which had caused me to cross an ocean despite my fears. Caused me to remain in a city that was in a constant hunt for the man who'd fathered me. Caused me to acknowledge the man before me with a softening sigh.

"So are we a team?"

The irony was not lost on me. The offspring of rivals joining forces. Yet only I knew the stakes. "It appears there's no other alternative." Maybe if I cooperated in a minor way, I could gain some major information concerning Papa. "What's my part in this?"

"I'll do all the investigating. You answer my questions and pretend to be hopelessly head over heels for me." His rogue smirk now unleashed, lingering on the dangerous side of handsome, making me wonder if I'd made the right choice.

"Follow my lead." He offered his arm, and I reluctantly slipped my hand through the crook of his elbow. "And remember, we're madly in love."

CHAPTER 5

"That's an awful idea."

Peggy's voice seemed amplified in the narrow cloakroom, making me wish I'd chosen a more secluded place to tell my friend about the detective's plan. Said man remained in the hall, guarding the door, ensuring our privacy. Since Peggy was the only other person aware of today's events, it was necessary to let her in on the ploy. I had assumed she'd be tickled at the notion. My fellow broadcaster took to matchmaking with all the devotion of an athlete in a professional sport. But Peggy's flustered plump face and narrowed gaze revealed her disapproval.

I grabbed my wool hat from the rack and secured it on my head. "It could be worse." I'd rather embrace a fake romance with Rhett Jennings and remain hidden from the public than have word get out and merciless men like Big Dante hear about it. Yet being in the detective's constant presence held its own risks. Prisoning a sigh, I peeled my light coat from the hanger, slid it on, and knotted the belt. "It's important you go along with this."

"I can't." Peggy shook her head so hard the tassel on her turban smacked her eyelid. "And neither should you."

"I have to." I tried to sound convincing, but my tone fell flatter and thinner than a Victrola record. "You were the one who told me the dangers about the "S" card. By pretending, no one will ask questions why Detective Jennings is always around me."

Peggy tugged on her fringe cape and tied the strings at the base of her neck. "You don't want to do this. I can tell."

My arms wilted to my sides. "No, it's not the ideal situation. But I don't want the extra attention this could bring about." Though how could I act in love when I'd never experienced such emotion?

"I understand." Her tone softened. "I'm concerned because you don't know Detective Jennings's character. The man is like a Steel City Casanova."

Not surprising. Stella couldn't have been more awestruck than if he were Calvin Coolidge. That was, until the man had fibbed about our false relationship. Then her admiration had melted into abject shock.

Peggy glanced toward the door, lips peeling back from her teeth in disgust as if she saw a spider. "His former landlady used to go to my parent's Bible study and every week she'd ask for prayer for him. She said the man brought home a different lady every week."

How could I judge him for his sins, when my family was known for much worse? "He's been completely professional. And I can assure you, he's not interested in me."

Peggy clucked her tongue three times. "Your dated and over-sized wardrobe can't mask your prettiness. But ..." She centered my belt with a maternal expression. "Perhaps you're right. Men like him are superficial. I never thought I'd be thankful for your poor fashion sense."

I smiled at the insulting compliment. After all, I knew more than anyone how bland I appeared. My colorful and stylish gowns collected dust in the back of my closet as I donned the bleak clothes that made me fade into my surroundings. "It will turn out all right, Peggy."

Though my twisting gut said otherwise.

Rhett's arm stretched along the yellowed back of the wooden trolley bench. He brushed Kate's shoulder, and she wriggled so far forward he was certain any good bump would catapult her into the seat in front of them.

A smirk played on his lips, but all amusement fled at the remembrance of the situation. Kate hadn't the luxury of acting repulsed by him, or his touch. The success of this case—and more importantly, her safety—depended on her cooperation. The world couldn't know the famous "S" card had landed in her mailbox.

Yes, it'd be less complicated for him to do his job without becoming a false Romeo, but it was for the lady's sake. And his own. He'd had enough press attention after his father's death. And maybe if he had free reign to investigate Kate's life, routine, and hangouts, he could determine why she'd received the threat. Gain ground in the search for the phantom crime boss.

His business partner had lamented about how valuable nabbing Hugo would be for boosting their detective agency, but Rhett's motives surpassed that. He'd finally get closure, freedom, and perhaps a decent night's rest away from the chaos of his mind. And if Rhett had to pose as the smitten beau for the sake of this case, he'd give it his all. Though he couldn't say the same for Kate, who right now—with her closed posture and down-turned mouth—appeared as affectionate as his partially-bald cat. At least Kate hadn't hissed at him. Yet.

He flicked a glance over and caught her staring at him. She averted her eyes and melted against the trolley's inside wall, putting as much distance as she could between them, gluing her attention out the smudged window.

A groan rumbled his chest. He scanned the tight space, studying the various passengers. Seven more people had boarded at the last stop, filling the cable car half-full. Rhett had made certain no one had followed them and had remained watchful. Nothing had been out of the ordinary, no fugitive mobster ducking between seats and waiting to massacre. Just the standard folk, commuting to the small steel town of Braddock, where Kate's apartment was evidently located.

He leaned closer to his pretend-sweetheart and kept a low tone. "Think Miss Whitmore will go along with our plan?"

She jolted at his voice.

"Forget about me already?"

Her teeth sunk into her full lower lip and she gave a slight nod of the head. "She agreed to." Her eyes met his. "Though she was a bit hard to persuade."

Miss Peggy Whitmore wasn't the only one. Rhett had overheard the conversation, and while Kate had said all the right words, she hadn't sounded too convinced in her own argument. Her backward actions since then only reinforced Rhett's assumptions. As for Miss Whitmore, her condemning remarks about his past had burned into his skin. Though what had she said that wasn't true? No one was more acquainted with his mistakes than himself.

The trolley braked at their stop. Rhett stepped off first, scanned the area, then helped Kate down the lofty step and onto the dusty walk. Even though Braddock was ten miles from Pittsburgh, Rhett never had cause to visit the mill-driven town. Immigrants flocked to work at the massive steel plant, visible from where Rhett stood.

He shot a glance behind him.

All clear.

"Where to?"

Kate inclined her head to the left. "My apartment's only a few blocks that way."

"I believe I owe you dinner first."

Her eyes widened. "Oh, that's not necessary. I'm not at all hungry." The early May breeze danced upon her collar and played in the wisps of her dark brown hair. "I appreciate all your concern, but I can manage from here, Detective."

"Call me Rhett. Remember?"

Her lips puckered into a perfect O. "Sorry. I'm still not used to the idea of ..." She motioned between them.

"I know this day has thrown your world off-kilter." They started walking in the direction she'd indicated. "But I'm going to do everything I can to get things back to normal for you." Though he wasn't sure how since his own Earth had spun off its axis the day his father had breathed his last. Or ... maybe even sooner than that. He pushed the shadowy thoughts back into the dark corners of his mind. "So let's get some matters out of the way. Tell me, what do you know of Hugo Salvastano?"

Her step hitched on the uneven sidewalk, but she caught herself. "I've read about the ... um ... killings in the Gazette." She stilled, and her shoulders lowered with a delicate exhale. "I'm sorry about what happened to your father."

Sympathy laced her voice, but it was her movements that gave him pause. Skittish. Was she uncomfortable around men in general or

The Mobster's Daughter

was there more to Kate Chamberlin than intriguing brown eyes and fidgety mannerisms?

He received the condolences in his usual manner, with a tight nod. "What time is your shift at KDKA?"

"Why?"

"Because I'm going to walk you from your place to the station and then home again until this case is solved." Hadn't they gone over this already? Granted, the woman had a lot to process over the past few hours.

A handful of men staggered out of an unmarked building ahead. The clashing of their cackles and shouts told Rhett all he needed to know. "That's a gin joint."

She nodded.

How often had Kate been forced to walk by this place alone? Every day it seemed. The early twilight sky elongated her shadow on the sidewalk, but Kate couldn't be taller than five-foot-three, four at the most. Would she be able to defend herself should one of these men act obscene?

The pungent stench of liquor and unwashed bodies became stronger as they approached. A lanky fellow, with untucked shirttails, hooked his gaze on Kate and swept her form with a lazy perusal. Rhett instinctively settled his hand on her lower back, locking his glare on the man.

He could sense Kate's struggle, but she didn't pull away, though she walked like her spine was made of old railroad spikes—stiff and somewhat rusty.

"Act natural." He whispered in her ear. "Don't let them see your fear."

"I'm not afraid." She countered. "Your cufflink is stabbing me."

He glanced down and sure enough, the left sleeve of his sport coat had crept up, revealing a broken cufflink with a jagged edge. "My apologies." Once clear of the speakeasy, he withdrew his hand and shirked down his cuff.

"There it is." With an abrupt start as if he'd pinched her, Kate increased her pace toward an apartment complex.

Gaze alert, he lengthened his strides and followed her up a flight of steps, down the sun-weathered walkway to the last door on the second floor.

Number 11. He moved past her and leaned over the bannister, taking in the view to his left—a patch of grass, an empty clothesline, and a lopsided burn barrel. A small stream glistened in the distance, and were those ... ducks?

"What are you doing?"

"Keep your voice down. You never know who could be watching."

Kate stood there gawking at him as if he'd sprouted ten heads.

"I'm checking the perimeter." He stretched further and this time, spied to his right. Rusted steps of a fire escape led to the trash-strewn ground. He straightened and dusted off the front of his coat. "Secure enough. Now to look inside." He turned in time to catch the color draining from her face.

"Inside?" She mouthed. "But I don't know you."

Why shouldn't the lady be apprehensive after the picture Miss Whitmore had painted of him? "My motives are only for your safety. There could be someone in your apartment aiming to follow through with their threat."

She fidgeted her purse strap.

"I need to check." He held out his hand for the key. "I'll enter first and make sure no one's inside. Then I'll leave."

She flicked a glance to the door, her mouth pinched so tight, her pouty lips disappeared.

"You don't know the Salvastanos like I do. They hide and wait until the perfect time to strike." Which meant the longer they lingered outside on this open walkway the easier of a target they became.

She blinked so hard he feared her lashes would tangle.

"Please." His brusque tone made her jerk, pulling her from whatever dreamland she'd been wandering.

Hesitancy marked her features, but she relinquished the key.

"Wait here." And with that he unlocked the door and readied for the possibility of coming face to face with a killer.

CHAPTER 6

My gaze fused to the pistol Detective Jennings withdrew from the holster on his hip. Dread crawled over me, seeping into my bones and locking every joint. He hesitated at the entrance of my apartment for a second as if waiting for his sight to adjust to the darkened space. Then with furtive steps, he disappeared through the doorway.

I held my breath, inclining my ear, but all fell silent. The shaded porch allowed enough light for me to peek into the entryway, but anything beyond that tangled into a hazy blur. Papa wouldn't be in my apartment. How would he even know where I lived? There was no possible way—

My heart lurched in my chest.

Papa wouldn't be within those walls, but someone else very well could be. And the detective had a gun.

My purse thudded to the floor.

I launched into my apartment. Darkness engulfed me, but I was no stranger to the shadows. My feet navigated through the small parlor.

"Rhett!" The volume of my own voice made me tremble, but I had no option.

Footsteps charged from the bedroom, but I continued toward the small nook beside my kitchenette.

The lamp to my left switched on, and I swirled toward the man breathing as hard as I was. My fuzzy eyes snapped clear at the sight of a gun barrel aimed at me.

Rhett's shoulders heaved with a low growl. "Man alive, Kate." He lowered his pistol, but his eyes remained like loaded bullet casings ready to shoot his fury. "I thought you were in danger. Why didn't you stay put like I told you?"

"I forgot to warn you." I motioned to the obvious lump in my curtain and then pointed at his gun. "Please hide that."

A shaft of air burst from his lips, and he holstered his weapon. "I could've hurt you. Can't you see that?"

"Better me than him." I rushed over, knelt on the hardwood floor, and placed a gentle palm on the boy-sized bump in my muslin drapes. The small form shifted, and I caught sight of red-stained fingers as he tugged back the cloth.

Alarm registered in youthful eyes. The scar tissue on his face had paled, almost bluish, probably from fright. His hazel gaze darted back and forth between Rhett and me.

"Everything is okay, Charlie." No doubt he'd felt the tremors of our steps through the floorboards. He wasn't used to two sets of footfalls. Only mine. Why hadn't I thought to warn Rhett? And since when had I regarded the detective as Rhett? Oh, this day had been a whirlwind, but that was no excuse for being forgetful about my young friend. Too many have forgotten him already. I motioned toward the window but kept my face in Charlie's line of vision so he could read my lips. "Were the ducklings out today?"

Charlie scooted toward me, and with his chin tucked to his chest, he raised his tablet, showing his latest creation.

He'd sketched the baby ducks with meticulous detail. By varying the pressures of the pencil strokes, he'd shaded the feathered bodies, giving the picture impressive depth. Charlie couldn't read nor write, yet his skill in drawing went beyond his eleven years. While the picture itself seemed the handiwork of a seasoned artist, the sticky patches on the paper from his candy feast revealed his youth.

"This is amazing. And I can see you liked the taffy I left for you." I gave a light tap to his nose which he playfully swatted away.

Merriment lit his eyes, but then his gaze strayed to Rhett, and his grin wobbled into a grimace.

"I brought someone I'd like you to meet."

Charlie scrambled to his feet and pulled off his oversized newsboy hat, revealing a flop of dark blonde hair. His fingers wringing the cap like a dishrag, Charlie observed Rhett with a vulnerability that made my stomach knot. I wished I'd had time to prepare Rhett to greet Charlie. Most would take one look at the child's warped skin, and their faces would say the rest—repulsed. But they didn't understand what Charlie had gone through. The tragedy he'd overcome.

A survivor, like me.

But while I harbored a scarred soul, the traces of trauma were visible on Charlie's face, neck and arms.

Rhett's eyes turned soft instead of wary.

I released my pent-up breath and stood. I smoothed out my skirt but kept my face turned toward my young friend. "Charlie, this is Mr. Jennings."

His small mouth twisted, and I pointed at Rhett, then signed our newly learned word. Charlie relaxed and rewarded me with a relieved smile, making his scars pucker. He then aimed that same expression at the detective. I stepped behind the boy and placed my hands on his shoulders. "Charlie lost his hearing in an accident, but he's brilliant at reading lips. Only be sure he can see you."

Rhett removed his derby with his left hand and extended his right toward Charlie. "Glad to meet you."

Charlie wiped his palms on his trousers, leaving scarlet streaks on the faded tweed. He shrugged and shook Rhett's hand. I covered my smile with my fist. Maybe my next lesson with Charlie should be about manners.

I glanced at the wall clock above Rhett's shoulder. "It's a little after six, Charlie. Your father should be heading to work." I'd leave out the part that I'd spotted Jack Davenport carousing outside the Thirsty Thunder. The way he'd ogled me made the hairs stand on my arms. Rhett must've observed the man's lewd attentions as well. The small of my back still tingled from his protective touch. And now to see him respond to Charlie with such kindness? Was this the same shrewd detective that had entered the archive room not too long ago?

Rhett strode to the front of my apartment and stood at the open door, gaze searching. These past moments with Charlie had made me forget about that ridiculous "S" card, but the stern set of Rhett's jaw and determined steps revealed he hadn't.

With a sigh, I moved to the counter and withdrew some biscuits from the bread box. I angled my face to stay in Charlie's view. "Do you still have the deli meat I gave you yesterday?"

He signed, "No."

His father no doubt had devoured it all. Not surprising. If I ever caught that man sober, I'd have a few choice words for him. Unfair as it was, Charlie shouldn't be the one to suffer. "Not a problem. I have plenty." A lie. But at least this deception was for the good of someone else. Not that it made any difference in God's eyes. But what else could I do?

The truth will set you free. Madre Chamberlin's reedy voice echoed off the brittle places of my heart. My lashes lowered, but I could still see my former guardian's pale eyes—always filled with conviction but never love. A sigh rattled my chest, but I wouldn't give it place. In my life, the truth wouldn't free me, only destroy.

Taking in a calming breath, I pulled the paper-wrapped ham from the ice box and handed it to Charlie. "Maybe try to hide it this time." I handed him the food then ruffled his hair.

Gratitude shone in his eyes, and I decided I would starve if it made this boy's world easier. Charlie gave a cheery wave and skipped to the door only to halt when he reached Rhett. The detective patted his small shoulder, and the tenderness in his eyes was almost my undoing. Charlie stood a little taller as Rhett stepped aside to let him pass.

I turned my back to the pair. Over the past months, I'd embraced a motherly role over Charlie, and watching Rhett's unreserved acceptance did something strange to my heart.

The hinges of the door creaked followed by the recognizable click of the deadbolt. I'd never been alone in my apartment with a man, and though the circumstances weren't normal, it didn't stop my nerves from tangling raw.

Peggy's final warning floated to the forefront of my mind. *He might have the charms of Al Jolson, but he has the manners of a wolf. Don't let him paw you.* All the more reason for me not to take my eyes off him.

At the sound of approaching footsteps, I unfurled my spine and notched my chin. Even though he'd treated Charlie with endearing approval, didn't mean I should let down my guard. I had an identity to protect. Secrets to shield.

Rallying the shreds of my confidence, I whirled around to find the detective only a few feet away.

"I believe this is yours." He held out the purse I'd dropped earlier.

"Thank you." I received the black bag, and our hands brushed, his thumb briefly sticking to my little finger.

The taffy.

I set aside my purse, withdrew a cloth from the drawer beneath the counter, and dampened it with the lukewarm water in the basin. "Here. To wash off the candy."

He gave an appreciative nod and cleaned his hands. He returned the cloth, and I offered him a towel. He dried his fingers, and I gestured to the counter where I'd just set the washrag. *We've had enough finger-touching already.*

"May I ask what happened?" He set down the towel. "To Charlie?"

"At the steel works." I nodded in the direction of Wilmington Rolling Mills. "A furnace exploded, and Charlie barely escaped. He survived, but as you see, it cost him."

"You need to be at least fourteen to work there. That boy's no older than twelve."

"He's eleven." I relaxed my weight against the counter. "His father must've forged his birth papers." My heart shattered every time I thought of Charlie and others like him facing dangerous work conditions to earn a penny an hour. *To me, even fourteen years of age is too young.* "I confess I'm not fond of Charlie's Papa. The man turns violent when he drinks. That's why Charlie comes here. Everyone needs a safe place."

Rhett's jaw worked. "Can he talk?"

"I'm not sure. I think he was able to before the accident." And I had never pressed him on the subject. If the trauma had made him mute, then he'd speak if or when he was ready. I'd offer him the patience I'd never been gifted. Not that the Chamberlins had mistreated me, but how different would my life have been if Papa would've stayed instead of abandoning me? If I had been allowed to grieve my mother? If I'd been given longer time to recover from the accident rather than been pressured to do the lung exercises that fatigued me for days on end? But … maybe that was what had made me a stronger singer.

"What's this mean?" Rhett's deep timbre yanked me from the pit of my memories. He hooked his index fingers together—the word I'd signed to Charlie earlier.

My mind spun at the shift in conversation.

"You motioned that, and he changed."

"It means *friend*." I picked at a loose thread on my sleeve, anything to avoid eye contact with the man. "I'm teaching him to sign. Well, we're learning together. No one ever bothered to teach him another means of communication. And …" Now I was rambling. My gaze lifted to find his piercing blue eyes on me. Had I said something wrong?

After a few long seconds, he cleared his throat. "There's an issue that needs addressed. Follow me."

He cast a vague look my way and then strode toward … my bedroom. My chest tightened. Had I left Papa's letters out? How would the detective had time to read them? I forced my feet into motion, crossing the faded parlor room rug, hoping with all hope I'd left nothing in plain sight that would betray my identity.

With a gulp, I stepped into my bed chambers. My gaze darted to my vanity. The letters were out of sight, and I allowed my lungs to take in air again.

The intimacy of the situation was not lost on me, especially with the space being the size of a storage closet and the detective's commanding physique only a touch away. I pulled my elbows into my sides, making myself as small as possible.

"That needs to be closed and locked." He pointed at the open window. "And keep the curtains drawn."

"I can't." My only glimpse to the outside world.

"You must."

"I'm on the second floor." I crossed my arms. "No one can get to me."

"Really?" He stepped toward the window, allowing me space to breathe, and cast a knowing look. "That rusted fire escape says otherwise."

I spied my lacy nightgown folded atop my pillow, and shuffled in front of my bed to keep him from spotting it. But something told me he'd already seen it. Heat climbed my neck. "The fire escape doesn't reach the ground."

He rolled his eyes.

Even I knew my argument was flimsy. All one needed was to stand on those discarded wooden boxes littering the alley, and they could pull themselves onto the metal landing. But I wouldn't—no, couldn't—close my window. How could I get that across to him without revealing the details of my trauma? The day when the black monster had smothered me, suffocating my screams. Even the memory made my lungs burn and the air rattle in my coarse throat. "George." I rasped. "I have George to protect me at night."

"Pardon?" His gaze flew to my ringless hand, and I could only imagine what thoughts whirled in his mind.

I stooped and retrieved the baseball bat from under my bed, my heart settling at the possibility of a compromise. "I present you my wooden defender."

Detective Jennings received the bat, his eyes focusing on the black ink before his jaw went slack. "George 'Babe' Ruth." His hushed tone signified wonder. "That's signed. By Babe Ruth."

"It is."

"But … how did you …" His gaze widened as if the signature had been etched in gold. So the detective was a sports fan. I could play this to my advantage and hopefully a distraction to get the man out of my bedroom.

"Harold Arlin interviewed him. He signed several of them. I took it for means of protection." I shrugged. "If you find me another bat, you can have this one."

His eyes met mine, disbelief swirling in the blue depths. "I couldn't possibly."

"Truly." I made my move toward the door. "I don't care for such things." I tossed a glance over my shoulder and almost rejoiced to find the detective following me into the parlor. "Did you know he has 'mike fright'?"

"Really?"

"According to Harold, the Bambino froze the moment he was 'on air'. So Harold took the speech from the man's hand and read it aloud."

"Completely fooled me." His eyes lit with amusement. "I remember listening to that segment. I had no idea that wasn't Babe's voice."

"Neither did all of Pittsburgh. We received several letters complimenting Babe's kind voice. Harold still laughs about it."

His mouth hitched in a lopsided grin. It was easy, natural, and made my mouth drier than a vibrato-rich song.

No, no, no. I couldn't allow even the slightest thought of admiration. The danger proved too great. The man before me could never know—

"You feeling okay?"

"Hmm?" My fingers stilled … on my temple? Oh dear. I'd been unconsciously massaging my head. As if trying to physically subdue the unbidden rush of awareness. My hands fell to my sides. "Yes. It's been quite the day." And that had to be the explanation for my erratic heartbeat and jumbled thoughts.

He returned the baseball bat, and I shifted under the weight of his gaze. This time he wasn't peering at me with suspicion. No, worse. His eyes registered a compassion that hooked my heart, its luring grip ebbing as the tide of truth swept in with a numbing chill—he'd have no sympathy if he knew my real name. One that matched his father's murderer. I took a step back as if increasing the distance would detach me from the kindness in his expression.

"I understand." His deep voice filled the small space. "I'll leave so you can rest." He angled as to turn away, but then paused and faced me. "I would ask that you not leave your apartment without me."

I opened my mouth to object, but he silenced me with a look.

"I deal with enough guilt as it is, Kate. I won't have your blood on my hands." That ghosted expression from earlier resurfaced.

"But this could stretch on and on. What if you never locate the person who gave me that card?"

"I'll find him." His jaw tightened in a steel determination that made my chest squeeze. "And you're going to help me."

CHAPTER 7

R hett shifted on the padded barstool and downed the rest of his vanilla soda. K's Drug Emporium was empty, save a couple of older women discussing foot powder brands loud enough to make Rhett's toes itch.

After seeing Kate safely to her apartment for the second evening in a row, he'd ridden the trolley to Pittsburgh only to get off several blocks before his destination. Sure he was pressed for time, but walking had always been the best way to clear his mind. Questions filled his head faster than the Monongahela after a deluge, and his thoughts were just as murky.

Yesterday had brought about the mysterious "S" card, causing Rhett to hope today would mark the appearance of the elusive mobster himself. Having persuaded his investigative agency partner, David, to help scout the expansive Westinghouse plant, Rhett had been more than ready.

They'd remained discreet, lingering on the outside of the many buildings, staking out the entrances with their firearms loaded and ready.

But nothing.

The lead had been sizzling hot yesterday, but now seemed cold as a day-old firecracker. Could this have all been a mistake like Kate had claimed? After all, why would a wholesome broadcaster appeal to a vile crime boss? He folded his arms on the metal countertop and grimaced at his empty soda glass. He wouldn't have splurged on the syrupy vanilla drink, but a part of him almost needed it.

Nothing like a touch of sugar to sweeten our blandest thoughts, Mom had said whenever Rhett'd been in a glum mood. Like the time he'd been seven and had turned his ankle climbing a tree, causing him to miss the Pirates game against the Cubs. Or when he'd been eleven and his terrier had died. She'd never needed an excuse to bake dessert, but it'd seemed she always had something ready for Rhett when he'd needed a spoonful of sweetness and an earful of her sound wisdom. If only he'd been there for *her* when she needed him most.

Same with his father.

They'd saved Rhett from a lifetime of shame, but he hadn't been able to help either of them. Absent when they'd gasped their last. A fine son he'd been.

With a scowl, he yanked a napkin from the dispenser and wiped his mouth.

Better get home.

He had a grumpy cat waiting on him for dinner and a long evening ahead. Rhett tossed the crumpled napkin onto the counter beside his soda glass and stood. He cupped the back of his neck, the taut muscles beneath his palm evidence of the hours cramped inside his Model-T last night. Keeping an eye on Miss Chamberlin's apartment complex so far had produced nothing but a dull ache that his twenty-eight-year-old frame should've been able to tame. And he had another bout to look forward to tonight.

A squeaking noise to his right pulled his attention. The soda jerk, who appeared around sixteen, was wiping the exterior glass of the penny candy display. Rhett dropped a nickel in the tip jar as an idea formed in his head. The click of Rhett's oxfords seemed to bounce off the tin-plated ceiling, but the white-capped youngster didn't seem to notice.

Rhett cleared his throat, and the dishrag stilled on the smattering of finger smudges.

His pointed chin angled toward Rhett. "Need somethin', sir?"

"I see you have some taffy." He gestured to the vanilla and chocolate bars. "Would you happen to have any strawberry flavored?"

Green eyes squinting, he studied the various boxes of candy, then regarded Rhett with a shrug. "May be some in the back. Let me check."

"I appreciate it." Rhett browsed the display again, only this time with Kate in mind. What kind of sweets would she like? In his experience, chocolate had been the typical preference for the women he'd dated. Yet Kate wasn't the *typical* female. She didn't slap on the war paint like other ladies, and certainly didn't dress to attract notice. He'd bet most men he knew wouldn't grant her a second glance, and from what he'd witnessed of Kate, the way she'd cowered away from his attentions, she seemed to actually favor disregard. What kind of female relished in being ignored?

"See anything you like?" A feminine voice poked into his thoughts.

He glanced over. "Miss Kromer?"

Her slender fingers clutched a box of strawberry taffy, her lips stretching into a luring smile. "I have what you're craving."

Mercy. Rhett didn't have to be an investigator to figure out that blatant clue. "What happened to the kid?" He tossed a thumb at the door where the lanky soda jerk had disappeared through.

"Oh that's Henry. My baby brother." She set the box on the counter beside the display case and lowered onto the nearby stool. Her long legs took their good ole time crossing. "I told him I'd manage the front while he takes the rubbish out to the bin." She glanced around, her expression taking on a bored tone. "My parents own this place."

Rhett nodded, marking the resemblance between the two siblings. They both had emerald eyes. "About the taffy, I'd like to buy—"

"Where's the new love of your life?"

"At home." Safe. He shouldn't linger any longer. David would start wondering where he was. Rhett was thankful his partner had offered to watch Kate's place for a couple hours, but he didn't want to take advantage of his generosity. Goodness knew he owed David more than he could repay already.

Her gaze swept over him with amused interest and then to the candy box. "Kate doesn't seem like the strawberry taffy kind of girl to me." Stella crept to her feet and trailed her finger over the glass case, so near Rhett caught whiff of her floral perfume. "She's more of a Sandy Chew." She pointed a manicured fingernail to the plainly wrapped confection, also nicknamed "Sawdust Square" for its lackluster flavor.

"Now what makes you think that?"

She leaned over with a conspiratorial curl to her mouth. "Because I know she put you up to this."

Huh? "Up to what?"

She tipped her head back with a laugh, her bobbed curls dancing on her shoulders. "Come on, Rhett. It's so obvious."

Rhett scratched the turn of his jaw. Maybe he should play along. "Looks like I can't get one past you."

She gave a casual shrug. "It's not hard to see. You coming in here and pretending to not know my parents owned this place. Don't tell me that you're not here to fish for information."

"Worth a shot, right?"

She turned, placing her back against the glass case, and tilted her chin. "I like the bait. So I'll nibble a bit."

"What if you get hooked?"

Stella leaned forward, her pearl necklace dipping just below her collar bone, a wry smile tugging the corners of her mouth. "I've escaped sharper snares than this."

He didn't doubt it. Rhett wasn't sure as to what she was implying but he was certain this woman was equal parts shrewd and beauty. The former Rhett would've enjoyed her flirtations and no doubt have explored beyond that.

He opened his mouth to speak but Stella silenced him with a raised finger. "Besides you'll have a hard time proving it's me." Her tight smile wobbled, a crack in her brazen façade "Kate had it coming to her. Though maybe it was a bit beneath me."

What was this woman getting at? Had Stella started all of this? Forged the "S" card? A sliver of him burned with agitation at the possibility of this not leading to Hugo, but relief eased the fire. At least Kate would be safe. "Why would you do such a thing? Do you hate her that much?"

"What do you care?" She straightened and took a generous step toward him, but Rhett held his ground. "The whole thing failed. She wasn't even rattled by it."

Her breath steamed against his neck, but Rhett only stared down at her. "I never thought you capable of something this low, Stella."

Her mouth hitched to the side. "Gotta fight for what I want. If it takes sabotaging her performance to get it, then I will. That broadcasting position should've been mine. Not Killjoy Kate's."

His eyes narrowed. Being the devoted beau, he probably should put Stella in her place for her condescending remarks, but his brain snagged on her other words. Broadcasting position? What did Kate's job at KDKA have to do with the "S" card? Something wasn't adding up.

"Switching the music in her folder was simple." She studied a fingernail and then raised her sultry glare to him. "I even sat in to watch her blunder her way through, but of course Kate managed to have the song memorized. But like I said, you don't have any proof."

So Stella hadn't anything to do with Rhett's investigation. The woman was innocent of planting the card in Kate's mailbox. Her only crime had been jealousy, making her resort to a juvenile prank.

The older ladies by the foot medicine passed by, their voices only a little louder than their scuffling steps. The jingling bell above the door noted their exit.

With a pert smile, Stella stepped around Rhett. "It was beneath me. I realize that." She glanced over her slender shoulder. "When you go back to report this to Kate, let her know that not everybody sung her praises last week."

His brow spiked at her obvious disdain. "What happened last week?"

She adjusted a few bottles of hair tonic, acting as if she hadn't heard him. He knew better. The rigid line of her shoulders betrayed her ruse of nonchalance.

After a handful of seconds, she turned around, gaze settling on him. "Mr. Arlin was supposed to interview an opera performer, but she didn't show. Kate swept in and saved the day with some kind of lullaby. Everyone has been doting on her since." She eyed him. "Seems to be the trend now."

"I remember that segment." Rhett always listened to Arlin's broadcasts and had indeed heard the song, rather the voice, that had enchanted Pittsburgh. But he hadn't been aware it was Kate who'd been positioned behind the microphone. How could the woman who'd sung with so much emotion be the same stiff, controlled person he walked to and from the station today? Such varying degrees of personality made her all the more intriguing. Which was the true Kate Chamberlin? He'd have to tune-in to her performances from now on.

"I'm back." Henry reemerged, dusting his hands off his aproned thighs. He glanced at the box on the counter, then to Rhett's empty hands. "Stell, why didn't you ring the man up already?"

She rolled her eyes. "Because the gentleman was interested in something else." With a knowing smirk, she sauntered to the back, disappearing without another glance back.

"Did you change your mind about the candy?" Confusion riddled the kid's brows.

"Nah. I still want the taffy." Rhett dug in his pockets for some money.

"How many, sir?"

"I'll take the whole box." He'd buy an entire truckload for Charlie if he could. Rhett's heart had cracked upon seeing the boy's scarred skin and then broke entirely at the vulnerability in his innocent eyes.

Henry told him the amount, and Rhett had exact change. After a nod of thanks, Rhett grabbed his taffy box and strode out the door. He'd gotten more than he bargained for with this visit. Never would he guess a quiet girl like Kate could rack up enemies. Stella wasn't one to take defeat without a fight. Would she try something more dangerous next time? And what about Charlie's dad? Kate had told Rhett the jerk of a man was the same who'd ogled her yesterday in front of the gin joint. The look in his eye had been downright predatory. Rhett's jaw tightened. Then there was Hugo Salvastano, who had a history of vengeance.

Question was, which of these three would strike first?

CHAPTER 8

R hett Jennings had clung closer to me than my shadow, and it was unnerving. The other women in the Westinghouse building seemed to adore the handsome detective with his broad shoulders and eyes the same color as the Tyrrhenian Sea. But the gentleman's presence made my insides uneasy. How long could I keep avoiding his questions? Surely he'd soon see through my veil of deception.

I gripped the edges of the wooden chair inside the *Jennings & Wilson Agency* on Forbes Avenue. Why had I ever agreed to this? Because I'd gotten swindled. Rhett had figured out my weakness and had played it to his full advantage. He'd arrived at my door this morning sporting an enchanter's grin and clutching a box of Charlie's favorite sweets. A whole box! My mind had been so distracted by his thoughtfulness that I hadn't realized until *afterwards* that I'd unconsciously agreed to Rhett's request of accompanying him to his office after my shift.

He'd made it clear there were things I needed to understand about the man who'd sent me the card, saying information he'd possessed went beyond public knowledge.

While I had done my share of investigating my father's and uncles' dealings, I hadn't found much beyond newspaper articles and faulty gossip. And I hoped upon hope the rumors swirling just today were as false as Stella's eyelashes.

My gut twisted.

No, the awful story I'd heard on my lunch break today couldn't be true. If the dead man that'd been found in Rumrunners Row was Papa, then there'd be no need for Rhett to bring me here. No need to further the investigation.

I shirked the nagging thoughts by allowing my gaze to roam the modest space as I waited for the detective to return from the adjoining room. The opened blinds provided a slanted glimpse of the five and dime store across the street. His desk situated in front of a picture window, papers splashed all over the top. The need to straighten them into neat piles surged. Perhaps I could tidy them a bit. I removed my gloves and paused. *What am I doing?* Resting my gloves on my lap, I slid my hands beneath my thighs, holding them captive. That was, until I spotted a brass picture frame. After a quick glance at the door, I retrieved it from his desk.

A younger Rhett Jennings, maybe age six or seven, looked back at me, a large grin splitting his small face. Even the photograph's faded gray cast couldn't dull the glimmer of happiness in his youthful eyes. A woman stood to his left with light hair and a gentle smile. His mother? Now a widow. Sadness pricked my heart. But then ... there hadn't been a wife's name listed in any of the articles I'd read concerning the police commissioner. Nor had Rhett mentioned her. Now her smile, so soft at first inspection, seemed delicate and those light eyes frail. Whatever happened to Mrs. Jennings?

In the photo's far right stood a well-dressed man with a hand set upon Rhett's tiny shoulder. The commissioner. I pulled the picture closer, studying his sturdy frame and friendly face. While the detective seemed broader, the father was taller, towering his wife and child.

The Jennings family.

I blinked back the moisture stinging my eyes. I glanced at child Rhett, then to the door the grown Rhett had disappeared through. He'd lost his world. His father. And perhaps his mother, too. That glimmer resident in his adolescent face was gone. Yes, he'd been blessed with handsome features that could fluster an entire legion of woman, but I had noticed an emptiness in his expression. One that came from the burden of loss. One I'd glimpsed in my own reflection. I shared yet another unspoken bond with the detective.

I knew how it felt to stitch the pain together until it became a tapestry of wounds. A picture of all my anguish. Though the delicate binding of my memories threatened to snap if I pressed my mind upon it. So I must direct my thoughts elsewhere before everything unraveled in Rhett's presence.

The entrance door creaked behind me. I scrambled to return the frame. With a deep exhale, I twisted in my chair to find an older man entering the office.

"Oh." His steps stilled. "I didn't know Everhett had company." His amiable smirk offset the gruff tone of his voice. He tipped his hat, the movement bringing attention to a cross-shaped scar on his left cheekbone. "I'm Major Gordon Ford, Everhett's former boss and current chess partner."

Before I could mutter a response, Rhett emerged from the other room, box in hand. He flicked a glance toward me as if to make sure

I hadn't escaped on him, though I was acutely tempted. His gaze settled on the gentleman standing behind me. "Ah good. You're here, too. I might need your expertise."

Major Ford's mustache twitched. "Since when do you ever take my advice? Especially when women are involved?" His teasing glint made a tight band stretch between my shoulder blades.

Rhett's chuckle was low and deep. "I might have met my match with this one."

I struggled against a frown. Surely I hadn't given him any reason to suspect *me* trouble.

"Have a seat, Major. I brought out the archives for this young lady's sake."

Young lady? What happened to the *happily in love* scheme? Were we not pretending anymore? I could only hope. Rhett'd claimed our fake relationship had to appear believable, but when he'd held my hand and looked into my eyes, he'd been almost too convincing.

"Your Salvastano collection?" Deep grooves settled between Major Ford's brows. "What's the occasion?" He lowered onto the chair beside me, but not before sneaking a glance in my direction.

"She got a card."

"An S?"

"The very kind." Rhett claimed the plush seat behind the desk and set the box atop the scattered papers. "I'm trying to persuade her that this family is not one to take lightly."

I opened my mouth then snapped it shut. I wasn't taking it lightly. In fact, I'd never been more confused in my life. Why would my own father send me a card? And if —God forbid—the rumor I'd heard this afternoon about Papa was true, then who else would send it to me? Who else knew I was a Salvastano?

"By the way, Major, this is Kate Chamberlin." Rhett's casual introduction seemed out of place, but I still nodded a greeting to the older gentleman.

Major Ford's attention fixed on me, his gray eyes studying. "What makes you such a danger that Hugo Salvastano feels the need to threaten you?"

"I'm at a loss." At least I could speak one truth.

Rhett lifted the box lid and withdrew a notepad. "This was my father's." A tinge of sadness marked his tone, making it huskier. "He didn't log much, but the notes he made are important." He flipped to a page and handed me the pad. "Look at the list."

I reached over accepting it, and our fingers brushed. His gaze locked with mine, and once again the intensity of his eyes made my heart jump. I lowered my lashes, breaking the connection, and focused on the paper.

I scanned over a dozen names the title read—*Men Killed By The Salvastanos*. A gasp burst from my lips, and I winced at the marked sound.

"Granted, none of those men were on the right side of the law." Rhett reclined in his chair, stacking his hands behind his head. "Actually most of them were murderers or gang lords."

I forced my gaze on the names of men who no longer drew breath and prayed that somehow all of this was a colossal mistake. "Are you certain these people were ... um ... killed by the Salvastano family?"

Rhett's brow quirked. "They all had a card somewhere on their person."

"But couldn't that have been planted there? Is that your only proof?"

Rhett straightened and exchanged glances with Major Ford. "The names on that list are men who were involved in activity that went beyond rumrunning. Like prostitution rings or hitman soliciting. There's evidence suggesting the Salvastanos repeatedly warned the goons to quit. Threatened that if they didn't shut down their operations, then … well you see what happened. They took the law into their hands."

I handed him back the notepad, trying my best to keep my fingers from shaking. "Did they go after the innocent?"

He drilled me with a look that went for a direct hit into my gut. "No. Which is why I'm curious about you."

"You're scaring the dear child." Major shot Rhett a warning look. The same one he'd given when Rhett had begged to drive his Model-T years ago.

But unlike back then, this wasn't fun and games. No, if striking terror in Kate Chamberlin got her to see reason, to understand the amount of danger she was in, then so be it. It'd been three days, and he still hadn't been able to get her to talk.

Maybe there wasn't any connection between her and this family. Maybe this all had been a mistake like she'd claimed, but he couldn't risk everything on a couple *maybes*. Keeping air in this woman's lungs was his responsibility. And the weight of it pressed like a dozen locomotives on his chest.

Rhett palmed the back of his neck and slid a glance to his right. The picture frame had been moved. He always kept it facing full forward but now it was angled. He reached across and adjusted the picture, not missing Kate's sheepish expression. Quite nosy for a woman who'd been closed-off in all her responses. "I'm trying to find a connection here. The more information you provide the easier it'd be to keep you safe."

She wrung the gloves that'd been resting on her lap. "I see no reason for them to hurt me."

True, she wasn't a whiskey peddler invading their territory. Yet to be fair the Salvastano trio had never bumped off any of those who lingered on the lowest rung of the racketeering ladder. They only went after the ones at the top, those who'd been trying to scale the high walls of their twisted kingdom. As if trying to keep their domain safe from the ne'er-do-wells.

Irony at its best. "Neither do I. Unless there's something you're not telling me." He leaned forward. "The last time Hugo Salvastano was seen, he was on a killing spree. My father was included in that final victim list." He exhaled. "What I'm saying is that men like that can't be tamed. Not even for a pretty face like yours."

A gasp squeaked from her unpainted lips, turning to a cough. She clutched her gloves, using them to cover her mouth. Rhett stood and poured her a drink from his water cooler. She waved off his concern, her gloves fluttering, the movement resembling a crazed bird flapping its wings.

"I'm sorry," she rasped. Her glossy eyes flickered shut as if composing herself, her long lashes resting atop mottled cheeks.

Major's brow dug deeper by the second. Rhett offered her the glass which she refused with a shake of her head. He held it out to Major who still held that disapproving scowl. With a shrug, Rhett downed the water in two long gulps.

He set the empty glass aside and reclaimed his seat, his focus sharpening on the young woman who'd become as puzzling as the case itself. Gloves still pressed to her face, she raised her chin, her glossy gaze colliding into his like an elbow to the gut.

A handkerchief.

He *had* seen her before. She'd had a white handkerchief covering most of her face, except for her distressed eyes. Those vulnerable gold flecks of her eyes had been pressed into his soul. But where? Where had he and this woman crossed paths?

Some detective he was. He ground his jaw. Rhett had always prided himself about his immaculate memory, but right now his so-called *steel trap* had a faulty hinge. Could his run-in with her have happened right after his dad died? That had been the only time when things had become blurred. He took to grief like a drunk to the bottle, guzzling every somber thought, intoxicating his mind with heavy gloom, until the darkness settled in.

"Feeling better, Miss Chamberlin?" Major's concerned tone brought Rhett back to the moment.

The lowering of her hands, still clutching the gloves, revealed her pinched mouth. Her taciturn expression had been so constant these past few days, that it gave Rhett the sudden urge of wanting to glimpse her smile.

She cleared her throat and gave a small nod.

"Don't let him intimidate you, dear." His father's best friend put a gentle palm on her shoulder, her cream-colored sleeve rumpling under his veined hand. "He's only like this when he's stumped."

As if Rhett needed the reminder. "Thanks for that."

But Kate seemed to have missed their exchange. Her attention rested on her hands in her lap, faint lines rippling her forehead. Was she finally realizing what grave danger she was in?

Major shifted in his seat, the wood creaking with his movements. "Now Miss Chamberlin, he's correct about the company that gave you that card. They're not to be trifled with. Is there any information you can offer as to why you'd receive this card?"

And they were back to that again. Rhett wanted to drag a hand over his face. This conversation was getting nowhere. Like yesterday. And the day before that.

Kate pulled an envelope from her bag and placed it on the desk. "The card was in this. There's no marking. I don't think that would help much."

Rhett picked it up. Turning it over, holding it up to the light, he inspected it thoroughly. Nothing.

Grimacing, Kate squirmed in her seat. "I heard a rumor a few hours ago that Hugo Salvastano is …"

Rhett motioned with his hand. "Go on."

She swallowed. "Dead."

Rhett shirked loose his tie-knot. Gossip traveled like a cable car on iced rails, way too fast and dangerous. "A body was found in bootlegger territory. The person who reported it in claimed it was Salvastano. The deceased has been identified. Not Hugo."

Kate exhaled as though … relieved? "Maybe someone else sent me the card."

His temple throbbed. "Why?"

Her gaze fastened on him. At a quick glance her eyes seemed the average shade of brown, but upon closer inspection, he could see an amber ring around the pupil with gold flecks swirling about, like a whirlpool pulling him in. "That's your job to find out. Is it not?"

The older man beside her placed a fist in front of his mouth, smothering a chuckle.

Rhett gripped the box, wrestling with the retort dancing on his tongue. Why did he invite Major again? He reached inside the small pine box and withdrew three photographs. Men whose faces had been seared into his mind. He slid the first two across the desk. "Take a look at these."

She leaned forward, strands of her dark hair whispering against her cheek.

"The one on the left is Pedro Salvastano. The right is Lorenzo. Did you ever meet these men before?"

Small lines crimped the skin framing her eyes as she inspected the photos. Her mouth pressed tight, then relaxed.

"Have you ever seen these men?" Rhett scratched his jaw to keep from scowling. All he wanted was a simple *yes* or *no*. He didn't ask her to study each picture as if there'd be an exam.

Major glanced at the photos and shook his head. If any person could identify the Salvastanos, it'd be Major. He'd been the reporting officer on several cases involving the brothers—all of which had insufficient evidence to convict. Rhett's father had accompanied Major for at the final confrontation with the Salvastanos. Hugo betrayed his own blood, killing them then turning his wrath on the two men that had made a difference in Rhett's life. Only one of them escaped.

"No." Kate spoke up. "I've never met them."

Finally, they were making progress. "What about this man?" He handed her Hugo's picture, and she blinked once. Twice. Then all emotion drained from her face.

She stood, chair legs skidding, her gloves falling to the wood-planked floor. Eyes haunted, she moved near the window as if that area held the only pocket of air in the room.

Her mannerisms identical to that first day in the archive room. When she'd hustled into the hallway.

Ah, tight spaces.

He gave a reassuring nod to the baffled Major, launched to his feet and pulled the blinds open, giving her a full view of the soot-crusted buildings.

"I apologize." Her voice was soft. Almost practiced. Her gaze never strayed from the window. "This has been a lot of ..." Her breath shuddered.

What woman wouldn't react negatively to the face of a killer? Rhett should've prepared her more. Yes, he wanted her to realize the danger involved, but he didn't mean to shove the girl into a fit of panic. "I understand all of this has been difficult for you."

The sharp rise and fall of her shoulders. The way her mouth bowed down at the corners. The blanched fingers pinching the edges of the crime boss's photograph. All spoke of a woman who could use some rest. And maybe a friend. Rhett would take her straight home. As for the latter, what harm could happen from getting more personable with Kate?

But first ... "I need to ask, does that man look familiar at all?"

Her gaze lowered to the picture, then rose, albeit slowly to Rhett. "I told you days ago, and I'm sorry, nothing's changed." Her eyes wept without shedding a single tear. "I can't help you."

CHAPTER 9

I played the Italian concerto with a finesse that would've made Madre Chamberlin proud. Since the piece the song director had chosen for the broadcast was one I had memorized, I slid my eyes closed and allowed the music to sweep me away.

My fingers paraded across the ivories with the flair of the Calabrian pasture dance and visions of my homeland overtook me—the lush hills behind the Chamberlin's cottage, the velvety grass pillowing my back as I'd lay beside the whispering brook.

I approached the *vivace* segment of the selection, and my memory livened with the faded laughter of the village children, the rhythm like the slap of my feet against the old dirt roads when I'd race to the center of Spirelli for the weekly reading lessons. Oh, how I missed them.

But then ... the tempo slowed, my heartbeat quieting along with the mood of the transition. A somberness drifted into the delicate measures, carrying me even further back in time. The tone became one of grief. The methodic strike of keys were like the shovels of dirt smacking Mamma's wooden casket. The grit of the damp, packed soil pushing under my fingernails as I tried to dig Mamma out from the grave. How could they've buried her without allowing me to say goodbye? I had only wanted to see her face one last time, but Papa's knobby hand had tugged me away. The pain etched in his dark eyes would forever be carved into my soul.

The final bars of the song crawled to a close, but I couldn't end on the morose minor note. And who would know if I changed the progression the slightest bit? I pulled in a shaky breath and finished the piece, my heart thudding dully in my chest.

Tears gathered in my eyes, and I blinked them away. My homeland was now a distant memory, an ocean away. The Salvastano family that had once graced its surface now in shambles—the best parts of it dead while the other pieces were broken beyond repair.

In my loneliness, I couldn't even write to my former guardians in fear of exposing them. Mussolini wasn't fond of Protestant missionaries who proclaimed a Power greater than him. I shuddered at the horrors now invading my precious Italy.

"Ladies and gentlemen, the moving melody you just heard was played by none other than KDKA's sweetheart Kate Chamberlin." Harold shot me a wink and refaced the microphone. "On today's special I have the privilege of making some very important announcements."

I quietly grabbed my music folder and padded toward the door. When another musician struck the chimes for the signature opening of Harold's segment, I exited to the adjoining room. Thankfully no one was in there.

I slouched against the wall, eyes slipping shut. The heat from the electric lamps hovering above was enough to chase the chill down to my numb fingertips. Who would have thought playing one song could be so draining?

"Enchanting, Kate." The unmistakable deep voice seemed to echo off the wall and knock me in the side of the head, making me drop my folder onto the floor. Rhett ambled into the room with a gait Madre Chamberlin would call a swagger. "I listened to your version of Aldenberg's Movement Number Four on the radio in Conrad's office and—"

"My version?" I straightened at the censure in his words. "You speak as if I altered it." Which I had, but how on earth would he know?

Quick as a blink, sturdy arms wrapped my waist. I squeaked and slammed my hands against his solid chest. "What are you doing?" I hissed.

"We're finally alone." His voice raised, and I winced. "I've missed you all day."

This past week, he'd only act smitten when others were present. Now it seemed his attentions progressed to include when we were alone. If Rhett thought for one second I would fawn over his charms, give in to his kind of pleasure like scores of other women, then he'd another thing coming. And what was *coming* would be a slap against his rascally handsome face. I locked my fingers together, primed to strike.

His head dipped and his voice pitched low. "Someone's listening at the door."

What? My gaze flew to the entrance and caught sight of the tips of shoes poking out from the doorjamb. All the fight left me. Who was that? Hadn't Peggy worn black pumps today? But so had dozens of others.

His breath fanned against my earlobe, sending shivers to my toes. "And if I have my perfumes correct, it's Stella."

I didn't exactly want to know how Rhett had gotten familiar with Stella's perfume.

"Play the part." He quietly urged. "Relax against me."

I inched closer, but probably not enough to meet his approval. How was I supposed to act in love if I'd never been? It was like telling a person who'd never been taught piano to play Chopin. It just wasn't possible.

"If I recall …" Whispering should be outlawed. For it stirred something in me that I wished to remain solidified. "The original score is marked andante and you played it adagio."

Hmm? Oh, my performance. Yes, Aldenburg intended the tempo to be somewhat quicker than what I had played, but my heart hadn't wanted to leave the depths of my memories. It was all I had left. "I wouldn't guess you to be an expert on music." I glanced up at him. Big mistake. For his lips pulled into a smirk that made his blue eyes twinkle like a star-drenched sky.

"There's lots of things you don't know about me."

I could reply the same, but his reaction to my secrets wouldn't be quite as impressive.

"I'm fond of all of Georg Aldenberg's works." His face softened, and my heart ducked behind my iron resolve of never harboring attraction to this man. "Your performance was expressive. No wonder Pittsburgh has fallen in love with you."

If I wasn't so dumbfounded by his statement, or flustered by his sturdy grip resting comfortably on my waist, a scoff would've erupted from my lips. No one had ever fallen in love with me. Or cared for that matter. Had I been worthy of love, Papa wouldn't have left me behind, the Chamberlins would've embraced me as part of their family. Having no children of their own, I had insisted, during my later childhood years, on calling them Madre and Padre Chamberlin— hoping it would create a bond between us. But no. I'd been a burden.

He glanced over and I'd followed his gaze. The shoes hadn't budged.

"I found your manner of playing that piece intriguing. The last portion especially. It held a sad tone, almost mournful."

I averted my eyes, lest he peer into my soul and glimpse the wreckage. "Music gives the heart a voice." And spoke what could never be uttered. Could he feel my hands trembling against his chest?

Amazing how only a seven-minute performance could rattle my emotions. Though, his nearness, the bulge of his muscular arms pressing against my goose-fleshed ones, could also be blamed. How long had it been since I'd been held, wrapped in an embrace? Seventeen years. Not since Papa had left. The Chamberlins had never offered comfort through physical touch. Not even a pat on the head or a squeeze of the hand. Figured the first person to break the drought of this affectionless season would be the only one whose touch I couldn't indulge in. Though I could hardly call his embrace affectionate, it was born of duty. But still, something about it offered warmth to the parts of my soul that'd been left drafty for far too long.

"But then, you changed the final E minor chord progression." His tone held no condescension but rather conversational. Then I realized what he was doing. He was distracting me, engaging me on a subject where I'd feel safe—music. I leaned into him more, somehow acting like I'd cared for him wasn't so difficult at present.

"I never liked for the way it ended without resolve. After such a moving piece, it should conclude on a hopeful note." His eyes trained on me. "And that's what you did. It's like you gave it closure."

Because that was exactly what *I* needed at the moment. But how had he detected all of this? I played with an openness because that was the only area I felt safe to express myself.

My gaze darted to the door. The shoes had disappeared.

Rhett's hands dropped from my waist, and he took a step back. "Well done, Kate."

The eavesdropper's identity would remain a mystery, but that didn't stop my chest from swelling at his praise. Yet it deflated just as quickly. I couldn't let Rhett past my defenses. I was still the daughter of the crime boss, and he the son of my father's victim.

Somehow I had to numb myself to the kindness so evident in his eyes. And steel myself against his touch. Because no doubt he'd be in contact with me again. Oh this wretched charade!

A familiar hunched silhouette appeared in the same doorway the unknown snooper had disappeared from. "Fernando." My heart lightened at the sight of him. "I thought you might've gone home already." I rushed to the table where I'd placed the basket. "Excuse me a moment, Rhett." I cut a quick glance at the confused investigator and approached the aged janitor with my warmest smile. "This is for you." I presented him the basket which he received with an arthritic grip.

"What … is this?" He stumbled on the words. How easy it would be for me to communicate with him in Italian, but that would draw questions for certain. He peeked into the basket and his dull eyes brightened. "Cannoli."

I nodded and couldn't tamper my grin at his childlike expression. "For your birthday."

White brows spiked, then sunk in realization. "You … remembered?"

My heart tore at the edges. "I'm sure they won't taste as heavenly as Rosa's, but know I gave my best effort. Flora Conrad helped as well." Helped as in my boss's wife had given me full access to an equipped kitchen. My own oven was about as predictable as the days of sunshine in this soot-laden city.

He placed a wrinkled hand on my elbow, emotion welling in his eyes. "Grazi, signorina."

Prego. "You're welcome."

He nodded his appreciation and ambled down the hallway.

Someone cleared a throat behind me.

Rhett.

I turned on my heel to find his eyes on me. At least I hadn't given into the urge and conversed with Fernando in my native tongue.

"So you're a musician *and* a baker?" He looked at me strangely.

"I'd hardly call myself a baker." *Unlike Papa.* His likeness from yesterday's photograph popped in my mind like flash powder. The grainy image contained a man I almost hadn't recognized—his weathered and lined skin, his saggy jowl, and his hair which had appeared lighter than the flour forever coating his hands. All different from the father I'd once known. The mole on his upper cheek had even faded. It would've been like glimpsing a stranger if not for those eyes. His eyes. *Oh, Papa.* I tugged a loose thread from my sleeve and tossed it aside. If only I could disregard the pain just as easily. "Fernando once said his wife used to make him cannoli on his birthday. She passed last spring."

"That was kind of you." His voice held a warmth that could've melted a hole in my iron resolve had I not turned my gaze to my T-strap shoes.

"It's nothing really. Not anything worth broadcasting." I hoped he'd take the hint and not press the subject. Last thing I needed was him asking how I learned to make cannoli.

"Well I do have something worth broadcasting. A breakthrough in the case."

And he'd waited this long to mention it?

My eyes darted to his, and he shot me a smile I hadn't seen before. I wouldn't label it flirty, but it wasn't the wry smirks I had grown accustomed to. My heart pounded a wild song. What kind of breakthrough? Dare I ask?

"Hugo Salvastano has a child. One that's right here in Pittsburgh."

CHAPTER 10

A tremble rocked so fiercely through me I feared my stockings would collapse at my ankles. Rhett had discovered my identity. My secret. My past. All I'd fought to keep hidden, now unveiled and exposed before the very man the truth would impact—and hurt—the most. A large piece of me niggled with guilt over deceiving him, and an even larger portion wanted to sprint toward the exit. But Rhett blocked the door.

I forced myself to meet his penetrating gaze. "How did you find out?"

His brow dipped a fraction. "It wasn't too difficult. I was—"

"Does anyone else know?" I had no grounds to ask him to remain quiet. I was at his mercy, and it'd been all my own doing.

"I heard it's been submitted to the bulletin. I'm sure the broadcaster already has the news. Possibly delivered it already."

"What?" I dashed to the studio door and pressed my ear against it. I couldn't hear anything. I gripped the knob, ready to burst inside.

Clang the gong, utilize my opera voice, steal the microphone anything to mute Harold's words. Though it wouldn't do any good. There was another news broadcast an hour from now. What was I going to do then? And what about the thirteen Pittsburgh newspapers that were no doubt running their presses at top speed to get a special edition out? I couldn't very well stop all of them.

My shoulders curled forward with a heavy exhale, and I released my intense grip on the doorknob. This was what I deserved for living the facade. Madre Chamberlin had always said what was spoken in secret would be shouted from the rooftop. Well in this case, from the eighth floor of the Westinghouse building.

Soon all of Pittsburgh would know I was Catarina Salvastano.

I glanced out the door, my gaze latching on the hall window, then slowly my attention crept to Rhett who appeared ... amused? Small lines of skin fanned from the corners of his eyes, while his mouth tilted in a lop-sided smirk. Was he so vengeful that he'd rejoice at my downfall? I expected him to be furious with me, to lash out at me. Not to mock me with a wry smile. His odd behavior struck fear in my joints. Would he take me to jail for lying? Did he even have that authority?

"No need to listen at the door. I can give you all the details." He lowered onto a chair by the small table next to the wall and kicked out his heels. So casual. As if he hadn't just upended my world. "Would you like to know the name?"

Now he toyed with me. Like the time my cat Biscotto had caught a mouse. The tabby had let it go, only to trap it again. Well, I wouldn't play this kind of game with the detective. I squared my shoulders ready to face the consequences.

"Have you ever heard of Vinny Salvastano?" He removed his bowler hat and slapped it on his knee.

My strained mind took several seconds to register the shift in conversation. I was not the target. Rhett wasn't taunting me. Harold wasn't muttering my name through the 'tomato can.' The waves of fear fell silent, but the waters of my circumstances weren't exactly still. Rhett just launched a new stone, one wholly unexpected, troubling the surface, leaving ripples of confusion.

Vinny?

The familiar name rolled through me. I angled away from the detective as my fingers flew to my parted lips.

How could anyone find out about my dead brother? My parents had hidden his existence even from me. I would've never known about him if I hadn't found the infant's picture in Mamma's drawer, the single word "Vinny" written on the back in Mamma's feminine script.

Feeling dizzy, I claimed the seat beside Rhett.

"It's a possibility she sent you the card."

Wait. She? I turned, facing the detective and his sky-blue eyes. The question danced on my tongue in such a wild cadence I couldn't restrain it from bursting past my lips. "She who?"

He leaned toward me, keeping his voice low as if the eavesdropper had returned. "Her real name is Delvina Salvastano. But she goes by Vinny."

Rhett's eyes were on my face, and I struggled to hide my shock. The only Vinny Salvastano I'd known had been dressed in an infant christening gown. I had always assumed the child was my brother, but—

"Apparently Delvina was left to the care of an America-bound family during the eighteen-ninety-eight famine in Italy. Hugo gave her up to offer her a better life."

Of course I had heard stories about the famine. It'd hit fierce but hadn't lasted long. But that meant … Oh, My poor parents. What anguish they must've endured in giving up their firstborn.

All the times I'd heard Mamma whisper about Vinny being gone. Or that one night when I had woken to Mamma's sobs only to discover her a shivering heap on the dirt-crusted floor wishing an absent Vinny '*Buon compleanno*', a good birthday. Mamma hadn't been grieving her child's death but missing her.

"Interesting though," Rhett continued. "This Delvina never mentioned a word about her mother. But that's not surprising considering the father. Her mom was probably some tramp."

His cutting words pulled me to my feet, the toes of my beige shoes stepping on the folder I'd dropped earlier. I picked it up, taking the moment to gather my senses. I couldn't defend Mamma's honor without giving myself away. The deception I'd wrapped myself in was lined with biting hooks, sheltering me one moment, leaving me in pain the next.

But the sting of Rhett's false remarks soon gave way to the miraculous truth.

My sibling was alive.

I had a sister.

"Are we really going to meet Delvina?" I shifted on the wooden-slatted trolley bench. My slip had crept up my leg as we'd rushed down Perry Avenue to catch the cable car enroute to the heart of Pittsburgh, and I hadn't the privacy to tug it in place. I wiggled again with no success.

"No. We're going to *see* her." He pulled his gaze from the exuberant toddler two rows ahead of us and fixed his attention on me.

I squirmed again, but not due to my errant undergarments. No, the full force of the man's intense gaze made my insides hum, bringing every cell to life with nervous activity. Fake romance or not, I should've backed away from his embrace earlier. I'd just discovered I'd had family nearby—a sister!—and my traitorous mind kept revisiting those moments cocooned in Rhett's arms.

"I'm curious if you'll recognize her." Rhett angled forward to glimpse past me out the window. "Maybe you've seen her around the Westinghouse Plant. If we can place her there, then it's possible she's the one who delivered the card."

I nodded while new questions surfaced, none of which I could voice. Wouldn't Papa have endeavored to locate Delvina after his arrival here so many years ago? Maybe he'd tried and hadn't been successful. But then why hadn't he mentioned that in his letters? Though, my parents had never openly spoken of their firstborn. Papa could've believed I had been oblivious to the fact I had a sibling.

And as for me being able to recognize Delvina? The only time I'd rested eyes on my older sister had been through a yellowed picture of an infant bearing the same birthmark across her neck as the one stretching across my stomach.

Perhaps Rhett was right. What if I happened upon her at the plant? Or somewhere else? How odd it would be to pass a blood relative without any hints of recognition. Though I suppose it was possible.

Rhett leaned against the seat and tipped his head toward mine. "My informant tells me Delvina made a reservation at The Regent for half past six."

"The Regent?" One of Pittsburgh's fanciest restaurants. My gaze crept from my faded dress—now creased in several spots from sitting on the trolley for almost an hour—to Rhett with his pinstriped suit and felt hat.

Yet it was more than his impressive wardrobe that had arrested the attention of every female on this cable car. No, his confidence shone in every angle of his commanding profile. What would that even be like? To brim with self-assurance? To be comfortable within the confines of one's own personality? Though I held claim to two personalities. Two conflicting identities. And I must remain the taciturn Kate even if that meant arriving at a lavish restaurant dressed in a garment two sizes too big and cloaked in a falsehood even larger than that.

We arrived at the Forbes Avenue stop, and Rhett offered his hand as I descended from the lofty trolley step. Warm fingers wrapped my bare ones, the skin-to-skin contact jolting me to recall I'd forgotten my cotton gloves at the studio.

The detective withdrew his hand as soon as the soles of my T-straps met the bricked road, but it didn't stop the shock of tingles from racing up my elbow. I fought against a grimace. First the embrace and now this. Could I be any more pitiful? Who shivered at a mere touch of someone's hand?

Perhaps my emotions should bear the blame. This past week had acted like a dull knife to my nerves, serrating, leaving them raw and blistered. And now I was only seconds from seeing my estranged sister.

I willed my breaths even, but the anticipation made my mind as clear as the mud puddle I'd just stepped over.

The Regent's green and gold striped awning came into view, and Rhett glanced over, a reassuring look on his face. I stared a little longer than usual, drawing strength from his Spirelli Sky eyes until I almost tripped on a crack in the sidewalk. Thankfully I caught myself.

"You okay?" His words seemed to stretch deeper than my clumsy falter. Had he noticed my distress? Or had he been aware that I was relying on him as a comfort—something foreign to me and equally dangerous.

"I'll be fine." And would possibly be better if the sidewalk split wide and gobbled me whole. Could I really keep composed knowing I was about to encounter my older sister? And in the presence of a man that hated everything that I had once been proud of—the Salvastano name? I'd soon find out, for Rhett held open the door and gestured me to enter first.

One foot. Then another.

Cigarette smoke swirled the air, and the ceiling fans did nothing but tangle the ashen vapors. Rhett approached The Maître D with a friendly handshake and a clap on the shoulder, addressing the older gentleman by his first name. My brows rose on their own volition, but I soon learned the men attended the same fitness club. While the two of them conversed, my gaze roamed the elaborate room in search of Vinny.

The soft glow from the hanging electric lamps reflected off the ornate tin ceiling. Several couples were seated near the center aisle, but each of the women at the tables had fair complexions, not olive-toned like mine. There was a larger table in the back, though the patrons were on the more mature side of life, all with silver hair. The rest of the tables were filled with men of varying ages.

"She's not here yet." Rhett whispered and then motioned for me to walk with him.

We followed the Maître D to the table in the corner—dimly lit and easily the most intimate spot. Given Rhett's reputation, I wasn't convince being seated at this cozy nook was much of a coincidence.

I took the seat opposite of the detective and set my purse on the chair beside me. "So is there a strategy behind all this?

"There's always a strategy." Candlelight from the silver center-piece flickered across the angles of his face, highlighting his smile. "I just learned from Frederick"—He jerked a thumb toward the Maître D—"that the other name on the reservation is Julian Prove."

"That reporter from the *Gazette*?" I had never seen the man, but everyone knew the name *Julian Prove*. He always covered the important features for Pittsburgh's leading newspaper.

He nodded. "She's meeting with him to discuss her story."

The notion of seeing my name in the paper made my toes curl in my shoes. Remaining far from the spotlight had been the only reason I'd agreed to Rhett's crazy fake lovers scheme. Yet my older sister seemed to crave the headline. Why else contact the biggest name in journalism this side of the Ohio River?

A small party of men and women had been seated at the adjacent table. All were primped to perfection with their lace-overlay dresses and matching hats. Meanwhile my boring beige dress coordinated quite nicely with the folded napkin.

"Don't be uneasy." Rhett offered a comforting look. "All you have to do is get a good glimpse of her. See if you recognize her or not."

"You think she's the one who sent me the card?"

"Anything's possible." He sipped his water. "If you can identify her, it might show a link between you two. Maybe that will bring more clarity to this case."

Oh there was most definitely a link. Sisterhood. I'd been alone for so long and in a few moments another human who shared the same blood would be in this very room. Fighting the rising emotion, I angled away from Rhett and watched the chamber orchestra—a cellist, two violinists, one flutist, and timpanist. Though we were situated on the other side of the room, the delicate strums of *Who's Sorry Now* could reach my ears with perfect clarity. I cherished the classics, but I'd had to perform this popular song several times over since America couldn't get enough of it.

"The server's approaching." Rhett's lowered voice caused me to glance his way. "It's important to act casual."

How many times would he emphasize that? I stuffed my sigh back where it belonged. The man wouldn't say it if I hadn't given him reason to.

"Ah, Mr. Jennings, nice to see you. And at your usual table, I see." Usual. Knew it.

"Hendrick." Rhett raised his water glass in greeting. "Where else could I get Delmonico steak the way I like it?"

The server eyed me, skepticism weighting his gray brows, and slid his questioning gaze to Rhett. Apparently I wasn't Rhett's *usual* type of date.

Rhett's good-natured smile spread wider. "Hendrick, my girl here has never tasted what this place has to offer." He winked at me with such flirtation that I had the unholy urge to throw my napkin at him. I found it rather irritating that he could always be ease and confidence while I was so nervous that I fumbled with the simple task of spreading a napkin over my lap. "She deserves only the best, so I trust you can recommend something noteworthy."

The man twisted the edge of his waxed mustache. "May I suggest the sea bass for the lady? It's the chef's choice."

I reached for the menu and nearly caught my sleeve on fire. Was the nickel-plated candelabra always this close? I yanked back my arm and my elbow smacked the small serving dish. I barely missed coating myself with butter.

"She may need a few moments, Hendrick." Rhett dismissed the server and moved the flickering centerpiece closer to him, causing me to feel like a child. Though I'd rather be keeping Charlie's company than Rhett's. I'd missed his signing lesson for the second evening in a row. Did he feel like I'd abandoned him? I would be certain to tell

Rhett I couldn't go anywhere after work tomorrow. And then ask Charlie if he wanted to join me for the visit to St. Paul's on Saturday.

Rhett peered around the room, as if studying every space, and then focused on me. "I know I sprung this on you. But please allow me to treat you to a meal while we wait for Delvina. You won't find anything better around."

"Looks like you should know."

A flash of wounded surprise shown in his eyes, and I wished my words unsaid. I pretended to peruse the list of dishes on the menu and forced an even tone. "I mean, you have an ear for music and a knack for selecting great food."

"I'm very cultured that way."

"I appreciate the offer, but … I'm not hungry." And I didn't want to owe the man anything. "Though I'm curious, does the server look at all your dinner guests as though they have four heads or only me?"

Rhett dismissed my question with a shrug. "He didn't mean anything by it. You're different than my past dinner dates."

Thought so. Rhett, of course, chose women like Stella, who'd sensually smile at all his winks, hang on his every word, and favor him with several bats of mascara-laden lashes. Making Rhett feel like Al Jolson, Aristotle, and Casanova wrapped into one. But women like the stylish secretary were also the ones who'd snicker over my every flaw, look down on precious souls like Fernando, and on occasion seek attention from the married Westinghouse employees. So being different was much more preferable. Rhett just handed me the best compliment ever.

"Best ever, huh?" Something sparked in his eyes.

My fingers splayed across my lap. Had I said the last part aloud? What was wrong with me? Maybe this entire thing was a bad idea.

I obviously had forgotten my wits back at the station along with my gloves.

"How about a dance while we wait?"

"A what?"

"I'm asking if you'd like to dance with me?"

My gaze darted to the polished wood floor directly in front of the orchestra. Why hadn't I spied that clearing before? Biting the inside of my cheek, the invitation in Rhett's eyes and the beckoning of his outstretched hand pulled the confession straight from my lips. "I don't know how. My guardians never allowed it."

Thanks to Madre Chamberlin's zealous teaching, I could speak English fluently, recite American presidents, and understand the three branches of government, but I couldn't dance the Charleston or any other popular dance. I expected Rhett to tease me, but instead his eyes registered a tenderness that turned my insides mushier than polenta.

"I didn't know you were an orphan."

Another blunder. But this one was costly. I opened my mouth to respond, but a flash of red strolling by caught Rhett's attention. My gaze followed his.

A well-dressed woman—with her slender hand tucked inside the crook of a tall gentleman's arm—was being seated several tables down from them.

Rhett leaned in, the candlelight dancing across his features. "That's Delvina."

CHAPTER 11

R hett reclined against the plush seat and observed Kate's reaction. "Do you recognize her at all?"

With hands fidgeting the napkin, she squinted in the direction of the Salvastano heir, her gaze turning distant as if lost in thought. Rhett glanced at Delvina, and something niggled under his skin.

A Salvastano was in the same room as him.

His muscles flexed, ready to stalk up to her table and demand information about her killer father. Had she been in contact with him? Did she know where he was hidden? Rhett ground his molars, his jaw aching. The promise he'd made hours ago held him captive to the seat. Kate, pulling in air as if it were on short supply, remained his only hope. "Do you know her?"

Her brown eyes snapped to his, her abrupt movement causing his brows to knit.

Was she insulted? He could never tell with her. "Look, I know she comes from a criminal family. I'm not trying to offend you by saying you'd associate with someone like—"

"That's not fair." Her fingers clenched the napkin, then relaxed.

"Pardon?"

"You're implying I should be disgusted with her based on who her father is. Isn't it wrong to despise someone simply because of a last name? It's not her fault."

Her tone was as sharp as his steak knife, but something else snagged his attention. Her "r"s. Did they hint of an accent? Or was he imagining it? His tactic of being patient—gradually earning her trust—wasn't working. He knew about as much as Kate as he did Delvina—next to nothing. He poked his tongue into the side of his cheek to keep from voicing the mounting frustration.

"She could be devastated by her family's criminal history. Have you ever considered that?"

"No. I haven't." He kept his tone even. "Mostly, on account that I only became aware of this woman's existence three hours ago. The only thing I've wondered so far is if you recognize her or not."

"Well your *usual* table also happens to be the dimmest. How could you expect me to get a decent glimpse of her?" She strangled the napkin again. "I need to see her better."

Rhett straightened, unsure of what had gotten into the timid broadcaster. "You can't approach her. It's too risky." It helped having connections to the police force through Major, but if he botched this and made a scene, his mentor would never feed Rhett leads on his cases again.

Kate abandoned the wrinkled napkin and stood, the gold flecks of her eyes sparkling with determination. These past moments, he witnessed an unexpected boldness in her that was both intriguing and alarming. What was she intending to do? Surely Kate wouldn't go speak to Delvina. Palms flattened on the table, he pushed to stand, but Kate pressed her hand on his, stilling him mid-rise.

Mouth parted, she regarded her fingers barely covering his and withdrew her touch faster than one can say 'sea bass'. Their gazes locked, and for a quick breath, he glimpsed what she'd been trying, yet failing, to keep veiled—vulnerability. His chest squeezed even as the fringed-curtain of her lashes closed, breaking their eye contact, shutting him out once again.

Her shoulders lifted with a ragged inhale, and her lids slowly opened. That twinkle resident only seconds ago in the brown depths of her eyes was now masked by something completely different—not quite hesitation but not exactly confidence. She flicked a glance at Delvina and then to him. "Would I have to walk past their table to visit the powder room?"

"Ah, nice thinking." Rhett sunk back onto his chair, impressed by her quick presence of mind. Kate could get a good look at Delvina without appearing suspicious. In truth, he hadn't been able to grab a good glimpse of the woman when she'd strolled by. He'd noticed her raven black hair cropped below her chin and her slight frame overshadowed by the tall journalist. But nothing beyond that. "Go through those doors behind them and down the hall. The powder room will be on your left."

"Thank you." She retrieved her small bag from where she'd set it earlier and walked away. The crooked back-seam of her stockings pulled his attention to her legs. Nice, slender, and ... what in blazes was he doing? He cleared his throat with a slight shake of the head.

She neared the area of tables where Delvina chatted with the reporter, and Kate slowed her pace. The smoke from lighted cigarettes casted a strong haze, blurring Kate's expression, allowing Rhett only to make out her form. She disappeared through the door, and Rhett relaxed.

Hendrick approached the table, and Rhett ordered for them both. Kate could claim she wasn't hungry, but he'd taken her straight here from work. If she'd been home, wouldn't she have eaten dinner by now?

And despite their recent altercation, he couldn't get past her kind exchange with that widower at the station. It stirred something in Rhett, making him want to do something nice for her. To make her grin exactly like she'd made that Fernando fellow beam when he'd discovered she'd baked him something for his birthday.

Over the past week, her rosebud lips had been fixed in a somber, downward tilt. Had she used up all her smiles or was she saving them for special occasions? He shook his head at his own foolishness. The offspring of Pittsburgh's leading mobster sat only a handful of yards from him and all he could focus on was Kate Chamberlin's lips? He finished off his drink, hoping the crisp water would help clear his thoughts.

He needed all his focus to be on nabbing Hugo and keeping tabs on any Salvastano—Delvina included.

I pressed a clammy palm to my collarbone and rested a shoulder against the expensive papered-wall of The Regent's powder room. The soft electric lamps only served to highlight the pale blue circles under my eyes as I grimaced at my reflection in the oversized mirror.

I appeared past my bloom, too withered and worn for only being twenty-four years' old. Yet the woman calling herself Delvina seemed at the peak of her beauty—with brown eyes framed by high cheek bones swathed in an olive-complexion.

But no birthmark.

Cosmetics could hide the blemish. So how could I determine if the woman was truly my sister? With a heavy sigh, I ran a hand down my dress then pushed open the powder room door. The walk down the hallway seemed longer than I remembered, but I was soon met with the clanging of silverware and soft chatter.

My could-be sibling skimmed the menu, slender neck bent, head slightly bowed. I bit my bottom lip and stepped into the main room. It'd been seventeen years since I'd watched my father sail away to America, and I hadn't been near a relative since. The loneliness that'd shadowed me begged to be addressed. I needed to know the truth. Yet I was powerless.

Or was I?

Before I could talk myself out of it, I forced my feet into motion.

Heart pounding in my throat, I took long strides in order to reach Delvina's table at the precise second the server would. I held my breath and fell forward, letting my bodyweight do the rest. My shoulder collided with the server and the two pitchers of water he carried spilled onto Delvina.

A feminine yelp pierced the air as my knees smacked the ground.

"Mademoiselles!" The server's mortified gaze bounced between me and Delvina as if confused as to whom he should assist first.

I launched to my feet and swiped a napkin from the table. "I'm sorry. It's all my fault." I pressed the napkin to Delvina's soaked neck.

"I'm drenched!" Her shocked eyes met mine before she wrung the bottom of her dripping dress.

The server muttered apologies in French. Julian Prove scrambled to gather napkins from the adjacent table. I inspected Delvina's damp neck, the truth scoring deep into my bones.

CHAPTER 12

No birthmark. She wasn't Delvina.

Only a fraud.

Tears welled my eyes, blurring my vision of the congested avenue. I swiped my cheeks with the heel of my palm. The sidewalk teemed with early evening traffic, but my feet moved to the swift pace of my pulse.

Seconds after I'd realized the ugly truth about the imposter sister, I had dashed out of The Regent. I'd never done anything so impulsive. Crashing into a defenseless server? Blotting a stranger's neck with a coarse napkin? Sprinting toward the exit like the place had caught fire?

No doubt everyone had thought me a madwoman.

I tossed a look over my shoulder, making certain I wasn't being followed by the overbearing detective. I licked my lips, tasting salt from my tears. Where could I go? The only route home was the trolley to Braddock. If I waited for the cable car, Rhett would catch up to me.

My stomach clenched. Rhett had made it clear that anyone related to Hugo Salvastano wasn't worthy of any respect. Such a man's judgment wasn't easily swayed. If my secret emerged, I would be branded with the same fire stick as Papa. I'd be punished for his crimes simply for bearing the same name.

My gaze flicked upward. The pressing prayer on my lips would go unvoiced. Again. How could God rescue me while I lived in sin? I'd clung to lies. Surely that was enough to make God turn his ear from my pleas. Now I must be my own defender.

Pivoting on my heel, I turned my back to the trolley stop and made a sharp right. Yet another spontaneous move which wasn't like me. But then I hadn't felt like myself for quite some time. May never again.

Four blocks later, my feverish walking stalled on the corner of Prescott Avenue. A husky lamplighter blocked the crosswalk. Extending the lighting stick as if it were a scepter, he illuminated the gas-fueled lamppost. I almost pitied its weak glow. How could such a feeble light ward off the burden of the hovering gloomy skies. I cut a glance to my left and took in all the other lamps. The collective light proved bright enough to cast my shadow on the sooty walk. Loneliness ran a jagged claw over my soul, exposing the bleeding truth. I stood alone against the darkness. How much could my flickering strength endure before my life extinguished altogether?

"Need by, miss?" The lamplighter stepped aside, a warm smile splitting his weathered face.

"Thank you." A breathy reply was all I could muster.

I crossed the street, pinching my collar to my neck even though the drafty chill had nothing to do with the gentle breeze. A woman carrying an infant hustled past, her dress the same bold red shade as the fake Delvina's. A stony fist wrapped my heart. Why would anyone pretend to be a Salvastano? I'd been desperate to obscure my familial ties while that woman exploited false ones.

Why? What would she benefit by this pretense?

Yet one thought drowned out all others—there was no way to expose the imposter's identity without uncovering my own.

♦ ♦ ♦

"I still can't find Kate." Rhett squeezed the neck of the candlestick telephone with a grip that made his knuckles throb. How could he have lost her? When she hadn't returned to her apartment last evening after the restaurant fiasco, Rhett had scoured every place imaginable. He'd forfeited a night's sleep, but that was nothing compared to what was at stake—Kate's life.

He'd returned home to grab money for gasoline, feed Chimney and check in with David. Soon he'd venture out again, hunting for any trace of her.

"Relax." His agency partner's calm tone through the phone wire splintered Rhett's brittle nerves. "She'll turn up."

"Turn up? I'm sure. It's *how* that has me concerned." Receiver in one hand and base in the other, he paced the small area of his den, the cord stretching taut with his movements. "If he got to her, David ..." A million scenarios screamed from the dark corners of his mind. *God, please let her be okay.*

"Have you contacted her boss?"

"Not yet." Because that would be accepting defeat. Rhett didn't want to inform Frank Conrad of his failure to keep an eye on his prized musician. Not until he had to. "I was hoping I would've found her by now. Her shift starts in two hours. I'll head back to her place, and if she's still not there, I'll go to the plant and face Conrad."

David's sigh crackled through the earpiece. "Let me see what I can do on my end."

"Thanks." He rolled his shoulders and the nagging tension slid to his lower back, sore from the hours on his feet.

Rhett ended the conversation and hung the earpiece on the candlestick base with enough force to make the flimsy table wobble.

He had to find her.

Desperation gnawed his gut. Hugo Salvastano was still on the loose, and heaven knew what the monster was capable of. Just the thought of that man's hands on Kate ignited fire in Rhett's veins. He grabbed his hat from where he'd tossed it on the worn sofa and slapped it on his head.

If he left now he could swing by Major's office before heading to Kate's place. Maybe his father's old friend could give him some quick advice. Or at the very least an aspirin.

"Sorry, pal." Chimney ears twitched at Rhett's voice, but the cat didn't move from its favorite spot between the coffee table and the sofa. "I have to be on my way again."

Chimney's eyes drooped shut with a shiver. Grimacing, Rhett strode toward the front closet and grabbed his scarf. Careful not to disrupt the dozing feline, he'd tucked it around its hind end where the fur had been burned off. The kitten Rhett had discovered frightened and wounded in the blazing Halloway Building had come a long way. Chimney hardly ran from him anymore and had been eating more regularly. He offered the cat the space needed to trust him, and it paid off.

The ticking clock on the wood-paneled wall pressed into Rhett's skull. He had to go. Kate depended on him.

"How about the noise box to keep you company?" Rhett wasn't convinced that Chimney cared, but it made Rhett not feel as guilty leaving the house so quiet. He turned the radio's dial and static rattled the speakers. A groan rippled his chest. He didn't have time to mess with the frequency. He jerked it again, and the disturbance shifted to something else.

Her voice.

Kate Chamberlin's pure soprano tone filled his living room. The ball of tension that had weighted his gut crumbled with his deep exhale. She wasn't in distress, not at the mercy of Hugo. She was singing at the KDKA station.

But then why had she not returned to her place last night? Where had she been?

Relief sparred with annoyance, making him rub the dull ache in his temple.

She was safe. She. Was. Safe. That was all that mattered. Not that she'd put him through an emotional wringer for the past twelve hours. Or that she'd taken a direct hit on his pride by switching shifts, no doubt to avoid him.

Rhett made a brief call to David informing him of Kate's unexpected whereabouts, then he bounded toward the front door. He needed to confront her, yet in a way that wouldn't make her back arch in defense. Maybe he could learn from his dealings with Chimney. Rhett needed to find a way to get Kate to trust him.

CHAPTER 13

The sky rejected its prison gray uniform and unveiled the glories of gold studded in hazy blue.

For about two minutes.

I savored the splash of light from my place on Building K's roof, but just as the clouds pulled its ashen curtain over the sun, my thoughts had the same gloom tugging on my mood.

I shouldn't have taken the coward's way out. Should never have switched shifts. But my heart couldn't stand seeing Rhett so soon after yesterday's disaster at the restaurant. Even now I wished my spine was stiffer than a bowl of Jello. Because while I'd often visited this rooftop—so much that Frank Conrad had brought up a stool for me—I was fully aware it was approaching my routine arrival time for work.

I hooked the heels of my shoes on the seat's rung and rested my elbows on my thighs. Might as well get comfortable. I wouldn't be moving from this spot until I was certain a run-in with a handsome investigator would be ruled out.

Hinges creaked behind me and I jumped.

The paint-chipped door yawned open and Peggy poked her head out, squinting. "I knew I'd find you here." The rest of her petite form emerged, and she walked across the puddle-dotted space toward me. "Thought I'd come in early to check how you were faring."

"Thank you for swapping shifts with me." I stood. "And for giving me a place to stay last night." I had nowhere else to turn, and Peggy had received me like family.

"You're welcome any time." The steam whistle screeched, and Peggy winced, pressing a finger to her earlobe. "Wow, that sounds way louder up here.

I agreed, but the view was worth the aching eardrum.

A gusty breeze pulled wisps of strawberry blonde hair across Peggy's face, and she smoothed it back. "I enjoyed spending time with you. It was kinda refreshing hearing you chat about boys. Proves to me you're human after all." She gave an exaggerated wink and I smiled.

We'd talked late into the night. Well, mostly it'd been Peggy bombarding me with questions about Rhett, and me answering the best I could without revealing too much. It'd been Peggy who devised the idea of swapping shifts so I could sidestep Rhett.

"This wind isn't good for your hairstyle." Peggy stood on her tiptoes, studying my head, then moved closer. "Stand still. A pin's loose."

Fingers dug into my hair, and my scalp paid the price.

"There." Peggy took a step back and admired her work. "I like seeing most of your hair down. I never realized how long it was."

This morning Peggy had armed herself with a hairbrush and a cosmetic bag, determined to make me resemble one of those porcelain dolls stacked on her bedroom shelves. I hadn't been enthusiastic about the idea, but Peggy *had* lent me a dress to wear today, sparing me from wearing the same outfit two days in a row. Add that kindness to all

Peggy's other noble acts over the past twelve hours, and I had relented. The only condition had been that Peggy wouldn't apply too much cosmetics. Which she hadn't.

"You know what I really want to know, right?" Peggy nudged my shoulder with a growing smile. "Tell me how many jaws dropped at how lovely you look? Did Robert Fuller see ya?"

"I'm supposed to be happily in love with Rhett, remember?" And I had no interest in the KDKA sound man. Matchmaking wasn't a hobby Peggy should pursue.

"Yeah, well, Detective Dashing isn't going to be sticking around long. Soon he'll realize that Salvastano card was a strange mistake like you said, and he'll go bother someone else."

If only it were that simple.

"Now tell me." Peggy clasped her hands together and hugged them under her chin. "What did everyone say when you walked into the station?"

Did I really look that different?

Yes, yes I did.

There was no mistaking how the lavender dress complimented my complexion. The stylish drop waist with lace accents was different than anything I'd worn since assuming the role of Kate Chamberlin. Problem was, the moment I had slipped on the dress, I'd felt pretty— something I couldn't chance anyone else considering. I needed to be overlooked. Being ignored kept me safe.

"The only attention I got was a reprimand in Frank's office." On Fridays, I wasn't needed on the secretarial side. So it would've worked out perfectly to exchange shifts if not for the song director getting flustered and complaining to Frank. "He was kind, but firm. Telling me to talk to him before adjusting my schedule." Which had been fair enough. Frank had been so generous in giving me the position in the first place.

Peggy's nose wrinkled. "Did Robert at least drop the microphone stand when he saw you? Walk into the wall? Come on, you have to give me something to squeal over."

"He told me I looked nice."

Peggy's arms collapsed against her sides. "That's it?"

"This is the first time he's spoken to me since he discovered I was dating Rhett."

"But you're not *really* dating Rhett."

"He's not supposed to know that."

"Right." Peggy released an exaggerated sigh. "I should probably head to the studio. Are you going to be okay?"

I nodded, appreciative for the concern in Peggy's tone. "I've survived way worse than this."

Peggy smiled and squeezed my hand. "Just in case you see Detective Dashing, don't let him sweet talk you into doing anything you don't want to do." This would mark the fifth—no, sixth—time my friend had warned me in these exact words about Rhett's suspicious reputation.

"Rest assured. His only interest is this case."

Peggy gave a satisfied nod and started for the door, but then stilled. "Now Robert on the other hand—"

A laughed ripped through me. "Enough talk about Mr. Fuller."

"I'm only reminding you of the possibilities." Peggy giggled and exited the rooftop.

I inhaled the sulfur-laced air. The black cable attached to the small shack on my right swayed back and forth, like a giant metronome keeping time with the wind, stirring my heart with gentle remembrances as to why I loved this particular spot on the globe. The sun broke free from the clouds again, making the wire glisten in its rhythmic dance. No one would know by looking, that the black cord helped make world history and dreams come true. I released a wistful sigh. Would it ever be possible for me to have dreams? What I wouldn't give for my life to be different.

The door creaked again and I shook my head. "Peggy, if it's about Robert." I called without bothering to glance back. "I don't want to hear it. He told me he doesn't like fig pudding and that kind of negativity doesn't make for a lasting relationship."

"I've heard of worse faults." That voice.

I catapulted to my feet and spun.

Rhett stood in the doorjamb, hands holding a brown paper sack, eyes staring. He tipped his hat to me. "I passed Miss Whitmore on the way up here." He took a few strides forward. "She asked me to give you a message." His gaze swept my borrowed attire with a curious perusal.

"She did?"

Another step. "Miss Whitmore says—*Don't let him sweet talk you into doing anything you don't want to do.*" His brow raised, disappearing beneath his bowler. "Why do I get the impression she's talking about me?"

"Because she is."

"Ah, that explains it."

I wished the delicate wind would turn into a gale and whisk me far away from here. The confrontation I'd been skirting was now inescapable. I took in his jawline, darkened with stubble, and the weariness in his eyes. My breath lodged in my throat as I took in his suit. It was the same one he wore yesterday. The stylish Rhett Jennings would never wear the exact suit for two consecutive days unless... he never changed. Surely he wasn't searching for me all night. Was he? Guilt poked my gut with an accusing jab. The weight of my actions pressed against my ribs, making it hard to take a full breath. "I … um … feel I should apologize."

"On which part?" He slacked a hip against the brick barrier. "Leaving me at the restaurant? Having me wander the streets of Pittsburgh in search of you? Or pulling a shenanigan at work so you can avoid me?"

He *was* looking for me. My mouth swung open, my tongue poised to release a thousand excuses, but I offered the only truth I could spare. "I handled everything poorly."

"I think we both have." Rhett straightened, and his two generous steps ate the distance between us. "I propose a truce." His eyes met mine, and he held out the brown paper sack.

Hesitant, I accepted it from him. "What's this?"

"A peace offering."

More candy for Charlie? I peeked inside. A handful of strawberry taffy bars settled around a familiar tin can. My smile broke free. "Fig pudding." I glanced over and found Rhett watching me with a strange expression. "How did you know?" Just a few minutes ago had been the first time I'd ever mentioned my sugary weakness to him.

"You had about a dozen empty cans in your garbage bin the other day."

"Did not." I teased back, but it couldn't be helped. Neither could the smile now growing rampant despite my heart's objection. "Only about five or so. Besides I didn't know you liked this, too."

"Can't stand the stuff." Cloud-speckled sunlight hiccupped across his relaxed form. "Looks like Robert and I will never measure up in your eyes." He let out an exaggerated exhale. "By the way, who's Robert?"

My lips pressed together, hiding my smile. I set the bag atop the stool. "He works at the station."

"Ah, I see." He peered out over the expanse of the Westinghouse kingdom. "Your boss told me you were up here. In case you've been wondering."

Oh I knew. Frank and Peggy were the only ones aware of my favorite spot. Peggy wouldn't dare give away my location to Rhett, which left my boss.

"It's interesting up here."

"Would you like the grand tour?" Anything to not speak of what happened last night. I didn't trust myself to keep the emotion from my face. Knowing there was a woman traipsing about Pittsburgh and claiming to be a Salvastano, unnerved me every passing second. The helplessness turned overpowering if I didn't force my mind onto something else.

"Only if you're my guide." His tone, though not flirty, still released butterflies into my stomach. Or more like crazed bats.

"Let's start with this shack." I stepped to the white-slatted structure.

Rhett followed. "Looks like it's seen better days." He flicked a piece of chipped paint off the siding. "What's in it?"

"It used to hold a hundred-watt transmitter. And see this antenna." I pointed to the black wire attached to the shack's roof. "It stretches all the way to that smokestack. That helps give additional range for broadcasting."

He scratched his stubbly cheek. "I didn't know this was up here."

"They moved on to a five-hundred-watt transmitter, but this was where it all started." I assessed the soot-crusted railings and the grimy rooftop floor. "Coming up here has been a good reminder for me."

"And why's that?"

"People doubted radio from the beginning. Would it work? And if it did, who would spend their money on listening sets? Odds were against it, but the dream proved bigger." Maybe there was hope for me. Opposition had ruled me ever since the earthquake. Could I dare to believe my life could be filled with happiness again? "This humble place reminds me, it's okay to dream big." I risked a glance his direction, fearing I'd spoken too much, but the kind smile on his face revealed I hadn't.

"Well said." But just as my eyes soaked in his pleasing expression the fix of his mouth turned serious. "Speaking of dreams, makes me think of nightmares as well. Kate, when I couldn't find you last night, it rattled me. You could imagine all the awful thoughts running through my mind." Something in his dark tone made the breath stall in my chest.

How inconsiderate I'd acted. Rhett had not only been searching for me, he'd been fearing the worst. I placed a hand on his arm, and his muscle tensed beneath my fingertips. "I'm sorry. I shouldn't have ran." I withdrew my touch and angled away. "I was embarrassed at the scene I made. With all the attention on me, I panicked."

"Kate?" The way my name rumbled from his lips was like a peal of thunder in the distance—hushed but powerful. "I want to be the one you to run to. Not away from."

His words drew my gaze and the silent plea in his eyes beckoned a response. But what could I say?

He removed his hat, revealing a flop of disheveled wavy locks. Rhett had always been as pristine as one of those fashion plates I'd seen on a Kaufman's display with his gleaming, slicked-back hair, but this? The untamable curls—including the wayward one tumbling over his forehead—made the man more appealing.

He placed the derby over his heart and regarded me with an intensity I didn't have the strength to examine. "No matter what Peggy, or even all of Pittsburgh says, you're safe with me. And I aim to prove it."

CHAPTER 14

Rhett didn't bother to control his smile. When he'd given Kate the box of taffy the other day, he hadn't been around to witness Charlie's reaction. But today he was.

The kid's grin shone brighter than the sunshine filtering through Kate's apartment window and was just as rare. It made the earning all the more worth it.

"I have another surprise." Rhett kept his face in Charlie's line of vision, reached inside his pocket, and withdrew the Faber-Castell tin. The man in the store had said the product was the newest craze in the world of art. "These might help bring your drawings more to life." One would think Rhett opened a pirate's treasure chest rather than a slim box of a dozen colored pencils.

Charlie accepted the gift with careful hands as if it was made from delicate glass. Rhett would empty his wallet ten times over to view the look of appreciative wonder on Charlie's face.

Kate pressed a hand on his small shoulder, and he glanced up at her.

"Sandwich and signing lesson first." Charlie would miss her motherly tone if it hadn't been evident in her expression.

The boy huffed like any other kid not getting his way, but Kate signed something, and his frown softened. He stepped in front of Rhett, and his flattened hand touched the bottom of his small chin then lowered, looking like the opening of a drawbridge.

"He said, *thank you.*" Kate clarified.

Ah. "You're welcome, kiddo."

Charlie skipped to the table where Kate had placed cards depicting several hand motions.

"Would you care to stay and eat with us?" Her hand paused on the ice box. "It's only ham, but you are welcome." The flicker of hope in her eyes was enough to sway him.

"I'd be glad to." Something had shifted between them earlier. When he'd stepped foot on the rooftop, he'd been taken back by her appearance. The dress she wore was so different than anything else he'd seen her in. The color reminded him of his mother's beloved lilac tree. But what had entranced him the most was her hair—the sides had been swept off her face, leaving the rest cascading down her back. The rich brown locks had a coppery tint in the sunlight.

Though it hadn't been Kate's outward change that inspired this new friendship, but her inward. She'd appeared remorseful about last night. He still hadn't the chance to ask about Delvina, but for the first time since Monday, he had hope for this case.

They all ate at Kate's tiny circular table. Kate on one side of Charlie and Rhett on the other. The bread wasn't that fresh and the ham was a bit on the salty side, but he would give every compliment to Kate if only to see her smile like she had when he'd given her the pudding. Charlie devoured his sandwich faster than Rhett, making his brow raise. Was this the only time the kid ate?

Charlie tugged on Kate's sleeve and gestured to his empty plate.

She still had half of her meal left. "All right. You can go draw with your new pencils while I finish." Her mock sigh wasn't fooling Rhett.

Charlie jumped up and scrambled to the sofa, grabbing the tin along the way. Kate shook her head, but amusement danced in her eyes. Her foot jittered under the table as she fixed her attention on her plate. Even after those moments on the roof, she still couldn't relax in his presence. Might never be able to.

Rhett flicked a crumb off the tablecloth. "So what did you think about Delvina yesterday?"

She froze mid-bite. Wrong topic. For being a detective, that sure wasn't tactful. Kate placed the sandwich down and wiped her hands on a napkin.

"I've never seen that woman before last evening."

He leaned back in his chair and studied her, searching her face for sincerity. "Looking back, I see what happened at the restaurant as a good thing." He shoved the last bite of sandwich into his mouth.

"Why?"

He swallowed. "Because we also discovered she didn't recognize *you*."

Her expression turned thoughtful. "You're right. She didn't." Her fingers traced one of the flowers on the tablecloth. "How do we know Delvina is who she says she is?"

"What do you mean?"

She cast a quick glance at Charlie and then back to Rhett. "Is there any proof besides her word that she's Hugo Salvastano's daughter?"

Rhett shrugged. "I'm sure the proper authorities will check into it. But in my opinion, she came forward too soon. No one has even found it yet."

"Found what?"

His gaze traced her face. The confusion pinching her brows revealed she had no idea. "You haven't heard about the Salvastano fortune? No doubt Delvina wants to claim it."

"What fortune?"

"The one that's missing."

Her pale fingers pressed against her temple. "I don't understand."

"The Salvastanos never trusted in banks. So the money they've made over the years is somewhere." He finished off his glass of water. "After Hugo's disappearance his bakery was raided and so was the speakeasy they ran. Delvina's not the only one that wants the loot."

A tinge of something unnamed darkened the gold flecks of her eyes. "If the fortune is missing, then how can she claim it? And how does anyone confirm she's his daughter?" Her shoulders slumped. "There are too many questions."

"I know who we can talk to for answers."

Her eyes widened. "Who?"

"Franco Cardosi. The Salvastano family lawyer."

I hooked the cookie-filled basket on my left elbow and snuck a sideways glance at Rhett as we climbed the steps leading to St. Paul's Asylum for Orphans. Charlie had visited me early this morning, and with the saddest frown, signed his father was sick. So while Charlie took care of an undeserving, ailing father, Rhett would act as my stand-in guest at the orphanage. Though the man's solemn eyes and downturned mouth made it appear as if I'd asked him to accompany me to a funeral.

He'd barely spoken a word to me since we'd left my place. Was he upset about not being able to speak with Papa's lawyer because the man was out of town? Or was Rhett's silence from something else? Maybe from his past. Grief had the manners of a discourteous houseguest—it arrived unexpected and overstayed the welcome.

I rapped on the orphanage's large wooden door. Rhett's gaze flicked upward and his lips moved as if he were praying. And from the bob of his Adam's apple, he was struggling at it.

The door cracked open, revealing Sister Rosemary dressed in her customary nun's habit and clothed with the kindest smile. "Greetings, Miss Chamberlin. The children will be delighted to see you." Aged blue eyes settled on Rhett. "I see you brought a different visitor today."

"Indeed." My fingers squeezed Rhett's arm. He'd been adamant that I shouldn't leave my apartment without his company, so here we were. "This is Mr. Rhett J—"

"Just Rhett." His wooden smile was unconvincing.

Then it hit me. Rhett's tense praying. The awkwardness around a woman of faith. Could Rhett Jennings be sensing the Lord's conviction? Or *Heaven's tug* as Madre Chamberlin had always said.

Too bad I couldn't offer him any advice. God and I hadn't been on speaking terms since I'd become a walking lie. "Are the children through with their lunches?" I raised the basket of sugary treats.

She nodded, her wimple slightly dipping on her forehead with the motion. "They finished a few moments ago. They're still in the great room."

I thanked the nun and tapped Rhett's elbow, signaling him to move.

A muscle ticked in his jaw, and he followed my lead down the hall, the slap of our footsteps against the wood floors the only noise against the silence. My hand may be curled around his arm, but from the distant look in his eyes, he was at a place I couldn't reach.

Maybe he needed space, room to gather his emotions. It was possible my nearness brought him agitation rather than comfort. I flexed my fingers, releasing my touch, but his other hand cupped over mine, gently pinning my palm to his arm. The look in his eyes both pleading and haunting—as if he needed me. He didn't. He needed someone way stronger than us both. If only I could guide him to that Mercy Seat. But how dare I when my own sin screamed from the dark recesses of my soul?

We were both lost. And it was tragic.

The whir of children's voices grew louder as we approached the door.

I gripped the tarnished doorknob, though I couldn't bring myself to open it. "It's all right to wait outside if it will make you more comfortable."

"No, I need to stay."

Because of me? The man was like a watch dog when it came to my safety. "Rhett, no harm will come to me inside these walls."

"It's not that." His lips pressed together then relaxed. "I'll be fine. Let's get this over with."

His words stung but I wouldn't let them affect me. I opened the door, and Rhett stepped behind me. It took less than a handful of seconds for the children to notice us, but once eyes landed on me, the precious hoard of children dashed forward. Sister Kathleen clapped her hands to gain order, but gave up when they continued their advance.

Rhett's hand settled on my lower back, no doubt sensing the impending stampede. The man couldn't help but protect, guard me from anything and everything, but this was an invasion I welcomed. I turned, handed him the basket with a cheeky smile, then knelt, arms outstretched.

"Miss C.! Miss C.!" Lucy reached me first. Her red curls bobbing as she bounced on her toes. I wrapped an arm around her in greeting.

Jacob and his brother Douglas, with their matching toothless grins, fought for space on my other side. I laughed and stretched to embrace them both. Several more children joined in, almost knocking me over. Oh how these little ones refreshed my soul.

I stood and dusted off my skirt. "I've brought a guest with me today. Allow me to introduce you to Mr. J—"

"Just Rhett."

Again? Why wouldn't he let me say his last name? I shot him a sideways glance.

His lips wobbled into a smile. "Nice to meet all of you."

Lucy tugged my elbow and pointed to the basket in Rhett's hand. "What's in there?"

"It's filled with goodies, of course." I patted Lucy's head.

Rhett stood stoic, like one of the garden gnomes on the back lawn. I still wasn't sure what was causing the shift in his mood, but I'd do what I could to brighten it. When I'd been anxiety-ridden the other day in his arms, he'd used music to distract me. Would the same strategy work for him? "How about a song?"

Cheers erupted, and I took that moment to lean into Rhett. "How about a wager?"

"Pardon?" His brows spiked.

I held up a finger and addressed the children. "Find your seats around the piano. I'll be right there."

Chaos ensued.

While the sweet sisters managed the raucous, I turned back to Rhett. "Let's play a game." My mouth curled in a saucy grin. "I'll choose a familiar song and alter some of the notes. If you have a trained ear as you claim, then listen for the note variants and tell me the word I spell. That is, if you can?"

Blue eyes sparked, and that was all the encouragement I needed. I relieved him of the basket, setting it on the nearby table, and grabbed his hand. If he had any objection, I couldn't hear it over the children's exuberant squeals.

I inched the bench forward so I could reach the pedals, then sat. This instrument was hardly in tune, but I adored the baby grand for the amusement it brought to little hearts. I glanced over my shoulder, and Rhett stood, face impassive.

I wasn't sure if he'd actually play along, but I'd make it challenging for him just in case. Most children's songs were simple, so I'd have to flavor the melody to mask any note changes. I decided on a popular tune, and then allowed my fingers to fly across the keys. The children sang along, their sweet voices clashing with the tinny piano. After several rounds through, I varied enough notes to spell a word. Satisfied, I ended the song.

The children clapped, and I acknowledged their applause with a smile. In my peripheral, Rhett hadn't budged from his spot. A wave of embarrassment flushed through me. He probably thought me the silliest creature on earth by creating such a foolish game. I'd only wanted to cheer him up. Why had I believed—

"F-A-C-E." Rhett spoke from behind me. "You changed the notes to spell *face*."

My breath left me. "Well done." I twisted on the bench to catch the softening of his expression. "I wasn't sure you were listening."

His large hand cupped my shoulder. "I believe it's my turn now."

"You play?" I'd imagined him only to be an enthusiast, not a musician.

"Not as well as you." And oh, that lost smile returned to his face in all its pulse-pounding glory. "But I'll give it my best shot."

I started rising, but he motioned for me to sit.

"There's room for both of us."

No, there wasn't. But who was I to disagree? Thankfully whatever had been distressing him had subsided. He eased in beside me, his side brushing mine, sending a rush of warmth to the ends of my fingertips.

The children's chatter muted to an anticipating hush. From the way my breath flitted about my chest, I was just as eager.

"So you know." He leaned toward me and met my eyes. "I don't intend to make this easy."

My lips pulled into a smile on their own accord. "I'm hoping you won't." This was my game, and I intended to be its champion. But then ... I wasn't familiar with all the American songs. What if he chose one I'd never heard? How would I explain that?

Posture set over the keys, he tossed me one more look and pressed the ivories with a comfortable flair. I exhaled relief. It was a nursery rhyme. To play fair, I didn't watch his right hand as it pounded out the melody, though his left hand did an excellent job exaggerating the supporting tune. He was trying to throw me off, but I prided myself on my keen sense—oh, there was a 'C' out of place.

I inclined my ear, eyes sliding shut, focusing on the music. The children clapped along, which would've distracted me had I not been fixed on winning. There was another one. *An 'A'.*

So 'C' and 'A' so far. A slow smile spread. With the limited number of letters, there were only so many words that could be formed. I committed them to memory. He played the melody through several more times, and I'd collected the rest of his secret code along the way. The letters strung together to form …"Cabbage." I blurted out as he was closing his song. "What made you think of cabbage?"

"Wrong." His smirk turned mischievous, and he punched the final note. It clashed horribly, making me wince. The last variant—a 'D'.

I'd spoken too soon.

"Cabbaged, sweetheart." His grin was one of triumph, but I felt like the winner.

I was able to brighten his dark mood. And while his endearment stemmed from good humor, I couldn't help but relish the way it caressed my heart. Oh heavens, I was in trouble.

He leaned closer, eyes on me. "Is there a prize for winning?"

The need to escape propelled me to my feet.

If only to catch my breath and remind myself that he poured out charm like bootleggers with moonshine—and it had a similar heady effect. I couldn't take it personal, no matter how much my affection-starved soul craved it.

"Is it cookie time?" One of the kids called from somewhere opposite the piano.

I welcomed the valid excuse to move from this man's presence and scurried to retrieve the basket. I lifted the cheesecloth and ushered the kids to the tables in the corner of the room. My eyes found Rhett without my brain's permission. He was watching me, intently, and the warm approval in his gaze was something that could give me a third degree burn if I wasn't careful.

CHAPTER 15

Darkness smelled like dirt and blood.

Something had crashed onto me, trapping me to the ground, crushing my chest. I dared not squirm or the splintered daggers sliced deeper, knifing the air in my lungs. Oh, why had I sneaked out of the house in search of my kitty? Now Mamma and Papa wouldn't know where I was.

If only I could yell without the blackness swallowing my cries. My throat burned, but I hummed anyway. I needed a song, craved Mamma's lullaby more than the thinned air. Imagining her gentle face and soothing touch pushed away the crowding fear.

My eyes drifted shut, but the darkness remained. Voices drummed against my temple, loud at first then growing silent. No one saw me. They were leaving. I struggled against the choking sob. The numbness in my chest stretched to my shoulders, my neck, crawling down my spine. How easy it would be to surrender to it, but my gut told me to fight.

Someone called my name.

The debris lifted, freeing my mangled frame. Shafts of sunlight blinded my aching eyes, but I welcomed the pain. Papa reached for me, smiling though tears welled his eyes. He was here. Everything would be okay.

He stooped lower, and his face turned angry. A meanness I'd never glimpsed before. Unable to move, I cried for him to love me, to hold me like he always had.

The sun slipped behind the clouds and a storm swept in. He reached for me again, but then grabbed his chest, pain twisting his weathered face.

I was losing him.

"Papa!" My yells didn't affect him.

He collapsed beside me.

"Kate." Papa's eyes were lifeless, but his cracked-dried lips moved. Calling. "Kate."

Wind rustled around me. Movement. Shadows.

The edges of my consciousness blurred. I groaned into my pillow. The softness of my sheets against my clammy skin informed me the nightmare had ended. At least for now.

"Kate. Are you okay?"

My eyelids popped open, and I shot up. A man *stood* beside my bed.

I shrieked, and the form bent toward me.

"It's me. Rhett."

My pulse thudded so hard, it seemed to echo through my being. Why was he in my room? What was going on?

"Talk to me." His voice hitched. "Are you hurt?"

My vision slowly adjusted to the dark surroundings. "I'm fine. But—"

Strong arms swept me into an embrace. "Thank God," he whispered, pulling me closer, the fierce rise and fall of his chest matching my own staccato breaths. "Someone broke in. Could still be here."

My heart catapulted into my throat. An intruder? My gaze flew to the open window.

He released me and a rustling sound followed. "I need to check the other room." Pale moonlight glinted off his gun.

"What are you going to do?" My voice was low and reedy.

"Where's the bat?"

I reached under my bed and pulled out George.

"Keep it close to you. No matter what happens. If you hear me yell, go down the fire escape and get help. But *only* if I say so, okay?"

"Yes." My voice quivered, along with the rest of me.

He squeezed my hand, then stood. My gaze followed his shadowed outline as he moved from my room.

Lord, please keep him safe.

Would God listen if my prayer was for someone else? Or was He deaf to all my pleas? The darkness pressed in beside me, and I was torn as to where to fix my gaze—on the door or the window.

Who could have intruded? What did they want? I eased off the bed and inched toward the door, clutching George with slick palms. A shuffling noise was all I could distinguish, followed by the recognizable sound of the front door closing and locking.

"It's okay, Kate." Rhett called from the other room. "Whoever it was, left."

My shoulders sagged.

Needing the comfort of light, I flicked on the electric lamp. Rhett rejoined me. A few steps in the bedroom and he froze, causing my anxiety to return.

"What's the matter?"

His gaze swept over me, and he swallowed. Hard. Oh, I was in my nightgown. Rhett angled away and preoccupied himself with investigating the window. With swift movements, I grabbed my robe and wrapped myself in it.

"The person came in through here." Rhett studied the sill as if the answers to the mystery were engraved on it. "That's how I came in, too." He finally looked at me. His eyes weren't stern but regretful. "You need to keep the windows closed. I'll get you an electric fan to keep you cool."

I worried my bottom lip. Someone was here. In my room. The backs of my knees trembled, and I lowered onto the bed.

Rhett pulled over the vanity stool and straddled it. "Are you sure you're okay? You're not harmed in any way?"

I gathered the robe tighter around my throat. "I'm fine. I had no clue anyone was here. Maybe that was why I had the—" *Nightmare.* But I wouldn't tell Rhett the horrid night vision that had blended my childhood and my present. "How did you know?"

He palmed the back of his neck. "I saw him come in."

"What?" Rhett's home was in Pittsburgh. What was he doing in Braddock at this hour?

"Kate." A shaft of air blasted from his lips. "I've been watching your apartment every night." The dark circles under his eyes confirmed his words.

What would've happened if Rhett hadn't shown up? I didn't believe the intruder had been Papa, but what if it was someone from the gin-joint down the road? Someone with cruel intentions? I placed a hand on Rhett's arm, and his gaze crashed into mine. "Thank you."

He nodded, and I withdrew my hand.

"When I saw him come in, I-I … thought that—" He launched to his feet as if the stool had caught fire and paced the floor. Stopping mid-stride, his penetrating eyes settled on me, the deepening blues making the breath snag in my chest. "I thought I was too late. Like I was too late with my father."

He knelt before me, his gaze tracing my face with a tangible intensity, as if ensuring I was real, alive.

"I'm here." The words felt foolish, but somehow I knew they needed voiced. For him.

His hand stretched toward me, stilled, then fell to his side. Behind the thin layer of relief lingered wells of guilt. And the shame transferred to me. It was my papa that'd been the source of Rhett's sorrow.

Maybe it was time to abandon the hope of my father's innocence and accept reality. Though embracing the truth wouldn't help anything, only throw me in harm's way. Big Dante's men wouldn't be merciful to the daughter of their rival. The police would hound me for information I didn't have. And as for Rhett? I cut a glance at him—now standing with his arms barred across his expansive chest. *Those arms*. They may have held me a few moments ago, but they'd be the first to push me away if he discovered my lies.

I swallowed the hurt and flicked my gaze at the clock on my vanity. "It's two in the morning?"

"Yeah."

I smoothed a hand over my disheveled hair, the movement pulling Rhett's interest. I'd worn it half-unbound the other day, but this? It was all down and everywhere, probably shocking him at the wildness of it. My mind searched for something—anything—to say. "Did you get a good look at him?"

"No." His focus drifted to the ceiling, to the dresser, glancing everywhere but on my unsightly self. "I was a fair distance away. I couldn't distinguish anything beyond a vague profile." His attention snagged on the vanity. "Perhaps it wasn't a *him* at all." He grabbed something off my grooming tray and inspected it.

"What do you mean?"

"Another 'S' card." He held it out, and my eyes caught sight of a name ...

Delvina.

CHAPTER 16

"*Watch*" Rhett read aloud the lone word above Delvina's name. The messy script didn't strike him as one from a feminine hand, but maybe it'd been jotted in haste? Or ... in the dark. That would account for some of the letters being scrawled atop each other. Probably was written right here in Kate's bedroom.

"I don't understand." Confusion bled into her words, her lowered brows a rumpled line across her forehead. "Is this woman threatening me?"

"Appears so." Why would she single Kate out? The other day at the restaurant there'd been no sign of recognition on Delvina's face. Rhett would have to ask David to trail the Salvastano daughter tomorrow and look into her activities. He'd always suspected Hugo to be the culprit, but ...

He glanced at the card, resting in the hollow of his palm. Had the shadowy profile he'd spied entering Kate's apartment been a woman? Rhett couldn't be certain. What kind of game was this intruder playing? Breaking in with the sole purpose of leaving a card? It didn't make sense.

Kate lowered her head, and a lock of hair whispered across her cheek, pooling against the slender column of her throat.

Man alive.

He hadn't been prepared for this. When he'd spotted the person going through Kate's window all he could think of was getting to her, keeping her from an attacker. He hadn't considered happening upon her in a pale pink nightgown, dark hair flowing over her bare shoulders, vulnerability shining in her eyes. Thank heavens, she'd put on her robe, but still, he needed to inspect the area and get out of here before he lost his mind. He crossed to the window, pulled in a healthy lungful of night air, and slammed it shut. Locked it. Kate's gasp pricked his ears, but there was no other option.

Her safety came first.

He scanned the room, pacing methodic lines, making certain no other clues had been left behind. Satisfied, he propped a shoulder against the door jamb, leaving a comfortable space between he and Kate.

While he'd been scouring every inch of her room, he completely missed one important detail—Kate. Silent tears flowed down her face, his heart wrenching at the sight.

"What's wrong?"

"I can't say." Her gaze darted from the window to the door behind him, lips snapping shut. She ran a hand over her hair, stroking the rich tendrils with her fingers, as if self-soothing. So distracting, he forced his gaze on her glossy eyes.

"Kate." Her name rumbled off his lips. "You can tell me anything."

The skin bunched around her pained stare as she sat motionless. Like a grieving statue. "I'm not ..." Her voice was pleading. "I'm not the woman you think I am."

What? She's not the woman I . . .

It hit him like an elbow to the jugular. He'd locked the window, and now he stood by the door, blocking any means of escape. She'd heard the rumors of his jaded past and had just caught him staring at her. What else could she be thinking?

"I never once thought you a woman ... like that." Heat crawled up his neck, but she needed to realize the truth. "I would never be forward with you. Ever."

She blinked. As if his frank words weren't expected. Great, she didn't believe him. What else could he say?

He took a step back from the threshold as if removing himself completely from her bedroom would help convince her. "I have a history I'm not proud of. But—"

She held up a hand. "You don't have to. I didn't mean it to be taken—"

"No. You have every right to know." Didn't she? After all, Rhett was standing in her bedroom at an ungodly hour. It would be the only considerate route to take, especially if he were to gain her trust. Though what he was about to say, he could lose her respect. Blast his mistakes. "Maybe we can chat in here." He jerked his head toward the main area of her apartment.

She readily agreed and followed him into the parlor, but instead of squeezing onto the tight sofa, Rhett decided sitting at the table in the small dining area would give her more space. She claimed the same chair she'd used the other day when they'd eaten sandwiches with Charlie and Rhett took the seat beside her.

He cleared his throat, hoping the words he was about to say wouldn't scare her off forever. "My mom died of tuberculosis when I was fighting in the Great War. I wasn't there for her. I didn't get to say goodbye. Wasn't there for the funeral." He traced small circles on the tablecloth with his finger, gaze lowered. "She'd always been my anchor, so when she was gone, I drifted. Badly. Then after Father was killed, I was lost at sea completely." He hazarded a glance at her.

She offered him a delicate smile—one that said she was listening.

"I'm not proud of my sins."

Her face held no judgment, giving him courage to continue.

"I regret every one of my mistakes. And there were many. Women I met overseas during the war. Some from dance halls." His gut sunk lower and lower with his confession. "But I can tell you this, I never took advantage of any of them. They were willing. But it didn't make it right." No doubt he looked vile compared to her high standards, using his parents' deaths as excuses for his waywardness. "My partner, David, helped me get grounded again. He introduced me to Jesus."

Her eyes widened.

"I'm new at this faith stuff, but I'm grateful for mercy."

Awkward silence stretched between them. He'd said too much. Maybe he should've never mentioned his dark days.

"I never said goodbye to my mother either." Her words pulled his gaze, and he spotted the anguish instantly. "When I was six, she died in an ..."

"In what?"

She paled, eyes closing. "A wall collapsed on her. It crushed her. So much so, they wouldn't let me see her. I had to bid farewell to a closed casket." Her lashes, glistening from tears, lifted and her eyes fastened on him. "This isn't easy for me to say. You're going to look at me differently from now on. And I'm sorry for it."

Something twisted in his gut and a thousand questions rattled his brain, but he forced them silent. "Go on."

"It's about my papa." Her voice held a sob. "After Mamma died, he struggled. Being a widower filled with grief, he left me behind.

Another couple raised me. I haven't seen him in all these years, but …"
Her voice choked. A hand splayed to her collarbone as if it physically
hurt her to speak.

Her father had left her. Abandoned her.

The urge to comfort Kate with his touch—pull her into his arms,
hold her trembling fingers, anything—pulsed through him, but after
his admission of weakness with women, he kept his hands clamped to
his sides.

"You don't understand. My father is—"

"I do understand. Kate, I'm an orphan, too."

"What?"

He nodded.

"But I thought …"

"I never talk about it." He ran his hand through his hair. He wasn't
accustomed to opening up to people. But the goal he'd set—to win her
trust—had been achieved. She trusted him with the story of her aban-
donment. He would return the gesture. Tell her what he hardly said to
anyone. "I'm sure you noticed my odd behavior at St. Paul's earlier. The
last time I was in that building, I was a resident. An orphan, like you."

She gasped. "You were placed at St. Paul's?"

"The first five years of my life. I was left at Nelson theater when I
was an infant."

Understanding lit her eyes. "So that's why you didn't want me to
introduce you."

"It was silly. I didn't see any of the same sisters, but yeah. That was
why. I didn't want anyone to recognize my adoptive name Jennings."

Her fingers cupped her cheek. "I'm so sorry. Had I known, I
wouldn't have forced you to come."

"You didn't force. Until this case is over, I go where you go. It's as
simple as that." The sadness in her eyes, prompted his touch, reaching

for her without his mind's permission. He placed his hand over hers, still resting against her face. "More so, it was something that needed done. I came to grips with my past."

That building, each soot-layered stone, every slate shingle, was as much a part of him as any vital organ. It'd been the place that'd kept him alive—provided for him—but also the site he hadn't been able to return to. Until Kate came along.

"And I have you to thank for it." His hand fell to his side, but their connection remained tangible. No wonder since they shared a common thread. She'd understood the misery of being rejected, being left behind.

"You faced something difficult. That took a lot of courage." Something flickered in her eyes. "I admire you for it."

His heart warmed at her approval. "When you sat at the piano, I realized I had more to be thankful for than to be ashamed of. You see, I played that instrument before you did. It's where I had my very first lesson with Sister Agatha." He smiled at the memory. "You helped remind me of how blessed I was to have had a place like St. Paul's."

Her delicate smile blossomed, and it was all he could do not to reach for her again. When had she become special to him? When had she passed the line from client to—dare he admit—something more than that. A friend.

"Who would've thought you and I shared a unique bond?"

She stiffened. "There's something you need—"

"It's uncanny how similar our situations are. Like you, I had a kind couple raise me. They took me in as their child." His mind traveled back to the day Sister Agatha had told him the Jennings family decided on him to be their little boy. Not a cute infant. But him.

"William Jennings had given me a new life. He gave me his name." Rhett stared at his knuckles, pressing past the emotion clogging his throat. "He raised me like I was his own. Called me his son. We couldn't have been any closer than if we shared the same blood."

"You lost so much."

"That's why this case is important to me. I need to avenge his death and bring the man to justice who'd ripped him from my life."

She drew in a sharp breath.

He was too passionate. But how could he not be? "I'm sorry if that sounds harsh. But I won't apologize for my purpose. If Hugo Salvastano is still breathing, then I'm going to find him. If he's dead …" He exhaled deeply. "Then it's no better than he deserves."

A tremble rocked through her.

Perhaps the conversation was too heavy for what she'd just gone through. He should let her rest. "I'm going to check the perimeter of the building and then return to my post." He stood and tugged the hem of his vest. "Are you okay? Is there anything else you need to talk about?"

She peered up at him, a sad slant to her feeble smile. "No. There's nothing more I can say."

CHAPTER 17

"To what do I owe this privilege, Detective Jennings?" Franco Cardosi's heavy accent made him sound like he resided in the heart of Florence rather than the belly of Pittsburgh. The Salvastano lawyer took a long drag on his Toscano cigar, his thick eyebrows barely raising over aged brown eyes.

The leather chair I sat in screamed luxury, but for all its plushiness, I couldn't be more uncomfortable than if it'd been upholstered with metal spikes. The high, bone-colored office walls would intimidate me if not for the gold-leaf framed pictures of the Coliseum and the Pantheon dotting the massive space. While I'd always worked to conceal my heritage, he seemed proud to display his. A piece of me mourned that. Would I ever be able to return to Catarina again?

I had almost confessed everything to Rhett last night. The lies had pressed so hard against my sternum, swelling to the point of difficulty taking a full breath in the man's presence, feeling like I'd snap if my secrets weren't released. Then Rhett had confessed his own, his heart so bent on vengeance, widening the chasm between us.

"We'd like to discuss the Salvastanos." Rhett removed his hat and capped it on his knee, that familiar rogue curl toppling onto his forehead.

"Haven't we been over this before?" The lawyer didn't so much as blink. "I have nothing new to report." He leaned forward, stretching his right hand over his desk as to give a parting shake.

Rhett didn't stir. "No. But we do." He cut a quick glance at me then sharpened his stare on the older man. "Your client may have been in contact with this young lady."

Mr. Cardosi's hand drooped, and his gaze swung to me. "May have?"

I opened my mouth, but Rhett spoke first. "She got a *calling card*."

"May I see it?" Hugo wiggled his knobby fingers.

Rhett gave me a nod, and I withdrew the one I'd received at the plant from my purse. Hesitant, I handed it to the man, his weighted stare making my insides squirm.

He inspected the card with half-lidded eyes and tossed it on his desk with shrug. "That could be from anyone."

"True." Rhett scooped it up and handed me back the card. "But it could be from Hugo."

Why would Papa use this person as his solicitor? There was a coldness in the older man's expression that made my palms clammy. He didn't seem one to trifle with, but Rhett's stony jaw revealed he was up for the challenge.

"How come this woman receive a card?" The lawyer's mouth bowed with an amused smile, and his hooded stare lingered on me. "Are you a rumrunner, young lady?"

"Leave her alone, Cardosi." Rhett's tone was cool, but his fingers gripped the chair's armrest. "We didn't come here to play your games."

"I'm not sure Hugo's behind all of it." I was careful not to let my accent slip. Being around another from my homeland almost drew the inflection out. I took a stabling breath.

Rhett's gaze caught mine, and he held it for a brief second before turning his focus back on Mr. Cardosi. "It's possible Delvina Salvastano gave Miss Chamberlin the card. Though we don't know why."

The lawyer took another puff on his cigar, the smoke climbing into the air like gnarled fingers. His gaze shifted between Rhett and me as if calculating his next move. "She's a fraud."

My pulse thudded. How'd he know? Did Papa speak to him of Delvina? Of me?

"You say that with such conviction." Rhett leaned forward. "What makes you so sure the woman's an imposter?"

He shrugged. "Simple. Hugo had no children."

His words withered my heart like a rose against a wintry gust. Papa had never mentioned me? Not even once?

The man had to be lying.

Or maybe it was Papa who'd been the liar. He'd lied to his attorney about my existence. Lied to me about his life in America. Maybe all of his letters hadn't been sincere. He'd kept me in a mindset of make believe, always portraying himself as the golden-hearted father yet he'd had blood-stained hands.

But how could someone maintain such a falsehood for so long? For seventeen years? I'd barely been able to manage my own fake persona for nine months.

What if Papa hadn't mentioned my existence as means to protect me from all of this? Yet I'd stepped into his world. A world he could've avoided if he'd only stayed with me in Spirelli.

"Delvina has a very strong case." Rhett's counter brought me back to the present. "Saying she'd come over on the S.S. Genoa in eighteen ninety-eight when her parents struggled because of the famine."

"And so what?" Mr. Cardosi scoffed. "Instead of being concerned for her dear papa, she's trying to get Hugo declared legally dead? All so she could claim his fortune? A treasure hunter is all she is."

I couldn't disagree there. But how had this woman known the nickname Vinny? Or all the facts about the family? That was difficult information to unearth. I was at an extreme disadvantage with more questions than answers.

"What about the fortune?" Rhett asked. "I thought no one could find it? What good would it do for this woman to get the courts to declare him dead if she couldn't locate the fortune?"

Maybe the fake Delvina knew where it was? Maybe she was also aware the only other person with a rightful claim to such an inheritance was me.

"That's not entirely true." Franco set his cigar on a copper tray and folded his knuckly hands. "There's a nice sized account in the Federal Union bank."

"But I thought the Salvastano's didn't trust the bank—"

"They didn't." Franco interrupted with an agitated tone. "But they set it up to render monthly payments to those in their service."

"Like you." Rhett's smirk would hardly be considered friendly, but more accusing.

Franco tapped his cigar on the ash tray in slow movements as if he had all the time in the world to answer. "Yes. Like me."

"So if Hugo was declared dead, then that would stop your continual stipend, correct?"

I could almost choke on the tension suffocating this place. I folded my hands in my lap before I reverted into my habit of wringing them raw. Hands that only a dozen hours ago had been tucked beneath Rhett's strong ones for the briefest of moments. I should've pulled away from his touch like I'd done before, but at that moment I couldn't. With this morning's dawn also came the enlightenment that I had to withdraw from him.

I forced my stare out the window, peering through the slits of blinds. Even the solace I'd glean from glimpsing the outside world wasn't deadening the snaring emotions. I'd been trapped by something internal, the walls of my lies were closing in on me.

"You okay, Miss Chamberlin?"

I stiffened at the lawyer's words. His gaze bore into me. Could he see a resemblance? I always thought I favored my mother, but even those images were hazy in my mind. "I'm fine. Just a bit warm."

He nodded and took another drag on his cigar. "To answer your pert question, Detective Jennings. Yes. If Hugo was found dead— which I don't believe he is—then I would administer the will and testament. After that, my services would no longer be needed."

Rhett lazily drummed his fingers on the armrest. "Has Hugo Salvastano been in contact with you?"

"The law is after him."

"That didn't answer my question. Has Hugo contacted you in any way?"

"No." Franco said the word with a snarl that'd make even Mussolini cringe. "Now if you don't have any further questions, I have other matters to attend. I bid you good day."

I collected what was left of my confidence and stood. Once outside, Rhett faced me. I could almost see the thoughts churning behind those determined blue eyes.

"So what did you think of all that?" I motioned toward the office building.

"He's lying."

CHAPTER 18

R hett approached the front desk of the River Oaks hotel. A woman, he presumed by the white tuft of hair stacked atop a narrow head, hid behind the afternoon paper. "Good day, ma'am."

The newspaper didn't even flutter, but Rhett could've sworn he heard a huff.

"I was wondering if Miss Salvastano was receiving visitors today?" If David hadn't successfully trailed the crime boss's daughter yesterday, it would've taken longer to discover her lodgings, precious time Rhett already felt slipping through his fingers.

The paper inched lower, revealing an older woman with a disgruntled face. "Who wants to know?" Her head tilted, and she gave Rhett a good onceover. Her dress, black in color and severe in style, made her look more like a warden matron than a front desk operator.

"The name's Everhett Jennings." He'd been to this hotel on several occasions when he'd worked on the force. This establishment was known for its cheap furnishings and even cheaper rates, attracting patrons who needed to stretch their dollars, including those of questionable integrity. The way Delvina had been dressed at the restaurant, draped in fox fur and strings of pearls, one would've thought she'd rented the penthouse of William Penn, not holed up in a place where rat droppings soiled varnish-stripped floors.

"She's not in." The clerk snapped the paper in front of her again, not-so-subtly hinting the conversation was finished.

But Rhett was only getting started.

Between Delvina and Cardosi, the mystery had grown in intensity, involving more factors than Hugo and his crimes. It was up to Rhett to untangle the questions, separate truth from lies. Plus keep Kate safe above everything else.

She'd been invading his mind on a regular basis, thoughts ranging above the usual concern for her welfare. He was getting attached. While he considered her lovely, his attraction would've been the same if he'd been blindfolded. Because while most women, like Delvina and Stella, flaunted their mink stools and painted smiles, Kate clothed herself in kindness—and it was breathtaking.

Since he'd become a Christian, he hadn't allowed his mind to consider a relationship, too much temptation involved. Could he harness his physical cravings, when he'd given in so easily before?

God help him.

"Did she say when she'd be back? I'm prepared to wait." Having just saw Kate to her shift at the plant, Rhett had a generous pocket of time before having to meet her again.

Another huff. "She left a note saying she'd be gone all day."

Probably a lie.

Rhett leaned on the counter.

The woman peered at him from above the crinkled newsprint, eyes as inky as the text she read.

He studied his fingernails as if he had nothing better to do in life.

"Fine." She slapped the paper on the counter, edges rumpling with the movement. "Maybe this will convince ya." Her spindly fingers held out a small note.

Rhett raised it by the dust-coated lampshade and read the loopy script.

> *Have a lot of errands today*
> *If anyone calls on me*
> *take a message.*
> *Delvina*

He conceded the grumpy hotel clerk had been honest, concerning this instance at least. What a turn of events. While he wasn't thrilled to miss his chance with Delvina, he now had in his hands a sample of her handwriting.

The way she'd written the "D" in her name looked nothing like the one on the card Kate had received. Granted, the person in her room had been in a hurry and it'd been dark, but shouldn't there be some similarities? Unless Delvina disguised her handwriting. But then why mask her script if she'd planned on signing her name?

Could he have interpreted the "S" card wrong? Maybe it hadn't been intended to read "Watch" signed by Delvina. What if it was supposed to say "Watch Delvina"? As if it had been a note of warning? To be on guard against the gangster's daughter? He scanned the feminine script before him.

Who would warn Kate? Was it Hugo? Rhett couldn't imagine that man as anything but vile. Hugo Salvastano wasn't capable of decency. No. It was all a mind game. And Kate was somehow involved. Rhett didn't have all the pieces, but he would work to collect them. Then he could beat the old man at his own devices.

"Bout done yet?" A snarling voice jabbed Rhett's ear drum. "The girl thinks this place is the Waldorf Astoria. I'm to take a message for the duchess? Humpf." She snatched the note from Rhett's hands with a scowl deeper than the wrinkles lining her face. "You believe me now?"

"I appreciate it, ma'am." He tipped his hat, and his gaze snagged on the afternoon edition, the lower left corner was puckered but the headline was crisp.

Big Dante to Reopen Salvastano Speakeasy Tonight.

"Oh my stars, you look like Greta Garbo." Peggy tilted the cheval mirror standing in the corner of her bedroom and stepped aside, giving me my first glimpse of the transformation from plain broadcaster to flapper. "It worked. No one will know it's you."

I gawked at my reflection. "I don't believe it. This can't be me." Of course I was buried under layers of cosmetics and Peggy's wig from her playacting days. The red gown was accented with so much fringe, any movement tickled my inner arms and legs. Yet all of this pulled together to create a woman I hardly recognized. A woman who would soon step a bulky heel into a speakeasy once owned by my family.

Peggy adjusted my headband, the silver sequins scratching my forehead, and stepped back. "I'm amazed we were able to fit all your hair under that wig."

Thirty-seven hairpins stabbed my head, pinning and flattening each lock to my scalp. A dull throb trailed from my temples to the nape of my neck, a constant reminder of the false blonde tresses that itched the tops of my bare shoulders.

A small frown tugged at Peggy's mouth. "Are you sure this is a good idea?"

It was a terrible idea. But how else would I get to see Papa? The entire western side of Pennsylvania hummed with the news about the reopening of Saluti—the Italian word for cheers. The rumor spread that Big Dante was making a statement by overtaking the Salvastano speakeasy, trying to lure Papa out of hiding.

"Think he'll be there?" Peggy's word made me jolt.

Did I say the last part aloud? I'd done that once in Rhett's presence and thought I'd been careful since. "Who?"

"Your pretend main squeeze." Peggy rolled her eyes. "Detective Dashing."

I released a breath. "I'm not sure. All he said was he has something important going on tonight. Then asked if I could stay with you."

He'd escorted Peggy and I back to her parent's house, Peggy making snide remarks throughout entire trip here and Rhett remaining silent despite her attacks.

"Wait. He doesn't guard your apartment every night, does he?"

I fingered the fake pearls at my neck, heavy against my collar bone, and nodded. "He's been my guard dog round the clock."

"You got the dog part right."

Peggy was unfair to Rhett. Yes, he'd made mistakes, but the sorrow in his eyes when he'd told me his past had revealed his regret. His conversion had been genuine, making him a much better person than I was.

I missed God. I missed reading His Word. As one would bestow an heirloom, Madre Chamberlin had given me her Bible to take with me to America, but I hadn't cracked it open since assuming the deception. Wouldn't God strike me dead or something for even touching something so holy? Madre Chamberlin had always said He was a severe judge, ready to punish sinful hearts.

"Wow, that must be some awful daydream." Peggy nudged my elbow. "You missed half of what I said and I think your right eye was twitching."

"I'm sorry." I pressed my lips together, tasting the grit of the crimson pomade. "I have a lot on my mind."

"I'll say." Peggy handed me a matching purse. Ugh. More fringe. "Big Dante is claiming Salvastano territory which is possibly the most dangerous move in crime boss history and you're going to be there for it." Hazel eyes filled with concern. "I don't like it. Can't I talk you out of going?"

My heart pounded. Territory or not. That wouldn't be wise for Papa to make an appearance. He stood one man against Big Dante and all his underlings. Everything about it spoke danger. If I perceived it as a trap, surely Papa would. Shouldn't I try to head him off and warn him? Yet what was I going to say to him when—or if—I found him? "I'm just going to find answers. I doubt anyone would notice me. I'll fade into the background as usual." All the other women would be dressed like me, only they would clamor about for attention, something my personality never allowed. I was confident my awkwardness would work in my favor.

"Pfft. You look like a Hollywood starlet."

"Hardly."

"Although." Peggy tapped her chin and zeroed in on my legs. "We should probably roll down your stockings."

"What?" My knees pressed together at the very thought.

"I saw it in the gossip magazine. Clara Bow rolled down her stockings and slapped rouge on her knees."

"Clara Bow *is* a silent film star, I'm only sneaking into a speakeasy to get clues about this case."

"Which is Rhett's job." Peggy countered. "Not yours. This whole thing makes my stomach all twisty. I don't see why it's up to you to go tonight."

"Like I said earlier, it's one of those things I *have* to do. I want this case to end. I want this charade to be over. You have no idea how miserable it is—" Everything almost leaked out.

Peggy placed a hand on my arm. "I imagine it's not fun at all masquerading as that man's sweetheart. But putting yourself in danger doesn't seem like the best route to take. Will you at least let me go with you?"

"I'm not planning on staying long. Just to go in, use my wallflower status to my advantage by listening to the gossip, then get out." And maybe keep Papa from eminent death.

Peggy sighed. "Okay. But my parents will be home soon." She walked over to her window and unlocked it. "How good are you at climbing trees?" Said so casually I almost missed it.

"Trees?" I joined Peggy, glimpsed past the sheer, ivory curtains, and caught my friend's meaning. The oak tree boasted several branches, especially a sturdy one leading up to the window. "I think I can manage it." It'd been a while since I had scaled anything like that, but my carefree days weren't too far behind me.

"I'll leave it open." Peggy gave me a hug and squeezed my elbows. "I'll be praying for you."

I slid my eyes closed, keeping the pain at bay. If God was bent on punishing me, praying would only make it worse.

CHAPTER 19

Electric lamps hung over a crowd blowing their cigarette smoke in the face of the prohibition. Sitting at the bar, Rhett pulled his hat lower and allowed his gaze to roam the congested space. From the gold paisley-papered walls to the ornate tin ceiling, Saluti could rival any high-class establishment in New York City or Chicago.

Big Dante must've shelled out some dough to get this gin joint in working order. Perhaps he'd finally show his face tonight. Rhett had always found it odd that the leading crime boss had never made a public appearance. The man operated through his network of hoodlums, which easily kept him from exposure. Though Major had boasted the other day that he was gaining ground on the gangster. Rhett would be sure to keep his friend in his prayers.

The last time Rhett'd visited here had been the night of his father's death. Driven by grief and rage, he'd searched all over Pittsburgh for the murdering outlaw. The building had been in shambles, vandalized and ransacked like Salvastano's bakery. Rhett hadn't found Hugo then, and doubted he'd see him tonight. No way the former crime lord would be foolish enough to walk into his enemy's hands.

But something in Rhett's gut had told him to come. So here he was. An untouched glass of Pittsburgh Scotch in front of him, and a loaded pistol strapped to his waist.

Given the amount of broad-chested bouncers creeping about, Rhett was sure this place was as much an arsenal as it was a gin joint. Not exactly a comforting thought.

Thankfully Kate was safe at her judgmental friend's house. No doubt Peggy was filling Kate's mind about Rhett's every flaw and for some reason, it rankled him. He'd never been friends with a woman before to the point of confessing long-kept secrets. But Kate had this honesty about her. Those large brown eyes beckoned his trust, and he'd freely given it to her.

A sultry jazz melody thrummed from the seven-man band to his left, the throb in his temple keeping time with the base drum. The barkeep eyed Rhett's drink in his hand. The lanky man would lose patience before long with a patron who'd been sitting at his bar for over an hour and hadn't taken a single sip. Rhett gave the man a nod, and he continued checking other customers.

Despite the upheaval caused by the recent trolley strike, the masses hadn't let that deter them. The mingling of perfume and per-spiration, combined with cigarette smoke, created a nauseating atmo-sphere, but Rhett had been in worse. If he could lie in the trenches in France, he certainly could face a bunch of locals.

"This seat taken?" A brunette, decked out in a heavily beaded dress, rubbed a gloved hand on the barstool beside him, eyes half-lidded and suggestive. The amber drink swished in the flapper's glass as she swayed to the music, the fringe on her scooped collar dancing along.

Rhett hadn't any inclination to entertain young ladies who took enjoyment in violating the law. Assuming his silence as a nod in the affirmative, she scooted onto the stool, cozying so close beside him the feather in her cloche hat tickled his nose.

Rhett sat taller, placing distance between them. Not too long ago, he'd taken pleasure in bold women by flirting with them and enjoying all they'd wanted to give. The only thing he ended up with was emptiness.

The band struck up a popular tune, and couples abandoned their seats, hustling onto the already-jammed dance floor. A taller man approached the brunette beside Rhett.

"Dance with me, Millie." The brute tugged her wrist, making Rhett's eyes narrow.

The woman jerked from his grasp and curled into Rhett's arm. Her gloved fingertips quivered against his bicep. Interesting. The young lady didn't seem to welcome the gentleman's presence.

"I already got a dance partner." Her thumb dug into Rhett's sleeve. "Maybe another time, Gio."

Gio Pitrello? As in Big Dante's nephew? Rhett stole a glance at the gentleman, sizing him up.

If the lady's dismissal bruised the fella's pride, he didn't show it. Instead he tipped his hat and ambled away.

Rhett leaned closer and pitched his voice low. "Is that Big Dante's nephew?"

"Yeah." She glanced at Pitrello's retreating form, her shoulders relaxing. "But don't worry about him. All he has to do is snap his fingers and a dozen dames flock to him."

"But not you?"

She shivered. "No. He doesn't date fair."

Rhett wasn't sure what that meant, but he was certain Millie wasn't comfortable around the man.

"Thanks for being a good sport." She offered an appreciative smile. "Care to dance?"

Rhett's gaze floated over her shoulder to find Pitrello peering their direction. "Why not."

◆ ◆ ◆

I arrived late, slightly dehydrated, and limping.

Of all the points in time for there to be a trolley strike, why this evening? Instead of being able to catch a cable car, I'd been forced to walk over an hour to get here, earning a fiery blister on my left heel. With the sun having set long before, most of my journey had been in the dark. The muscles in my neck ached from flinching at every noise along the way.

Fortunately, I'd already been at Peggy's when the trolley workers had decided to close their operations, otherwise I would still be in Braddock with no chance of coming here tonight.

Saluti.

A man with a shiny forehead and arms the size of barrels held the door for me. I nodded my thanks and stepped into the speakeasy.

Indistinct chatter hummed as loud as the band. Orange dots from lighted cigarettes speckled the dim, smoke-laden air. With a shaky breath, I wove around dancing couples and meandering drunks.

A portly man stumbled forward, knocking me in the shoulder, sending me reeling. I smacked into someone's back. I muttered an apology. The throng seemed to press in on all sides. I took a step to my left, but was cut off by a scantily-dressed young woman clutching a bulky tray of cigars and cigarettes. There was a wall of gentleman to my right, their cackles rattling my brain. My feet shuffled back only to run into the same gentleman I'd just collided with.

The air thinned. I flicked my gaze heavenward, the tin ceiling hazily reflecting the crowd. My hand tightened on my purse, palms growing clammy within my black satin gloves.

My gaze scrambled for a window. There was none.

I pressed a finger to my collar bone, my heartbeat thudding faster than the music's rushed tempo. Gnawing the bottom of my lip, I turned. Where was the door?

I spun a full circle, but people blocked my view. My elbows squeezed into my sides. How could I lose the direction of the entrance? What was I thinking coming tonight?

"You look in need of assistance." A deep voice cut through the blur.

It was the man I'd bumped into. Twice. "I'm so sorry. I need to leave." Only I would find a way to get lost in a single room.

"Here. Take a seat." He gently guided my elbow to a large corner booth away from the chaos.

With a deep breath, my lashes fluttered shut, and I pictured my usual open skies, but a different image of calming blues flashed—Rhett's eyes. Oh, what I wouldn't give to gaze in those starry depths rather than being stuffed in this speakeasy. But it was my own fault. I seemed to have a knack for finding trouble.

A soft touch grazed my hand, and my lids cracked open, the blurred edges of my vision clearing to reveal the stranger.

"Are you okay?" He leaned forward giving me a good glimpse of gray eyes set in a boxy face.

"Yes. I'm not a fan of crowds."

He took off his hat, revealing wavy black hair. "Me either." As if at once shy, he fiddled the brim of his bowler. "Want to go someplace else? I brought my car."

The interest in his tone made me blink. This wasn't supposed to happen. Kate Chamberlin never attracted men. "I was hoping to meet someone tonight."

His brow dipped slightly then settled in place. "A date?"

"No, nothing like that." My gaze roamed the place, but it was hard to distinguish anything but roving forms. "Though he might not even show." Which would be a good thing.

"Date or not. If the man leaves you on your own, he's the biggest fool alive. If I may say so, Miss …?"

Oh. *Oh.* "Miss…uh…Jennings." The name blurted out, and I regretted it. Why hadn't I thought of a fake moniker? I'd been prepared for everything else. The gown. The wig. Then again, I hadn't counted on anyone talking to me. I'd expected to be the wallflower, overlooked and ignored.

"Miss Jennings, delighted." He gave me a smile with dimples. "I'm Gio Pitrello."

"Nice to meet you." I acknowledged him with a friendly nod and continued my search for Papa. Men in felt hats bumbled about, some with women hanging on their necks, others with faces buried in beer mugs.

"Care for a drink?" Mr. Pitrello snapped his fingers, summoning a waiter.

My brows rose, making the headband pinch my skin. I fought against a wince. First, my heel, and now my temples. This attire was not conducive to my wellbeing.

My attention drifted to the man across the table watching me with an amused smile. He probably could tell I was a novice at being a rebellious flapper. "No thank you. I reached my limit for today."

He gave me a curious look. Maybe he'd observed me walking in and knew I hadn't drunk anything yet. But no matter, my lips wouldn't be imbibing anything that this country deemed wrong. Call it penance for the sins of my family.

"How about something small to quench your thirst? It's blasted hot in here."

I couldn't disagree there. After my three-mile trek, my coarse throat felt as if it'd been scraped with sandpaper, but any form of liquid in this place came with a lawbreaking price tag.

The waiter approached our table, and Mr. Pitrello ordered a drink for him and ... "The fruit medley special for the lady."

A refusal skittered upon my opened mouth.

He raised a hand. "I insist. It's only juice."

Only juice? Then perhaps it'd be okay. I'd know right away if it was laced with alcohol, right?

My gloved finger traced a seam on the plush cushion, my thoughts as hazy as the atmosphere. *Focus on why you're here.* "I've heard Saluti is run by Big Dante."

"Yeah. He gave it new life. The joint was all rubble before he took over." The man spoke as if he knew the gangster, an almost proud glint shining in his eyes.

Nervous energy swirled through me. I fidgeted the fake pearls draping my neck. "I've heard rumors about Hugo Salvastano coming."

His eyes flashed, then a corner of his mouth lifted. "It would be kinda hard for the old man to make it. I've never seen a corpse dance the Charleston."

My sharp breath stabbed my lungs.

"That's the latest rumor anyway." He shrugged and relaxed against the seat.

I willed my joints to ease, but they rebelled, tightening with every heartbeat. It was only a rumor. One I'd heard plenty of times. "What about Big Dante? Is he here tonight?"

"Uncle never comes to these things."

The hair spiked on my arms. Of all the men I could've bumped into tonight, it'd been the mobster's nephew. A member of the family that rivaled mine. I had to keep my wits about me. This man couldn't figure out who I was. If Big Dante had reopened Saluti to bait Papa—taking something important to him and using it against him—then heaven knew, what they would do to me.

"You're a curious one." His gaze searched mine, and he leaned forward. "Be careful about asking too many questions. Nosiness has a tendency of attracting unwanted attention."

My heart punched my ribs. "Then I'll stick to my own business." Too bad my business involved the very man they were hunting.

"Atta girl. I would hate to see anything unfortunate happen to a cute thing like you."

Despite the sweat beading at the nape of my skull, my blood chilled.

The waiter returned with our drinks and served me a cranberry-colored concoction before giving Gio his glass.

Hesitantly, I took a sip. Tasting only pure juice, my lips relaxed around the rim. I needed to thank him for the drink and invent an excuse to leave. The longer I stayed in his presence, the more dangerous it became.

"Good, ain't it?" Gio winked and took large gulp of whatever it was he drank. "It's refreshing on hot nights like this."

I forced down another sip. "Thank you. It's delicious."

"And you're pretty." He flashed a smile. "So where are you from?"

My eyes burned at the corners, and I fanned myself with my free hand. Could it get any more stifling in here? "I live around Pittsburgh."

His head tilted and a smirk crept over his lips. "I didn't ask where you lived. I asked where you're from."

"Is it not the same?"

"Darlin', I think it's better to dance to this jivey music than turn circles in conversation. If you allow me to hold you in my arms for the next song, then I won't bring up your cute accent."

CHAPTER 20

R hett ran a thick finger along the inside of his collar. With all these breathing bodies clustered within four walls, the temperature climbed from toasty to sweltering. Most men had already shed their jackets, but Rhett's concealed his pistol.

"Maybe we should dance another." Millie playfully tugged his arm. "You were kinda stiff during that one."

Because he didn't want to shoot himself in the thigh. "I think I'm done. But don't let me spoil your fun."

Her lips pinched, and she met his gaze with apologetic eyes. "You sure?"

He dipped his chin. "It's been a pleasure meeting you, Millie."

She gave a cheery wave and joined a band of giggling women, a few tossing glances at him.

He turned away from their high-pitched clamor in search of his hat. If these folks had no regard for the Volstead Act, they sure wouldn't think twice about swiping his derby. Rhett snaked his way through the throng to the bar. Retrieving his hat, he slapped it back on his head, then glanced at his pocket watch.

Midnight.

If Hugo hadn't turned up by now, he probably wouldn't make an appearance. Same with Delvina. This place was void of any Salvastano presence. What a waste of an evening.

Fatigue stretched into his bones, reminding him of a week's worth of little to no sleep. With a grimace, he started toward the exit, but froze in his steps.

Kate.

She wore a blonde wig and a ridiculous amount of warpaint, but he could pick her out of any crowd.

And she was not alone.

Opposite of her in the booth was Gio Pitrello, Big Dante's repulsive nephew. Rhett's blood pumped fast in his veins. What was she doing here? With him? And why the disguise?

With determined steps, his legs ate the distance between him and their table. Pitrello spotted him first, his eyes sharper than Rhett's pen knife. Kate, however, fussed with her pearl necklace, as if she hadn't a care in the world.

"Do you need something?" Pitrello's jaw was steel hard, his tone even more so.

"Am I interrupting?" Rhett's voice made Kate's chin lift.

"What a nice surprise!" She practically sang the words. "And so handsome in that sportscoat." Her hand stretched towards him, and she almost fell out of the booth.

Sweet mercy, she was drunk.

"You know each other, Miss Jennings?"

Jennings? Was that the name she'd told him? Rhett took in her glazed eyes, her scarlet dress that she filled out a bit too nicely, and that outlandish wig. What had she gotten herself into?

Pitrello leaned against the cushion, draping an arm along the seat-back. "We've been getting closer acquainted."

It wouldn't be wise to grab the man by the collar and pin him to the wall, but Rhett's hands tightened at his sides anyway.

"He wants real close, I think." Kate took another sip of her drink, then hiccupped. "Want some?" She held up the half-empty glass to Rhett. "It's fruit."

"Sure it is."

Her full lips pouted. "It is!"

"I'm taking you home."

With that declaration, Gio stood, chest thrusting out. "Who are you to her?" His penetrating glare shifted to Kate. "Was he the one you're supposed to meet?"

A flash of guilt swept her features, but soon gave way to the brightest grin he'd ever seen on her pretty face. "Did you bring me fig pudding?"

He sighed. "I'll get you some. Let's go."

"Hold on." Gio reached across the table and grasped Kate's wrist.

Rhett took a bold step forward, widening his stance.

A lazy smirk played across Gio's face. "I can't let you leave with a stranger."

"How chivalrous," Rhett said, dryly. "Why don't you let go of her and I'll show you my identification which also bears the name Jennings?"

Pitrello's hand fell to his side, but his jagged brows conveyed challenge. Exchanging punches with him meant taking on the entire Dante clan. Not the wisest of choices.

God, help me. "Kate's my sister. We'll be leaving now."

Her eyes clouded. "But—"

"Now." Rhett's firm tone caused her to launch to her feet.

Then she stumbled.

Rhett caught her by the elbow, her skin cool and velvety against his burning palm. He gave Pitrello one last glower for good measure.

Noting the exit, he began guiding her through the congestion.

Kate tugged his jacket, and then she walked her fingers up his lapel, hooking her hand around his neck. "I'm not your sister."

His gut tightened. "Believe me, I know. But you are for tonight. Someone has to look out for you."

She snorted. "Coming from a man with two noses." Her touch lingered on the raised knot of his spine above his collar, then wandered to the area behind his ear, leaving a fiery trail. The pad of her thumb caressed the flesh beneath his lobe.

He swallowed a groan. *I'm trying here, God.*

Every nerve sparked to life. He shouldn't—couldn't—let her attentions stir him. Kate had no idea what she was doing, and the longing in her eyes could easily shift to any man in this room. Even a high-class idiot like Gio Pitrello.

His jaw hardened and that was the exact thought needed to switch focus.

They weren't in the clear. Not by any stretch. Pitrello had a lot of underlings milling about. It wasn't irrational to think the man might still try to have his way. To have Kate. Sneaking past the bouncers at the gate could prove the biggest challenge. Grimacing, he tightened his hold, then realized she leaned against the side his gun was holstered.

"Kate, you need to move to my left."

She yawned, and her head drooped onto his shoulder.

He stilled and gently shifted her limp frame, jostling her forward enough to loop her in front of him. This seemed to rouse her, for she stood a little taller, but planted her feet, toe to toe with his. She released a deep, contented sigh and wrapped her arms around him, placing him in a soft chokehold.

Her body melded to his, and she nuzzled into his chest. "Are we dancing?"

"Not quite." He blew out a labored breath. "You can't hang on me like this. We're supposed to be related."

"I haven't been around family in years." Her left arm swept through the air in an exaggerated circle, making her lose balance, her body pressing more against his.

Of all the ways he thought this evening would unfold, this hadn't been one of them. It was important to get her out of here before Pitrello alerted his cronies. Rhett may already be too late.

Could he toss her over his shoulder and storm out? No, that would garner attention. But how could they fade into the background with Kate looking like some kind of glamour girl?

"My gloves." As if jolted with renewed energy, Kate jerked away. "I need them." She launched forward, almost toppling into a waiter.

Rhett reached for her, but only caught a couple pieces of fringe, which easily snapped off her dress. If she was bent on retrieving her gloves, she was staggering the opposite direction than the booth—good because it increased distance from Pitrello, but bad for it placed them farther from the exit. Her arms thrashed through the air like crazy propellers. For Pete's sake she was going to hurt someone if not her self. He circled her waist, and she squirmed in his arms.

"My gloves." Her voice held a sob.

"I'll buy you new ones. We need to leave."

She turned into his chest, shaking her head, fast at first then slowing. She wilted against him, all the fight leaving.

He pressed a hand to her back and reoriented himself. The exit was now to their far left. Maybe there was another way out besides the main doors. His gaze searched the room. A hallway stood next to the bar, but that probably led to the washrooms. His molars ground. It looked like they'd have to risk the front gate.

"You did a good thing." A feminine voice rose above the chaos. Millie stood on his right, concern creasing her brow.

"Pardon?"

She stepped closer. "Taking that girl off Gio's hands. Like I said, he doesn't date fair." Her lips formed a sad smile, and Rhett saw the ugly truth.

Kate wasn't drunk, she'd been drugged.

"I overheard Gio telling the bouncers at the door to keep an eye out for you." Millie stood on her tip toes and whispered into Rhett's ear. "He told them to look for a blonde in a red dress with her brother in a beige sportscoat."

Rhett's eyes squeezed shut.

Think.

Kate's head rolled to one side, her chin resting on her shoulder. She could collapse at any moment. Then what? He needed to move. But where could they go? Pitrello identified Kate as a blonde in a red dress. There wasn't anything he could do about her attire, but …

"Millie, can I buy your hat?"

He stabled Kate against him with his left hand, reached into his pocket, and pulled out some bills. "I'm not sure how much this is." He pushed a wad of cash into Millie's hand. "But it should be enough."

Confusion marking her light eyes, she quickly pulled off her cloche hat. "It won't help much since she's still a blonde."

"No, she's not." Rhett glanced around and spotted a small alcove behind them. Motioning Millie to follow, he hoisted Kate by the waist and carried her to the abandoned nook filled with racks of table linens and glasses.

Balancing Kate against his chest, he went to work removing the false hair.

Kate moaned and weakly swatted at his hand.

Millie stepped forward. "You're ripping the poor girl's hair out. Let me help." With quick movements, she untacked the wig and let loose some of Kate's locks. With all the pins in her hair, they'd be here all night. "That's good enough. Now for the hat."

Millie wedged the wig under her arm, slipped the bell-shaped hat on Kate's head, and pulled some curls to frame her face. "There, sugar." She gave Kate's arm a friendly squeeze, to which Kate didn't respond, then glanced at Rhett. "Is she really your sister?"

"Not at all. Thanks, Millie, for everything. Can you dispose of the wig?"

She nodded. After a pat to Rhett's shoulder, she was gone.

"Kate? You still with me?" He cupped her upper arms and pulled back to check her pupils, but her eyes were closed, and her head sagged forward.

She'd soon be unconscious.

"Come on, sweetheart. Wake up for a few more minutes." He curled his arms around her and maneuvered her to his left side.

A faint giggle erupted from her lips. He glanced at his hand. She was ticklish. His fingers danced along the side of her ribs, and she let loose a howl of laughter. Her lashes fluttered open.

"That's it, Kate. Stick with me."

Her right cheek pressed against his shoulder, and she peered up at him. Her eyes were dilated and glossy. Pure and naïve Kate. What would've happened if he hadn't shown up here tonight? A fire kindled in his gut and Rhett half-wished he could empty his wrath on Pitrello.

"Let's walk." He urged her forward and—bless God!—she moved with him. They cleared the dance floor and were almost to the door.

A couple of bulky men stood at the entrance, stony and stoic like two gargoyles, but their gazes were searching.

For them.

Kate returning to a brunette should help them pass undetected, but they still ran a risk because of her red dress and his beige sportscoat. Plus, Millie overheard Pitrello identify Rhett as her brother.

A well-dressed couple cut in front of them, hands all over each other and whispering in intimate tones. An idea sparked, but Rhett resisted, scrambling for a better option. One that didn't require so much of him and his emotions.

Only a few more steps, and they'd be positioned in front of the bozos.

The bouncer on the right of the door spotted Rhett then peered at Kate, his eyes narrowing. The ogre nodded at his counterpart, gesturing toward them.

Rhett's gut clenched. If these men were on a hunt for a pair of siblings, it was time for him to act unbrotherly, and he better make it convincing.

He bent low to her ear. "I'm sorry, Kate. This is to protect you." And with that, he gathered her in his arms and nuzzled her satiny cheek.

Her head lolled back, lashes fluttered shut. Rhett cupped the base of her neck, stabling her, hoping she appeared as if she savored his caress rather than being moments from passing out.

His lips pressed to her temple and trailed kisses along her jaw. His conscience wouldn't allow anything beyond, and he prayed it was enough.

Kate's face tilted toward him, and her chin brushed his. Her fingers clamped his collar. He eased back, but not far enough. Her mouth captured his with a pressure of fervency, ravenous in pursuit.

Shock pulsed.

Kate was kissing him.

Nothing about her execution was graceful. Her thumbnail dug into his neck, and she missed his mouth when she came back for seconds, landing only on his lower lip. She reconnected, and Rhett tasted the longing in her touch, heat purling through his entire system.

Her fevered boldness surprised him. Her slight frame had been drugged and even that couldn't fully dull her. But what did he expect? He'd heard her play, knew her capable of deep passion. He never imagined being on the receiving end of such intense feeling, and in front of an audience no less.

Blast it all.

But this was for her safety. He pulled her into his chest, drawing on the desire to shield her from every villain. Her frail whimper feathered his lips, and any lingering hope of detaching his emotions vanished.

"All right love birds, keep moving." The same bouncer flicked his shoulder, and Rhett jerked back, keeping a gentle grasp on Kate. "Go carry on somewhere else."

Warm air greeted them outside on the sidewalk. Rhett drew in a relieved breath, holding on to Kate and keeping them at a steady pace.

"You're safe," he murmured against her temple, hoping that she'd forgive him for what he'd done.

CHAPTER 21

Rhett walked closely behind Kate, propelling her forward by a gentle palm to her back. He glanced over his shoulder again. They'd cleared Saluti's front gate, but Pitrello could still send out his thugs in search of them, and Kate's slogging pace made them effortless prey.

He wouldn't be at ease until they were in his Model-T, which stood a frustrating block-and-a-half away.

Kate expelled a deep sigh, and her knees buckled.

With quick movements, Rhett scooped her up in his arms, her cloche hat falling to the sidewalk. She curled against him, using his chest as a pillow. The thud of his heart matched his rapid-fire thoughts. He would not look down at her angelic face. Would not sneak a glance at her full lips still swollen with his kiss. He pressed his own together, trying to shake the memory of her touch and the encroaching shame. He hadn't intended on a smooching session on the gin joint floor any more than he'd expected to find Kate in a booth with a mobster's nephew.

Boy did he have a lot of explaining to do tomorrow.

The fringe of her dress grazed his knuckles. Then again, so did she.

A swishing noise behind him made him slink into the shadows of a store awning. A rumpled flyer tumbled along the walk in the wind. He'd flinched at a slip of paper? *Brother.*

He couldn't clog his mind with the morning, not when they still needed to get through tonight. If anything, that rolling piece of garbage reminded him to keep vigilant. With Kate in his arms, he was at a disadvantage, not being able to defend them or even access his pistol.

He quickened his pace. His lower back tightened, straining from the pretty bundle he hauled. Kate was slender, but her limp weight hatched more difficulty.

He stepped off the curb and crossed the street.

She groaned.

Was he jostling her too much? He steadied his grip, fully aware that her every curve was in contact with his body.

Thank God his vehicle was parked ahead.

It took some maneuvering, but he settled her in the passenger seat. He cranked the car and started the engine, all the while keeping alert of the shadowed surroundings.

Soon they were driving down the avenue. Every stop sign he checked her pulse. *Nice and strong.* She just needed to sleep it off. His own pulse thrummed at the realization that the place she'd be sleeping would be his own bed. He couldn't return her to Peggy's parent's house in this condition. He couldn't get into her apartment in Braddock. His home seemed the only option.

He stole another glance at her. The rhythmic rise and fall of her chest told him she was peaceful. He, on the other hand was far from tranquil. With a swallowed groan, he set off toward his place.

Choosing a longer route, he utilized the side roads and back streets, ensuring they weren't being followed. Twenty minutes later, he pulled in the drive. The neighboring houses, dark and quiet, offered a stitch of relief. Last thing he needed was nosy Mrs. Fisher seeing him carry a young woman across his threshold.

He'd never taken a woman to this home—the memory haven of his deceased parents. Dragging a coarse hand across his face, he killed the engine and accepted his fate.

He lifted Kate from her side of the car and managed to get through the door. He notched the light switch with his elbow. His cat glared at him from its lazing spot on the sofa.

"Chimney, meet Kate."

Feline eyes blinked at him, even its tail hooked as in a question mark.

"Don't look at me like that. It was a desperate situation."

And a delicate one. Reminding himself of how he'd rescued Kate from a danger no woman should ever encounter, he resumed the mission of taking her to his bedroom.

She grumbled gibberish and buried her face in his jacket, his lapel streaked with cosmetics. He approached the bed and settled her on the mattress.

Probably should've turned down the sheets first. *Smart, Jennings.*

She grimaced against his pillow. The shifting of her head only deepened her frown.

The hair pins.

Millie hadn't removed them all. He slid a hand behind her slender throat, gently coaxing her forward. He could see why she was uncomfortable—the pins seemed to push into the nape of her neck. Working his way around her crown, he gingerly tugged each pin, freeing the locks that had held him captive several evenings ago.

His fingers threaded her hair, searching for more metal, trying to ignore the silkiness of her tendrils, the rose fragrance taunting his senses. Fire scaled his spine. This was the most intimate situation he'd been in for seven long months. And the woman was unconscious.

The rhythmic rise and fall of her chest told him she was in deep sleep. His gaze roamed the length of her. She was adorned with color. Red. Like her lips. Her sultry appearance soured Rhett's stomach. He'd grown to admire the natural Kate.

It was no wonder why Pitrello chose her among all the other women tonight. Her eyes were always alluring, but the dress she wore revealed the gentle curves he'd seen in her night dress. An image he'd tried to scrub from his memory without success. The other night he'd been in her room, tonight she was in his. If they kept this up, he'd have to marry her within the week.

And for once, the thought didn't terrify him.

He peered at his trunk by the door, untouched since the day he'd quit the force. Since two weeks after his dad's death. Rhett had been itching for the day he could wipe off the dust and scram. His mind had been consumed with finding Hugo and then getting as far away from Pittsburgh as possible.

But now …

He ran a hand through his hair. What was wrong with him? He glanced at the woman who'd catapulted into his world, shaking its foundation.

Why had she gone to Saluti's?

He'd have to have a long talk with her tomorrow. For now, she needed rest, something he could use, too. He made sure his window was locked and then turned on his fan. But what if she chilled easily? He grabbed the light-weight blanket at the foot of the bed and draped it over her, tucking her in.

He'd be sure to shut the door, keeping Chimney from invading. It was going to be awkward for her to waken in his bed even without his hairless cat snoozing on her feet.

"Feet." He should take off her shoes. He lifted the blanket and unbuckled her left shoe. Then her right. Her toes responded by flexing then relaxing.

"Grazie," she said on a groan and rolled to her side.

My head felt heavy as if stuffed with bricks. Pressure mounted behind my eyes, and I curled on my side, only to clutch my swirling stomach. What was wrong with me? Why did everything ache?

Had I fallen ill?

I pulled in a rugged breath, and a masculine scent pushed into my nose.

My lids cracked wide. I yanked the unfamiliar sheet to my neck. The jerky movements cost me. My vision swam, and the taupe walls surrounding me appeared to ripple like a flag in the wind.

Where was I? How had I gotten here?

Daylight mocked from the lone window to my left. The cruel truth trembled through me with fresh fear.

I'd spent the night in this place.

My hands searched my person. I was fully clothed—a drop of relief against the flooding panic—but the itching fringe stole any bead of comfort. For I laid shivering in the same gown from last night.

I sat up, the mattress groaning beneath me, and pressed a finger to the hammering in my forehead. The final thing I recalled was sitting in Saluti's with Big Dante's nephew. Talking and sipping the juice—

Oh no! The drink!

Could I have been any more foolish? How could I have gotten drunk? The juice hadn't tasted any different than what I'd always known. I couldn't detect any alcohol whatsoever. Plus I only recalled having only one drink. What if there wasn't alcohol in it, but something else? What if I had been ... drugged? My face sunk into numb hands, sobs threatening to overtake me.

Had I been assaulted? Was this that *man's* bed? My gaze dashed to the door. Could he be out there? My shaky legs protesting, I climbed to my feet, the cold floor shooting ice through my heels.

"Kate?"

That voice.

I could weep at the sound of it. But was it truly Rhett or my mind playing a harsh trick? My fingers wrapped the knobby bedpost. It couldn't be. How'd he even know I was here?

"Are you awake?"

Hope renewed. The deep timbre was unmistakable. Ignoring the nausea, I rushed across the room, threw open the door, and launched into his arms.

Unprepared for my impact, he stumbled back a half-step. But his strong build sustained us, and he anchored me to his chest.

"How'd you find me?" I barely rasped the words. Emotion swelled at his nearness. Though how could I relax in his comforting embrace when we were still in danger?

We needed to escape.

I tried to twist away, but his secure grip didn't budge. "We need to leave, Rhett. If that man even—"

"It's okay." Softening his hold, he smoothed a hand over the crown of my head, down the length of my hair, settling again on my lower back in one soothing motion. "This is my house. That was my room. You're safe."

Harnessing the tears was like trying to catch a sky-full of rain in my hand.

Rhett gathered me closer, the ticking of his heart a steady solace against my ear. He pressed a handkerchief into my hand.

I dabbed my drippy nose. "I thought ..." The words were too horrible for utterance.

"I know."

I felt more than heard his bass voice. Everything was okay. My virtue hadn't been stolen. Rhett had been there for me. But then that meant ...

I angled to peer up into his face. "You were at Saluti's?"

"I was."

My head drooped. "I'm so ashamed." Add this mistake to the mountainous pile of errors I'd made since boarding the S.S. Columbo last fall.

The pad of his thumb nudged my chin, raising until I met his compassionate gaze. "Don't take the blame for Gio Pitrello's vile behavior. You're the victim."

The tenderness in his eyes was palpable. If only I could lean into it, savor it, sketch the image of his warm expression into the pages of my mind. So when loneliness taunted I could revisit the memory of when someone had cared.

"Let's talk in the parlor. I think you'll be more comfortable in there." He motioned me down a hallway covered in an inviting floral wallpaper.

Still in my stockinged feet, I followed him into a larger room flooded with natural light from an enormous picture window. Gilt-framed oil paintings hung from a picture rail. This area alone was the size of my entire apartment.

"Your place is really nice." My voice was still a bit frail, but at least my head had stopped its fierce pounding.

"It was my parents." He was quick to dismiss ownership.

The parlor boasted several wing-back chairs and a sofa currently housing a rather peculiar looking cat blanketed with a … tea towel?

"That's my roommate. Chimney." Rhett smirked at the feline with a small, bald head and torn left ear. "A still exploded on Rumrunners Row, and I rescued it from the burning building."

Of course he did. Because that was how Rhett Jennings operated. He found pathetic creatures, like me, and saved them from tragedy. I keenly knew what would've happened had not Rhett intervened. "I'm sorry for all the trouble I've caused you. I shouldn't have gone to a place like that."

He gestured to the sofa. I claimed the side opposite the cat, and Rhett settled beside me. The cat took offense and hopped to the floor. I'd assumed Rhett would slide into the extra space, but he remained close to me, our knees almost touching.

He angled toward me, and his piercing eyes made it difficult to breathe. "Kate, may I ask why you went? And why the disguise?"

My hand plucked at the fake pearls, now heavy around my neck. "I borrowed all this from Peggy." I gasped. "Oh dear, Peggy! I never went back to her place. How she must be worrying."

Rhett braced a hand on my shoulder. "I called her earlier this morning and told her what happened." A wry smile eased on his face. "I'm sure she'll feel better hearing from you though. She wasn't exactly convinced with my version of the story."

I could imagine. "Peggy gets something in her head, and it's hard to sway her. But she wasn't happy with me going last night."

He removed his touch, and I willed away the disappointment. "Yet she dressed you up like a flapper?"

"I feared if I went wearing my usual clothes, I'd stick out as an outsider."

"Well, you still stuck out." He rubbed the turn of his jaw, and his gaze swept my form. "You attracted the nephew of the biggest crime boss in all of Pittsburgh."

Heat shot through me. "The drink didn't taste like alcohol. I thought I'd be able to tell."

"You were drugged."

"But how? The drink was in my hands the entire time. I don't understand when he drugged it."

"He didn't."

"But you said—"

"Pitrello had one of his cronies drug it before it even reached your table."

The fruit medley special. The words sank into my stomach with such force I could almost hear the thud. "Here I was thinking I was clever. Asking him questions, and all the while he knew I was drinking a laced drink."

"What kind of questions?"

I ducked my head. "About the Salvastanos."

"Was that why you went there last night?"

My bottom lip sunk beneath my teeth. "I thought I could find some answers. Help the case." Help keep Papa from injury, when it was me who had almost landed in harm. The wave of nausea in my gut could be lingering effects of the drug, but then it could be the realization that this was all there was. Hope of finding Papa had been exhausted, and it was time to move on.

"I see." His blue striped shirt had darkened spots from my tears. How easy it'd been to fall into his arms and take the comfort he'd offered. What would it be like to have the welcome of his embrace every day?

"Kate. This is a dangerous case. These are dangerous people. You can't do this anymore."

I forced my focus on him and was met with his compassionate eyes. "I'm so grateful to you for what you did last night. This all could've ended another way. A terrible way. And you protected me." Defended my innocence. I leaned closer and cupped his freshly shaven face. "Thank you."

He swallowed. "You're welcome."

The moment stretched. I floundered in his deep gaze. The ocean blue of his eyes a fierce current, ready to pull me under. My growing feelings like mighty waves, crashed against the brittle resolve in my mind. After all my resistance, I'd fallen in love with him.

My fingertips withdrew from his face, slow and forced. My palm was the last to retreat, peeling away with rebellious submission. Before I could pull away fully, Rhett caught my hand in his, his fingers wrapping around mine.

"I can't take full credit." His voice was husky. "I wasn't planning on going to Saluti, but God wouldn't leave me alone about it."

"What do you mean?"

He stroked his thumb over my knuckles. "Just that. I kept having a feeling that I needed to go to the gin joint. It was slight, but often. David calls it the *God-nudge*. I can see it was for you. God wanted you safe."

"That can't be true."

"Why not?"

Rhett didn't understand. If he were aware of my sins, he'd agree with God and disregard me. I gently eased my fingers from his. "Because there are better people than me to look out for. Trust me, God had nothing to do with last night."

"I beg to differ on both accounts." He palmed the back of his neck and stared at a spot on the rug. "If there's one thing I learned about God, it's this—we can't earn His favor, or in my case, His forgiveness. It's freely given. So is His love. He loves us no matter what we do."

That went against everything I'd ever learned. "He's a just God. He punishes the wicked."

"He is and He does. But He's also merciful. Nothing you can do is beyond His mercy." He relaxed against the cushion. "Don't take my word for it. Read the scriptures for yourself."

I wouldn't dare. I knew from what Madre Chamberlin said. I couldn't even approach the Almighty, even open His holy word, until I got rid of the sin. And I couldn't get rid of the sin until I abandoned the deception. "No matter how our opinions differ, *you* were there last night and kept me from danger. I can't thank you enough. I've never even kissed a man, let alone what Gio Pitrello had in mind."

Rhett abruptly stood and muttered something. I hadn't meant for Rhett to get distressed over Big Dante's nephew. Yes, it was a close call, but I was safe—because of him.

With a heavy exhale, he pinched his eyes shut and ran a hand through his hair. After what felt like forever, his dark lashes opened, his wearied gaze searching mine. "We should get you home."

Maybe he was tired of dealing with me. Understandable. I'd put him through unnecessary trouble, but the idea of me being a bother made my chest twist. "I left my key at Peggy's."

He gave a tight nod.

I stood, my hair brushing against my bare arms. Wait. "My wig's gone. You removed my hairpins."

"The wig is somewhere in Saluti. I had to remove it to ... um ... get us out the door." His gaze flicked to my lips and the haunted look returned. "As for the pins, you looked uncomfortable. I wanted to help."

Over the past week, this man had lost sleep watching my apartment. He'd risked his life pursuing the intruder who'd left the card. Last night, he'd protected my purity. Yet it hadn't stopped there. Rhett had sought my comfort in the smaller things, like removing my numerous hair pins.

The ache for him grew within me. I had a heart that'd been built to outlast earthquakes, withstand stormy seas, but to stare into the eyes of a man I could never have?

That was a pain beyond recovery.

CHAPTER 22

Rhett had been Kate's first kiss.

And she hadn't remembered.

He tightened his grip on the steering wheel, his mind spinning faster than the tires beneath them. All morning he'd been primed to tell her about the kiss they'd shared, but when she'd opened his bedroom door and lunged into his arms, his well-crafted plans had melted in the moment. Her body had trembled against his as hot tears soaked his shirt, kindling an affection he'd never experienced before. What had crowned it all was the admiration shining in her glossy eyes—the gold flecks brightening against the rich brown. She'd gazed at him as if he'd been her hero. A man could get used to that.

Might as well relish the feeling while it lasted.

Soon he'd tell her she'd wasted her first kiss on him. With Rhett's sordid past with women, she wouldn't believe she'd been the one who'd initiated the lip-locking. Maybe he should lie and take full blame.

He stole a glance at Kate sitting beside him, his side humming from the warmth of her closeness. Her pale skin contrasted the crimson dress, but her blanched complexion didn't give him pause as much as her silence. She'd been quiet since they'd left his parents' house. Though not surprising, considering what she'd been through over the past fifteen hours.

"Where are we, exactly?" Kate's gaze skimmed the surroundings. "I've never seen this area."

He glanced in the rearview mirror. A steady stream of cars piled behind them. On Saturday, traveling into Pittsburgh was always headache-inducing traffic. More so today with the recent cable car strike. "We just left Brookline."

Her eyes widened. "On the other side of the river?"

"Yes."

Her shoulders spiked so high she could wear them for earrings.

"Are you okay?"

"I'm not used to being in this part of town." She twisted in her seat and practically glued her forehead to the window.

Was she afraid of the area? His parents had chosen this location because of the nice distance from the chaos of the city. Brookline was safe and sought-out real estate. "I'm not sure I understand—"

"The Liberty Tunnels." The words clipped even as the dual tubes approached. "Please turn around. Go a different way."

He couldn't.

The congestion had them sandwiched between cars. There wasn't a place for him to pull over. Kate must've realized that too, because she slammed her eyes shut as if accepting her doom.

She'd mentioned before she didn't like tight spaces. Why hadn't he thought about the recently opened tunnels? They were the longest ones in the entire city no less.

"I'm sorry, Kate." He reached over and squeezed her hand. Her skin felt like ice.

Eyelids cracking open, she twisted toward him and gave a lousy version of a smile. "I'll be okay. You took me to your home last night, and I made it through those tunnels, right? I didn't die. Nothing caved in on me."

Her rambling made his brow wrinkle with worry, and an unfamiliar lilt infused her words. A definite accent. But before he could contemplate further, her fists clenched in her lap, her usually delicate jaw rigid like stone.

He gentled his tone. "We'll be through in no time." A quiet prayer passed his lips. They entered the mouth of the tunnel, and except for the weak glow of the automobile headlamps and taillights, darkness enclosed them.

She let out a muted welp.

Could Rhett be any more of an idiot? He should've been more aware of her needs. Now she faced another source of discomfort so close to the trauma from earlier. He opened his mouth to apologize again, but brake lights shining ahead alerted to a problem.

He slowed the car, then stopped it altogether.

"What's going on?" The quiver in her voice made him glance over.

"Only a bit of traffic." Blasted trolley strike. The thirty-two hundred men who'd walked off the job last night were to blame for this upheaval. "Things should clear up soon, and we'll be on our way." He cranked down the window, inclining his head out the open space.

Cars stacked bumper to bumper, unmoving.

Curling forward, Kate hugged her arms to her stomach.

"Are you doing okay?"

She let out a string of words he didn't understand—all filled with panic and in another language. "Cielo. Cielo. Cielo."

Yes, she'd mentioned her dislike of closed quarters, but this? Her eyes locked tight as shadows and fear ravaged her taut face.

Kate Chamberlin was claustrophobic.

Questions surfaced, but now wasn't the time to ask about her foreign expressions. He needed to keep her from falling into hysterics. But how? Her sobs throttled the air from his chest. He rubbed her back in steady, circular motions. "You're safe, Kate."

Rhett peered out the windshield. Smoke twisted the shadows, writhing like the devil's fingers. No, they weren't safe. Exhaust from all the cars was overrunning the tunnel, choking their oxygen supply. He yanked his handkerchief from his pocket and pressed it into Kate's hand.

"Breathe into this." He killed the engine. "We have to get out of here. Now."

He launched out of the car and yelled between the blaring horns. "Everyone turn off your engines!"

The cars directly in front of him obeyed, but what about those behind and farther ahead? This place had become a death trap, and no one was aware of it. He rushed to Kate's side, jerking open her door.

She was crouched over, her nose almost to her thighs.

"Kate, let's go."

"It's … closing in." She heaved the thinning air. "I can't move."

"Hold the handkerchief to your face."

She didn't move. Precious seconds wasted. With every breath, more poison seeped into their lungs. He slid his arm under her knees and the other around her back, lifting her. She didn't protest, but sank into him, almost like a child.

"Let's get to safety." He rushed forward, calling to motorists to shut off their engines and abandon their cars. Some were already aware of the danger and joined Rhett in pursuit of the exit. Electric lamps cut a weak line through the darkness, providing enough shine to navigate the narrow passage between the tunnel wall and the chain of vehicles.

Kate's cries slid into muted whimpers. He offered soothing words, unsure if she could hear over the chaos. His calves burned and chest fought for breath, but seeing the light ahead pulsed renewed strength into his veins.

More and more people cut into the frenzy, shouldering in from all sides. Some moved slower than others, causing a few cuss words to erupt. The panic was as tangible as the smoke filling his airways. Someone slammed into his back, nearly knocking him forward.

A truck idled to his left. He glanced inside. A man about Rhett's age slumped over the steering wheel. To his left was … a small child. He adjusted his grip on Kate and jerked closer to the wall, allowing the madness to flow around them.

"Kate, I gotta set you down."

She answered by clutching his lapel.

"There's a child that pickup. She's not moving." He coughed. "Kate, she needs your help."

Her chin notched higher, and she pushed against his chest, angling her head over his shoulder.

"Where is she?" Her voice cracked with a flicker of courage.

Despite the severity of the moment, Rhett's dry lips broke into a smile. "That's my girl."

Kate Chamberlin could slay her dragon, she just needed the right sword.

The blackness sank into me with familiar dark fangs.

Rhett gingerly set me on the ground, and I braced a palm on the cool stone of the tunnel wall. The handkerchief acted as a flimsy defense against the pressing haze, but I had been more prepared for this fight than I'd realized. Madre Chamberlin's vigorous diaphragm training years ago had seen to it that my lungs had not only recovered from trauma, but strengthened. Holding my breath and pacing its release was as strategic as holding a high F note.

No, the venom that crippled me was the result of my infected imagination.

The walls warped in my blurry vision, mocking me. I pressed harder against the stone, the rough surface nicking my skin, my fingertips processing what my mind could not—nothing was caving in.

Rhett yanked open the door on the passenger side of a truck. I pushed forward on shaky legs, focusing on the target. Through mild beams of light, I spotted a cherubic face lulled to sleep by death's fumes.

A spark of that December day flashed. The rumbling of earth. The pressure against my chest. My cries being swallowed by the shadows. I wouldn't allow the darkness to claim this sweet child. Not if I could help it. With a guttural moan, I reached inside the truck's cabin and gathered the small one in my arms.

"Can you lift her?" Rhett called as he rounded the truck to the driver's side.

"Yes." The child seemed only about three years old, so weight wasn't the issue. No, it was her delicate condition that concerned me. I needed to get this darling to fresh air. And fast.

"Go." Rhett's voice was coarse but firm. "I won't be far behind."

I hated to leave him, but the young girl needed aid. I took off, fueled by purpose and the milky dot in my line of sight. The exit. I fused my gaze to it, like I had the windows, drawing strength from the promise of open skies. The light spot grew bigger, and I only hoped I could reach the end of the tunnel before my legs gave way. And now, strong diaphragm or not, the battle for breath raged fierce.

Choking coughs clashed with piercing shrieks from those surging forward like me. Someone's elbow connected with my upper arm, and I shirked away only to smack my hip off an open car door. Pain cracked like lightning through my bones. Eyes watering, I pulled the child closer, a nurturing instinct propelling me.

For every one step, my lungs pinched twice as hard. My chest ruptured with a fit of coughs and my muscles weighted as if stuffed with rocks, making my strides slower and shorter. Even my pulse, so rapid a moment ago, throbbed a slow dirge in my ears.

Fatigue pressed in, unrelenting, but something inside me pushed back. *No, Darkness, you will not win again.* A fury tore into me, rage against the shadows, against the fear that had hemmed me in for years. Jaw clenching, I forged onward.

Within fifteen feet we were out of death's snare, the daylight gouging my vision with a welcomed pain. Another cough overtook, pressuring me to sink to the ground. But I couldn't. A string of patrol cars and firetrucks parked along the road. Men in uniform pushed past, entering the tunnel. Firemen with masks and oxygen aided several people who'd escaped before me.

Lungs burning with each scrape of air, I called out. "Over here." My voice, weak against the swell of chaos, didn't attract a passing glance. I staggered through the crowd until a fireman, armed with an oxygen tank, spotted me.

"Let me help, miss." He rushed toward me and relieved me of the girl. Lowering onto the ground, he set the cylinder tank beside us and pressed the leather mask to her small face. Hopefully enough air pressed through the hose, giving this young one a fighting chance.

I dropped to my knees, my gaze flicking between the limp form beside me and the entrance of the tunnel. Maybe Rhett had come outside already.

The fireman shifted and glanced at me. "Can you hold this mask in place, while I tend to others? 'Sides this little one could get no better care than from her mamma."

I nodded, not possessing the strength to correct him.

"Hold the mask like so and don't touch the tank. I'll be back to check on you." He disappeared into the bedlam.

With one hand I secured the mask and with the other I stroked the girl's arm. Her ashen complexion contrasted her red-checkered, gingham dress, making a sob jam in my throat. "C'mon, sweetheart. You have to pull through."

The next stretch of minutes seemed like several hours as I critically watched for signs of movement from the girl and every so often scanned the crowd for Rhett. Tiny fingers twitched, pulling my attention to the child. Her right leg jerked, and I fought tears.

The adult-sized mask extended over the girl's eyes, so I tucked back the edges in time to see the flutter of blonde lashes, revealing ice blue eyes.

The sleepiness lasted only a handful of heartbeats until her dazed expression turned frightened.

"Everything's okay. You're safe now." I ran a calming hand over the child's forehead. "Keep breathing into this mask until you're all better." I offered a warm smile.

The girl blinked at me twice. Then must've decided I was trustworthy because tiny fingers wrapped mine.

Another fireman attended to an unconscious gentleman adjacent to me. *The driver from the pickup truck.* The one this child had been with.

"You there." I raised my voice, and the uniformed fellow glanced my way. "Where was the gentleman who carried him outside?" I motioned with my chin to the man who had the same shade of hair as the girl beside me.

"Oh him?" The fireman's squinted gaze shifted to the tunnel. "He went back in to help some more."

My gut clenched. Rhett was still inside.

CHAPTER 23

The burnt odor of exhaust fumes clung to Rhett. That thirty-second stint in the open air hadn't seemed nearly enough to recover before dashing back in. But while he'd been gulping clean breaths, people inside the Liberty Tunnels were crawling to death's door.

Men, some he'd recognized from his years on the force, had joined him, but Rhett knew which cars held people. He directed some officers to the Ford Touring which housed a family of four. And to the Oldsmobile with a middle-aged couple inside. Meanwhile Rhett dashed toward the elderly man slumped in the Lexington sedan.

Rhett blinked, but the haze dotting his sight remained. Ignoring the nausea swirling his gut, he managed to sling the man's arm over his shoulder and hoist his slender frame out of the vehicle. The exit wasn't far from where Rhett stood but it seemed like miles.

A violent cough exploded in his chest, and Rhett almost dropped the poor fellow. He adjusted his grip and with joints tingling like fire, he forced one foot in front of the other.

The outside world was within reach. Twenty more strides or so. Every muscle screamed, and his movements edged towards clumsy. Thoughts of Kate pressed his mind. If she'd overcome her fear of closed spaces, he could survive a handful of yards to freedom.

A lanky officer rushed to the older man's other side, assisting Rhett for the last few steps. With another round of coughs, he emerged from the toxic trap. People buzzed about, but his gaze searched for Kate. Colors blurred, voices dulled, even the pounding of his own heartbeat seemed distant.

He stood in daylight, but the shadows pressed into him, stretching across his vision until all went black.

◆ ◆ ◆

I reunited the fully-recovered girl with her father who'd woken from his unconscious state. After pressing a kiss to the top of the child's head and nodding my thanks to the fireman attending the small family, I scurried through the fray in search of Rhett.

My gaze scanned the bustle. Workers aided dazed victims. Mothers cradled wailing children. Shouts of panic clashed with authoritative commands depending on which way my face angled. My head ached with a dull throb, no doubt the lingering residue of the carbon monoxide, but I pressed on, hunting for that familiar profile. I shifted toward the tunnel and caught sight of him, emerging from the darkness like a wearied soldier from battle.

He needs oxygen.

I increased my pace, side-skirting a road sign and nearly tripping over a divot in the cement. "Rhett." My strained voice blended into the chaos. Forcing my feet faster, I spotted a discarded tank and scooped it up without slowing my steps.

He stumbled backward, and I dove behind to catch him. Not the wisest of moves, for he toppled atop me and we tumbled to the concrete. By trying to break his fall, my spine received the brunt of the impact, knocking the air from me. A sting bounced between my temples, but all I could think about was helping the man currently pinning me to the oil-stained ground. I squirmed from beneath his weight, wriggling until I could get into a sitting position with the top half of him resting on my upper legs.

A hissing sound emitted from the mask, blessedly telling me it still had oxygen in the metal cannister. But how much was left? After positioning Rhett's head face-up, I set the mask over his mouth. With my free hand, I stroked his sweat-soaked hair.

Dark-fringed lashes eased open, as if wakening from a long nap. Though he'd only been passed out a mere minute, if that.

He blinked, disoriented.

Leaning over him, I continued to run my hand over his hair. His foggy gaze cleared, and I'd never been so thankful to be reacquainted with those beautiful blues. I didn't bother tapering my relief, allowing my shaky smile to break free. "Hello, there."

While the mask covered the lower part of his face, I could see a glimmer in his eyes while happy tears stung the backs of mine. "I thought you were going to be unconscious longer. I was fully prepared to sob over you for a while." I forced a light tone despite the emotion welling in my chest.

With slow movements, he raised a hand to cup my face, thumbing away the lone tear that had escaped. I pressed my fingers over top his and before I could think twice, shifted my head and kissed the inside of his wrist. Such a small gesture compared to what my heart felt, but this was all I could give. And by the flicker of pleased surprise in his eyes, it was enough.

He left his fingers intertwined with mine and with his free hand he pointed to the mask.

"I'm your self-appointed nurse, Mr. Jennings, and I say keep breathing into it."

What a way for a man to come to.

Rhett's head nestled in the softness of Kate's lap and his first clear view of the world had been that of her lovely face framed by cascading dark locks. He had half a mind to fake slipping in and out of consciousness just to keep reliving the moment.

Besides a lingering ache behind his eyes and the roll of nausea in his stomach, he felt fine. The oxygen stopped its flow against his mouth, and Kate wrinkled her brow at the empty tank.

"You should probably have more. I'm sure I can locate another." She leaned forward and cupped the back of his head. "If I can maybe slide from beneath you."

He pulled the mask from his face, earning an adorable scowl from his nurse. "I'm fine, Kate. But thank you."

Her mouth pinched. "You sure? I'd feel better if maybe you—"

He settled his hand on hers, silencing her concerns. "Trust me, I'm all right."

She gave a slight shake of her head, the crinkled nose a sure sign of her disapproval. He shouldn't derive so much pleasure from seeing her distressed concern for his wellbeing, but it inflated his chest more than the crummy oxygen. His mind flitted back to a few moments ago when her lips had pressed against his wrist. She hadn't been drugged that time. Kate Chamberlin cared for him.

His gaze locked with hers and his thoughts strayed to all she'd gone through today. "You're the strongest woman I know."

She blinked. "What made you say that?"

"You waged war against more than carbon monoxide."

She bit her lip and lifted her gaze from their locked hands. "I don't think I would've managed well on my own. You helped me face that fear and showed me how to look beyond myself. I needed that." Her lips tipped in a small smile and Rhett wanted to press his own to them. "Thank you."

He acknowledged her words with a squeeze to her fingers. "Have to say though, I feel bad for all the other fellows. I nabbed the prettiest nurse."

She pulled her hand from his and smoothed the hair from her face. "The poison is still in your blood stream. You should wait a bit before making such declarations."

"What if I told you I thought you were pretty, before I breathed the carbon monoxide?"

Her head tilted, but she said nothing.

"I've never seen a woman dislike attention as much as you. It makes things more of a challenge." He cracked a smile. "And I never back down from a challenge."

Chapter 24

Rhett grabbed an extra sportscoat off the wooden rack in his office and draped it over Kate's shoulders. She thanked him with a gentle nod. The weather was on the warm side, but this morning's events seemed to have pressed a chill in her. Though her frame shook like a leaf caught in the wind, Rhett didn't know a stronger woman alive.

Kate Chamberlin had conquered her fear today. He couldn't be more proud.

On the way here, they'd retrieved Kate's belongings from the Whitmore residence. Kate's friend had launched more questions at her than a seasoned investigator. Kate had answered with grace and kindness, but he could tell the recollection of all she'd been through recently had started to affect her. Rhett had invented the excuse of having to check in at the office and so here they were. Truth was, he needed a few moments to collect his thoughts and strength. Not to mention grab an aspirin for the lingering headache hammering his temples.

While many in the tunnel had been knocked out by the carbon monoxide, no one had lost their life. A miracle to be certain. But until the authorities could install a proper ventilation system, the tunnels would be closed. A fact that would make his commute more tedious, but necessary.

He led Kate to a small sofa in David's office, grateful his agency partner hadn't arrived to work yet.

She reclined against the plush cushion, weariness carving into her delicate features.

He claimed the seat beside her and stretched his arm alongside the back, his fingers brushing her shoulder. "What does *cielo* mean?"

She tensed. "Sky."

"In Italian?"

"Yes." Her chin sagged. "I wasn't born here."

"In Pittsburgh?"

"In America."

Given the stream of Italian words that'd flowed from her mouth this morning and the hints of accent that'd surfaced even before that, he wasn't surprised. But why hide it? The majority of Pittsburgh was comprised of immigrants. Polish, Italian, Irish. And the list went on. So much so, that many haven't bothered to learn the English language. Not only did Kate know it, but she spoke like a true native. Hadn't she said another couple raised her? Maybe they were American. "There are many Italian Americans around. Why do you hide your heritage?"

"For a number of reasons," she said on a sigh. "I was born in Spirelli. A small village off the coast of Southern Italy." She tugged the collar of his jacket snugger around her neck. "When I was six, there was a massive earthquake. It leveled the coastal town of Reggio and was so large that it reached our village. Thousands upon thousands died."

Rhett remembered hearing about that. Though he'd been young, he recalled his church had gathered in prayer for those affected by the disaster. Little had he known he'd been praying for Kate and her family.

Her lips formed a sad smile. "That's how I lost my mother."

The hurt behind her voice was enough to make his heart clench. Kate had told him her mother had died but hadn't explained much further. She was opening up to him, offering the tragic pieces of her past. "I'm sorry."

"My ... uh ... father was making his morning deliveries while our house and small shop were demolished. Everything caved from the inside. It would've claimed me, but I lost Biscotti, my cat." Her glazed eyes stared into the distance, and he knew she wasn't seeing the walls of David's office. No, she was back in Spirelli, reliving the pain. And it was torture to watch. "My birthday was only days before and for my present, my parents allowed me to keep a stray cat. We didn't have much, but that cat was all I wanted."

"I tried to tame him, but Biscotti often wandered off. He did that morning, and I chased after him. It was then the earthquake hit." Her bottom lip trembled. "The ground beneath my feet shook as if there was some terrible monster beneath the layers of earth, wanting to swallow me whole." The words rasped from her. "The world tipped sideways, and somehow I got trapped beneath a pile of debris. I was pinned there for two days."

His breath stalled. Two days? Unimaginable. "Oh sweetheart." His fingers wrapped her shoulder in a gentle caress, but she remained numb to his touch.

"All I remember was blackness and the struggle to breathe. The weight on my chest made it hard to cry out or even talk. I survived by humming Mamma's lullaby and picturing the sky."

What hardships she'd faced at a young age. She'd survived an earthquake only to discover her mother had not. Then to be abandoned by her father? Hadn't she once said he'd left because the grief had been too great? Rhett's teeth ground. He had half the urge to track down the no-good chump who'd forsaken his own daughter. But his frustration with her idiot father wouldn't help Kate. He gentled his voice. "Tell me more about these Italian skies."

Her dark-fringed lashes glistened as they lifted. "It's different in Pittsburgh than in Spirelli." She stood and crossed to the window. "Here, everything is clogged with smoke and soot." She gestured to the ashen clouds then tucked her hands behind her elbows. "The skies in Italy were vast and stretched forever. I would lie in the tall grass and stare at the heavens."

"Sounds beautiful." He itched to move to her but remained seated.

"It was. I hardly remember any rainy days. Only the times when the sky was the perfect shade of blue. Just like your—" Her mouth snapped shut, her features tightening.

"My what?" He rose to his feet.

"Your eyes." Her lips pressed into a straight line then relaxed. "The color of your eyes reminds me of the sky in Spirelli."

All those times he'd wondered the reason behind her intense stares. Now he knew. He reminded her of home. As an orphan who'd once dreamed of having a sense of belonging—a home—he'd become that very thing to Kate. A safe haven for her to escape. Something inside him broke. "Cielo."

She moved closer, their gazes melding. "My sky."

Drawn by an invisible pull, he matched her distance, a step for a step. He brushed a knuckle against her cheek.

Her eyes—crimped with sadness a moment ago—now warmed with want. He recognized the desire as much as he could identify with it. Her breath fanned against his neck, his craving for her intensifying. Which meant, he should back away. If only his legs would budge.

"Rhett." His name rolled on her lips, heavily accented, as if she'd hungered to speak it in her native cadence. To bring him into her world. One she'd seemed to keep hidden from everyone else.

His hands slipped beneath the jacket cocooning her, and he explored the curve of her waist. Tugging her closer, his fingertips wandered up her spine, absorbing the shiver that rocked through her. The jacket fell to the floor. He cupped the back of her slender neck, easing her head to his.

His chin dipped, his mouth hovering mere inches from hers. Her lashes fluttered shut, lips parting, inviting his touch.

He moved to close the distance, but Kate inhaled sharply.

Her lids cracked wide, and she angled away.

He jolted back as if she'd slapped him. What had he done?

"I can't." Her voice wobbled as much as her chin.

Kate's eyes filled with regret, and his own slid shut. Why had he thought he was good enough for her? His chest hitched, and he withdrew his hold.

She shuffled back a step. "I shouldn't have let this go this far." Her soft rebuke proved she spoke to herself rather than to him. "I'm the biggest fool."

A fool? Because they'd almost kissed? Then it dawned on him— her first kiss. She didn't want it squandered on the likes of him.

But she already had.

He dragged a hand over his face. "Kate, I'm sorry."

She stilled. "No, it's me who should apologize. I have to tell you—"

"I know."

Her pulse throbbed in the hollow spot of her collarbone. "What do you know?"

"You mentioned about never being kissed. I know you're being careful. I tried to prove myself to you, but..."

She leaned toward him and placed a hand on his bicep. "That's not it, Rhett."

"No?"

Anguish tightened her features. "I can't kiss you because of my own convictions."

He'd been right all along. "You don't think I'd cherish your virtue. Cherish you." His fingers flexed at his sides. "Because I've been with other women."

"Rhett, you don't understand."

Blast his mistakes. "Believe me, I do." He shoved a hand through his hair. "Kate, I'm sorry. But you already kissed me."

She blanched. "What?"

"In order to get you away from Big Dante's nephew, I told him you were my sister. Pitrello alerted the bouncers at the door to look for a pair of siblings. And he gave them our descriptions."

She shuddered.

"The men were looking for us and we had to act ... non-related. I would never take advantage of you, Kate. I hope by now you'd know that. I only wanted to appear like a couple in love. So I pecked your cheek, your jaw, but then you—"

"What?"

"Kissed me."

I'd kissed Rhett. At Saluti's. And we'd almost shared another. Then, my mind had caught up with the moment, scolding me for my carelessness. Turning away from him had been difficult, but I couldn't allow him to kiss me. It wouldn't be fair to him.

The hurt in his eyes at my refusal, the pain etched in his voice had made the guilt triple its weight in my gut. I'd never sought to fall in love. I hadn't any idea how to search for such a thing, yet it'd found me. And my heart wouldn't look the same again.

I let out a self-depreciating laugh, causing Rhett to raise a brow. This was crazy. The entire thing. Of all the people for me to fall for? Why the son of the man my father had murdered? But then, perhaps I wasn't in love. It'd only been, what? Nine days of being in this man's presence. That was barely enough time to form an attachment. Maybe *I* was the one who was crazy. The trait certainly matched my family line.

"Kate." Rhett reached for me, then, as if remembering my rejection, slid his hands into his pockets. "How can I prove to you I'm not the man you believe me to be?"

He thought it was him. How cruel was this?

"Anyone here?" An unfamiliar masculine voice echoed off the wood-paneled walls, and Rhett mumbled his frustration.

"In your office, David." Rhett exhaled and turned hopeful eyes on me. "Can we continue this discussion later?"

I glued my stare on his crooked necktie, and kept silent. My voice wouldn't work anyway, so clogged was my throat. I followed Rhett to his side of the building.

"Hey there, Jennings." A tall, lean gentleman with arms loaded with files regarded Rhett then me, a small smirk lining his mouth. "I take it you are Miss Chamberlin?"

I gave a tight nod and offered what hoped could pass as a smile.

"I'm David. Charmed to finally meet you." A vague look passed between the men. "If you have a second." His hazel eyes were directed at Rhett. "I have a few contracts I need you to sign."

Rhett gave a solemn nod, and David retreated to his own office. As soon as the man was out of earshot, Rhett approached me. "I won't be long." His gaze roved my face, but it was a face he connected to another name. A name I'd claimed to hide from mobsters, police, and anyone else who'd harm me because of my family.

But my efforts to protect myself had failed. I was wounded in a way I'd never thought possible. And from Rhett's sullen expression as he walked into David's office, I'd injured him as well.

That was what Salvastanos did, they hurt others. Then they fled.

So I took off. Sprinting out of Rhett's office. I needed away. Away from him. Away from this city. From anything that reminded me of the misery of my life.

I bounded down the stairs, my heartbeat thrashing in my ears. Footsteps sounded behind me. My neck stiffened, refusing to allow a glance back. I exited the agency door, racing onto the walk.

"Kate. Wait."

I wasn't Kate. I was Caterina. I was a murderer's daughter. My feet pushed faster as if carrying me far from the torment.

"Kate!"

My foot caught in a crack in the cement, and I tumbled forward onto the ground. But it wasn't hard enough. The pain jolting my knee-caps, needed to pulse my body. I wanted the anguish to surge until I grew numb so I could be dead to everything.

A sob ripped through me and I lay curled on the soot-crusted walk. Exactly where I should be. A lump of garbage. Dirtied from birth.

Strong hands gripped my waist, and I struggled against him.

Why couldn't he leave me?

He pulled me to stand, and I leaned against the agency building. My vision blurred with the unyielding tears, my heart bleeding from the unchanging truth.

I could change my name. My identity. But at the end of the day, I was still the child of a criminal.

CHAPTER 25

His heart being ripped from his chest seemed less painful than viewing Kate, her shoulders heaving with sharp gasps.

He cupped her face. Her tears dampened his palm, and he wished her pain could seep into him just as easily so he could bear it for her. "I'm sorry." He should've told her first thing this morning about the kiss. Or maybe he should've waited and told her in a day or two. In the span of twenty-four hours, this woman had been drugged for cruel intentions, trapped in a poisonous tunnel, and told she'd forfeited her first kiss. Her emotions were no doubt stretched thin and then he added more strain. No wonder she'd reacted that way. "Let's get you home. So you can rest." He reached for his handkerchief and pressed it into her palm.

She dabbed the corners of her eyes, but their glossy sheen revealed more tears were on the way. He couldn't blame her. Even without the emotional pileup of this past several hours, she'd had a stressful week.

It wasn't everyday a woman got threatened by a crime boss or her apartment broken into.

He led Kate to his car. The long drive to her apartment had been painfully silent, except for her sniffles. He pulled into the small lot beside her complex and shut off the engine.

She angled away from him. "Thank you for taking me here." She threw open the door and scurried out of his car, her face buried in her hands.

No. He couldn't let her leave this way. Not when it was his recent doing that made her so upset. He caught up to her as she was sliding the key in her door. "Kate, don't leave me. Not like this." He placed a gentle palm on her shoulder, and she stiffened. "I can't say again how sorry I am—"

She raised a hand, silencing him. "Stop apologizing. This was never about you."

His brow dug lower. If it wasn't him, then what? "Is it about the case? I know that's been hard with all the unknowns surrounding it. But … Kate, will you look at me?"

She pulled in a deep breath and stared at the button on his jacket.

"I won't let anything happen to you. You mean more to me than just another client." *Don't say it, Jennings.*

She lifted her eyes to his. The vulnerability in her gaze struck him afresh.

"Kate, I'm in love with you."

CHAPTER 26

My heart leaped at Rhett's words, then plummeted so hard it shattered, the shards cutting deep.

Rhett Jennings was in love with me.

No, he wasn't.

He was in love with Kate Chamberlin. Someone who didn't exist. I locked my gaze on his. Those eyes. My sky. Only now they seemed clouded, and I realized I'd given no response to his declaration.

I clasped my hand around his large wrist and tugged him inside my apartment.

With a steadying breath, I closed the door, shutting us in.

Surprise etched his face. He removed his hat and fingered the rim, eyes on my every move.

I motioned for him to sit, creating some much-needed distance. He sunk onto the sofa while I chose to stand. A good four feet separated us, but soon it'd be much more.

"You can't be in love with me." The words burned so bad I gripped my stomach.

His hands stilled on his hat and his brows furrowed, deep and serious. "I don't understand."

"That is, you *think* you are, but—"

"No. I *know* I am."

I winced and Rhett's shoulders sagged. He'd taken my reaction as a slight against his affections, and something in me died a little. Oh, to be able to accept his love. If only I could acknowledge my own for him. But the course had already been determined for me, and I had to journey every heel-bruising step. Alone. Before I even placed sole in America, I'd been pitted against Rhett. The forces opposing were stronger than the brittle ties between us. My last name was the emblem of wickedness, uglier than the symbolic serpent on the card. Salvastano meant monster. And I carried its blood. "You don't even know my real name. It's not Kate. It's Catarina."

"So Kate's your nickname. That doesn't make any difference to me." Confidence flecked in his eyes and his tone strengthened. "I understand what you're saying. It's too soon. We don't know each other well enough to claim a deeper attachment. But here's the thing, Kate. There's no rush. I want to prove to you that I'm committed."

"We're not good for each other."

"Give me a chance."

I pressed my fingers against my temples, shaking my head. "It won't work."

"Why, Kate? I need more of a reason than that."

"I'm Catarina Salvastano."

Rhett gaped at her, words escaping him.

To his relief and agony, she continued. "I came to America nine months ago." Her lashes swept shut and her voice strained. "To find Hugo ... my Papa."

Rhett launched to his feet, his pulse thundering. "Do you realize what you're saying?" The question ripped from his lips.

"Yes." A tear slid down her cheek. "I should've told you sooner."

He paced the small area once. Twice. Then stopped cold in front of her. "I never thought you were capable of cruelty. Anyone else, but not you."

She swayed and sunk onto the sofa, elbows pinning to her sides.

"I tell you I'm falling for you and instead of letting me down easy, you invent the most ridiculous story I've ever heard."

Her steady eye contact faltered, her gaze crumbling to somewhere on the floor. "It's true."

He scoffed. "You heard the lawyer. Hugo had no children."

"He's wrong." Kate rose, legs wobbly as a newborn fawn, then made her way to the bedroom. Seconds later, she emerged, her pale fingers clutching a stack of mail. "Remember when I said the earth-quake took both my parents away? That my father left?"

He gave a tight nod, his neck so tense, it ached. He'd remembered the anguish that'd deadened the gold sparks in her eyes. The torment wracking her every syllable. He'd remembered the intense urge to pull her into his arms and hold her until every ghost faded.

Now she was claiming relation to the demon that haunted him.

"Papa had the Chamberlins take care of me. They were mission-aries from America. He sailed to the states to join his brothers, Pedro and Lorenzo." She held out a pile of envelopes.

He glared at the items "What are those?"

"Letters from my father. I've saved them all." Her voice fell quiet. "The last one he sent was why I came to Pittsburgh. He sounded desperate, and I was concerned."

Rhett took the top letter and slid out the contents. It'd been written in Italian, but he recognized some words. Something fell out of the pages and onto the floor.

A picture.

He scooped it up and glowered at a young Hugo, smiling like the devil himself, with his arm around a pretty woman who looked similar to Kate.

The realization sunk in with icy hooks, carving the chilling truth into his bones.

Kate was a Salvastano.

"Did he happen to mention he was a crime boss?" He flicked the corner of the letter and she flinched.

"No."

"Or that he murdered my father?" Venom drenched his words, but he was the one who'd been poisoned by her lies. Fine detective he was. All the while he'd been searching for clues to Hugo's whereabouts and his biggest lead was standing two feet away. Hugo's daughter. The woman he'd declared his love to.

He tossed the letter on the sofa beside him.

"I didn't know any of it. It was only when I came here. It was the day I met—" She flattened her mouth.

"Met who?"

"You. You saved me from a couple of Big Dante's men who were harassing me."

He jerked back, his chest squeezing so hard he feared its collapse. "That was you?"

She nodded, her frame shaking. "I always wanted to thank you for being there."

The day he'd met Kate in the archive room at KDKA flashed his mind. He'd had an inclination of having seen her before, but she'd indeed known. She'd been aware of who he was the entire time. Could he be any more of an idiot? And for her. Not giving any hints or clue to her true identity? She should be on the stage rather than hiding behind a piano. "You lied to me."

"I'm sorry."

Another lie. Everything from her lips, all of her actions, were a ruse. "You're sorry?" Fire gathered in his core, the flames spreading through him, consuming. "I trusted you. I told you everything. About my past. My adoption. Words I've never spoke to any other soul." He tugged at his tie knot, but the chokehold on his throat had nothing to do with a piece of fabric. "Your blasted father killed mine."

Her eyes slid shut, her fingers convulsing, as though the thought pained her.

A derisive laugh scraped through his lips. "You can drop the act." He'd lamented to her about the loss of his father. No doubt giving her a good chuckle later. That day in his office when he'd shown her a picture of Hugo. He'd thought her distressed reaction had been due to fatigue. Now he knew. It was because she was glimpsing her cherished father, a cold-blooded killer. "Have you no soul?"

She blinked.

"No, of course you don't. You're a Salvastano."

"I didn't mean to … to go this far. I was scared to mention it. I tried to tell you before."

"You had plenty of opportunities to tell me, Kate. Or should I say *Catarina?*" He drew out her true name in a mock Italian accent. "I've been exhausting myself trying to keep you safe. I've lost nights of sleep.

Turned cases over to my partner, because you needed constant protection. I bet you've had a good laugh at my expense."

She reared back as if he'd hit her.

"Spare me the theatrics." He sneered. "We both know you're not in any danger from Hugo." He slapped his hat on his head.

"Rhett, believe me. I never meant for things to turn out this way." The plead in her voice only fueled his irritation. "I care for you, too."

"Goodbye, Catarina." He forced the words through clenched teeth, his heavy steps carrying him to the door.

She wrapped her arms around herself. "I need to tell you that Delvina is a fraud."

He halted. "That makes two." He tipped his hat to her, hardening himself to the pain darkening her brown eyes, and stormed out her door.

CHAPTER 27

I had unveiled my deception. Any pinch of freedom from my disclosure had been crushed by heartache. My blurred stare fastened on the door Rhett had disappeared through. He could never forgive such a betrayal. Not that I'd ask him to.

I couldn't claim I'd held his heart for any sliver of time because he was in love with the image I'd created. The one of a woman who had no ties to the man who killed his father.

Oh, Papa.

I peered at the letters. Pages my father had scribed. Phrases I'd relished. In my hands contained every single word Papa had written to me in the span of seventeen years. All but the one I'd lost the day I'd met Rhett in front of Papa's demolished bakery.

How naïve I'd been thinking that coming over here, braving the voyage, was proof of my undying affection for a most beloved Papa. What had I learned? That I was insignificant. That I held no power to help anyone. Not even myself.

I didn't even resist the rush of tears. What was in my makeup that caused everyone I loved to leave? Why wasn't I worth the effort to stay? Mamma had been a victim to the earthquake. But Papa? He'd refused to say goodbye, claiming he'd see me again. He probably only had said that to halt my cries. Then the ocean liner, a giant coffin that carried the shell of a Papa I'd thought loved me, was gone.

I'd known Rhett would leave. There'd been nothing I could've said or done to make him stay. Before tonight, my mind's eye had envisioned his reaction again and again. But I'd pictured him filled with wrath. While fury had bulged a vein in his forehead, there'd been darts of hurt behind the blue flames in his eyes, sorrow lingering beneath the embers.

Sorrow cut through me with the force of a thousand knives.

I sobbed for Rhett and for our never-to-be romance. The tears that flowed told a story of our brokenness. Of the lies I'd lived. Of the bitter wound I'd inflicted upon him.

Rhett claimed I had no soul. I feared he was right.

Rhett launched punch after punch into the bag hanging in his basement. Knuckles throbbing, he kept at it, mercilessly.

"Don't break anything." Major's voice clashed with the click of his oxfords descending the wooden steps. "I could hear those swings from upstairs." The man was dressed in his Sunday best, while Rhett sparred against his striking bag in his undershirt and trousers.

"It helps relieve pressure." Rhett took another swipe, a sharp pain zinging to his elbow.

Major dragged a stool from under the workbench and settled onto it. "Your father would do the same thing, and bare-knuckled too."

That Rhett knew. His father had taught him how to make a fist so no bones would break. How to lead left to catch any opponent off guard. How to pull and deflect a cross-body punch. By the time Rhett was fifteen, he could defend himself against any assault. But his father hadn't taught Rhett how to protect his heart. That'd been an instinct Rhett'd possessed since day one. He'd refuse anyone past his self-imposed barrier except those he trusted—Father. Mother. The Major. And for a fleck of time, Kate.

"Missed you at church this morning."

Rhett threw a right hook, sending the bag swinging with the impact, shaking the support beam that held it.

"Anything you want to talk about?" Major removed his hat and set it on his knee. "How's the Salvastano case coming?"

"It's closed." *Jab. Jab. Jab.*

"Really? Then the broadcaster is out of danger?"

If Major was trying to distract Rhett from his heavy thoughts, he'd selected the worst possible route. *Jab. Jab.* But it wasn't the old man's fault.

It was hers. "Kate Chamberlin was never *in* danger." He still didn't know why she'd received the cards. Maybe it'd been a setup. What if Hugo had known Rhett'd been on the hunt and the mobster had used this as a ploy to keep Rhett occupied? And occupied, he'd been.

He took another swing. No, that couldn't be. Because Dr. Conrad had employed Rhett's help. Not Kate.

But still, something was off somewhere. "Hugo Salvastano wouldn't harm his own daughter."

Major coughed, clearly taken by the news. "His daughter?"

"Yeah. She showed me proof." Sweat gathered in the corner of Rhett's eye, and he swiped it away. "My services are no longer at her disposal." Another pain shot through him, not from a forceful punch but from the knowledge of the woman who'd lied to him.

Major scratched his scar. "Does Miss Chamberlin intend on taking over the family business?"

Rhett's arm was mid-swing but the question threw him off, the edge of his fist barely making contact.

Would she? Kate had deceived him on every other line of truth. He'd witnessed her compassion with the orphans and her tender interactions with Charlie. Had that all been an act? Had she been working with her father all along? If so, what was Hugo up to? "I'm not sure."

Major looked skeptical, and he had cause to.

Rhett's father and he had been the only ones on the right side of the law concerning the Salvastanos. He'd toiled many long nights with Father, trying to navigate the corrupt system to bring these men to justice.

"Is Kate her given name or did she assume another?"

"Her real name's Catarina. She adopted the surname of the couple who were her caregivers growing up." Why hadn't he put any of this together? All those questions he'd fired at her at the beginning of the investigation, she'd dodged so cleverly that it'd never once occurred to him that she'd been related to Hugo.

"I see." Major shifted on the stool and hooked the heel of his shoe on the low rung. "Had she mentioned being in contact with her father?"

"Said she hadn't seen Hugo since she was little. They communicated by letters. Though that could be a lie, too." He shook his hands at his sides, the tingling sensation leaving his fingertips. "Her story is, that after her mother died, Hugo sailed here and left Kate in Italy with American missionaries. She only arrived a little while ago. After..." *Father's murder.* "It happened."

Major gave an understanding nod.

"She claims to have no clue about her family's illegal activities."

"And you believe her?"

Rhett turned and threw a series of uppercuts into the pillowed bag.

"Son?"

He finished his rounds and exhaled. "I don't know. I came across her the first day she arrived." Or so Kate had said it was her first day. "She was being harassed by some of Big Dante's men."

"Did they know who she was?"

"Probably not. If they did, I'm sure they would've pursued her further." Having the daughter of their rival in their clutches would be a cruel but effective way to draw Hugo out of hiding.

"Interesting you didn't recognize her when you saw her again." Major's tone was light, but the meaning hit its mark.

Rhett stiffened. "Maybe I was distracted by my father's murder." He all but snapped the words.

Major raised a silver brow in a way that he could imagine his own dad doing.

"Sorry." His attention fell to the concrete floor. "It's been an awful week."

But Major had a point. What kind of detective was he? It was Rhett's line of work to be observant. His skillset included catching details everyone else overlooked. And yet, he hadn't placed where he'd seen Kate. Though that wasn't the case now. Each time he closed his eyes her face would flash. When he'd glanced at the radio he'd almost heard her angelic voice. Even sleeping in his own bed last night, his pillow had been rose fragranced from her hair. That alone was maddening.

"You're fond of her, aren't you?"

Rhett grabbed a towel off a rack against the wall and wiped his face, his neck. "She lied to me."

"Indeed, she did. But—"

"There's nothing else." Grimacing, he rehung the towel. "She lied to me, and that's the end of it."

"Good to hear it." Major stood and walked over to Rhett. "You don't need to be involved with that family." He clapped a veined hand on Rhett's shoulder. "I've never known you to be committed to one woman anyway. You remind me a lot of myself. A confirmed bachelor has definite perks."

Rhett would've agreed a year ago, but not now. His heart had a gaping Kate-sized hole. Yet there was no way he'd allow Catarina Salvastano to fill it.

I stretched and rolled right off the sofa. I landed onto the floor with a hard thud. Wincing, I flopped onto my back, my vision clearing with several blinks. I'd fallen asleep after hours of sobbing. Too bad it hadn't helped any. My father was still a murderer and Rhett was still gone from my life.

Something crinkled beneath my left leg.

Papa's letters.

With a sigh, I clumsily made my way to the bedroom and shoved the envelopes beneath the bed, my knuckle brushing the corner of Madre Chamberlin's Bible. I released a frustrated laugh as I withdrew my former guardian's cherished possession. The black binding looked so severe, and the weight of it was heavy in my hand.

This is your Heavenly Father's letter to you. Madre had said when she'd reverently packed it in my trunk alongside Papa's correspondences.

God's letter. I'd first learned to read and speak English on the commandments. I'd practiced talking without an accent by reciting proverbs. All the verses about what I shouldn't do. How I couldn't act. Madre Chamberlin had hand selected them to ingrain the fear of God in me. And it'd worked.

Rhett had mentioned about God being love. If only Madre would've instilled those verses in me instead. But then ... maybe I should've done that myself. What if I would've taken the time to learn the scriptures rather than being spoon-fed them by the Chamberlins?

My grip softened on the worn edges, my thumb skimming the spine. It wasn't too late. My breath snagged in my chest as I lifted the cover. Flipping through, the pages opened to the book of Psalm.

I knew that word meant *song*. In the center of the Bible, at the very heart ... were songs. That spoke to my musical soul. I skimmed several verses, taking in the psalmist's continual cries for help. I could relate with his distress, yet I'd never asked God to rescue me. My perspective of the Most High had been that of a strict judge. I'd never felt like I'd been good enough to win His mercy or secure His help. And just because I'd confessed the truth to Rhett didn't mean I was in His favor now.

I moved to close the Bible, but my gaze hitched on a passage.

Thou art my hiding place; Thou shalt preserve me from trouble; Thou shalt compass me about with songs of deliverance.

God sang?

Mamma's lullaby swept to the forefront of my mind. Even now I could hear my mother's gentle voice, washing over me, soothing my fears. I could imagine her face, filled with a tenderness that encompassed my heart with comfort.

That song had been *my* hiding place, clinging to it in times of trouble. This verse, the psalmist's refuge had been God. His lullaby that of deliverance.

I set the Bible on my lap and tried to form the picture. Could I replace the stern image of the Almighty with that of One who sings over His children?

I would have to ponder that awhile. As well as how to move forward. I'd remained guarded so long, hiding behind the cover of pretense. Could I endure the throes of peeling away the mask, so rigid and untouched for months? Would I recognize what's underneath?

My spine curled forward, shoulders slumping. Who was I kidding? I hadn't the luxury. Just because Rhett knew the truth didn't change the fact that revealing my identity would position me as a target.

A knock sounded at my door. I jolted. Or was it a knock? Over the past week I'd flinched at every groan and creak this old building had produced. I returned the Bible to its spot by Papa's letters and tucked my feet under my legs, waiting for another rap. None came.

Disappointment wrapped a gloomy band around my mind, tightening with each breath. Rhett wouldn't stop by today. Or any other for that matter. But hadn't I expected this? I'd known he'd want nothing to do with me upon discovering my identity.

How would Rhett proceed? Would he expose me to the world? My heart squeezed. I had no right to plead for his silence. But what if, Big Dante, or other crime bosses, found out?

Pressing a hand to my roiling stomach, I stood and padded into the parlor. The click of my deadbolt snatched my attention. The door eased open and Charlie slipped inside.

He shoved his floppy hat from his forehead and smiled when he saw me.

I rushed to him and squished him in a hug.

He glanced up at me.

"I've missed you." Guilt stitched through me. I'd hardly been home the past several days. By the way Charlie clung to my side, he'd felt my absence keenly.

The stack of drawings that'd been daily left on my table proved Charlie had been using my apartment as a refuge while I'd been gone. The knowledge brought equal parts pain and relief. I was thankful he had a safe haven from his father's drunken wrath, but saddened I hadn't been here for him.

At least that was one consolation out of all this. I could return to my normal routine with Charlie. But how would I explain Rhett's absence? The child didn't open up easily, yet he'd embraced Rhett's friendship almost from their introductions. Knowing Rhett had exited my world was painful enough. Now I'd bear the guilt of Charlie losing one of his only two friends in this universe.

Charlie raised an envelope, a curious expression lining his scarred face.

I pushed past the solemn feelings and adopted a smile. "Did you draw me another picture?"

He coupled a shake of the head with a finger point to the door. He signed *mail*.

"That was in the slot?" Odd. Mail didn't arrive on Sunday. But then, maybe I'd indeed heard a knock. Was this from Rhett? My heart pounded. Was he addressing what I'd told him last night? Perhaps I should read this in the other room. If tears flowed, I didn't want to upset Charlie.

I offered Charlie some bread and honey, then excused myself to the bedroom with the mysterious missive. The envelope itself was blank, reminding me of the one that held the first "S" card.

Drawing in a shaky breath, I pulled the single paper from the envelope.

My gaze sharpened on the unfamiliar script.

I know who you are. We'll talk soon.

CHAPTER 28

M y hands glided over the ivories as I poured my soul into the music. The song director had been preoccupied with preparations for the upcoming special broadcast to Norway that he'd allowed me to choose my own pieces all week. Each of my selections had been from Aldenberg's opera—all carrying the theme of overwhelming remorse. Today's segment would float through many speakers, but I intended this song to reach one in particular.

If I couldn't talk to Rhett in person, I'd allow music to communicate my regret. He probably hadn't listened to any of my air times. But I had to try. If by chance he'd tuned in, he'd surely know the pieces and what they'd represented.

The tempo was marked andante, but instead my fingers slowed. I pressed each key as one would form an apology, deliberate and heartfelt. The tone had the effect I'd wanted, somber with a trace of hope. Though I hadn't any reason to hope with Rhett. He hadn't contacted me, and I hadn't tried to reach out to him either, not even to inform him of the distressing note left at my door on Sunday.

The chord progression crept to a gloomy F minor, but I couldn't bring myself to play it. Rather I adjusted the sequence to something lighter, envisioning midnight melting into dawn. Turning the page, I flowed into the final portion, the tempo brightening, imparting a whimsical feel—as if the skies opened above me, and I could view the glories of daybreak. A fresh start. Like the past few mornings I'd spent reading the scriptures, my heart becoming awakened to God's whispers.

The final crescendo approached and I leaned into it, building the moment. The sunrise was now full and vivid, making my fingers dance across the keys like the fields I'd romped as a young girl, skipping through the open spaces, heart carefree.

What had begun as bitter regret concluded with traces of life.

This piece had become my prayer.

Harold's deep timbre took over the broadcast, and with quiet motions, I slipped into the overflow room, heart still absorbing the strums of peace.

I returned my music to its proper spots. Now would've been the time for Rhett to arrive and escort me home. I cast a longing gaze at the door leading to the hallway only to discover Robert Fuller standing there. How long had he been watching me?

He took my awareness of him as encouragement and proceeded into the room, a lopsided smile flashing. "Hey, Kate. Is your shift over?"

"Yes." I crossed to the table against the wall and retrieved my hat and gloves. I normally left my belongings in the cloak room, but I'd been running late this morning. Charlie had stopped by and I'd gathered he was hungry. I couldn't endure the thought of him going without food. So I'd rushed to make him breakfast and barely made it in time for my shift. Thankfully the trolley strike had ended early Monday otherwise I wouldn't have had transportation to work at all.

Robert drew beside me, close enough for me to catch whiff of his spicy aftershave. "There's an older gentleman here to see you."

I blinked at his unexpected announcement. An older gentleman was waiting on me? How odd. The only person I knew that fit that description would be Fernando. Perhaps to thank me again for the cannoli? But then, Robert knew the janitor and therefore wouldn't be so vague about it. "Did the gentleman give a name?"

"No. He flat refused to say." He shot me an annoyed look. "Had the cheek to say that you know who he was and that's all *I* needed to know."

Who could it be? Surely not Papa. The notion seemed ridiculous. Preposterous. But yet … why wouldn't this person offer his name? Unless he was hiding something. Only one way to find out. "Where is he now?"

"I told him to wait in Studio B. It's vacant for the next few hours."

"Thank you, Robert." I tossed my gloves into my hat and started toward the door, but masculine fingers cupped my elbow, stilling me.

Robert flushed and pulled his hand away. "I noticed Mr. Jennings hasn't been around this week."

This wasn't the conversation I wanted to have. But since everyone at Westinghouse believed Rhett and I had been romantically involved, I might as well get used to explaining. "No. Mr. Jennings won't be escorting me anymore. We're going separate ways from now on."

"I'm sorry to hear that." Words that could be believable had not his lips twitched. "Maybe we could grab ice cream some time. Klavon's has excellent egg soda."

Oh. "That's kind of you, but—"

"You don't have to answer today." His tone held a nervous agitation, so unlike Rhett's confident control.

I managed an awkward farewell and eased my way down the hall toward Studio B. Each step closer made my heart pound harder, my thoughts unraveling. The visitor couldn't be Papa. He wouldn't dare venture here in broad daylight. People would recognize him. Unless he was disguised.

I paused in front of the door. What if it was my father? What would I say? How would I respond? Hugo Salvastano was a fugitive, wanted by the law.

My hand wrapped the knob. Six days ago I'd looked Rhett in the eye and unveiled the truth. Now, I could very well have to face another decision. Would I turn in my own father to the authorities?

I inhaled deeply and opened the door.

"Catarina." A familiar voice spoke from inside the studio "I told you we'd talk soon."

The trunk stacked against Rhett's bedroom door had taunted him all week. How easy it'd be to shove the agency into David's capable hands and shake the soot off his shoes for good.

But Rhett had made a promise. He'd sworn to procure justice for his father. Abandoning the case and leaving Pittsburgh was the coward's route.

And he was no coward.

So today, he found himself standing in front of Delvina Salvastano's hotel room.

Kate had labeled Delvina a phony. Quite the statement considering what Kate—no, Catarina—had disclosed. Trying to stop thinking of her had been like willing the tide to stagnate.

It'd been six days since he'd seen her, but not since he'd heard her. He'd tortured himself by listening to her segment. Somehow he'd deluded himself into thinking tuning in to her broadcasts had been solely for investigative purposes. If she would be secretly communicating with Hugo through the airwaves, Rhett would know it. But she hadn't been signaling her mobster father.

No, she'd been reaching out to him.

He'd told her he was fond of Georg Aldenberg's compositions. So what had she done? Played them all week long. And not just any of the famed composer's works, but the ones from the Viennese opera with the centering theme of regret and bitter loss.

She'd been apologizing through music, her language. His eyes squeezed shut. *Enough.* He couldn't let her torment him any further. Fingers already in a fist, he lifted his hand to knock on Delvina's door, but the woman herself charged out, nearly barreling him over.

She jumped back with a yelp. Her gloved hands clutched a traveling bag to her chest as if it were a shield. "W-Who are you?" The netting from her hat draped over terror-stricken eyes.

"The name's Everhett Jennings, Miss Salvastano." He tipped his hat but kept his gaze on her. "I'm a private detective and have a few questions if you have time."

Her alarm seemed to settle, but not her distrust. "Don't call me that."

Had he missed something? "Call you what, ma'am?"

"Salvastano." She spat the word as if it repulsed her.

Odd, this one. Two weeks ago, she'd relished the attention attached to the name. Why now the disgust? Kate had said this woman was a phony. Instinct told him she'd been correct. Kate may have spoken truth on this minor key, but it no way cleared her on a major scale.

His gaze drifted into the hotel room. The furniture had been turned over. Broken glass and debris strewn all over the floor. "What happened?"

The woman's laugh was as humorless as it was high-pitched. "I got taught a lesson by Big Dante's clan."

His hand jerked to his holster. He pivoted a step back and scanned the halls. Apart from the flickering hanging lamp three doors down, there was no movement.

Her mouth parted then tipped into a thin smile. "At ease, handsome. As much as I enjoy playing damsel in distress, I think the brutes are long gone."

"Are you hurt?"

She shook her head. "I wasn't here when this lovely shindig occurred." She switched her bag to her other hand and sized him up. "You say you're a detective? Are you a boy in blue?"

"I'm not a cop. Just a private investigator." At the restaurant weeks back, Rhett hadn't grasped a clear glimpse of her. Even without Kate's claim, Rhett could see she bore no semblance to her. While Kate had prominent cheek bones and a heart-shaped jawline, the lady before him had softer features and a rounded chin. The deep brown eyes that had once entranced him were different in color to the pair of greenish-gray ones currently pinned on him.

"What did you come here for?" She smoothed a hand over her stylish dress, trimmed in the same color blue as the peeling wallpaper beside her. "I'm not up for an interrogation, mister."

"I only wanted to ask a few questions, but I think you should call the authorities. Let them know what happened."

"Well, thanks for your noble advice, but I'm going to stick with my plan." She lifted her bag. "I got a one way ticket to Albany and after this wonderful send off"—she tipped her head to the wreckage behind her—"I'm not going to miss this place." As if to punctuate her stance, she pulled the door closed with a definite click, joining him in the hall.

"So the charade is off?" He laid all the cards on the table.

"The final act's over and so is my performance as Delvina Salvastano." She did a mock curtsy as one would do in a curtain call on the stage. "The name is Gladys Cartwright."

Cartwright. The name skated the edges of his memory until it found solid purchase. "Is your mother Beulah Cartwright? The Salvastano's housemaid?"

"Sharp deduction, but she's my aunt."

That was one piece of the puzzle solved, but what about the rest? "What time's you train departing?"

She shifted her balance from foot to foot, as if weighing her next move. "Why?"

He had to think of a way to stall her. The questions piled like dirt on a casket. He couldn't let this subject die until he had all the facts. "How about I buy you a cup of coffee first?"

"Coffee?" Her lips pulled into a wry smile. "I think my nerves need something stronger, like a shot of bourbon."

"There's a nice café down the road. How about it?" He reached out his hand, gesturing to hold her bag.

Her lips puckered as she assessed him. "Well." Seconds slid by. "I've got two hours before my train leaves. If you keep me safe until then, I'd say you got yourself a date." She allowed him to relieve her of her belongings and slipped her fingers through the crook of his free arm.

Gladys held charm and beauty, but Rhett knew he was safe from her wiles. Because his heart was still smashed beneath the sorry heel of Catarina Salvastano.

CHAPTER 29

My gaze clamped on Franco Cardosi. It hadn't been Papa on the other side of the studio door, but his crooked lawyer. I hazarded a step into the room. KDKA had always been my haven, a solace away from the Salvastano frenzy. But it'd been twice in three weeks where Papa's world had found me. First the "S" card and now the man who looked twice my age and half amused at my shock.

"Mr. Cardosi." It was a miracle my voice worked. "To what do I owe the pleasure?" I repeated the same words he'd spoken to Rhett on Monday. Keeping my wits about me seemed pivotal. How would Rhett act? Speak? I held my sternum stiff and tightened my jaw, hoping my forced composure was believable.

Cardosi's calculating eyes resembled that of a serpent ready to strike. "I planned to speak with you on Sunday, but you weren't home."

It'd been him who'd left the note. *I know who you are.* I squeezed my hat so hard, the edge of my fingernail bent back. I'd rather bear the stinging ache, then let this man glimpse me trembling. Through these past weeks I'd felt like one continual tremor. A skittering leaf in the wind of my circumstances. And I was tired of it. Tired of living in fear. Something in me kindled hot.

No more.

I straightened, and that scrap of courage that'd had risen within me in that tunnel returned. This was a different kind of darkness, the shadow of Papa's past, but I refused to let it smother me. "Why did you call me Catarina just now?"

His waxed mustache flickered above a knowing smile. "That's your name, isn't it?"

Had Rhett told him? Informed this man of my identity? No, Rhett wouldn't. I may have hurt him, but the trait of fierce protector was the bedrock of Rhett's nature. He wouldn't allow me to be prey to men like Cardosi.

The lawyer took a step closer, standing adjacent to Peggy's xylophone. "You look like her." His Italian lilt snapped my gaze from the cloth-draped walls to his stormy gray eyes.

"Who?"

"Amelia."

Mamma. How could my gut soften and twist simultaneously? Mamma's name was like precious stone embedded in my heart, yet Mr. Cardosi had used it as a crude boulder for me to stumble over, to get me to confess my identity. I wouldn't give in. "Who is Amelia?"

"The woman who has your eyes. I've seen a picture of her, and you, Catarina, take after her." His tone was as definite as the deep lines of his face, the sharp edge in his eyes daring me to defy him. "The moment you stepped into my office I recognized you. Did you think I didn't know of your existence, *piccolo topo?*"

Little mouse. Papa's nickname for me.

Surprise must've registered in my eyes for his thick lips curled in a satisfied smile.

Rhett aware of the truth had been an injury to my heart, but with Cardosi knowing? A lot more harm could happen. Heaven forbid he'd *sell* this knowledge to Big Dante or another crime boss. "If you knew, why didn't you mention it the other day?"

"You were introduced as Kate Chamberlin. It was obvious the astute detective had no idea who you were." He withdrew a pocket timepiece, glanced at the time, and leveled me with a withering look. "Jennings wouldn't have gazed at you so fondly had he known you are Hugo's daughter. It was amusing to watch."

He made it seem like a parlor game. I bit the inside of my cheek, heat curling around my tight shoulders.

What should I do? Maybe it was time to leave. I'd exhausted enough hope for Papa's innocence. I hated abandoning Charlie, especially with his circumstances, but what other option had I? Cardosi knew where I lived. Knew there was something between Rhett and me. For Charlie and Rhett's sake, I needed to go.

"I'm guessing you wouldn't want all of Pittsburgh to know who you are, yes?"

There it was. He intended to blackmail me. I lifted my chin despite my queasy stomach.

Mr. Cardosi hooked both thumbs under his lapel, unaffected by my silence. "I think staying in obscurity is a good thing, young lady." He strode another step forward, his eyes never leaving mine. "After all, you have no proof of who you are. Therefore you can't claim any assets."

The fortune. "Who said I have no proof?"

The crinkles framing his eyes tightened. "I just assumed. Or you would be beating down my door like the woman that says she's Delvina. Who we both know isn't."

I refused to feed him more information. Knowledge was power, and I was already at his twisted mercy. "If you'd excuse me, I must be going."

♦　♦　♦

Gladys pressed the mug to her mouth, taking a long sip and leaving a red lip-print behind. This café had been Rhett's favorite stopping post during his early days on the force. The pastrami sandwiches with piccalilli had gotten him through the grueling hours walking the beat.

He bounced the edge of his shoe against the vacant chair leg opposite him. Gladys had selected the seat beside him, and they've bumped elbows twice already. "Why'd you claim to be Delvina Salvastano?"

She set her mug on the saucer and shifted in her seat, angling toward him. "If I answer, then do I get to ask a question in return?"

If there was anything he'd learned over the past weeks it'd been winning trust was crucial. Not that it had done him any good with Kate, but it could prove useful here. "How about I answer your question first."

Skepticism threaded her brows. "You say you're a detective, right? What's the motive behind talking to me?"

"I've been searching for Hugo Salvastano since last September." Which seemed like yesterday and a century ago. "I wanted to verify if you were really his daughter. Simple as that." Yet it wasn't simple at all. Since the moment she'd opened her hotel room door, Rhett had been studying her. Nothing about her seemed violent or malicious. Yet the card left in Kate's apartment had been a definite threat—directly from this woman or someone warning about this woman. Either interpretation led to the assumption Delvina was vicious.

The waitress refilled his coffee and Rhett nodded his thanks.

Gladys ran a manicured fingernail over the length of her sugar spoon. Back and forth. Pause. Back and forth. "My aunt worked for the Salvastanos for twelve years. She was devoted to them. In her eyes, they could do no wrong."

Of course her aunt would believe that, she'd been collecting a paycheck from them. "May I ask if she was law-abiding?"

If Gladys was offended by Rhett's words, she didn't show it. "She's a devout catholic. She clung to her rosary right until she passed away this last January."

"I'm sorry for your loss."

"Thank you." She accepted his condolences with a hint of surprise. "I lived in New York. So we mostly communicated through letters."

His mind spun to Kate. She'd clung to those letters from Hugo as if they were treasure. But those words had been scrawled by the hand that'd killed his father. She'd known Rhett's stance on Hugo. He'd made it clear how he'd loathed the man, how he thirsted for revenge, yet she'd continued to hide her identity from him. As if any length of time would change his mind about it all. She may have been apologizing through songs, but did she really expect his forgiveness?

Gladys removed a slender, brass-toned case from her purse and retrieved a cigarette. "My aunt was a determined busybody. All her letters leaked juicy details of the Salvastanos."

"And that's how you learned about Delvina being Hugo's daughter?"

The smoke stick pinched between her lips, she struck a match, lit the end, and shook out the flame. "My aunt overheard Hugo discussing her to his brothers. He was searching everywhere for the girl and hadn't been able to find her. The brothers supposed her adoptive parents hadn't told her anything, since she was young when brought to the states."

Which could be a possibility. Delvina's appointed caregivers may have raised her without revealing her birthparents. The Salvastano firstborn could be anywhere, going through daily life without any idea of the vile man that'd fathered her. "So you assumed the role."

"Can you blame me?" She blew a stream of smoke. "My aunt brags how rich these fellas are. With the real daughter out of reach, two Salvastanos dead, and the other an outlaw, I figured it'd be a cinch to step in and claim the dough."

"Which is illegal."

"Minor detail." She gave a dismissive wave, her cigarette dropping ashes onto the crisp white tablecloth. "I figured once I got the money, I'd travel to a far away land like a rich princess with a carriage full of expensive hats."

Gladys had succumbed to the same snare his officer friends had bowed to. Hadn't the Bible said the love of money was the root of all evil? In a way, Rhett felt sorry for this woman.

"The gig proved harder than I expected. First that no good lawyer threatens me and now Big Dante's men are destroying my room. I'd rather be Broke Gladys than Loaded Delvina."

"Wait. Cardosi threatened you?"

"The old man said I'm a fraud. Which he's right, of course, but he told me he has proof I wasn't the real daughter. Something about that man gives me the jumps." She gave an exaggerated shiver, her shoulders hiking, disturbing the tips of her bobbed hair. "But the man did give me some swell gossip."

"Such as?"

She leaned closer, her rose-scented perfume swirling his senses, and whispered. "Did you know Hugo had two children?"

Her words lodged like shrapnel in his stomach. Cardosi had denied Hugo having a family, yet he'd admitted this to Gladys. That shifty glint in his aged eyes had sparked Rhett's suspicion. He'd presumed the man had been lying, but had been clueless as to what falsehood.

Until now. Cardosi knew.

Could Kate be in danger? The shyster seemed protective over Hugo's money. Money that Kate held claim to. But … just because Cardosi was aware of Catarina Salvastano's existence, didn't mean he connected it to Kate.

Kate had seemed uncomfortable in the lawyer's office. Had she been worried the man would recognize her? Or … what if Cardosi and Kate had been working together all along, playing Rhett for a chump? Questions tangled like barb wire around his mind, squeezing.

He had to tackle one challenge at a time. Right now he had to disprove Gladys's hand in this. "If Hugo has two children, and Delvina can't be located, where's the other child?"

"Beats me." She shrugged. "He's probably lying low in some obscure location. Which seems ideal to me at present." Gladys rested her cigarette on the ash tray and adopted an innocent look. "Maybe I'll try to join some convent in the tropics. Think I could pass as a nun?"

"He?" Rhett steepled his hands and rested his chin on his fingertips. "What makes you so sure the other child is a man?" Because Rhett had definite proof to the contrary.

"I'm not." Her lips pulled to a slight frown. "It's my guess. Cardosi didn't relay the gender of the other Salvastano. We're not exactly bosom buddies."

The waitress drew near and set the order slip on the corner of the table, her bashful eyes and smile directed at Rhett.

Gladys observed the exchange, the crinkles fanning from her eyes revealing her amusement. "I'm beginning to think you're a fraud, as well." She took another drag on her cigarette. "You don't pound the table or threaten. Aren't detectives supposed to intimidate?"

"That's not how I operate."

"Mmm." Her lazy gaze perused him. "You better be careful with an approach like that. Others can take advantage."

"I can handle myself." He downed the rest of his coffee. "What makes you think Big Dante destroyed your room instead of Cardosi?"

Her mouth crimped around her cigarette. "I got paid a visit by the handsome Gio Pitrello last evening."

The mention of the crime lord's nephew set Rhett's teeth on edge. This time last week Rhett had been wavering with the idea of going to Saluti's. Until finally the nudge had been so strong, he couldn't ignore it. If God's direction had been so clear then, how come He hadn't warned Rhett about Kate being a Salvastano? None of it made sense.

"Gio told me it'd be in my *best interest* to let him know if Hugo's been contacting me." Grimacing, she tugged back the hem of her sleeve. Bruises colored her wrist. The four dark spots lined her skin as if branded by an iron grip. "I didn't need to be an investigator like you to get his message."

Every nerve sparked hot. Pitrello had grabbed Kate's wrist at Saluti's but not like that. Not hard enough to leave marks. Probably because Rhett had been there. "I'm sorry." Was all he could mutter without his chest exploding. Pitrello seemed to hurt every woman he came in contact with, by one way or the other.

"Guess I'll call it my punishment for lying."

"No man should hurt a woman." He ground out. If this was how they'd treated Gladys, what would they do to Kate? The coffee in his stomach hardened to concrete.

She'd been right to keep her identity a secret.

During his and Kate's heated exchange, she'd confessed she was scared to say anything. He'd taken it as her being afraid to tell him because of his father, but what if there had been more to it? What if she was terrified of the repercussions of gangsters like Big Dante discovering she was a Salvastano? His head had been stuffed with hurt and offense that he hadn't considered any of this. Yes, Rhett believed Hugo wouldn't harm his own daughter, but he couldn't say the same about any other crime boss.

Could he be any more daft?

"I returned from errands this morning to find my room looking like it'd been hit by a train. With *this* in the center of it all." She pulled a cigar sleeve from her purse and tossed it on the table. "Gio smoked that brand of stogies last night."

"I know many men that favor that kind." Not Cardosi though. The man hadn't parted from his Toscano the entire time Rhett and Kate were in his office. "But I can see it being more than a coincidence."

Rhett would be certain to tell Major about this. Though how the state expected Major to capture a crime boss no one had ever seen was beyond Rhett. Big Dante had been the ghost of the underworld, running the show through his cronies. Maybe Pitrello would be the weak link that could break the Big Dante crime chain.

Glady reached for the paper, cigar sleeve and crumpled it. "Know what I'm thinking, detective?"

"I'm not good at reading women's minds."

Her lips spread into a flirty smile. "I'm convinced you're good at many things that pertain to women. But let's not go into that now. Not when I have everything figured out."

"As to what?"

"I think Big Dante is Hugo Salvastano."

His head reader back at her ridiculous words. "What makes you say that?"

"Think about it. No one has seen Big Dante. No one has seen Hugo since the shootings. Why did the man plug his own brothers?

He wanted all the power. So the man worked behind the scenes setting the stage, getting fresh underlings, putting everything in place." The tone of her voice intensified even as it lowered. "Then at the right time, he shoots his family and takes on another identity. Has his little cronies doing all the work while he holds every ounce of power."

Gladys shot a smug smile, and Rhett sat stupefied.

He'd never considered such a thing. The very idea was absurd. But possible. He'd often wondered why Hugo shot his siblings. There never seemed to be a reason for it, but Gladys revealed a powerful motive. Hugo posing as Big Dante. Assuming a false identity. A family habit.

Of course, there were several snags to Gladys theory. Gio Pitrello, him being Big Dante's nephew, was one of them. Though that could be a hoax as well. But if that was the case, then why would Pitrello threaten Gladys, trying to scare her into confessing any information about Hugo? No, Rhett couldn't buy into Gladys's sketchy deduction. Big Dante and Hugo Salvastano were not the same man.

"Is there anything else you need from me, detective? You'll find I'm very obliging to those I like."

Rhett wouldn't indulge her inference. Instead, he withdrew his wallet, tugged out the "S" card, and handed it to her. "Since we're exchanging mobsters' *calling cards*, how about you tell me about this one."

"I've never seen this before." She pulled it closer, studying. "But I'll go out on a limb and say it's a Salvastano one."

"You deduced right."

"Kinda creepy if you ask me." She slid it across the table to him.

Rhett scooped up the café slip and turned it over. "One more thing, if you would." He fished his fountain pen from his trouser pocket and handed it to her.

"Why you sly dog." She purred. "I'm flattered you want my contact info in Albany."

"More like an autograph. Sign Delvina's name." He tapped the slip. "With your eyes closed."

CHAPTER 30

I stepped off the trolley onto Main Street in Braddock, my conversation with Mr. Cardosi haunting me. The parts of the mystery swirled like broken notes of a melody. If only I could string them
together to make sense of it all. Papa's lawyer knew where I lived.
Knew where I worked. Knew I was a Salvastano.

My strides slowed. Could he have been the one that'd left the "S"
cards?

Billows of smoke puffed from the nearby piles, the shadows twisting across the sky. If Mr. Cardosi had left the cards, the motive could've
been to frighten me. I resumed my pace. Maybe he wanted to run me
out of Pittsburgh before the fortune was found. Though fleeing town
was an option I'd devoted serious consideration to since hearing the
man call me Catarina.

The intersection approached, and I waited for the trickle of traffic to clear. How could I prove Papa's lawyer had been behind all of
this? Calling the local police was a gamble. Everyone in Pittsburgh

understood the corruption that tainted the badges. I couldn't contact Rhett. But what about his father's former partner? Major Ford. Would he be interested in my assumptions about Cardosi?

When I'd met him a few weeks back at Rhett's office, he'd been kind and gentle. I doubted he'd show the same sensitivity if he discovered who I was. As close as Rhett was to him, he probably was already aware.

My spine bent forward.

Alone. As always. The steam whistle screamed, indicating a shift change at the mill. Heavy decisions stretched before me. The glass jar holding my savings wouldn't get me far, but it may be enough to purchase a bus ticket. But to where?

I stopped in front of the variety store window. Through the smudges and soot, I spied a Westinghouse tube radio, and an idea took shape. Maybe I could travel to one of the sister stations down south. My boss held a great degree of influence in the broadcasting world. Would he help secure me a transfer? Waiting until Monday gave me a pinch of reluctance, but that'd give me extra time to pack and spend quality moments with Charlie.

My heart stung at having to say goodbye to him. But this was for his safety. With Cardosi aware of where I lived, it put Charlie in danger. I would be—

"Where's your sweetheart?" A slurred male voice staggered into my ear.

Charlie's father slouched against the lamppost, his cap scaled back, precariously close to falling off his head. His mouth curled around a cigarette, his languid gaze raking over my body. "No guard today?" He tsked three times then belched.

Lips pressed tight, I moved to cross the street. Better walk on the other side than to be within his grabbing reach.

He cackled and I fought against a wince.

"Sorry, princess. Didn't mean to scare you away." He jolted, arms raised high and fingers curved like animal claws. His hat flopped to the ground. With a loud cuss, he stumbled forward to retrieve it.

I hastened my pace. It'd taken two blocks before my pulse settled. Poor Charlie. How could he bear living in the same apartment with that man? When I removed myself from this steel empire, I'd also eliminate Charlie's place of shelter. If only I could take him with me. But I had no right. Awful as he was, Jack Davenport was his family, his legal guardian. If I were Charlie's relation, I would fight to gain custody by proving the man ill fit.

Which made me wonder ...

My feet skidded in front of Davis Pharmacy. Without hesitation, I yanked open the door and cut a direct course to the nickel payphones.

The sun broke free from the clouds. Despite the gentle breeze that added a chill to the air, heat crashed into Rhett as he stood on the corner of Crafton Avenue, watching Kate and Charlie climb the steps to St. Paul's Orphanage.

The fiery loss hollowed his stomach, but Rhett held no guilt in trailing her. He endeavored to discover the real from the fake regarding Kate. Why had she assumed the false identity? To work in cahoots with her father? With Cardosi? Or had she adopted the role for her own protection?

So far she'd been on course with the Kate he'd come to know. Last night from his safe distance on the street, he'd spied her sweeping her neighbor's porch. Later he'd watched her wave goodbye to Charlie, only to chase after him to hand him a covered dish of food. Now she headed into the orphanage.

"Excuse me, young man." A feeble, yet familiar voice swept over his shoulder.

Rhett tossed a look back, and Sister Agatha peered at him with the same kind—yet significantly wrinkled—face he'd remembered from his youth. His chest clenched though he doubted the nun would remember him. So many children had grown up through this program, and he'd been only—

"Everhett. Dear Everhett." Dull eyes glossed. Her habit swallowed her frame, but she managed to wrap him in a delicate embrace. "How I've missed you."

Surprise stiffened his joints, but the fragrance of peppermint oil transported him back, softening his muscles, reminding him of this woman's timeless love.

"Nice to see you, Sister Agatha." He broke away gently, keeping a steady hand on her elbow, so the older woman wouldn't lose her balance. "I didn't know you were still at St. Paul's."

"I'm not, officially." The effects of age made her jaw quiver when she spoke. "But I can never stay away from these children. They're God's blessings, and mine, too."

That was why he'd clung to her those formable years. She'd always viewed him as a treasure, and not a burden.

"Now." Her age-spotted hand slid wire-rimmed spectacles up the bridge of her nose. "Let me get a good look at you." She shuffled back as if to take in the whole of him. "A fine man you've grown into, Everhett. I knew you would succeed. You've always had such determination and energy even as a baby."

"I'm grateful for St. Paul's and for you, Sister." He cast a glance at the stone building right now housing dozens of children, several nuns, an eleven-year-old furnace blast survivor, and a woman with an angelic voice but a devastating last name.

"Come sit." She waved him toward the park bench a few paces away. "We have twenty-three years to catch up on."

Rhett hesitated. The bench was in full view of the orphanage. If Kate happened to come outside soon, then there would be no mistaking an encounter. But after all Sister Agatha had done for him, couldn't he spare a few minutes? He lowered onto the iron seat, the cold metal pressing through his trousers.

"I'm sorry about what happened to Commissioner Jennings. I've been praying that your faith fail not."

"Thank you." His throat shouldn't thicken with emotion. He hadn't seen Sister Agatha in over two decades, but knowing she'd never forgotten him, that she'd been praying for him, warmed his heart.

"Have I ever told you what your name meant?"

That familiar pang twisted into his ribs. He'd arrived at St. Paul's when he was a couple months old. Knowing he'd not only been forsaken but also left nameless like some mutt on the street, gnawed continually until it'd left a gaping hole in his core. Which was why he'd purposed so long not to think about those days. "If you'd mentioned it, I don't remember."

"I've always took my role in naming arriving infants seriously." She stared into the distance, then as if remembering his presence, attached her rheumy gaze on him. "Sister Claire bundled you in one of the blankets and you hated it. You squirmed and squirmed until your arms broke free. Right then, I knew your name. Everhett, the strong and brave one."

The irony pulled a small smile. He'd been the scrawny kid, the runt that'd become an easy target for the bigger and tougher children.

Sister Agatha had once caught him hiding behind the piano bench and that was how he'd received his first lesson.

How about you sit on the stool rather than behind it? She'd asked, then proceeded to teach him the basics of the instrument. Music had become his companion. His gaze traveled to the third window on the first floor of St. Paul's. The curtains were drawn but behind that pane of glass stood the piano. Was Kate there at this moment? Or was she reading to the children?

He directed his attention on Sister Agatha. "Thank you for sharing that story."

Warmth lit her eyes. "Remember strength doesn't always mean brawn. Some of the strongest people I know are the ones who appear weak in the world's eyes. But to forgive those who are underserving. To love without limits. To try again when we fail at both. Real strength doesn't come from here." She tapped her arm. "But is found here." She pressed her palm over her heart.

A milk truck rattled by, a dog barked from somewhere close, and a flock of Canada geese passed overhead in the span of the following silence.

How could such a delicate voice carry enough force to pierce right through him? He'd struggled with forgiveness for as long as he'd remembered. Hugging his grudges so close to his chest—he'd fed them, pet them, and dared not set them free. But their bites had eaten into his soul. His birthparents, the Salvastanos, Kate. They all had done him wrong, but harboring bitterness wouldn't destroy anyone but him. A peace settled, smoothing the frayed edges of his mind.

The journey to wholeness would take some time, but he'd made great strides. Thanks to Sister Agatha's wisdom. "I'm sorry it's taken me so long."

"You came." Her beautiful, aged face shined with a smile. "And that's what matters."

But he wouldn't have been here, if not for trailing Kate. Even when oblivious, she still caused goodness.

"I need to head inside." With gentle grace, she stood. "Care to join me? Usually around this time a young lady comes and entertains the children. I'd like to introduce you." She faced him with … a wink? "She plays piano with a skilled ear like you. I think you'd like her."

Kate.

"Thank you, Sister, but maybe another time." Forgiving Kate would be difficult enough, letting her back into his heart would be impossible.

CHAPTER 31

Rhett slunk behind the garden shed at Shadyside Park, keeping Kate in his line of sight. Her hair was unbound, cascading down her back. The same breeze lifting the wispy ends of her locks also pulled at her dress, making prominent her curves.

He blew out a shaft of air.

Tracking Kate's activities had gone from being part of the investigation to him feeling like a peeping schoolboy. Plus his trip to Braddock early this morning had caused him to miss church for the second week in a row. No doubt he'd soon get an earful from Major.

Though the older man seemed interested in Rhett's findings. Thankfully there'd been nothing to report. Yesterday after the orphanage visit, Kate had stayed home the rest of the evening. Today, she'd gone to the market, and while he'd expected her to board the trolley back to Braddock, she'd taken the one west toward Shadyside. Why?

She crossed the stretch of lawn, steps appearing hesitant. Her chin swept slow from left to right as if searching for someone.

A rendezvous perhaps?

Every cell snapped alert. He scanned the area, searching for anything out of the ordinary.

A handful of children flew kites in the open space. Several families enjoyed picnic lunches at the pine tables framing the tulip patch. A middle-aged gentleman sat on a park bench browsing the paper.

Kate's gaze fixed on the giant maple about twenty yards from Rhett. Her strides quickened. She reached the towering tree in seconds. Her lips moved. She talked to someone on the other side of the trunk. Someone Rhett couldn't see.

He craned his neck, stooped lower, and even dared a step to his right, but still couldn't get a glimpse of her mystery companion. *Blast.* With the openness of the park, if he stepped farther in any direction, Kate would spot him. Agitation lodged in his sternum. He was trapped.

Hugo wouldn't risk meeting her in daylight. Out in a public setting no less. Though he could be disguised. Absurd, but Rhett couldn't throw out that possibility.

Kate seemed to be commanding the conversation, every so often pausing. Her features strained, she swiped at her cheeks.

Was she crying?

Heat gathered in his chest. The unknown visitor was distressing Kate, and Rhett stood helpless.

A hand became visible, followed by the dark sleeve of a suit jacket. The movement stopped but it was enough. Kate had come here to see a man. The fellow's fingers held out a handkerchief to which she accepted with a nod of gratitude.

Kate didn't appear threatened, but it didn't halt Rhett's fist clenching at his sides. He watched her converse several more minutes. The longer she was in this man's company the more relaxed she became.

Her tears ceased. Her shoulders weren't spiked. And now she had a charming smile on her face.

He rubbed a hand over his mouth. This was torture.

Finally she dug into her purse and handed the mystery man an envelope. The hand extended toward her, as if trying to return the letter.

Kate held up a palm, a definite refusal on her face.

The hand lowered as if in defeat.

She took gradual steps away and gave a parting wave. With quick strides, she came toward Rhett. He darted back, pressing his spine flat against the wooden shed walls.

He heard her brisk steps and even a sniffle. She crossed on the other side of the shed, which had been too close a call for Rhett. His breath escaped slow and steady. There had to be a better way to go about this. He angled toward the maple in time to see the mystery man emerge.

His gut bottomed out.

David. His partner.

Rhett stalked toward David, his shoes sinking in the soft ground, his heart rate climbing past human levels. He'd confided in his partner four days ago, enlightening him about the case, telling about Kate's identity. And what had the man done? Had a clandestine meeting with the woman behind Rhett's back.

Rhett advanced like last night's thunderstorm, full fury and without warning. "What are you doing here with her?"

"Jennings." He didn't even recoil. "I was wondering when you'd show yourself." David adjusted his homburg with a rascally grin

"That's all you're going to say?" He never thought he'd sock his friend, but every knuckle begged to strike. "I tell you about Kate being Hugo's daughter. Even ask you to pray for me because I was struggling. Then you meet her in secret?" He jerked a thumb the direction Kate had left. "What else are you hiding from me? Maybe I should reevaluate our partnership because—"

"It's about Charlie Davenport."

Rhett's hot blood iced over. "What about him?"

"Kate asked if I could locate his extended family. She felt they should know about the way Charlie is being treated."

All air left his chest. She'd contacted David on Charlie's behalf. She was to be his voice when he had none. This woman kept proving herself completely different than the traits of a Salvastano. Where they'd stolen, she gave. Where they'd no regard for others, she was an advocate for the broken. Where they'd destroyed, she created hope.

Rhett removed his hat, allowing the breeze to kiss his forehead. "Sorry, I got heated."

"You hold quite the torch for that lady." He shrugged. "It stands to reason those sparks would get outta hand."

Rhett opened his mouth to deny it, but couldn't. The motive behind shadowing Kate had been to expose her craftiness. He'd never considered that in trying to prove himself right, he'd end up wrong. He'd stuffed his affections for Kate behind a mask of anger. Convenient, until little by little her goodness chipped away at it.

"Have you met this Charlie?" David inclined his chin, gesturing Rhett to walk with him.

"Yes. He's a remarkable young man. Several months back, he suffered an explosion over at the steel mills in Braddock. He can't speak." Rhett waited as a pair of giggling children darted past. "I'm not sure if his muteness is from physical injury or trauma. He also has severe scar tissue burns on his face and arms."

"She mentioned that." His blue eyes clouded. "She also said the boy's neglected by his father."

"The man wastes money at the speakeasy instead of feeding his kid."

David scowled. "She'd said she tried to report the dad months ago, but the police never took any action." He rolled his eyes. "No surprise there."

"Are you going to take the case?" If not, Rhett would look into it. It rattled him that he'd never thought of it before. But then again, his mind had been dominated by finding justice for his father that it'd choked any other imposing thought. Since his talk with Sister Agatha, he'd begun to see that his thirst for vengeance had been acting as a poison to his soul.

"I told her I'd do my best." He patted the envelope sticking out of his breast pocket. "She insisted on paying for the service though I told her it wasn't necessary. One thing about it though, Jennings." His expression sobered. "The reason she wanted this done quickly is because she plans on leaving Pittsburgh for good."

Early evening sun hiccupped through swollen clouds, ever so often dappling my apartment with a hazy glow.

Charlie sat at the kitchen table, studying the pictures for a new greeting from the sign language book. He was so focused on mastering the challenge his reddish blonde lashes barely blinked.

From all my experience teaching children, Charlie had been the most dedicated. Signing had given him a channel to speak just as drawing had given him an outlet to express. Who would guide him in signing once I was gone? More importantly, who would give him food?

My meeting with David had gone well. Unsure of what Rhett had shared with him concerning me, I'd been worried he'd refuse to help locate Charlie's kin. Though I couldn't be certain there were any relatives to be found. All the information I had to give the detective was Charlie's father's name. Could it be any more of an impossibility?

David had assured me he'd give his best effort. He'd even tried to decline my payment, though I'd insisted. His manners were friendly and approachable, but he had a sharp wit about him. I could see how he'd be an asset to the detective agency.

Charlie glanced over.

"Are you ready to try it?"

He nodded and signed, *Nice to meet you.*

"Why, thank you very much." I gave an exaggerated nod since he couldn't hear the approval in my tone. "I'm glad to know you as well."

His grin stretched wide, and even his freckles seemed to brighten. I matched his expression with a blooming smile of my own, but my insides wilted like it'd been hit with a wintry gust. My dear, young friend. How could I leave him?

But how could I stay?

I'd hidden my trunk in the bedroom and shut the door so Charlie wouldn't see. The timing of my departure all depended on what Frank Conrad would say tomorrow. I decided to wait until I had a fixed day before informing Charlie. But how would I even begin to tell him? My ribs squeezed. This child had faced a lifetime of rejection in only a span of eleven years.

His threadbare shirt frayed at the elbows and was missing three buttons on the front. Early on, I'd bought him nicer clothing, to which his father had snatched and sold to feed his addiction. Charlie's gangly frame didn't appear as gaunt as the first day I'd met him, but his bony wrists and sharp cheekbones told of hours of hunger when not in my presence.

Oh God, please help David find someone who would care for this precious boy.

Charlie had taken my silence as permission to sketch again. Leaning closer, I caught a glimpse of what he'd been so diligently working on in between the signing lesson.

It was a likeness of Rhett.

Surprise whooshed through me. I'd never seen Charlie sketch a person before. He hadn't left out any detail. The graphite-colored contours of Rhett's face, the strong slope of his nose, and even that curl toppling over his forehead. But beyond Rhett's appearance, Charlie captured the man's demeanor. The determined slant of his eyes coupled with a jutted chin had been Rhett's signature look—that air of confidence which made my heart twist.

I tapped the edge of the paper bringing his attention to my face. "This is impressive." And heart-wrenching. I hadn't worked enough nerve to tell Charlie that Rhett wouldn't be visiting anymore. When I left, Charlie would be friendless.

David had to succeed.

Charlie pointed at the clock then signed, "Chores."

I tousled his hair with a smile. "Thank you for spending time with me." I grabbed the covered dish and handed it to him. "I put extra honey on the side so be careful not to tip it."

He gave an enthusiastic nod and was out the door before I could sign goodbye. I bolted the door and went to my bedroom. My cash jar remained on my bed where I'd left it this morning before meeting David. The meager lump of money, even less now that I'd paid the detective, seemed to mock me. If I didn't need every penny and nickel,

I'd somehow find a way to set up an account for Charlie so he could have means to buy food.

For the first time the thought of the Salvastano fortune wasn't nauseating. It could help Charlie and other forgotten children. I could give to St. Paul's.

But then, those funds had been from bootlegging. Was it right to use that money even for compassionate purposes? I bit the inside of my cheek. Probably not. Besides, I wouldn't—no, couldn't—let the world in on my secret. I prayed Papa's lawyer wouldn't either.

Knock. Knock. Knock.

I pitched forward to see the clock. Seven.

This was the exact time Cardosi had rapped on my door last week. As if he'd known I had just been thinking of him and his twisted game, the wicked man had come again.

No doubt to present his terms of blackmail.

CHAPTER 32

I clutched my baseball bat with a fierce grip. I wasn't certain if Cardosi would physically harm me, but with George in hand, I felt more in control. Keeping my footfalls quiet, I moved toward the door.

Though what if the person knocking wasn't Cardosi? My mind whirled like the motors on the enormous generators at Westinghouse, my thoughts screeching just as loud. What if he'd sold the information to other crime bosses? Those men carry guns and came in packs, like wolves.

My reflection in the decorative mirror in the entryway made me pause. The frail set of my shoulders paired with my gangly arms hardly made me look intimidating. My fingers wrapped the bat, and I hefted it, my precarious stance a far cry from the legendary slugger who'd signed it.

"Kate. Are you there?"

The bat dropped to my shoulder. Heaven help me, that voice. I'd been convinced that husky rumble wouldn't reach my ears anymore.

This scenario resembled last Saturday's when I'd woken in his bedroom. He'd called to me, and the panicky confusion had spiked to beautiful relief. But not this time.

Why was he here?

♦ ♦ ♦

Rhett's knuckles pounded Kate's door. Again.

David hadn't been sure when she'd planned on leaving, and so for Rhett, it'd been a race against time. Then his Model-T had gotten stuck behind a horse and wagon that'd rivaled the pace of an aged mule. He'd felt his window narrowing with each slow, tired clop of the horse's hooves. The delay had made him desperate, which in turn, made him realize … he needed her.

But he may be too late.

He flattened his palm on the jamb, resting his forehead on the door, and his eyes pinched shut. *Idiot.* He'd been trailing her since Friday, for Pete's sake. It wasn't like he hadn't the chance to speak with her. Yet he hadn't. And he'd lost out.

He missed the chance to make things right, of hearing the music in her voice. Missed those eyes that once held a world of secrets, but now were just his world.

The deadbolt unbarred, jolting his forehead.

The door eased open. Every joint locked. Every muscle froze. He dared not breathe. As if any movement would cause the door to slam in his face, separating her from him.

Then she appeared.

That breath he'd held, vaulted in his chest, nearly making him cough.

The soft evening glow danced upon her features. A shaft of light, slanting through the porch beams, gave her dark locks a deep reddish cast. Her eyes pinned on him, as rounded as they were cautious.

"Evening." He rasped. His eyes fell to her hand clutching the baseball bat. His chest that'd swelled to impressive proportions at the sight of her, deflated. He never expected her to be afraid of him. Though the last time they'd spoken, he'd been harsh, ugly. "I'd never harm you, Kate."

She followed his line of vision. "Oh." The bat's barrel rested against her leg, her fingers fidgeting the rounded knob. "Never mind that." She set it aside and returned her heavy stare on him. "Why are you here?"

He toed a dead leaf from her doormat. "Because I need to talk to you."

Confusion splashed in her eyes, a hazy swirl among the golds and browns. "Why?"

He stood close to the threshold, the symbolism not lost on him. Last week he'd blindly said he'd fallen in love with her. A phrasing he no longer cared for. He didn't want to fall into love, tripping, grappling for purchase. No, he wanted to step into it, footing sure, eyes open. Knowing full well who she was, and choosing her not despite it, but because of it. For *who she was* made her the beautiful soul he craved. "Can I come in?"

Her chest rose and fell in a choppy rhythm. She regarded him for several brutal seconds, her expression pained. "I'm still a Salvastano." Her whispered words cut through awkward formalities, straight to the mountain between them.

Their fathers had been rivals. Each out for the other's neck. Hers had succeeded. For months, pain's dull edge had sharpened itself against the blade of anger, both chopping away at his peace until only bitterness remained. But Kate couldn't be responsible for her parents' choices any more than he could for his. Rhett hadn't any clue of how his birthparents lived. They could've been saints or sinners. If the latter, should Rhett be forced to carry their shame?

No.

And neither should she.

Sorrow splayed across her features. She'd read his stretch of silence as dismissal. The door creaked as she moved to close it.

Rhett's foot jutted forward, stilling it. "What's in a name?"

She blinked. "Everything."

"A rose by any other name wouldn't it still smell sweet?" Sorry, Shakespeare. He'd botched that, but her fragile smile revealed he was making progress.

"*Romeo and Juliet* may not be the best story to mention." She leaned a shoulder against the jamb. "Don't you remember the ending?"

He shrugged. "I stopped reading after the wedding scene. I have no idea how the rest of it goes." He risked a step toward her. "Which means, I can rewrite my version however I want."

Sunset sparkled in her eyes. "I don't think Shakespeare would appreciate that."

A grin tugged, and he surrendered to it. "I won't tell him, if you don't."

From beneath the thick fringe of lashes, she watched him, studying his face as if searching for any hint of disdain. The smallest of smiles teased her rosy lips and she opened the door wider, granting him access.

Her apartment was tidy, yet felt cold. The few wall hangings had been taken down, and all the personal affects, like the sheet music that'd been piled on the counter, was gone. His heart slowed to a dull thud. It seemed David had been right about her aspirations to leave.

She closed the door, shutting them in, her gaze reclaiming its skeptical slant. Her feet were in no rush to join him a few yards away in the parlor. Instead, she hung back in the entryway.

He doffed his hat, aware his hair was disheveled, but no less than his mind at the moment. "First, I want to confess something." He set his hat on the sofa's armrest. "I've been following you since Friday evening."

Her mouth turned down. "Why?"

"The initial motive was to see if you'd lead me to Hugo."

She swallowed and averted her eyes.

"But then I saw the truth." He took a commanding step toward her, jerking her attention from her shoes to him, though her stare landed somewhere on his collar. "I realized you're the same now as you've been the entire time."

"A liar?" The brokenness in her voice pulled him closer, eliminating any space between them.

His knuckle slid under her chin, lifting, beckoning her gaze flush on him. "Just because you've used a different name, doesn't change who you are at heart."

She tensed, and he winced, making him wish he had the way of words Shakespeare had.

"I didn't mean that as a slight." He skimmed his fingertips along the curve of her jaw, framing her face so she couldn't turn away. "Last time we spoke, I said you had no soul. I couldn't have been more wrong. You visit orphans, feed the neglected, even sing apologies over the airwaves to a man who treated you harshly."

Her lips parted, eyes revealing her hope. "You listened?"

"I did."

"I should've told you sooner." Her tone was soft like her skin beneath his palm. "If I could go back and change things, I would." A feeble laugh escaped. "Though if I could time travel, I wouldn't have left Italy."

The thought pained him. "Then I would've never met you." He couldn't help it, his hands glided behind the tender flesh beneath her ear, lingering for a greedy second, then slipping into her hair.

Her eyes drifted shut, whether from physical pleasure or emotional pain, he couldn't tell. "Wouldn't that have been better?"

"No. God knew I needed you." He was only five, maybe six, inches from her full lips. How easy it'd be to let his mouth roam hers, answering her questions with definite action. To leave her in no doubt that his life was better because she was in it. His fingers curled around her hair, wayward wisps tickling his knuckles, feeding his want.

But he couldn't give in.

Not when she remained unconvinced and hesitant.

Her lashes lifted, uncertainty present in her eyes.

He relaxed his grip, untangling his hands from her locks, every muscle fighting him as he forced a step back, giving her space. "I followed you to the park and found out why you met with David."

"Because of Charlie."

"Because you're leaving and wanted him taken care of."

A crease puckered between her brows, but she didn't deny it.

"Don't." And just like that, the distance he created he broke with a single stride. "Don't go." How could he explain that she sparked a fire in him, and it only seemed to burn when in her presence. How drafty and cold his days would be without her.

This week had been misery. He couldn't imagine a lifetime.

"I have to." She retreated back. One step. Two. "Leaving would be better for you, for Charlie, and anyone else that could be put in danger because of me."

"Kate, we could work this—"

"Franco Cardosi knows who I am."

The words punched dread into him. "How do you know this?"

She grabbed her black bag off the table, fished out a paper, and handed it to him. "This was left at my door."

Rhett read the typed script. It was short, but the malicious intent was evident. "*We'll chat soon.*" Anger tightened his jaw. "When did you get this?" He handed back the letter, the urge to wrap protective arms around her throttling him.

"Sunday."

The day after Rhett'd stormed out. She'd been left to face that alone. He could call himself every ugly name.

"That's why I had George at the door." Her hand, still clutching her bag, motioned to the bat leaning on the entryway wall. "I thought you were Mr. Cardosi. This was about the time he'd knocked on my door last week." Grimacing, she tossed her purse on the sofa behind them. "Then Friday after my shift, he came to the station."

His chest seized. "What did he want? Did he hurt you?"

"No, but he knows I want to keep quiet about all this. I think he intends to blackmail me."

He gouged both hands into his hair, squeezing his scalp. Cardosi had arrived the time Rhett would've been there to escort her home. He'd decided to shadow her late Friday evening after his meeting with Gladys. If only he would've come to his senses sooner. "I'm sorry, Kate." His apology felt pathetic and weak compared to what she'd gone through. "He won't get away with threatening you. We'll figure this out."

Her smile was glum. "There's no solution."

If Hugo was alive then Cardosi wouldn't dare harm her. But that left her bait for Big Dante's men. Gladys's bruised wrist and shattered hotel room flooded his mind. Those men wouldn't blink about hurting Kate if that meant drawing Hugo out of obscurity.

As long as things remained undetermined with whether Hugo was in hiding or in the grave, Kate would be in jeopardy.

The only solutions that would secure Kate's safety would be the undeniable confirmation of Hugo's lifeless body or his breathing carcass placed behind bars. In those circumstances, Hugo wouldn't pose a threat to Big Dante's territory and Cardosi wouldn't be able to swindle the system anymore.

But Rhett had been searching for the man for nine months with no results. His gaze met Kate's, the sadness in her eyes making him wish he could sweep her away, leaving this mess behind. But they couldn't.

He tugged her hand in his, intertwining their fingers. "Running isn't the answer. These men are powerful. They have connections all over the country. It's only a matter of time before they'll find you again."

Fear took hold in her eyes, and Rhett hated that his words put it there. But it was true. "I need you to be honest with me, Kate. No secrets between us. Deal?"

Bottom lip tucked beneath her teeth, she nodded.

Still holding her hand, he led her to the sofa. "Has Hugo been in contact with you since you arrived in Pittsburgh?"

"No."

"Not at all? No letters? Telegrams? Anything?"

She shook her head. "I don't think he even knows I'm here."

"But what about the "S" cards?"

Her shoulders lowered with a heavy exhale. "I think that was Mr. Cardosi's doing. Only he knows where I live and work. Plus, besides you, he's the only one that knows I'm a Salvastano."

Surprise hiked his brow. "You haven't told anyone else about your identity?"

"Just you."

Her words knocked him with the force of a right hook. Her secret. One—that if leaked—could destroy her. And she'd trusted him with it.

"Though if Cardosi gave me the cards I don't understand why he'd care to warn me about Delvina. She doesn't even know who I am."

Realization jolted him. "He wasn't warning you at all." He released her hand and stood. Pacing back and forth across the area rug helped untangle his mind, the situation becoming clear. "No Cardosi was telling you to watch Delvina. Watch what was going to happen to her. It was a threat."

Her eyes narrowed as if processing Rhett's theory. "Like if I don't comply with him, the same would happen to me?" She shifted and he could see the questions piling in her unfocused gaze. "But nothing's happened to her."

"She skipped town Friday."

"What?"

He pulled a hand across his face. How much should he shield her from? If he told her the details it could scare Kate off for good.

"Rhett." Her voice that had sung to him all week, now held a plea. "Tell me what you know."

He settled beside her and stretched his arm around her shoulder, anchoring her to his side. She stiffened in surprise, but then melted into him.

"Her name is Gladys Cartwright. I arrived at her hotel room as she was leaving. Her place had been demolished." He felt her shudder. "Before that, Gio Pitrello had visited. He gripped her wrist so hard it left bruises. Something tells me, he was being *kinder* than normal."

Though she hadn't budged a centimeter from his side, he could sense her pulling miles away. The silence between them grew, the sun's rays through the window changing shadows with each passing moment.

She angled toward him. "Rhett, would you drive me to Union Station?"

CHAPTER 33

I had heard enough. The dangers of going out on my own seemed less risky than sitting in my empty apartment waiting for the bad guys to pronounce punishment for the name I bore. After what Rhett said they'd done to the imposter Delvina, how could I expect I would fare any better?

If Rhett refused to take me to the train depot, I'd have to figure a way to haul my trunk onto the cable car to the heart of Pittsburgh.

"Please reconsider." Rhett's hand cupped my shoulder, and I sensed an urgency in his caress. "I've seen the destruction these men cause."

I eased away, scooting on the sofa until out from under his touch. His nearness only clouded my reasoning. When he'd spoken moments ago while standing on my doorstep, I'd been nearly overcome with the admiration in his eyes. His bad attempt at quoting Shakespeare, only endearing him more to me.

A week ago he hadn't been able to stand the sight of me. Yet tonight his eyes didn't seem to get enough, boring into me with an intensity that made my heart warm. He'd asked me to stay. And how I wanted to. But I couldn't satisfy my longing without injuring everyone around me.

"Please?" His voice broke as if raked over sharp glass. "What can I say to change your mind?"

"Don't you see? They could come after you."

His eyes flashed, reminding me of lightning against angry ocean waves. "I can handle it."

"But I can't." The force of my words surprised me. But I wouldn't take it back. Rhett didn't deserve to be in the middle of this chaos. He'd already lost so much. "My family has already done enough to you."

"So you're to take the penance for it? You think it best to sacrifice your safety by going who knows where, and being completely unprotected?" He launched to his feet and paced the rug like he had earlier, hands running through his hair, brow furrowing deeper with each measured step. He stopped midstride and barred his arms. "Tell me, where did you have in mind to go?"

I hesitated, and it cost me.

"You're not sure, are you?"

No, no I wasn't. I'd considered WKN in Memphis or the newly established station in Wichita. "I hadn't decided yet because I wanted to talk to Frank Conrad about getting me hired on somewhere." But those plans to relocate would have to wait. It could take several days, maybe even weeks, to secure a position. Time I didn't have the luxury to waste. Those men had already gotten to Gladys Cartwright. How long before they reached me as well?

I scraped together the meager flakes of conviction and shoved it into my tone. "When I arrived in Pittsburgh, I didn't have a home or even a job. I survived, and I can do it again."

My forced confidence didn't fool him. For his perceptive eyes took me in, his scowl showcasing his disapproval.

"Even if I chose to stay. I'm here by myself." My gaze swept my soon-to-be-vacant apartment. "I can't expect you to watch me here at all hours."

Rhett blew out a breath and collapsed onto the sofa, his side flush against mine. "No, you shouldn't stay here by yourself."

"And I won't put Peggy or the Conrads at risk either. That's why I haven't told them who I am. The less people know, the safer they'll be."

His glare, so sharp and cutting a few seconds ago, dulled as if the fight wasn't worth it anymore. As if I wasn't worth it.

I'd won the argument, but oh, how I'd lost. My exit from his life was what had to happen, but it didn't stop the hole in my heart from gaping wider.

Warmth from Rhett's side pressed into me, and I savored it, leaning closer until my cheek pressed against his powerful shoulder.

"Last year at this time, I was still in Spirelli. Lying on my simple cot and imagining a beautiful life in America." I let out a sardonic laugh. "Could I have been anymore foolish? The land of opportunity they called it. It was to be a place where all my dreams can come true. But I've only seen nightmares." I shifted, cuddling into him. "Except for my time with you."

Everhett Jennings. The man who'd protected me against henchmen. The man who'd seen me at my lowest struggling with claustrophobia. The man who knew my true self and yet, in spite of it all, now accepted me.

A kiss pressed against the crown of my head, lingering. "Stay with me."

My eyes slid shut. "I told you I can't. This apartment is—"

"No." His breath fanned against the part line of my hair. "Stay with me at my house."

Oh. *Oh.*

I jolted upright, almost knocking him in the chin. "That's not a good idea." Especially with how I felt at present. His gallant demeanor, the protectiveness in his voice as if he dared anyone to hurt me while he was near, the way he'd just kissed my head, such a small gesture, lit a fire of yearning in me.

"It's an excellent idea."

I could almost see Madre Chamberlin's judgmental glare. "We'd be unchaperoned." Not like I should care about what others thought. Some choice words from Cardosi and my name could be smeared all over the papers, maybe even broadcasted through my beloved KDKA.

"Kate, these aren't normal circumstances. This is life and death." His serious tone matched his eyes. "These men are dangerous."

"Yeah, but ..." I searched for another excuse.

"There's nowhere else you could stay. You said yourself you don't want to put anyone in harm's way."

"*You* were included in that list."

He pushed a lock of hair behind my ear, his fingertips trailing along the ridge of my lobe, the curve of my neck, stilling on my shoulder. "Let me help. You've carried the burden of it all far too long. It's time you realize you're not alone anymore."

"I'm not?" My voice was reedy.

His hand slid behind my neck, coaxing me forward until I was inches from his face. "No, you're not." He was close. Kissably close. "I think together we have a fighting chance."

Together. How beautiful that sounded.

"You're safe with me." He fixed his stare on me. "On every level."

I knew better than to question him on his intent. If he'd wanted to satisfy his pleasure, he would've done so last week when I'd been drugged. But he hadn't. More over, he'd been the one who'd defended my virtue.

"But what if this lingers on? I can't stay at your house indefinitely."

His lips twitched as if he knew he was winning me over. "Let's take things one day at a time. I'll have David clear his schedule and have him dig up stuff on Cardosi, Pitrello and—"

"Charlie's family." I flashed my palm. "We can't forget about him."

"We'll make sure we do everything to find his relatives." He smiled but his eyes registered his commitment. "So what do you say?"

"Can we keep me staying with you a secret?"

"I'm not exactly planning on putting a bulletin in the Gazette."

My limp hand gave his chest a feeble slap. "You know what I mean. I don't want *anyone* to know."

"I can keep it from everyone but David. Major visits usually once every couple weeks, but I can tell him I'm busy with cases." He scratched the shadow of stubble on his jaw. "Though we may want to enlist Major's help. He has access to officers and knows which are honest."

"And one more request."

His smile held enough charm to bloom a flower in December. "Anything."

"If I stay, can we keep checking on Charlie and bring him food?"

"I insist we do." His tenderness could very well make me melt into the floor cracks. "Any other objections?"

"Can I still work?" If I remained in town, I needed to keep collecting a paycheck. This scheme could flop into a failed endeavor, and I'd be back to my original plan of moving out on my own. The more money in my pocket, the better.

"Cardosi knows you work there."

"He can find me at your place too." I countered.

"I don't like it." He considered me a moment, then released a sigh. "But I'd rather you stay than run off. So I'll agree to your terms. Only if you promise to keep to Conrad's office or the studio. No wandering off to rooftops alone. Deal?" He stuck his hand out as if to shake on a business proposition.

I regarded his steady gaze, the determined set of his jaw, and my fingers itched to clasp his.

But this was crazy. The entire notion was ludicrous. Yet it felt ... right.

I wet my lips. "Are you sure about this? I don't want any decisions you make today to become your regret tomorrow." Because while he may be heroic and protective in this particular moment, that didn't mean his feelings wouldn't shift. "I realize more than anyone the complication of us ... together. We're star-crossed." I'd tacked on the famous phrase from Romeo and Juliet. But really, it fit us. We'd been doomed from the start, opposing forces set against us.

"And I told you, I intend to rewrite the ending. My way." He stretched his hand farther toward me. "Our way."

He shouldn't be so adamant. It only made me hope when I knew I shouldn't. Getting involved with Rhett was similar to singing a melody set out of my range. I'd be a fool to give voice to it, but that didn't mean I didn't want to strain to try. With a hard swallow, I shook his proffered hand, his thumb stroking my index finger before he pulled away altogether.

"Besides, we don't look to the stars to determine our destiny. We have a more definite Guide."

The Mobster's Daughter

Rhett gave Kate space to collect her belongings, a peace settling in for the first time all day. He'd almost let out a victory whoop when she'd finally agreed to stay. Though she drove a hard bargain. He still wasn't comfortable letting her go to work, but maybe he could ask Conrad to help keep an eye on her. And maybe Rhett would speak with the security department at the plant. Since he couldn't reveal the true reason, he'd have to expound more on the risk of receiving the "S" cards.

Right now though, he should check on Kate. Knowing her, she'd probably try to lug her trunk by herself. He moved from the sofa, crossing the parlor, almost passing the kitchenette when something caught his eye on the table.

A picture. Of him. Disbelief marked each step closer. He picked up the paper and studied the penciled drawing. Charlie had captured his likeness.

Remarkable.

Rhett had always prided himself on his eye for detail, but Charlie seemed to best him on that subject. The kid had noticed Rhett's left ear hung slightly lower than his right. He'd caught the exact placement of his eyes. Even included that blasted curl that currently itched his forehead. A low chuckle stirred in his chest. That crazy lock of hair had always been a source of irritation, but Charlie's depiction almost made it endearing.

How could he have drawn this without a picture for reference?

"He left that for you." Kate emerged from her bedroom, sporting a proud maternal look.

"It's amazing."

She sidled next to Rhett and admired Charlie's handiwork "I think it's his best sketch yet."

"You do, huh?" Surprise hiked his brows. "Is it the subject or the artist?"

"Both." She clasped her hands behind her back and leaned in as to get another take on the picture. Her eyes sparkled. "Though I think your nostrils are much larger in real life."

"Kate." His grin unleashed, and he set the picture down. "I learned something about you at Saluti's."

She froze, eyes widening. "What?"

"This." He reached and pressed his fingers along her ribs like on keys of a piano.

A gasp escaped her lips followed by a fit of laughter. In effort to escape she turned, but it worked against her, making it brutally easy for him to tickle her other side.

With shrieks of amusement, she shouldered into him, pressing, as if trying to pin his hand between them so he couldn't move. But he pulled his arm at the last second and curled it around her waist.

The contours of her body melted against him. Her head tipped back, and the merriment in her eyes faded to something else entirely. Want. His own desire sparked. Though before he could process his next move, her brows scrunched in confusion.

"I remember this." She pinched her eyes tight then slowly opened them. "Or do I?"

"What do you mean?" His throat squeezed so tight, it made his voice deeper.

"Were we positioned like this at Saluti's?" Her gaze tacked on him. "When we, um, kissed?"

His Adam's apple dipped. "Yes." Though how could she remember? She'd been drugged and semi-conscious.

"I've been thinking about it a lot. You know, that kiss."

He could guarantee not as much as he had.

Her fingers wrapped his lapel. "Could you tell me what I missed?"

His hand tightened on her waist, some of the fabric of her dress wadding beneath his clutch. "You really want to know?" He supposed she'd every right to. Though heat sluiced his veins at the recollection of it.

"Maybe start at the beginning. What exactly did you do?" Pink dusted her cheeks, and he knew she felt as awkward as he.

He took a deep breath. "I caressed your cheek." *Man alive.* "With my ... uh ... nose."

She placed a hand on her flushed left cheek.

"This one." He abandoned his hold on her waist and trailed a knuckle in a slow circle on the soft spot beneath her right cheekbone.

She held her gaze on him. "Then what?"

"I kissed your jaw. Here." He pressed a gentle finger under her ear. "Then here." He placed a series of light taps, running the delicate curve of her face, then settling just shy of her chin.

Her sharp inhale almost unraveled him.

"That was it. Anything else would've violated my conscience." Even now he had to remain guarded. The urge to claim her mouth grew exponentially with every one of her breaths tickling his neck. But he'd won a major victory in getting her to stay with him, and he wouldn't risk it. No matter how beautiful she looked. Or how good she felt against him.

"Then I took over?" She eased in, curiosity dancing among the golds of her eyes. "Here?" The pad of her finger traced the soft flesh of his lip. His upper, then lower.

Mercy. "Yes."

Her stare locked on the wanderings of her touch, then her fingertip stalled in the dip just under his mouth.

Don't move, Jennings.

Her head tilted. Her eyes flicked to his and he saw it. Hunger consumed her gaze as it no doubt shone in his.

Do. Not. Move.

She leaned an inch. Paused. Then moved closer, her mouth painfully near his. He held his head so still, the tendons in his neck ached. His body thrummed while his mind screamed. *She is staying in Pittsburgh.* She needed to trust him, but heaven help him he wanted to crush her in his arms and show her exactly how he felt.

She remained a touch away, eyes engaged on him. If she was testing him to see if he could keep himself in check, she was making it viciously difficult. But he would do this. For her. So she could rest easy at his place. After several excruciating seconds, her shoulders slouched, and she stepped back.

He waited for the haze to clear in his mind. Though he wasn't sure when his heart would retreat back to its normal place beneath his ribs instead of in his throat.

"I thought so." She muttered.

So he'd been right? Kate'd been challenging him, ensuring he'd keep his hands—and lips—to himself? "Thought what?"

"Nothing." But by her defeated tone, it was definitely something.

Rhett blinked. He'd just withstood temptation. He deserved some sort of medal. Especially given his track record. Instead she tossed him a sad smile for a reward.

He palmed his sore neck. "What did I do wrong?"

She took a step toward her bedroom, then stilled. "You confirmed what I knew. That's all."

"Which was?"

Those eyes, so vivid a few seconds ago, now shaded with something Rhett couldn't pinpoint.

"Didn't we agree to no secrets between us?"

Her chin snapped up. "It's obviously not a secret, Rhett, since we both know. Let's agree that I'm a lousy kisser. That I don't know what I'm doing and move on."

"Who said you were a lousy kisser?"

"You refused to kiss me just now." Hurt reflected in her down-turned mouth. "I could see the disgust in your eyes."

His laugh rolled out before he could stop it, earning her icy glare. "Kate, if you only knew."

Her hands plopped on her hips. "Knew what?"

"How hard I was trying *not* to kiss you." He took a commanding step toward her, and to his relief, she didn't back away. "Keeping your trust is important to me. I didn't want to lose it by kissing you senseless."

"Then I wasn't terrible at it?" Her innocent tone undid him.

He ventured another stride, standing toe to toe with her. "You executed your kiss like everything else you do in life—with all your heart and with deep passion. It was unforgettable. Just like you, Catarina Salvastano."

CHAPTER 34

The fists I had dug into my hips weakened, my arms falling limp to my sides. "Can you say that again?"

Rhett chuckled. "What, that you kiss like a woman on a mission, even when your seconds shy of passing out? That's impressive for—"

"No, not that." I braced a palm on the doorjamb of my bedroom, keeping my knees from turning soft. "When you said my full name." Something I hadn't heard outside of my own head in over nine months. Yes, Cardosi had spat out my first name. So had Rhett last Saturday night standing almost in the same spot as he was now.

But no one had said it in its entirety for such a long time. And it soothed like balm over a blistered wound.

When I'd stepped foot in this steel jungle, the name Salvastano had been smeared all over. It'd been slandered like a curse. But this past moment, when Rhett attached my first name to the last, he'd said it with such a flood of affection that all the rot layered upon that word washed away.

As if understanding the impact it had on me, he outstretched his arms, inviting and accepting. I stepped into his waiting embrace and clutched him for all it was worth.

He bent lower and kissed my temple. "Catarina." He honored my request in a whisper against my skin. "Salvastano."

I had heard more than a thousand songs in my lifetime, but nothing sounded more glorious than my name spoken in Rhett's deep voice.

My fingers unclenched the bunched fabric of his sportscoat, and I anchored my arms on his thick shoulders. Shoulders that'd bore the weight of grief over his parents, carried the guilt for his past mistakes, and now took the brunt of my problems.

He slid his hands over the curve of my waist, settling on my hips. A few moments ago I'd misread his gaze, but there was no mistaking now. The intensity igniting the blue depths of his eyes, so steady and trained on me, the definite parting of his perfect lips, the way he slightly hunched so I'd be able to reach him, all spoke of my welcome. Yet he waited for me to make the move.

With a measured breath, I lifted on my toes and my lips brushed his. Such a feather of a touch, but shocks of heat rippled through me. I lifted for another, lingering still, then roaming. His patient lips let me explore the same areas that'd made my fingertip tingle in fascination.

Rhett had more experience in this matter, but he acted in no rush to take command. Rather his mouth, so pliable beneath mine, seemed to savor my unpracticed caress, giving me more confidence.

My fingers skimmed his hair at the nape of his neck, and his own hands flattened on my back, pressing me closer until I melded against him.

A soft whimper escaped me, and he answered with the gentle coax of his lips, parting mine, and guiding us deeper into the kiss.

This dizzying rhythm of give-and-take went beyond the senses, to the shared song between us. That delicate circumstance that'd brought us together yet also had tried to wedge us apart. Rhett's hold tightened as if reading my thoughts, ever trying to protect me. But he couldn't guard me against the unknown, and that was what we faced.

But we'd do so together.

Rhett eased back, keeping the embrace intact, and I rested my head on his heaving chest.

My own lungs burned as if I'd sprinted up Building K's eight staircases.

After several seconds of comfortable silence, I dared to ask the obvious. "Do you still think it's wise for me to stay with you?"

"I do." His voice rumbled in my ear, his tone allowing no challenge. "But we should set boundaries." He dropped a kiss on my forehead and his hands abandoned their post at my waist. With sure steps, he moved across the parlor to the entryway. "We'll take the Bambino as a chaperone." He grabbed the baseball bat and waggled his brows.

I laughed. "How will that help?"

"Number one." He widened his stance as if he stood at home plate and took a half-swing. "We have to always be at least a bat length away from each other when inside the house."

"Okay." I nodded. "What's the second rule?"

"We keep the bat with us as a reminder. Maybe set it in the middle of whichever room we're in. That way we're always mindful." He pointed the bat at me as if I'd be the one who'd be the rulebreaker.

My lips tugged into a full smile. I could only imagine how out of place George would be in Rhett's fancy sitting room. "Are you serious about taking it with us?"

He settled the bat on his shoulder and approached me with a swagger that'd send scores of women to their fainting couch. "Absolutely.

Because I have serious feelings for you." He handed over George, his other hand wrapping over mine, our eyes locking. "And I want you to always feel safe with me."

◆ ◆ ◆

The last strums of twilight swept through Rhett's opened front door. He gestured for Kate to step into his home and followed behind her with her things. Chimney tossed an unamused look at their newest houseguest, then pranced away, turning its tail to them with an air of indifference.

"I've never had such an affectionate pet." Rhett said dryly and flicked on the electric lamps, bathing the parlor in a soft glow.

Kate, lazily clutching their wooden chaperone in her left hand, moved toward the side wall and studied the two family photos hanging from the picture rail. "Your mother was beautiful."

Rhett's father had always said mother had left the legion of angels to join his side, even going as far as saying she'd stored her wings in the garage. Having been only five at the time, Rhett had sneaked to the outbuilding in a determined search for them. Looking at Kate and all her goodness, he understood his father's sentiment.

She leaned closer as if to take in every detail of his family. His mother would've been smitten with her. His father would've clapped him on the shoulder and welcomed him to the "Goners Club." Because once Rhett gave his heart, he was indeed a goner.

He swallowed. "I'm sure you're tired. Let's get you settled." He hauled her trunk into his room and tried not to think about her sleeping here. In his bed. In her pretty nightgown. He winced. This was going to be torture. Especially after that kiss they'd shared.

Her innocence during that exchange only made his heart all the more protective. She was everything moral and good. She deserved someone who valued her purity, and he would give his fighting best to be that man.

"What's this?" Kate leaned the baseball bat against his dresser and motioned to his trunk by the bedroom door.

He scratched his cheek. "That's been there for a while."

She gave him a curious look. Probably because he avoided her question like Chimney avoided human interaction.

She ran a finger over the black box, such a contrast to the eggshell walls behind it, her touch carving a trail in the dust. "I don't remember this being here last week." Then she glanced over, a sheepish smile lining her mouth. "But then I was a bit emotional at the time."

"Understandable." He positioned her belongings in the corner by the window and hoped she'd forget about—

"Why do you have this here?" She motioned to the trunk.

He expelled a sigh. "I'd tell you, but then I don't want to appear a hypocrite."

Her dark brow arching, she leaned against the spot on the wall beside the trunk as if to say she wouldn't budge until she knew all. "I remember someone saying something about no secrets."

Right. He removed his hat and tossed it on the dresser behind her. "I've hated this place."

"The house?"

"This city." He fixed his stare on the navy braided rug beneath Kate's feet. "My father devoted his entire life serving. He was a cop for thirty-five years. Probably would still be if he was alive. It's in his blood, like Major's." He loosened his tie knot. "After he died, there was a time I was more angry than sad."

Her chin lowered and that familiar guilt splashed in her eyes. "I'm sorry."

"Don't apologize for somebody else's sins." He tried to balance his tone with equal parts gentleness and adamance. "I was angry at Hugo, but also the crookedness as a whole. I had enough of it. Not even three weeks after Father's death I caught officers—ones that worked under him—taking bribes from bootleggers." He blew out a frustrated breath. "Those men I thought so loyal to the cause of cleaning up Pittsburgh, Father's life work, were padding their pockets. It was like spitting on his grave." He sunk onto the edge of his mattress. "So I quit."

His gaze wouldn't stray to her eyes. He'd never been the one to walk away from a challenge. From day one, life had forced him to face hard things, and he had. But staying on the force would've been a fight he'd never win. The corruption had spread like a tumor, killing the entire system. With Rhett being the son of the commissioner who'd declared war on all who'd violated the Volstead Act, the bootleggers and crime lords had known better than to bribe him. Though if his father would've turned a blind eye to the Salvastanos, he'd probably be alive today. But he'd be dead in ways that mattered to him most.

Rhett squeezed the edge of the mattress, keeping the emotion from his face. "I came home that night and packed my trunk in a blind rage. I can't tell you what's even in there." He finally glanced over and found brown eyes fastened on him.

"You haven't opened it all these months?"

He shrugged. "If I found myself needing a shirt or something, I'd buy a new one. I refused to unpack, because that meant I would be staying."

Her features softened. "Yet you're still here."

"I made a vow to stay until I found the man who killed him."

She gave a sad nod.

Could their relationship be any more complicated? While Rhett's edge of bitterness had dulled since his conversation with Sister Agatha, he wouldn't apologize for wanting justice for his father. But if Rhett would nab Hugo, would Kate be understanding? Or would he lose her forever?

That was a conversation for a different day. He was too exhausted to discover the answer. And perhaps a bit nervous as well. "David and I started the agency. Though he's always known my intent to leave town."

She hugged her arms to her chest, her lips pressed together.

"Here I am begging you to stay, yet I'd made an oath to myself that I'd leave this city the moment Father's death is avenged."

"If there's one thing I learned through all this." She pushed off the wall and stepped toward him. Then, as if remembering their rule, she lingered out of reach. "It's that it's important to remain true to your convictions."

For so long, he'd despised Pittsburgh and all it stood for, letting the resentment build and decay. But since he'd met Kate, the resolve head north hadn't been as appealing. His words at her apartment came back to him. *One day at a time.* This was a time to trust in a power greater than his own. A wisdom smarter than his own.

His cat picked this moment to enter the bedroom and to Rhett's astonishment, it brushed against Kate's shins. And was that purring he heard?

Her soft laughter was addicting. "I take it by the look on your face, Chimney doesn't do this often?"

"Almost never." His grin broke free. "Though Chimney knows a nice set of legs when he sees them."

She rolled her eyes, but her smile shone her amusement. "Wait. I thought the cat is a girl." Her gaze followed Chimney, who climbed onto the bed and padded around.

"Could be." He shrugged and stood. "I don't exactly know. We respect each other's privacy." Speaking of which, he needed to vacate his bedroom in order to give Kate her space. He grabbed his Bible off the dresser and tucked it under his arm. "Those are fresh sheets on the bed. If you need anything else, let me know."

She nodded and stepped aside, giving him a wide berth. Her hand absently stroked her hair, capturing his stare. His lips tingled. *Oh for the love. . .* He cast a look at the Bambino Bat and shook away the longing.

Rhett managed a *goodnight* and pulled the door closed behind him. He sure hoped she slept well, because he doubted he would for a while.

CHAPTER 35

I sat beside Rhett in his Model-T, thankful my shift had ended. With all that'd been going on lately, it'd been difficult to concentrate on work. I'd helped in the office most of the day, and had filed the log sheets incorrectly, costing me a full hour's time to amend. I could *not* afford to make any blunders tomorrow.

"What's that sigh about?" Rhett's hand slid over mine for a brief second before shifting gears.

"Frank's running a short-wave test in the morning. Norway is to pick up our signal." The whole station had buzzed with excitement. "The entire broadcast is in Norwegian."

"Impressive."

"It's more challenging than I imagined." I had to play and sing a difficult piece. During practice I'd stumbled over the language several times. My gut knotted. Maybe Rhett could bring me to KDKA early tomorrow so I could rehearse. "This program is important to Westinghouse."

"I'm sure you'll do great." He tossed me a reassuring smile.

Oh to have as much confidence as Rhett. I stilled my hands before they wrung more creases in the chiffon fabric of my skirt. It would be awful to ruin the outfit the first time I'd worn it. I'd forgotten about this drop-waisted dress until the other day when I'd been packing. With flutter-split sleeves and subtle tiered ruffles, it was different than all the other pieces in my wardrobe. But the look of masculine appreciation Rhett had given me this morning when I'd emerged from the bedroom was enough to warm me on this drafty day.

Rhett took the turn toward Braddock, and my chest pinched with guilt. "Are you sure it's okay to stop again?" We'd already gone to my apartment before my shift to visit with Charlie and bring him the breakfast I'd prepared at Rhett's place. He hadn't had much food stocked, so I had gotten creative with eggs, tomato soup, and crackers.

Before we'd left Westinghouse Plant, I'd suggested we fetch the groceries from my place. It'd be a shame for all my food to go to waste.

"It's not a problem." He shot me a wink. "Besides, I wouldn't want to stand between you and your fig pudding."

I smiled. "I fully intended to cook for you tonight, Rhett Jennings." The breeze from the open window made my hair pull across my face, and I tamed it with my fingers. "But for that remark you're now getting a plate full of your stale crackers while I eat Bolognese." I could use some of his tomato soup and gather the rest of ingredients from my cupboards. "Too bad, you could've feasted like a true Italian."

"Stale crackers?" He clutched his heart, his right hand gripping the steering wheel. "You're too good to do that to me."

I raised a challenging brow, my lips fighting against a smile.

He chuckled low. "Then I take back everything I said." Braking at the stop sign, he leaned over and kissed me.

I gave his shoulder a light smack. "You just broke your own rule." Not that I minded. But I wouldn't dare let Rhett know that his kisses were more savory than a vat of fig pudding.

"I did not." He eased the car down the side street leading to my apartment building. "I said we're to remain a bat-length apart while inside the house. This, my darling, is the car." He flashed a rascal of a smile, drawing my laugh.

"I still think that's cheating."

"It's a loophole." He drove onto the lot and shoved the car in neutral, pulling the brake. His strong arm wrapped around me and tugged me closer. "Big difference."

His lips pressed the crown of my hair for a delicious second, and then we both straightened. Rhett was out of the car first, rounded to my side, and opened my door. My arm in his, we walked the familiar route to my doorstep.

His muscles beneath my fingertips jerked as his feet skidded to a stop.

"What's the matter?" My gaze followed his, finding my apartment door ajar. My heart beat staccato against my ribs. I had locked the door when last here. I was sure of it.

Rhett's hand darted to his holster, and my fingers instinctively tightened on his arm.

"Be careful," I whispered. "Charlie could be inside." Though I'd cautioned him this morning not to visit my apartment, I couldn't be certain he'd obeyed.

Rhett gave a tight nod and nudged the door with his foot, the hinges groaning.

The early evening light shoved into the shadowed space, and I slapped a shaky hand over my mouth.

Demolished. Everything.

Images of Papa's gutted bakery flashed, reminding me of my horrid first day in Pittsburgh. Now the nightmare had reached my home.

"Whoever did this could still be close." Rhett's low caution caused goosebumps to prickle my flesh. "I'm not leaving you out here. Follow me, but keep quiet."

Trapping my lips between my teeth, I nodded.

Rhett withdrew his pistol and stepped into my apartment. I shuffled behind him, my eyes taking in the painful sight.

"Watch the glass." He rasped.

The entryway mirror had been shattered, the shards glittering on the tile. The sofa had been turned over, the lamps that had bookended it in pieces beside the torn cushions. My parlor rug had been pulled back as if the intruder had been checking the floorboards.

Why?

Rhett's gaze sweeping, he moved with deliberate strides toward my kitchenette. I followed so close my chest almost knocked into his back.

The cabinets gaped open. All its contents, the food I'd purposed to retrieve, lay in a messy heap on the floor, the litter extending to the drapes.

The drapes!

I sprinted to the curtains—Charlie's hiding spot—and yanked it back. My breath came out in a whoosh. The spot he'd always claimed was vacant.

Rhett's hardened glare softened as if realizing the motive behind my impulsive action. He motioned for me to get behind him as he eyed my bedroom. The door was closed.

Could the intruder be in there?

The veins on the back of Rhett's neck bulged. "I'm armed." His voice boomed. "Come out with both hands raised." He reached back and guided me so I stood directly behind him. With his shoulders set back and his stance wide, Rhett stood like a Roman gladiator, anchoring himself between me and whatever beast lingered opposite the door.

The wall clock ticked a slow dirge compared to my wild heartbeat.

"Stand back." Rhett gave a low warning. "I'm opening it." Pistol outstretched, he threw open the door.

No monster threatened within the room, but I looked in horror at its ravaged touch.

The window had been broken, the jagged glass like sharp teeth. Drawers had been emptied and thrown. The articles of clothing I hadn't packed littered the floor. My mattress had been pulled off the bedframe. My vanity moved to the other side of the room, all my grooming items scattered in the rubble.

Who could have done this?

Rhett stepped over the vanity stool and investigated the broken window, the sill, and the area around it.

"Anything?" My voice sounded feeble.

He stepped back and rubbed the turn of his jaw, his scowl deepening. "The intruder got in through the window and escaped through the front door." He glanced over. "The same way as before."

Which pointed blame even more toward Cardosi since he'd left both cards.

An eerie crunching came from the entryway. My head whipped toward the sound. A slim, dark shadow stood against waning daylight.

"It's Charlie." I dashed toward my young friend and squeezed him in an embrace.

His arms hugged my waist even as he trembled.

He shouldn't be in here. This place, his only refuge, had sank into devastation.

I pulled back and glimpsed the distress in his eyes. "Follow me." I led him onto the porch, away from the rubble. "Let me see if there's any salvageable food. Then you're to go straight home."

His fingers grasped my sleeve, tugging.

"Charlie, it's not safe here." At least he couldn't hear my voice crack. "Wait one second." I rushed toward the kitchenette. My plans of hauling my food to Rhett's house now lay in a puddle at my feet. The sugar and flour jars had been dumped, the bread in a soggy mush beside spilled milk.

My gaze searched for something—anything—to offer Charlie. The dessert tin leaned against the bottom of the ice box. I snatched it and lifted the lid. Peanut butter cookies weren't the most substantial supper, but it was better than him going hungry. I sorted through the produce bin, now tipped on its side, found the only apple that wasn't bruised, and moved swiftly to Charlie.

"Here, sweetheart. This is all I have." I handed over the food and strained for a smile I hoped appeared soothing. "Now you need to run along. I'll visit tomorrow after my shift." I kissed his head.

Something pressed into my palm.

A folded paper. One of his drawings.

Rhett joined us on the porch. He placed a comforting hand on Charlie's shoulder and wrapped the other around my waist, forming a small huddle. I held back tears. This small band of misfits. Not blood, but family nonetheless. For here stood the two souls I loved most. Rhett held his head high, and peered over Charlie, his swiveling gaze reminding me of the still present danger.

Charlie needed to get to safety.

I stooped to his level. "It's best you run home."

Scar tissue paling, Charlie gestured toward my apartment and his mouth quirked as if trying to say something.

My heart broke. "I know. It's awful. But it's just things, right?" I wound an arm around his thin shoulder, and leaned over so my face was still in his line of vision. "God kept us safe." And I prayed He would continue to cover us with His protective hand.

He signed, "Drawing."

He no doubt referenced his collection of pictures. To him, that sketchpad, with its worn binding and turned up edges, was his world, his prized possession.

"I'll find your drawings." The pad had to be among the debris. I only hoped it wasn't in shreds. "It's not safe here. Run as fast as you can, okay?"

He hesitated, and I motioned him forward with a loving smile.

His freckled-face frowned and something flashed in his amber eyes. Sadness. Frustration. The poor child had already dealt with enough, he didn't need to see any more of this disaster.

"I'll see you soon." I waved even while my gut twisted.

I watched him skitter down the stairs toward his home. *God, keep him safe.*

Over the next stretch of minutes, I cleaned the remains of the spoiled food while Rhett hunted for clues.

"What are you looking for?" I swept the ceramic pieces from my broken cannisters onto a dustpan and emptied it into the full garbage bin.

"A wrapper." He glanced up from his inspection of the parlor floor. "Gladys found a cigar wrapper on her rug. I think both of these break-ins are related. I'm just trying to find proof."

"Proof." My voice thinned and my palm flattened against my forehead. "I told him I had proof." How could I be so stupid?

Rhett vaulted to his feet. "Who?"

"Cardosi." I called even as I rushed to the bedroom. "I told him I could prove I was a Salvastano."

Thundering footsteps followed, alerting me of Rhett's nearness.

"They have to be here." I dropped to my knees, my hands scraping through the debris. *Oh God, please.* My gaze turned desperate, searching, refusing to yield to the greying edges blurring my vision.

There. The box.

I crawled toward the radiator, tearing my stocking on a jagged spot in the floorboard, the splintery pain shooting through my knee cap. My shaky fingers grappled the box.

Empty.

My lashes swept low, and then opened as if they'd magically appear. But no. "They're gone, Rhett." My heart might as well be tossed among the wreckage.

"What's gone?"

"Papa's letters."

CHAPTER 36

Rhett's gaze scanned Kate's bedroom. "Are you sure the letters aren't here?" His foot nudged the mattress that'd been separated from the bedframe. "They could be under this." He lifted the bulky thing and leaned it against the wall.

She searched the area, but even Rhett could tell there was only a few pieces of sheet music, a handheld mirror, and some feminine undergarments. The peach-colored nightgown inches away from his toe made heat scale his spine. He'd had his share of seeing those kind of pieces, but with Kate everything was different. Innocent. And he was thankful for it.

If Kate was unnerved by the exposition of her underthings, she didn't show it. Instead she sat back on her haunches, tugging her skirt modestly over her knees. "I think the letters are what Mr. Cardosi had been looking for."

Kate seemed convinced Cardosi was the culprit, but Rhett couldn't count out Pitrello, especially the way the room had been demolished.

With the slashed cushions, and the emptied drawers, this place was similar to Gladys's. "Your visit with Cardosi." He lowered beside her. "Tell me everything."

"He *advised* me not to seek Papa's fortune. He added it wouldn't do any good because I have no proof of being his daughter."

Anger twisted beneath his ribs. If Rhett had been there, he'd would've shown Cardosi what a real threat looked like.

"I told him I had all the evidence I needed."

"Did you mention the letters?"

"No."

So the crooked lawyer could've been on the hunt, searching for the proof Kate had spoken of. Cardosi wasn't exactly young, but it didn't take much strength to cause this sort of wreckage.

Her deep sigh pulled him from his thoughts.

"All this can't be easy for you. Papa's crimes have made me question if I ever really knew him." She glanced over. "But those letters were all I had left of the Papa I once loved. He used to lift me onto his shoulders when my legs grew tired of walking into the village. He never left my bedside when I was recovering from the earthquake. He held my hand when Mamma was being buried." A sad smile hung below her weary eyes. "The man I knew wasn't a villain. He wasn't a murderer."

But he was.

Rhett couldn't offer words of comfort. He'd only known Hugo as the crime boss, his dirty hands all over Pittsburgh's underworld and his bloody footprint on the planked hallway beside Father's lifeless body.

What Rhett couldn't supply in voice, he said with an arm around her shoulder. She rested her head on his chest. His eyes slid closed, shutting out the chaos and disorder. With Kate in his arms and God in his heart, they could establish their own peace, create hope when everything appeared destroyed.

His hand stroked the length of her hair, soft like satin beneath his fingers. "Kate, why didn't you bring the letters to my house?"

She snuggled closer. "Because."

Because of him. Because she regarded his feelings above her own. And now what was dear to her was gone. "I'm sorry you lost something special."

She straightened and wiped away the tears with the back of her hand. "I was careless with his last letter, and now this."

"What do you mean?" He moved a crumpled box so he could stretch out his legs.

"That last letter he'd sent was the very reason I sailed here."

His brow lifted. "Your father asked you to come to America?" If Hugo had painted himself as the loving father, Rhett couldn't imagine the man inviting his daughter to see the ugly truth.

"No, he never asked me to visit." Her tone was somber. "You see, his letters were always several pages long and included money for me to live on." She pushed back a lock of hair that'd been stuck to her damp cheek. "But not the most recent one. It was only half a sheet of paper with only a single coin. I thought he fell on hard times and needed me."

Of course she'd be driven by compassion. But the Salvastanos were by no means penniless. Or failing in health. Then why would Hugo send a dire note? If only Rhett could read it. Could Hugo have tucked a clue in his letter? "You said you were careless with it. What happened?"

"I dropped it that day we met. Probably when I was running from Big Dante's men. Or maybe even before—"

"Wait." His eyelids pinched tight, his mind scraping the recesses of the foggy memory. It'd been two weeks after Father's death. A few days before he'd quit the force. He could picture the two hoodlums chasing a defenseless woman. Kate. Her lacy handkerchief shielding most of her face, except those frightened dark eyes. Kate running from him. The letter at his feet. Rhett scooping it up. And that was where the memory stopped. "It's a long shot."

She blinked. "What is?"

"I somewhat remember picking up the letter." He stood, wiped his palms on his thighs, and helped Kate to her feet. "I still may have it."

"Do you think it's in here?" I swept a hand over the pile of clothes Rhett had dumped onto his bed. He'd already cleared out the closet in the foyer, the one in his home office, and now his bedroom. So far, we'd been coming up empty. My lips pressed tight, trapping the rising sigh.

"If I had the letter, it'd be in the pocket of my uniform." His hat ditched long ago, Rhett pushed back that wayward curl from his forehead, only for it to rebel and tumble over his left brow.

He caught me smiling, and his own smirk broke free. "I'm glad you find this amusing."

I'd embrace any opportunity to divert me from the ache in my heart. All those letters gone. Stolen. Rhett had told me it'd be a gamble for him to possess the last note from Papa, but still I'd clung to the thread of hope.

"The day you dropped it happened to be my last week of work. It was all a blur." He dug through the lump of clothes, eyes searching. "I don't remember what I did with my uniform. For all I know I could've chucked it in the garbage bin."

Then there'd be no chance of recovery. I was no stranger to loss. Like I'd told Charlie earlier, it was just things. Paper and ink. Maybe when the emotion dislodged from my system, I'd be able to believe my own words.

His eyes narrowed on a wool jacket with brass-toned buttons, and he snatched it from the bed. "Here's my patrolman coat. Could be in the pockets." He searched the inner, then the outer shell. The line of his mouth crimped into a white slash, and he shook his head.

Not there.

He sorted through more items. "The slacks should be here, too." One by one, he tossed the clothes onto the floor beside my feet. My courage dwindled as the pile shrunk to only a necktie and a pair of navy suspenders.

He pulled a hand over his face. "That's the last of it."

Disappointment sank like a brick in my gut, but I rallied a smile. "I appreciate you looking." For Rhett to hunt so thoroughly for the writings from a man who murdered his own father, said so much about his character, about his goodness. I didn't deserve his devotion, but I was grateful for it. "That means a lot to me."

He barred his arms across his chest, his eyes squinting as if in concentration. "I don't understand how I still have my coat, but not the slacks."

All of the clothes appeared laundered, so even if he did have the trousers, the letter was most likely long gone. It'd been a lost cause from the start.

"We've searched through everything I own." His gaze strayed over my shoulder and his blue eyes sparked. "Then again." With purposed strides, he moved to the wall and hoisted over the trunk.

I stepped aside so he could place the large box on the bed. Hadn't Rhett said he'd been in a fury the day he'd packed? Maybe, just maybe.

A few quick snaps to the metal latches, and the trunk opened. He withdrew several wadded shirts. A couple wrinkled ties. He yanked on a pair of tweed trousers and his long underwear spilled onto the bed.

Rhett's sheepish smile slanted into something more mischievous. "I guess now we're even." He referenced to my lacy chamise that had been only inches away from his feet in my apartment. When he'd said no secrets between us, I hadn't exactly figured that into the equation.

He tossed the underwear onto the clothing heap on the floor. "Though I must admit, yours is way more interesting."

"Rhett Jennings." My tone was half scold, half gasp. "I should slap you for such words."

"You can't. George is watching." He jerked a thumb toward the wall where the bat leaned. "That's a direct distancing violation." His smirk grew wider until his eyes gleamed.

"Someone told me it's key to find a loophole." I scooped up a pillow and launched it at him.

He deflected it with ease.

It could've been his deep laughter mingling with mine, or the familiar way our gazes knotted, that made me realize something I should've seen before—I'd been clutching yesterday so tightly, it prevented me from reaching toward tomorrow.

Those letters were my past. They'd represented a life I no longer knew, with a family I no longer had. It was one thing to look back on fond memories, but quite another to allow them to block my vision of the future. I needed to look forward, not behind. And maybe the man who now regarded me with the tenderest expression would want to be part of my tomorrows. "We don't have to search anymore." I crouched to start picking up the mound of clothes.

"Wait." Rhett's eyes narrowed, and he tugged the barely-shown hem of dark pants, sliding them out from beneath the pile. "Found 'em." He reached into the pocket and came out clutching the letter.

I straightened in disbelief. "That's it." I'd expected him to open it, especially since he'd told me on the drive here the letter might contain clues about Papa. But instead, he held out the envelope to me.

"I believe this is yours, Catarina."

CHAPTER 37

Rhett had expected Kate to be thrilled at finding the letter. Maybe squeal in excitement or throw her arms around him in joy. But instead, she stared at it, a crease between her brows as if in indecision. "What's wrong?"

She lowered the envelope. "Just moments ago, I purposed to move ahead. There's nothing left for me in the past." Her gaze met his. "Everything's in the future."

Everything. Could she mean him? He sure hoped, because now that he had her back, he wasn't about to let go. Not without a fight for her heart. "What if there's something in there that would help you move forward? I hate to crush your new resolve, but until you're out of danger, we need to explore every possibility of a lead."

Her soft eyes filled with understanding, and she slid the letter out from the worn envelope.

"Is it in Italian?"

"No." She skimmed the script then fastened her gaze on him. "That's another thing that makes this one different than all the others. Papa wrote it in English."

"Care to read it aloud?"

She nodded. "Dear Little Mouse." Her voice hitched on the paternal endearment. "I'm sorry it took so long to write. Things have been different here. Life is filled with twists that make you scratch your head. I know this wasn't how I wanted everything to be, but good will win out. Even though people may not think me good. But I know you do. Never forget how much I love you. Papa." She looked up from the creased page. "And that's all."

Rhett's heart crashed into his stomach. *Good will win out.* His father's famous phrase. He'd say those four words in speeches to the press and in radio interviews. He ended every meeting he'd conducted on the force with that signature phrase.

"The coin is still here, too."

Of all the distorted, twisted things for Hugo to write. He mocked his father. Ridiculed him to a daughter who hadn't a clue about his vile ways.

"I thought it would've be gone too."

All this proved was that Hugo had Father in his line of targets long before that bloody day at the Salvastano house. Rhett had always thought it'd been an impulsive slaughter. But, no. Hugo had been tracking Father. Watching his every move, listening to his words, and waiting to strike. A sourness, the familiar taste of bitterness, coated his tongue.

"Rhett?" Kate pressed a hand over his arm. "Are you okay?"

"I will be." As soon as he found Hugo.

And he knew the right person to enlist to help.

◆ ◆ ◆

With a sigh, I yanked open the cabinet outside Studio A. My stiff muscles protested as I bent over the folders, searching for my music. I'd hardly slept last night. From the red circles rimming Rhett's eyes this morning, he hadn't either.

Why had I read the letter to him? I'd known better. The strong nudge in my gut had told me to leave it all in the past, but I'd ignored it. Papa's words hadn't provided a clue, but rather stirred Rhett's anger. While Rhett hadn't voiced it, his fury shone in the granite set of his jaw, the fierce line of brow.

But what had I expected? Papa was responsible for his father's death. Of course, Rhett wouldn't enjoy listening to his enemy's sentiments. But he was the one who'd encouraged me to read it in the first place.

Though only paper, the music felt heavy in my hand.

Last evening, Rhett had promised to tune-in to my performance, but I couldn't be certain he'd remember. Because at the time, his focus had been on getting in touch with Major and setting a meeting for today.

I have something pressing to tell him, was all Rhett had said before bidding me a clipped goodnight and closing the door to his office in the spare room.

Shutting me out.

Perhaps I was overreacting. The stress of the past couple weeks, along with the commotion of last night's break-in, and now the pressure of this broadcast could all be working against my mind. Maybe I only imagined the distance between Rhett and myself.

I couldn't concentrate on the subject right now. All my attention needed to be on my music if I was to perform without error.

Robert entered the room in a flurry. "Three minutes until you're on." He brushed past me.

On instinct, I moved forward, giving him more space to enter Studio A, and knocking my hip on the side table. My purse fell to the floor, my compact mirror and Rhett's housekey spilling out. I scrambled to tuck them back inside, and my gaze snagged on the folded paper.

Charlie's drawing.

Guilt snaked across my chest. Yesterday, I'd been so caught up about the chaos at my place and then the quest to find Papa's letter that I'd forgotten I'd stuffed Charlie's picture into my bag. I withdrew the creased paper and leaned against the sliver of wall beside the studio's entrance.

I unfolded the drawing, and my throat thickened.

It was a man's profile.

His hat was pulled low, and he wore a suit as common as any other fellow walking the street. But his lined face held a distinction I'd seen once before—a cross-shaped scar on the left cheek.

Major Ford.

His slightly hunched silhouette stood beside a door marked with the number 11. My apartment.

My breath thinned. While huddled on my porch, Charlie had signed the word *drawing* and then urgently pointed to the wreckage. I could picture the plea in his eyes, the quiver in his hands. He hadn't been referring to his treasured sketch pad as I'd thought. He'd wanted me to look at *this* paper. To tell me who broke into my apartment.

My fingers worked to refold the paper. The monster was Major. He'd destroyed my things. Taken Papa's letters. But why steal what he could've easily seen with a simple request to Rhett?

Unless … he had something to hide. What if there was something in the letters that would've incriminated him?

My joints locked. Rhett intended to meet Major in less than an hour to discuss the last letter!

How could I stop him? There was a phone in Frank's office. Maybe Rhett was still at the agency. Blood coursing faster than the current of the Allegheny River, I sped to the hallway only to collide into Peggy.

"Kate!" She gasped. "What are you doing? The brass band's almost done. You're next!" She tugged my elbow.

I squirmed free. "I need to call Rhett." I started toward Frank's office, but this time Peggy's hand clamped on my wrist with the tenacity of a bulldog.

"You have an entire Norwegian country waiting on you." She yanked on my arm, pulling me back into the small room. "Detective Dashing can wait."

But then it may be too late.

My eyes landed on my Mozart folder, sticking out as if divine fingers had picked it from the pile. An idea swirled. I could inform Rhett through our discreet means of communication—the airwaves. Though this time, it could cost my job.

But not going through with this could cost Rhett his life.

CHAPTER 38

Rhett rested his heels atop his office desk at the agency and reclined in his chair. A brass ensemble boomed through the radio's speaker. He'd been listening to KDKA for the past twenty minutes waiting for his favorite performer to wow Norway with her talent. She'd mentioned this morning that the entire program was only an hour long, so maybe he could fight off the drowsiness weighting his eyelids.

He'd tossed and turned all night long. Hugo's words had rolled in the crevices of his mind, like a metal ball in a labyrinth, hitting mental blocks and walls in search of the right place to settle. He tipped his head back on the plush chair's cushion.

He was missing something.

Something important. But what? It was a good thing he'd see Major soon. His father's friend had always been a good problem solver.

He should've asked Major to meet him here at the office, then Rhett could've gotten in some more shut-eye. But the old man wanted to meet across town at a café Rhett had only eaten at once. And hated it.

But Major had carved out time in his hectic schedule so Rhett should be grateful. He still hadn't told his former boss about his relationship with Kate. Major would no doubt be skeptical. Maybe they could all get together soon. Then Major could witness firsthand Kate's goodness.

But Rhett needed to smooth things over with her first. He'd struggled with her father's letter and been emotionally detached last night. She didn't deserve that. She was a victim like him. Her apartment, the only place she'd called home while in Pittsburgh, was still in disorder. Someone had invaded, violated her space, destroyed all her belongings, and here Rhett was moping over Hugo's words.

He'd make it up to her. Tonight, he'd take her on an official date. Somewhere nice.

A masculine voice filtered through the speakers and announced Kate and the Norwegian piece she'd perform.

His eyes slid shut, waiting for her soprano voice to grace the air waves and seep into his heart. He probably wouldn't understand a word she'd sing, but he'd feel her emotion behind the music.

The first few bars from a piano sounded, and Rhett pitched forward in his chair, his feet plunking to the ground.

That wasn't a song from Norway.

But a piano sonata by Mozart.

Confusion rippled through him. She'd told him the entire program was to be in Norwegian, had stressed how important this broadcast was, yet now she played a completely different song? The sonata was a popular one.

Major F.

Why would she play Mozart's Major F? The song director had to have been oblivious to the switch, considering he just announced the Norwegian piece she was to play. So the adjustment had to have been Kate's idea. Something deliberate.

Was she trying to communicate with *him*? The notion seemed silly, but Rhett couldn't rule it out. Especially since the classical piece was such a drastic contrast to what she was originally supposed to perform. He listened for intentional variations in the melody, but he couldn't spot any. What if the message lay in the song itself?

Major F.

He rubbed the strain in his forehead. The only connection he could make was to Major Ford.

"Why?" He thought aloud. "Why would she tell me something about Major?"

"Because she knows something you don't." A gravelly voice yanked Rhett's gaze to a man standing in his doorway.

Hugo Salvastano.

My hands shook violently, but I ended the piece. Several pairs of eyes glued on me with mouths agape. But there wasn't time to defend my rash actions, I had to get ahold of Rhett. Quiet as possible, I stood from the piano bench, choosing to ignore the song director waving me over, and exited Studio A.

My fingers snatched my purse from the table without pausing my swift strides. As fast as my legs could carry me, I rushed to Frank's office.

Locked.

My palm slapped the wooden door in defeat. I didn't have time to search for him. The plant stretched across forty acres, my boss could be anywhere. I raced to the secretary station, bursting through the door like a crazed racehorse let out of the starting gate. Stella perched at her desk, receiver in hand, talking on the phone.

"Sorry," Squeaked from my lips as I grabbed the candlestick base and clicked the disconnect.

Stella gasped. "What on earth, Kate?"

"Can't explain." I gave the operator the exchange. I tapped my fingers against the phone's wooden base, willing the connection faster.

"That was H.P. you just hung up on." Stella snapped.

The vice president of Westinghouse, and I didn't even regret it. No doubt I'd already lost my job after switching songs for my performance.

Stella lunged for the phone, but I pivoted back as far as the cord allowed. *Come on, Rhett, pick up. Pick up!* I cut a glance to the clock by the door. Had he left already? I waited several more alarming seconds.

Nothing.

There was no way I'd beat him to the café where he was to meet Major. But I had to try. I surrendered the phone to Stella, who mumbled her displeasure, and took off toward the stairwell. My heels clicked a choppy rhythm against the concrete steps as I rushed down several flights.

My name was called in the distance, but I wouldn't stop. Any delay would be costly. Rhett needed me. I couldn't be certain he'd heard my song, caught my message.

God, please keep him safe.

I stumbled on the last step leading to the lowest level, grasping the metal railing, keeping me from tumbling into the stairwell exit.

The main floor of the building hummed with its usual activity. I sidestepped a worker pushing a cart loaded with crates and almost collided into a cluster of men entering the building through the double doors. I snaked my way through, earning a few grumbles as well as a couple 'pardon me'. Once outside, gray skies loomed over me, spitting rain.

Darting toward the parking lot, I came to the railway tracks and skidded to a halt. My gaze swiveled left to right, making sure the plant's shipping trolley wasn't approaching. High-stepping over the ribbons of rails, I continued forward. My mind caught up to my panic, and my momentum slowed. The cable car route went through homestead before entering the heart of Pittsburgh. It'd be at least an hour and a half before I'd reach the café. I'd never make it on time. Wouldn't even be close.

I could call the police. No, no I couldn't. Major worked on the force. Besides how would I know which cop was trustworthy?

What could I do? Maybe I could get ahold of David. He was closer to the café than I was. I needed to call the agency again. If I couldn't reach Rhett's partner, Peggy had a car. I could ask to borrow it.

A fancy automobile pulled directly in front of me and braked to a stop. I stumbled. My knee smacked against the metal bumper, darts of pain jarring my bones.

Of all the stupid things.

I could've been seriously injured. Maybe the driver hadn't spotted me because of the drizzle. But that didn't negate the dull throb rocking through me.

A man emerged.

My eyes took in Gio Pitrello, and I skittered back.

"What's the hurry, Kate?" His smile shoved a chill down my spine. "Or should I say Catarina Salvastano?"

My heart sank in my chest.

They'd come for me.

Nine months of hiding, of lying about my identity, and they'd found me. Rainwater soaked through my blouse, dread seeped into my bones, but I refused to shiver in this man's presence.

His gaze raked my wet body in a slow sweep before landing on my eyes. "I have orders to take you to Big Dante."

The phantom crime lord summoned me. No way I would get out of that alive. I glanced about. Maybe I could sprint to the main building. Or scream loud enough to attract a crowd.

With a smirk, Gio pulled back the edge of his rain-dotted sportscoat, revealing a side arm pistol. "This can be easy or painful. It's your choice."

Die now or die later. Was that even a choice? But the longer I cooperated, the better my chances of escape.

Smile widening, he rounded the car and opened the passenger door in a grand gesture. "Your chariot, princess. Big Dante will be pleased to welcome Salvastano royalty."

My gut twisted. I was to get into a vehicle with a man who'd once tried to assault me. Said man was to take me to the gangster who'd been bent on destroying the Salvastanos. Rhett had no idea where I was or who with. Little by little, my chances of survival drained like the rainwater into the sewer grates.

Thou art my hiding place; thou shalt preserve me from trouble; thou shalt compass me about with songs of deliverance.

I took a stabling breath and shuffled toward Gio's Rolls Royce.

"Kate!" Peggy ran toward me, face lined with worry. "Where are you going?"

Gio tugged my elbow and leaned close. "Get rid of her." He rumbled low in my ear. "She's too pretty to shoot."

I stiffened. "Gio's taking me to lunch, Margaret."

"Huh?" Peggy's eyes shone her confusion.

"Let's go, gorgeous. Time for our date." Gio adopted a charming smile that soured my stomach.

With one more subtle, but pleading, glance to my friend, I ducked into the passenger seat.

CHAPTER 39

Rhett had waited for this day. He'd coveted that pivotal moment of glaring into the face of the man who'd wrecked his entire world. But never had he thought the elusive mobster would stroll right into his office. Rhett gripped his gun, keeping his hand steady despite the shock raging through him.

"You have some nerve, old man, coming in here like this." At least the telephone had stopped its obnoxious ringing. Rhett wasn't about to take his eyes off Hugo's ugly mug to answer the blasted thing.

Hugo raised his hands in surrender. The mighty crime boss appeared nothing more than skin stretched across bones. The brim of his homburg threw a shadow over his eyes, but his gaunt cheekbones caught the daylight slanting through the blinds, revealing waxy skin. Yet he stood tall and proud, even with Rhett's pistol aimed at his heart.

He hobbled a step inside the room. "Your Papa reacted the same way."

Rhett's thumb pulled back the hammer, the click echoing. "Don't mention my father," he said through clenched teeth. How easy it would be to put a bullet through him. He could deal the same deadly card Hugo had given Father. But that kind of shuffled deck wasn't in Rhett's hand anymore. God was the dealer of vengeance. A sobering reminder Rhett needed to heed.

"Your Papa and I met at the baseball park. His hand never left his revolver." Hugo's upper lip hid beneath a bushy mustache, hanging unkempt over his mouth. "That day I told him his partner's a killer."

Major Ford. "I don't believe you." Because Hugo spewed lies like a black widow spit out webs, and Rhett wouldn't be snared in his twisted tale. He rounded his desk, keeping his gun trained on Hugo's every move. "You're the killer. You shot my father and your own brothers. Yet you shove the blame on a man who's given his life taking out garbage like you."

"I didn't do it."

Rhett's fists grew white hot. "You're a liar."

"Then believe Catarina." His head jerked to the radio. "She was warning you."

The sonata. Her strange behavior must've meant something. But not what Hugo claimed. "What do you know of your daughter? Nothing." Rhett approached the crime boss with slow, calculated steps, aware the man could withdraw a firearm at any moment. With a light jab of the barrel to Hugo's side, Rhett motioned him forward.

But instead Hugo winced and clutched his stomach.

Rhett's brow lowered. The gun hardly poked the man. "Are you armed?" With swift movements, he patted Hugo's person for weapons.

His sickly frame swayed like a sapling in the wind. Rhett gripped the convulsing elbow, stabling, then chided himself for doling out compassion. Satisfied to find Hugo unarmed, Rhett stepped back and observed the criminal. "You left Kate to fend for herself. You don't deserve to speak her name."

Sadness filled his jaundiced eyes.

As if the man had a heart. No, he'd been gutted from the inside out, a shell of the powerful crime lord he used to be. Rhett shook his head at the pitiful display, and Hugo's chin notched higher.

"We don't have time to discuss my mistakes."

"The state will give you plenty of time. Unless they choose for you to go to the chair." Or if Hugo's health allowed him to live that long. The man looked half decayed, and Rhett hardened himself to the pity swelling in his chest. Hugo wasn't worth a shred of sympathy.

"Catarina's in danger." His jowls, extending past his knobby chin, shook with his words. "They know who she is."

Was Hugo baiting him? Using his own daughter in his devilish schemes? "I'm driving you straight to Major Ford. And he can take your sorry hide to jail."

Hugo ambled farther into the room and claimed the chair Kate had occupied weeks ago. "I'm not moving until you call her."

A growl stalked his chest. "I'm not at your bidding."

"I know they're after her today. They'll kill her. Kill them both. Just like my brothers and your Papa." His accented voice hitched, his shoulders crumbling forward. The gaze he'd so steadily fixed on his dark-rimmed fingernails lifted to Rhett. "You can stop it, Radish Nose."

Rhett lunged forward and cinched Hugo's collar with his left hand, shoving the pistol into his chest with his right. "What did you say?"

The skin on Hugo's neck felt papery thin against Rhett's knuckles, but the determination in his eyes was tough as steel. "I said your code name."

Radish Nose.

The clandestine words from his childhood when he'd played "secret service" with Father. They'd made a pact inside Rhett's fort, constructed out of fallen sticks and branches, never to tell a soul about their undercover names. Only if it was life or death. And even then, with great caution. It had been all fun and games when he'd been eight.

But not now.

Rhett released him, and Hugo slunk into the chair.

"Father told you."

"Potato Lobes said you'd never believe me otherwise."

Father's code name. Rhett hadn't heard that spoken in decades, and now it was voiced from the person he'd hated. His father wouldn't have shared something so nonsensical—but sacred between them—to someone like Hugo Salvastano without a specific purpose. William Jennings had been a strategic man. It had been deliberate. Like Kate playing the sonata instead of the important Norwegian song.

Kate.

Rhett dove for the phone and rattled off the exchange to the operator. He glanced at Hugo who gave a solemn, approving nod. Could Rhett have had it all backward? What he'd thought bad be good, and right be wrong? Could Major Ford—the mentor Rhett'd welcomed into his home, considered as a second father—be the true killer?

A feminine voice greeted him on the other end.

"This is Rhett Jennings calling for Kate Chamberlin."

A huff sounded, crackling the line. "For goodness sakes, this is getting ridiculous."

"Stella." He'd know that hissing voice anywhere. "Where's Kate?"

"Your *sweetheart* was in here ten minutes ago. She disconnected me from a very important call trying to get ahold of you. Now you're calling for her. This isn't your personal line to play cat and mouse."

Kate had tried to contact him. That must've been her the moment Hugo had walked into the office. And Rhett had ignored it. "It's important I speak to her."

"As of two minutes ago, my lunch break officially started. Find someone else to be your—" Another voice spoke in the background. "It's none of your business." Stella's tone seemed distant as if she held a hand over the receiver. "Hey!"

A jostling noise crinkled in his ear. Two high-pitched voices argued. Silence followed. Had he been disconnected?

"Rhett? This is Peggy." She sounded breathless. "I thought you and Kate were now a real couple."

What kind of statement was that? "We are. I'd like to talk to her. Can you find her for me?"

"I knew something was strange about it all."

Rhett's pulse thudded. "What's going on?"

"Kate's behavior. First she plays a completely different song for her broadcast. Then she disappears. I finally find her running out of the building and talking to a man. Oh and she called me Margaret. She never calls me that. It was as if she was trying to tell me something but—"

"Was the man older, distinguished looking?"

"Not even close. This guy belonged in a pool parlor. He was young, handsome and drove an expensive car. Kate called him Gio."

Pitrello.

Rhett's fingers squeezed the phone. How could this happen? "Where is she now?"

"Gone."

After getting a description of Pitrello's car, Rhett disconnected, anger mingling with panic. Gio and Kate were alone together. The last time she'd encountered that man she'd barely escaped his evil intentions. If he harmed her, Rhett would rip the man apart. "Gio Pitrello has Kate." Not Major Ford. What in the world was happening? He slapped his hat on his head, his heartrate pounding as rapid as his swirling mind. He had to act fast, but helplessness put a chokehold on his throat. "I don't know where he's taking her."

Hugo stood, seeming to have more strength than when he'd first arrived. "I have a fairly good guess."

"It's Pitrello. I thought Major was our target." And the woman he loved was caught in the middle of this deadly game. Oh, God.

"This is larger than you know." Hugo's brow puckered. "Big Dante is involved."

CHAPTER 40

I melded against the passenger door, keeping as far away from Gio as I could. When we were still in town I'd contemplated jumping out of the car and making a run for it, but he could've easily shot me. I'd decided to wait for a better opportunity, yet the more we drove away from Pittsburgh the more alarmed I became.

He shifted gears, speeding faster along the country road.

Trees zipped past in a blur.

My fingernails dug into the edges of the cushion. The man was a maniac. Was he trying to kill us both? Gio's eyes flicked to my white-knuckled grip, and his lips peeled back in a smile.

The car sped toward a sign, my gaze trained on it for a clue to where we were. *Sewickley Heights.* My thoughts snapped back, to the newspaper articles, describing the wooded town located on the Ohio River where Papa and his brothers had lived. It was the place of the murders. "Are we going to the Salvastano house?"

"You're a clever one." He dimpled. "It's about time for a family reunion."

My breath snagged. Was he meaning Papa? Was my father at the house? Or were they going to use me to draw him from hiding? Like they tried to do with the reopening of Saluti's. At the speakeasy, Gio had hinted Papa had already passed on. But if that was the case, why bring me here? And why say a family reunion? And how did Major Ford play into all this?

So many questions, but thinking about the final answer, the end result, made bile climb the back of my throat.

Gio kept his glare on the stretch of dirt road before us. Silence reigned until we approached a winding drive leading to a large house surrounded by pines.

Papa's home.

It had stopped raining, affording me a clear view. The structure looked more like a fortress with its stone walls and high roof. But just like the bakery, it'd been vandalized. The windows had planks of wood nailed over them. The front door had also been boarded. Overgrown brush revealed the property's negligence.

The Salvastano castle looked nothing more than ruins. Their kingdom so mightily built on corruption had fallen like the pine tree now blocking the drive. Gio maneuvered the car around the commanding branches, the vehicles springs rattling on the uneven turf. He parked behind the massive garage located to the right of the house and aimed his gun at me.

"Get out." He motioned with the barrel at the passenger door.

I climbed from the car, my gaze taking in the Salvastano residence. There was a coldness to it, a chill which raised the hair on my arms. The wind stirred, and the trees moaned in response. The ghost gray structure stood silent like the dead that had been found within its walls.

Could Big Dante be planning on adding my death here as well?

Gio grabbed my elbow. "Walk with me and don't try to run away." He nuzzled my hair. "There are penalties for disobedience."

I fought against a shiver as he tugged me along.

If only I'd been able to get ahold of Rhett. It would be hours before he'd arrive at the station to pick me up. So much could happen between now and then. It was too much to hope Peggy had caught anything amiss. I had purposefully used her given name of Margaret, but would that be enough for her to alert anyone? Probably not.

Twigs crunched beneath my feet and tall grass, dotted with rain droplets, scraped my stockings as we bypassed the expansive front porch, rounding to the side of the house. A lone door, framed by ivy vines climbing to the second story, stood before us. Gio released me only to unlock the deadbolt, then returned his steely touch on my arm.

"Move inside and go down the steps. Remember my warning." Such a smooth voice for such a harsh heart.

I entered the dank entryway, and a musty odor assaulted my nose. Another door lingered to my left and a stairway to my right. With hardly any light, the stairwell reminded me of the tunnel—dark walls closing in.

This time there was no child needing safety. No Rhett to tell me I could overcome this. My chest squeezed, and I took a heaving breath, the moldy air stuffing my throat.

"Move." Gio all but growled.

The circle of his revolver pressed into my tailbone. His other hand grabbed the curve of my backside, as if reminding me of all the harm he could inflict.

God, you are my hiding place. He was with me in the darkness as well as in the light. In the depths and in the heights. As much as I wished for peace to melt over me like warm honey, I still felt cold and numb. But didn't the Bible say to walk by faith and not by sight? So without even the littlest twinge of confidence, I forced my feet forward.

Gio hung close almost knocking into me and sending me tumbling down the remaining stairs. The soles of my shoes smacked the damp floor, and I glanced around. A finger of light from a high, barred window on the other side of the basement, provided enough glow for me to establish my surroundings. I stood in yet another hallway with doors lining each side, making the Salvastano cellar appear more like a dungeon.

"The last door has your name on it, Catarina. Keep walking."

He followed behind me until we reached the end of the hall. His large hand reached around and opened the door. I was met with an empty room. Another metal barred window was set in the high corner and there was a stone hearth in the center of the back wall.

He shoved me forward. My knees slapped the dirt floor, and I turned my head in time to see the door close.

The click of the deadbolt echoed in my gut.

I was a prisoner in my own father's house.

CHAPTER 41

This was all Rhett's fault. He'd been the one who'd told Major that Kate was Hugo's daughter. He'd put her in danger. She'd been so careful, protecting her identity. She'd trusted him with her most guarded secret.

And he'd failed her.

He tightened his grip on the steering wheel. While he sped the country roads leading to the Salvastano home, Kate was at the mercy of Gio Pitrello. Rhett still didn't understand how Major and Big Dante's nephew were linked, but he had a feeling the man sitting beside him knew. Perhaps he knew Cardosi's role in this as well.

It was Hugo who'd advised Rhett to drive to the now-abandoned estate. Rhett prayed the older man was right.

There was no time for errors.

He thudded the pedal, increasing the car's speed.

Hugo peered out the front windshield, his collar lifting in the breeze pouring through the open passenger window.

"We have twelve miles until we reach your home." Which would be the longest twenty minutes of Rhett's life. He flicked a glance into the rearview mirror, making certain no one was trailing them. "Start from the beginning. Leave nothing out."

"Shouldn't we devise a plan first?" His voice barely registered over the rattling floorboards.

"Not until I have all the facts." Every facet of this puzzle was crucial to Kate's survival. The right piece of information could make the difference between life and death. *Please God, I can't lose her.* He hadn't been able to save Father. The weight of guilt had almost crushed him. If anything happened to Kate, it'd destroy him.

"The Salvastanos are not murderers." Hugo's tone, though weak, was adamant. "Bootleggers, yes, but not killers. Our business is alcohol, and that's all."

From the evidence Rhett had collected, the family hadn't been involved in drug rings, gambling dens, or brothels. While that part lined up with truth, he couldn't swallow everything being dished out. "How come any other bootlegger or rumrunner invading your territory wound up dead? With your calling card beside their bodies?"

He sighed, deep and long. "We used the 'S' card to scare them. It was important to have all the appearances of power, but we didn't carry out the threats. Someone else did and put the blame on us."

"And you say that someone is Major?" Rhett turned onto the wooded lane that would lead to the Salvastanos' driveway.

"At first, we thought the murders were done by our rivals in West End. We figured they were scheming to remove us by trying to get the law after us." Hugo pulled out a handkerchief and dabbed his forehead.

"Which wouldn't work because most of the force was on your payroll." Rhett added dryly.

He nodded. "Including Major Ford."

Rhett almost shifted into the wrong gear. Major had been taking graft money the entire time he'd been working alongside Father. This man had taken Rhett to boxing bouts, scolded him for missing church, stood beside him at Father's funeral. For almost fifteen years Major had been a hero in Rhett's eyes, yet in fifteen minutes' time he became an enemy.

Hugo removed his hat and set it on the cushion between them. "In order to get their cooperation, all the bribes were under the table. So there was no paper trail leading to Major Ford or anyone else."

Which made sense. Having no evidence of corruption would protect both sides if state investigators came around.

"Your Papa wouldn't have any part of it. He was a stubborn man with morals." A round of coughs erupted from the old man. "Believe me, we tried to buy his cooperation. Even sent him an 'S' card to frighten him into it." He shook his head. "That's how I knew later on that I could come to him about Major Ford."

Rhett pressed his mouth together. Father's honesty had gotten him killed.

"More and more people turned up dead with our trademark on their persons. We had to do something."

"So you investigated?"

"There was a detective already on the job." He leaned forward. "There's a rut up ahead, you may want to avoid it."

Rhett jerked the wheel to the right, missing a divot the size of a tire.

"She discovered that Major Ford was building his own empire. Using our threats as a cover, he got rid of the bootleggers who wouldn't cooperate with him."

Rhett's brows spiked. "She?"

Hugo scratched his neck. "Major has a weakness for beautiful women. And she used that to her advantage. She stole his private ledger that had logs of drug shipments, hitman transactions, other activities. That's what I showed your Papa."

"Where's this ledger now?"

"In the very house we're going to. I didn't have time to grab it when I escaped that day. Major Ford snuck up on us as we were discussing how to bring him down. He came in shooting. I managed to get away."

And that was it. The real account of that awful morning. Poor Father. Why hadn't he confided in Rhett about Major? Had he not thought Rhett able to handle the truth? If Father had told him, Rhett would've been at the Salvastanos that tragic day as well. He probably wouldn't be alive. It was as if Father had wanted to shield him from danger. Yet he'd face that same evil today.

Only another mile until the house, and Rhett still didn't have all the information he needed. Seconds ticked faster than his racing heart.

"Turn left up here." Hugo pointed. "See that large maple?"

"That's not the way in." Rhett squinted. "And I don't see a road."

"That's the point. We can't go any farther up the lane or we'll be spotted. Right here. Brake and turn." He leaned over toward Rhett as if he planned to take the wheel.

Rhett pulled left and the car jostled onto shifty ground. There wasn't a path for his tires to follow, but a narrow clearing. Rhett clenched the wheel tighter, lest one good bump send his fender curling around a tree.

"Keep straight." Hugo directed as if there was any other route to take. "There's a hill ahead with a shed built into its side. It's my brother Pedro's doing. He was always afraid of raids so he'd built secret hideouts. This is one of them." Hugo's voice had traces of sadness. For so long, Rhett had loathed this man. Yet in light of this new information, his perspective changed. Hugo knew pain. He'd lost his wife in an earthquake. His two older siblings had been murdered. And now his daughter was in jeopardy.

But Rhett would surrender everything, even his own life, so Kate could keep hers.

He followed Hugo's instructions, and sure enough, there was a garage camouflaged in the backside of a mound of earth. From the road it only appeared like a grassy knoll. Clever. Rhett shoved the car in neutral, pulled the brake, and got out. He lifted the hatch, painted in earth tones, and drove the Model-T inside. He killed the engine and threw open his door. One glance over his shoulder at Hugo told Rhett the old man wasn't moving.

Frustration mounted. Kate could be seconds away from drawing her last breath and here her father wouldn't budge.

"Would be nice to have a plan," Hugo grumbled.

There wasn't time. "How many do you suppose are in the house?"

"Don't know."

Rhett would be going blindly into a structure that could hold dozens of armed men. Not quite the ideal strategy, but he'd no other option. He'd left a note for David, but his partner was spending the day at the court of records a county over. "Do you think Major's inside?" He withdrew his pocket watch. It was one o'clock. "I was supposed to meet him about now. We were to discuss the last letter you sent Kate."

Hugo's eyes rounded. "Do you have it on you?"

"No."

"Good." He exhaled, and the deep lines in his face relaxed. "Major may be waiting for you because he'd want to know what information you have. On the other hand, he could've made that appointment to keep you away from Catarina, knowing he was going to kidnap her."

"But Big Dante's nephew is the one who took her."

Hugo leveled him with a grave look. "Haven't you figured it out? Major Ford is Big Dante.

CHAPTER 42

I wiggled my hairpin in the metal lock for the tenth time. The dime novel I'd read with the heroine picking a deadbolt using one of these had misled me. I sighed and tossed the mangled pin onto the floor.

The only other possible exit was the window—which was not only out of reach but had multiple steel bars. My family must've lived in fear of intruders to fortify this place like the Vatican Archives.

How long would I have to stay trapped in here? More terrifying, what would happen to me the moment the door reopened? If they believed I knew where Papa was, or was privy to the location of the fortune, I'd frustrate them on both accounts. Tension stretched between my shoulder blades. I didn't want to imagine the consequence for my ignorance.

Scratch. Scratch. Scratch.

The scraping was slight, barely audible above my thrashing heartbeat. It came from the direction of the hearth. I braved a few steps closer, and the noise intensified to a desperate clawing.

Someone needed help.

Crouching, I inspected the deep fireplace. Piles of ash darkened the pit, the walls framing it made of stone. Not the coarse limestone found on the exterior of the house, but smooth, rounded rocks like the ones found along a water bank.

But the constant scratching seemed to come from behind the right side of the hearth's wall. How could that be possible?

Unless …

I ducked into the belly of the massive fireplace. Once inside, I straightened to full height. I pressed my ear to the cold stone, the grating noise echoing, enlightening me to the brilliant deception.

There was a room behind the wall.

"Hello? Can you hear me?" I knocked and the scratching stopped.

Had I frightened them?

I searched for a point of entry, reaching as high as I could, skimming my hands back and forth. One of the rocks slid beneath my palm. I pushed it farther to the side until my fingers brushed a latch.

Uncertainty sparred with trepidation. Who would meet me on the other side of this door?

The feverish scraping had been replaced with chilling silence. But what if this room led me to an escape? With a determined breath, I pulled down the latch and shouldered the door back.

Quick as a blink, something scurried across my foot.

A rat!

My hand slapped over my mouth, stopping the rising shriek. The initial shock gave way to relief. With the anonymous scratcher being a strong-willed rodent, it gave hope of the possibility of an access to the outside world. Now to navigate through the darkness stretching before me. The familiar ache squeezed my chest. The shadows twisted like gnarled fingers.

I could do this. I had to do this.

God, you are my hiding place.

The prayer had become like a mending lyric to the broken melody in my heart. With one more gulp, I stepped into the blackness. The door clicked shut behind me, and I felt along the planked walls in search of a light. Something brushed my forehead and I jolted back. It felt too thick to be a spider web. With a rush of courage, I reached in front of me and my fingers wrapped around what felt like twine. With a gentle tug, light poured in from a single bulb.

Boasting a small table with a book on it, a couple of stools, and a corner shelf, the room was smaller than I would've imagined. A sweeping gaze of the walls and floors extinguished my hope.

No door or window.

Could there be another secret passage? My hands worked the grooves in the wooden panels. Using my hip, I budged the shelf, checking behind it. There were cobwebs and rat droppings, but no exit.

A dark circle in the upper right corner of the room pulled my attention. I dragged over the stool and stood on its seat. Wincing, I poked my fingers through the opening and felt damp soil. My shoulders sank. A rathole and nothing else. Unless I could shrink like Alice from that wonderland story the children at St. Paul's adored, then I was still trapped.

There was no other way out, and Gio could reappear at any time. I dug deep in my memory, trying to scrounge up anything that could help in this moment—Papa's letters, the dozens of newspaper articles I'd researched about this case, anything Rhett had said. Nothing rose to the surface in the quagmire of my mind.

I returned the stool beside the table, and my gaze lingered on the book atop the dusty surface. I picked up the crisp, leather binding and flipped it open.

Alcohol shipment, 50 cases whiskey

I rolled my eyes. It was my family's illegal record book. Of course they'd stored it in a secret hideout. My fingers flitted through a couple more pages until my eyes landed on something peculiar.

August 20, Bucklanders site, send Gio, collect 30 cases of opium.

Gio?

My brow rumpled. That man had never worked for Papa. He was Big Dante's nephew. And opium? Rhett had said my family hadn't been involved in drug dealing. I thumbed to another section. My eyes landed on Papa's name listed with my uncles. Just below was a sketched diagram of different areas of Pittsburgh, at the very bottom the words—*Take over Salvastano Territory by March.*

I gasped and almost fumbled the book. Could this belong … to Big Dante?

Why would it be here? In Papa's house?

My heart jolted in my chest even as my gaze flew to the door leading to my prison chamber. Was this why Gio had brought me here to this estate? Did he think I'd know where this was?

I thumbed over a couple more sheets. There were more logs of alcohol and drug deliveries. A few entries didn't make sense to me, but the next page had something I recognized. It was a record of the crime lords and bootleggers supposedly killed by my family. Beside each name was a date and two other words—Jimmy Townsend.

Jimmy Townsend!

If the rumors were true, he was a hitman. All his allegations had conveniently fallen through. Another mark of Pittsburgh's corrupt judicial system. I glanced over the list again. Could this be proof? I'd always hoped of Papa's innocence in the killings, but now it seemed I held evidence. Though with the courts as they were, did it even matter?

Still, I had to try.

A clicking noise sounded from outside. Someone was unlocking the deadbolt. I scurried to shut off the light. Maybe I'd have a fighting chance in the darkness.

"Catarina? Where the devil are you?" Gio's voice thundered through the partition, making dread forge my spine. "And how'd this rat get in here?"

Did he know about this secret room? He couldn't. Otherwise the ledger wouldn't be here. That gave me a slice of courage. But still … if I'd found this secret place, then so could he.

My hand fell to my side, my middle finger stubbing the stool. Pain zipped to my elbow, and I squeezed my eyes shut. I shook out the throb, and focused ahead where the fake wall would be.

"Well, lookie here." His shoes squeaked with his steps. "Footprints in the soot." The sound of banging followed. He was checking the walls.

My gut clenched. I had to do something. If I had George, I'd attack Gio the second he opened the panel. An idea sparked. I acted fast, hoping I had enough time.

A click sounded.

He'd found it.

"She better not have escaped." His voice was only above a grumble.

The door eased open. I lifted the stool over my shoulders and charged. I brought it down on Gio with a sickening thud.

He crumpled to the ground, unmoving. I grabbed the ledger, darted over Gio and zipped out of the hearth. Relief surged at the sight of the open basement door. With quiet strides, I approached the exit and peeked around. The hall was vacant. All I had to do was climb the steps and go through the side entry to freedom.

Heartbeat echoing in my throat, I dashed forward, passing the other rooms.

Soft singing made my feet skid. Someone was in the first room. I inclined my ear and my breath hitched at the feminine voice. I recognized the melody as familiar as my own face.

Mamma's lullaby.

My fingers unbolted the two locks, and I unhooked a chain. With one more glance around, I pushed open the door. The hinges creaked, and I cringed. I didn't know how long Gio would remain unconscious. Every second counted. I entered the room, so similar to the one I'd just escaped. A narrow beam of light angled through the high window, shining directly on a woman. I gasped. Not only because of the dainty wrists, bound behind the chair she sat upon, but because of the slender neck that revealed a familiar birthmark.

Between Mamma's lullaby and the matching skin discoloration, all the signs pointed to . . . "Delvina?"

Almond-shaped eyes squinted. "Catarina? Is that you?"

My thoughts clamored loud in my mind, yet I couldn't voice a single one. So I stared, taking in the slim figure that seemed to contrast my appearance in every way. Her bobbed hair, a few shades darker than mine, angled to frame her sharp chin. Her cheekbones were elegantly defined, curving toward a perfect nose sloping above an equally perfect mouth. The phony Delvina was beautiful, the real one was stunning.

The daze thinned, and I registered Delvina's words. She'd called me Catarina. As if she knew me already. How?

More questions surged, but answers would have to come later. I rushed to untie her. Needing both hands to work, I set the ledger on the floor.

Delvina stiffened. "Where'd you find that?"

"In a secret room." The muscles strained in my fingers, my arms, as I pulled at the rope, but the bindings were too taut to loosen. What could I do?

"Here." She kicked off her pumps. "Use the spiked heel to wedge into the tight part of the knot."

I snatched it from the floor and did as Delvina said. I dug the tip of the shoe into the coarse kink and applied pressure as I jerked. The knot slackened. "I think I got it." I tugged until the rope fell loose and winced at the raw abrasions left on my sister's skin.

Delvina stood, slipped on her shoes, and scooped up the ledger. "Well done." She pulled me in for a quick hug. "Now let's get out of here." Her long legs moved toward the door, and I followed. "How did you get in here unnoticed? Where's Pitrello?"

"I hit him on the head with a stool."

Dark red lips twitched into a smile then flattened. "Did you grab his gun?"

"No." Probably would've been the smart thing to do, but I hadn't thought of it.

Delvina wrapped a gentle hand around my elbow, leading me out into the hall. "The big lug took my pistol."

I wouldn't dare ask why this gorgeous, primly dressed woman packed a revolver.

"Stay close to me." She glanced over her shoulder at me. "We're going to sprint up the stairs and out the house. There's a residence about a mile and a half through the woods. That's our best bet."

I gave a tight nod and we raced up the steps. Once our soles hit the landing the other door swung open. A man filled the entryway.

Major Ford.

His slacked jaw revealed his surprise, but his rounded eyes narrowed on Delvina. "Why if it isn't the super sleuth. Ruth Talbert." He raised his gun. "Back to steal my heart again?" His gaze landed on the ledger in her hands. "Or after something more worth your while?"

CHAPTER 43

"Give me a moment or two." Hugo leaned against the weathered garden shed they currently used as a buffer between them and the main house located thirty yards away. His chest visibly heaved. His voice had sounded as fatigued as he looked.

Rhett withdrew his pocket watch. It'd taken them twenty minutes to journey here from where they'd parked in the woods, and Rhett had upheld Hugo the last half-section of the trek. At first Hugo had balked at the support, but Rhett had countered it'd take twice as long to reach Kate if he refused assistance. The man's shuffle rivaled the pace of an inch worm.

On the way, they'd discussed the plan. Hugo would enter the house in hopes to distract whoever was there. With the chaotic scene in motion, Rhett would sneak in using the passage—a secret tunnel installed by the paranoid Salvastano brother, Pedro—and search for Kate.

No more time could be wasted. He'd understood Hugo needed a quick break to regain strength, but every minute they dawdled could cost them. Could cost Kate. His blood burned in his veins. "Are you ready?"

Hugo clutched his chest. "Another second."

Rhett scanned the area. Pitrello's car, according to Peggy's description, was parked behind the garage. He hadn't spotted Major's Lincoln. Maybe he was across town still waiting for Rhett. He tightened his grip on his gun and glanced at Hugo's bare hand. "I think you should be armed."

"I don't care what happens to me. I've made peace with God." His countenance softened. "Just get them both to safety."

Wait. "Both?" This was the second time Hugo had said that word, first in Rhett's office, which he'd chalked up as a mistake, and now.

Hugo blinked at him as if the answer was obvious. "Catarina and Delvina."

"Delvina." Rhett repeated, letting it sink in. "She's inside, too?" Would've been nice to have known this before.

"That's how I knew Catarina was in danger. Vinny has been trailing Major for a while. Last night, she'd gone to shadow him, and hasn't contacted me since. He got to her just as he got Catarina." His eyes filled with sorrow. "All that's left of my world is within those walls."

Rhett could relate. He'd lost his foundation the day his father had died. Now, in the same house, he stood to lose his universe. He had to get to her. And apparently find Delvina, too. "Why was she trailing Major?" Rhett edged along the shed wall and cast a glance at the house. All seemed clear. It was time to act.

"She's an investigator." Hugo straightened. "The one I was telling you about."

Rhett digested the information as though swallowing rocks. Delvina was the one Hugo had been referring to earlier? The detective who'd schmoozed Major and had stolen the ledger? "How?"

"Does Ruth Talbert mean anything to you?"

Rhett's jaw slacked. Ruth Talbert—with her sleek black hair, curvy figure, and low smoky voice—had been the only woman Major had taken a serious liking to. Enough to have introduced her to Rhett. Then as quickly as the relationship had started, she'd dropped him. She'd also been the one who'd recommended Rhett's services to Frank Conrad only days before the first "S" card had been delivered. Coincidence?

Realization dawned. "Ruth, I mean, Delvina left the card at the KDKA station."

Hugo nodded. "We didn't know Catarina was in Pittsburgh. Not until we heard someone named Kate Chamberlin sing Amelia's lullaby." His voice grew soft. "Vinny arranged everything as best she could while keeping her cover. Catarina didn't know what she was up against, so we figured a way to get you in the picture for her protection."

And that *way* was through the power of suggestion with Frank Conrad and then placing the 'fatal' "S" card in Kate's KDKA mailbox. Then the scrawled message *Watch Delvina*. It'd been her actual signature. "Delvina broke into Kate's apartment and left the second card."

"Only because you were hot on her heels. Vinny intended to talk to Catarina that night, but you interrupted. So she warned her to be careful."

Rhett shook his head. When one question was answered, another took its place, but they'd already lingered here longer than he was comfortable with. "Time's up, old man. We have to get moving."

Hugo straightened his jacket and dusted the front of his trousers as if he was making a regular house call and not about to put his neck on the line. "Hopefully I'll see you soon, Radish Nose."

Rhett smirked despite the intense moment. "If we get out of this alive, I'll give you a code name just as ridiculous."

Something sparked in Hugo's dull eyes. "Looking forward to it." He turned on his heel and hobbled toward the house.

Rhett prayed the aged crime boss wouldn't get shot at initial sighting. At least he had the ledger as a bargaining chip. Major wouldn't dispose of Hugo without first retrieving the incriminating evidence.

With one last glance at Hugo, he opened the garden shed and ducked inside. The wheelbarrow Hugo had told him about stood in the corner. He moved it out of the way and lifted the dirt-colored mat, finding the trap door. Rhett lifted the hatch and a loamy odor assaulted him. A flashlight nestled between a lantern and a rusty spade on a shelf to his left. He snatched it, toggled the switch, and bathed the entrance of the tunnel in a soft, golden glow. With that, he descended the earthen ramp. Wooden beams ran the length of the underground passageway, calming his hesitation about being trapped beneath the surface. He raced the stretch of soil, passing a rat carcass and a broken moonshine jug.

Within twenty paces he was at a door. According to Hugo, this secret entrance was located in the side of the basement fireplace. Rhett had to hand it to the late Pedro Salvastano, he seemed to incorporate every trick in the book when it came to avoiding raids. Too bad all these shenanigans hadn't been able to help him when he'd really needed it.

But it served a purpose today, and Rhett was thankful.

Now to get his girl. And her sister.

He located the handle with ease and cracked open the door. Something blocked the motion. Was it a log? Or the hearth grate? Rhett shouldered into the rough plank, widening the expanse another two feet, enough for him to slip his form through.

Metal jammed into his side.

A gun.

Rhett stood almost nose to nose with Gio Pitrello. The man had a grotesque knot protruding from his right temple and an even uglier look in his eyes. "Drop your weapon, Jennings."

CHAPTER 44

Major trained his weapon on Delvina as if he suspected her opposition. The coldness between them hinted at an interesting history. He motioned me and my sister into another room.

With raised ceilings and arched entryways, the massive space reminded me of luxurious villas in Naples, but even touches of my homeland couldn't mask the sinister bite in the air.

The furniture was destroyed like my apartment. Canvas paintings sliced through, their wooden frames bowed and broken. Several lamps had been smashed, causing me to be careful where I stepped. Books were scattered along the marble floor, the spines warped or torn. Tall bookcases stretched across the side wall, my gaze crawling over the ornate mahogany that had been dented and scored. Were there any hidden rooms behind those shelved panels? So caught up on thoughts of escaping, I nearly tripped over an iron sconce.

Major snatched the ledger from Delvina and cinched it between his arm and side. "Now that I have this back, there's no need to keep you two." He spared me a glance. "Kate, I've nothing against you, but I can't take the risk."

I peered into his eyes. At the shades of evil in those onyx depths. I'd fought shadows all my life, but his darkness came from within. And for that, I felt sorry for him.

Major thumbed back the gun's hammer and his lips peeled back in a wicked smile directed at my sister. "You first, my darling."

Delvina's chin notched higher, her clipped dark hair sliding along her jaw. "What if I said there's other evidence against you. Proof you killed Pedro and Lorenzo Salvastano. As well as your own partner." Her rich voice was commanding, her poise unflinching. "The world will soon know who Big Dante really is. Not some hulking genius, but a puny old man who doesn't know how to kiss a wom—"

"Shut up!" Spittle shot through the air. "You have nothing."

I slid my hand into my sister's, and Delvina gave a gentle squeeze to my fingers, reassuring. My mind finally processed the jumble of words. Had Delvina just said Major was Big Dante? The phantom mobster was the same man who'd been the leader of the department bent on taking down such crime lords?

His outrage only seemed to embolden Delvina, for she took a step toward him. "The evidence is in my Papa's hands."

I gasped. Delvina had been in contact with our father? That would mean he was alive! Or … she could be bluffing. It was possible she'd made it all up to stall Major from pulling the trigger.

"You're lying." Major's ear lobes reddened. "Hugo's dead. I shot him."

"Yet I got away." A rusty voice sliced through the chaos.

Papa—my Papa!—stood in the corner entryway. Like when my aching eyes had focused on him after being rescued from under the debris after the earthquake, the rush of emotions overwhelmed me.

He was here. Alive. Yet as quick as my heart soared, it plummeted. Age had laid a silvering finger on his hair, had etched deep lines into his face, but he seemed far weaker for a man only sixty-five years of age.

Had he not recovered from the gunshot wound Major had morbidly boasted of?

Papa's once strapping frame was now skeletal. But despite the frailty of figure, there was a strength to his demeanor. The familiar confidence that had once made me believe he'd fight monsters on my behalf.

Our gazes met, and my eyes burned with tears. There was so much to say.

"Hugo." Major swung around, directing his gun on Papa. "Your arrival just made my life easier."

Delvina charged Major from behind, tackling him, sending them both to the ground. The ledger slipped from under his arm. The gun clattered to the floor. They scrambled for it, reaching. Major's hand knocked the butt of the pistol, and it slid beneath the bookcase.

He cursed and reached for Delvina. She dodged his grasp.

"Well, well. Looks like we're late to the party." Gio stood near the stairwell, his revolver pressed to ... Rhett's temple.

A sharp breath rammed my chest. Rhett's azure gaze collided with mine, a mixture of concern and regret. His pain-filled stare inched over me as if making certain I was unharmed.

I mouthed. "I'm okay." But I wasn't. Because the sole thing I'd dreaded all this time had happened—I'd put him in danger. How had he figured out I was in trouble? Known I'd been taken here?

"Stand by Hugo, Jennings." Gio shoved Rhett's shoulder. "But hands up and no funny business or I'll shoot your *sister*." He sent me a scathing look. "Nice racket you had going. Too bad you can't lie your way out of this one."

Jaw hardening, Rhett stepped beside Papa. The two men exchanged looks, and something passed between them. Rhett didn't seem at all shocked by Papa's presence. Had Rhett seen Papa before this moment? Why had he—

"Everhett." Major looked as confused as I felt. "What are you doing here?"

"I didn't want to believe it." His large hands clenched at his side. "All this time, it was you who killed him." His scolding held traces of hurt.

The older man expelled a weary sigh and scooped up the ledger. "I never meant for you to be caught up in this, son."

"Don't call me that." Rhett's voice boomed. "Let them go, Major. It's not worth it."

"But it is. Your father was a good man, but he had nothing. He had to marry your mother to get a shiny dime in his pocket. I have all the money and power I want. And women too." His tone soured, and he glared at Delvina. "Just have to be careful which ones I pick."

"Ha! Don't flatter yourself. I only went after you to get the goods on your dealings." She inched toward me.

"Take another step." Gio trained the gun on her. "And you get a nice bullet in your pretty head." He smirked despite his green-ish complexion and ugly bump on his head.

"Just do what needs done, Gio." Major urged. "But wait until I leave the room." He tossed Rhett a disappointed look. "This one hurts." With a dark scowl, he started toward the exit nearest to Papa.

"And here I thought you a smarter man than that, Pitrello." Rhett shook his head as in disbelief. "Here's your chance and you're bowing out like a coward."

"A coward?" Gio's brow raised and he now aimed at Rhett. "I'm the one holding the gun."

"But not the power."

His words made Major halt beneath the archway.

Gio thumbed back the hammer. "I have the power to kill you."

I bit the inside of my cheek. Provoking the man with the pistol didn't seem the wisest thing to do.

But Rhett seemed unfazed. "You have the golden opportunity to take control of Big Dante's empire. How easy it'd be to shoot Major and blame it on the Salvastanos." He motioned at Papa. "Since no one else but you knows or has seen Big Dante, you can keep the gig going. Why take a lousy cut when you can have it all?"

A vein bulged in Major's forehead. "That's enough, Everhett."

Rhett matched his glare. "If you could kill my father and blame it on Hugo. Then so could Pitrello. Everyone would believe the dirty crime boss did it."

Only Rhett would think to pit these men against each other. But whether the result would work in our escape? I could only pray.

"Shoot him first." Major's face registered anguish. "He's talking madness."

"Is he?" Gio hissed. "If this racket gets investigated by state, who's gonna be taking the hit? Me. Because you cleverly made me the face of the outfit while you hide and rake in the dough."

"I manage everything. Everything." Major seethed. "You stick to doing your job."

While the two men argued, Rhett toed the iron sconce toward him. I held my breath, hoping the metal wouldn't scrape against the floor.

Gio puffed out his chest. "You're not in any place to give orders, Uncle." He spat out the last word as if it were rancid meat.

"Or what?" Major scoffed. "You'll shoot me, Gio?"

Delvina was distracted by something out the window. Papa watched Major and Gio intently. Rhett also held his gaze on the men as he worked the candlestick closer.

"I've done your dirty work long enough, old man." He pointed the weapon at Major. "It's time I give myself a promotion."

Rhett scooped up the sconce, launched it at the gunmen, but Gio spotted the movement and swung his aim on him.

Papa lunged in front of Rhett.

The sconce struck Gio on the side of the head even as a shot pierced the air.

CHAPTER 45

The disturbing sound of steel ripping flesh throttled the air from Rhett's chest. But ... he hadn't been hit. The bullet marked for him lodged in Hugo Salvastano.

Hugo's weak frame crumpled to the floor.

Gio bellowed in pain. The sconce had struck his raised knot, making him double over, the gun hanging dangerously from his index finger.

Before Rhett could move, Delvina careened toward Gio with a guttural cry. She swiped the pistol from his loose grip, stilling Major from advancing.

Kate rushed to Hugo, sinking to her knees beside him, silent tears streaming her face.

Delvina glanced at her father. Her eyes glazed with fury. Her aim snapped to Major, and she curled her finger around the trigger. "You destroyed my family. You can burn in—"

"No." Hugo's fading voice stalled Delvina's words, though her glare remained channeled on Major. "No, child. Good … wins out."

His gurgled breathing was the only noise against the chilling silence.

Good wins out.

A shuffling noise came from the hall.

"David." Rhett breathed a sigh of relief as his partner and two other men he recognized as state agents barged into the room, revolvers raised.

"Got your note, Jennings." David and two other men barged into the room, revolvers raised. "Rounded up help along the way."

Delvina seemed miffed to turn over control, but Rhett couldn't be more appreciative. Operating on the state level was the only way to secure fair justice for Major and Gio. The two crestfallen mobsters were cuffed and led out. Major's eyes met his, and that familiar beast of bitterness stalked Rhett's chest. But he wouldn't give it a home in his heart this time. Rhett shook his head and turned to help Hugo.

Kate grabbed her skirt's hem, twisting and pulling. "I have to stop the bleeding." A sob wracked her desperate tone.

He lowered beside her and lifted the lapel of Hugo's jacket. His white shirt was stained crimson, the tinny odor of blood overpowering. The bullet entry hole was in the right side of his chest cavity.

Rhett had seen this kind of injury in the war and in his years on the force. Able-bodied men had barely survived. Hugo had lost a lot of blood, and with his previous weakened state? It could only be minutes.

Hugo's hooded gaze fixed on him, unmoving. "Radish Nose." Such a foolish term shouldn't make Rhett's heart choke with emotion. "I leave you with—" He coughed. "With what should've been my assignment."

Taking care of Kate.

"It's my honor, sir." And blast it all, a tear squeezed from his eye. It should've been Rhett lying here, fading into death. For all those punishing months he'd stoked his burning hatred for Hugo by picturing the man's demise. And now, Rhett was witnessing it, and wished with every part of his soul he could stop it all.

Hugo had taken Rhett's bullet.

The man he'd wanted to face harsh judgement was the same who granted him mercy.

Kate sucked in air, and pressed Hugo's age-spotted hand to her tearstained face. "We'll get you help, Papa." She jerked to move, but Hugo curled his fingers around hers.

"Stay." His right eye twitched, and his teeth chattered. "I just … want to look at you."

Panic tightened her features. "But—"

Rhett stretched an arm around her waist, anchoring her. Her shuddered sobs matched the heave of her shoulders, and he tightened his hold. Leaning toward her, he whispered into her hair. "The shot's fatal. He doesn't have much time left."

Papa was dying.

This man had witnessed my entrance into the world, and now I was watching him leave it. The walls of my soul tore wider with each of his labored breaths, leaving an aching cavern of emptiness.

Delvina stooped beside Papa, opposite of Rhett and I, and peered at him through slits of narrowed eyes. From her flaring nostrils to her locked jaw, my sister looked every bit rage-consumed. But then, in a swift movement, she leaned over, pressed a kiss to Papa's dewy forehead, and bolted from the room.

I called after her, but Papa raised a shaky hand. "She grieves differently than you."

We shouldn't be grieving at all. I should be squeezing him in an embrace, not watching his bloody frame writhe in pain. "It isn't fair, Papa." Tears gathered on my lashes, circular specks blurring my vision. Rhett stroked my back in a soothing rhythm, but I was far from calm.

"I just found you again." At once, I was six, watching him leave. Only this loss was worse. Back then, I foolishly believed I'd see him soon. That he'd return to me before even my tenth birthday. But this was the first time I'd set eyes on him since our parting seventeen years ago. "We've been separated so long."

"No, piccolo topo."

Little mouse.

His left arm bent at the elbow, and his hand clambered over his heart. "You've been ... right here." His dull gaze held mine. "Like last time, no goodbyes."

The day he'd sailed, he'd refused to bid me farewell.

Papa's jaw wobbled. "Because ..."

"I'll see you again." I finished for him, repeating the last thing he'd said to me on Naples' shores all those years ago. Now those would be his last words to me on this earth. But would I really see him again? Though he wasn't a murderer, he'd still lived a life of sin.

As if reading my apprehension, Rhett pulled close. "He told me earlier he was right with God."

His words uncorked another heart basin of tears. Only these were of relief and peace.

Rhett pressed a handkerchief into my palm. No doubt intended for my drippy nose and soggy eyes, but instead I wiped the sweat from Papa's brow.

His blinks were getting longer, his breaths clogging with more fluid.

"*Ti voglio bene*, Papà." *I love you.* My accented voice cracked and Rhett tugged me close to him.

The rise and fall of Papa's chest lessened, his eyes screwing shut. His lips moved, and I leaned forward, not wanting to miss anything if he chose to speak.

"Share your flowing hair ..." He sputtered blood. "With Vinny."

And then he was gone.

CHAPTER 46

I searched the vast estate for Delvina and found her slouched on a chair in a breakfast nook off the kitchen. With measured steps, I approached my sister and placed Major's ledger on the dust-layered tabletop. David and the state agents hadn't known to grab the incriminating book, so I determined not to let it escape my sight.

I placed a hand on Delvina's slender shoulder. "Rhett drove to the neighbor's to call the coroner." The day I'd become reunited with Papa, was to be the same he'd been torn from me again. I'd lost a father yet gained a sister. There was beauty even in sorrow.

"You must think I'm weak." Brow set low, Delvina peered out the window overlooking the wooded grounds. "Because I didn't stay and watch him die."

I claimed the seat beside her. "Not at all." Perhaps my sister had been wiser, because my mind would forever hold the image of the anguish in his eyes, the copious amount of blood. But then I would've missed the conviction in his voice when he'd spoken of seeing me again.

The sweeping peace that eased his twisted features when he'd surrendered to death ... well, more like, life. For he'd entered a place where pain didn't exist, only a freedom beyond anything I could imagine.

The afternoon sunlight slanted against my sister's face, making her high cheekbones more pronounced. "He told me he searched for me for years." Long lashes dipped then raised, and her ebony gaze was as sad as it was unfocused. "But I was the one who found him."

I remained silent, hoping my sister would share more.

"I knew I was adopted, but I wasn't told about my birthparents. I was three when I came to America." Her voice held no trace of the accent I had strained to conceal these past months. "I don't recall much from before that."

"But you remembered Mamma's song." And for me to have heard the lullaby in a voice other than my own had been surreal, beautiful, and no doubt the work of God because if Delvina hadn't been singing, I wouldn't have found her.

"Yes." Her lips tipped in a ghost of a smile. "But when I try to imagine their faces, it's a blur."

I had spent only six years with my parents, but I was thankful I had distinct memories that enabled me to conjure their likeness in my mind.

"My adoptive parents hid a letter from them. I found it when I was seventeen." She carved a finger through the dust on the tabletop. "They explained why I was given up, about the famine in Italy, and how they were scared I wouldn't survive. They included a photograph and signed their names."

If Delvina only knew the pain our parents had suffered. "Mamma would cry often for you. You were very much loved."

She angled away. "I thought they were still in Italy. It wasn't until I saw Papa's name in the papers. You can imagine how surprised I was to find him not only in America, but a notorious bootlegger."

I didn't have to imagine, I knew. I'd experienced the same devastating shock upon discovering Papa's activities. "I haven't seen Papa since I was six. He left me behind in Italy and came here to his brothers. His letters never said anything about his wayward life."

"So we both grew up without our parents." Delvina's eyes connected with mine. "You turned out well, Catarina."

"Only because God had His hand on me." I leaned forward. "And it looks like He's been watching over you as well."

Delvina's pinched lips was her only response.

"When did you finally contact Papa?" There were so many holes in this story, and my sister seemed the only one who could patch them.

"When the Salvastano name began being associated with murder." She straightened and the wooden chair creaked with her movement. "I left New York and came here. The truth was all I was after."

Delvina and I were alike in that respect. I hunted through KDKA transcripts looking for clues, and my sister took a bolder approach. Yet in the end, our pursuits had brought us here, together

"I trailed Papa without his knowledge."

I blinked. "You didn't tell him who you were?"

Delvina shook her head. "I didn't even let him see me. If he indeed was a murderer, I wanted nothing to do with him." She tapped her moon-manicured fingers on the grimy table. "But it turned out I wasn't the only one following him. Gio Pitrello hung around, too. It struck me funny, so I started shadowing him."

"And he led you to Major." I put it together.

"Precisely." She gave a definite nod. "It didn't take long for me to realize that Major was leading a double life. I just needed proof that he was Big Dante. So I got real personal with him using the name Ruth Talbert."

I shuddered. I had done my fair share of pretending, even claiming the false identity. But to place myself in that kind of danger? So close to such a man? That was another level of courage.

"Major hid his criminal secret with an impressive finesse. But I learned his habits," Delvina continued. "Discovered he went to the recreation center on Saturday mornings. That's when I broke into his house and found that." She motioned to Major's ledger. "Knowing I had the goods, I approached Papa. I revealed who I was and the knowledge I possessed."

I sat in amazement at my sister's bravery. Here I was hiding from the bad guys and Delvina was cozying up to them to get information. "How did Papa respond?"

"He cried." She looked away as if she didn't want me to read her emotion. "Then told me he would take care of it from now on, and to get as far away from Major as I could. Then he went to Commissioner Jennings."

Rhett's father.

Papa and the commissioner had not been rivals, but actually working together? How awful it must've been for Rhett's father to find out his partner and best friend had betrayed him. Had forsaken the law he'd sworn to uphold.

"They didn't get far in their scheming. Major realized his ledger was missing and it didn't escape him that I left him around the same time." She flicked the book with a look of disdain. "He didn't know I was Hugo's daughter, but I think he suspected I worked for the Salvastanos."

My gut clenched.

"Major came to this house and found the commissioner here. Then the shooting happened."

"But Papa escaped." Father had been spared only to be brought to his death nine months later.

"Yeah, but Major shot him in the shoulder." Delvina's tone cooled. "Papa refused to go to the hospital in fear of being arrested. I was able to dig the bullet out. He seemed to be okay for a while." Her gaze fell to the floor. "But then he battled infection."

That explained his yellowed complexion and weakness. Poor Papa. What misery he'd known in his lifetime.

"I found him a place to stay in an elderly woman's basement. She needed income and Papa needed a place to hide."

Papa had remained in Pittsburgh this entire time. If only I could've been able to see him sooner. Could all this have ended differently?

"I shadowed Major last night, and this time he caught me. I didn't check in with Papa, and he put two and two together. So Papa emerged from hiding and sought out your flame."

"And I almost plugged him." Rhett strode into the room, his intense gaze on me. "Then he said something that earned my trust and opened my eyes to see what was really going on." He pressed a kiss to my head. "Nice to see you again, Ruth." He extended a hand toward Delvina.

She shook it with a sheepish expression. "Um, about that, I—"

Rhett's friendly smile put her at ease. "Hugo explained it all. You completely fooled me. Nicely done."

Of course he would've met her since she'd been seeing Major. How ironic that Rhett had known Delvina before me. He pulled a chair from under the table and straddled it. "The coroner is on his way."

Delvina's shoulders slumped. "What are we going to do now?"

Rhett hooked his foot on the rung of my seat, pulling my chair closer and wrapping an arm around me. "The state's the best option. Let's just pray things don't get tainted before they get a chance to review the case."

Delvina let out a dry laugh. "Pray? Why do you think I never came forward, even with this evidence?" She sliced a finger through the air, pointing at the ledger. "Everything is corrupt. There's no chance this will get a fair shake."

"But the state operates differently." Rhett's tone was emphatic. "The governor's sent—"

"Soon as the police and city officials get knowledge of what happened, the truth will be twisted, and we'll be back where we started from." Delvina huffed a lock of hair from her face. "Major works with and controls most of the law around here."

I snatched the ledger, an idea taking form. "Where's David taking Gio and Major? Can you get ahold of him?"

"To the state station across the river." Rhett jerked his thumb to the left, where the Ohio cut through the city. "Those agents know what's on the line. They'll be discreet."

"Not good enough." Delvina grumbled. "Word of what happened here is going to get out sooner or later."

"Then let's be the ones to tell it before anyone else."

Both Rhett and Delvina looked at me with curious expressions.

With rushed words, I explained my plan. "But if this is going to work, we need to act fast."

"You two go." Delvina waved a hand. "I'll stay and wait for the coroner."

I stood, but the sadness in my sister's eyes made me pause. "You should know." I waited for Delvina to look my way. "Your name was his last word before he passed on."

Her fingers went to her birthmark, tracing along the dark raised ridges, as if gleaning comfort from the blemish. "What did he say?"

Should I even mention that awkward sentence he'd uttered? Being so close to death, his reasoning had probably waned, but it didn't forfeit the fact that my sister had been on his mind. "He said, share your flowing hair with Vinny." I winced at its absurdity. "I know it sounds ridiculous, but—"

Delvina paled. "You have it?"

I grabbed a clump of my long, unbound locks, my mind searching for any significance. "I'm not sure what you mean."

"The Flowing Hair." Delvina stood and braced both hands on my shoulders. "I've been looking for it everywhere. Do you have it? Do you have the coin?"

The image popped like a firecracker in my mind. The silver dollar. The one side of the coin displayed a woman with ... flowing hair. "I do. It was tucked in Papa's last letter."

Delvina sucked in so much air, I was surprised her lungs didn't burst.

Rhett palmed the back of his neck, confusion marking his brow. "Is that important?"

"That's one of the first minted coins after the Revolutionary War. There's not many in circulation." She let out a disbelieving laugh. "And here you had it the entire time."

Rhett and I exchanged looks.

Delvina stepped back and assessed us with a longsuffering countenance. "That coin is worth a fortune."

CHAPTER 47

I slid my eyes closed, bracing myself for the most important performance of my life—the moment I'd tell the world who I was. All the oxygen in the room didn't seem enough to fill the breathless void in my chest. Maybe because there were holes in my being. Papa's departure from this earth had left a gaping chasm I'd prayed God himself would fill.

Robert had fled Studio B in search of fresh bolts to secure the wobbly microphone, leaving me alone with Rhett.

Before I could speak, I was swept in his powerful embrace. His arms wrapped around me in a fierce, protective manner that left me short of breath once again. I pressed my cheek against his chest, stabling my emotions for what was to come.

He eased back to peer into my face. "Are you okay?"

"No." I shook my head and buried my face into his suit jacket. "But I will be." Someday the anguish would lessen, the pain would subside. But today the devastation was too fresh. I'd been kidnapped, held at gunpoint. The lives of the men I loved had been threatened. One survived, the other hadn't. I'd glimpsed undiluted hatred, but then … good won out.

Death might have stopped Papa's heart, but it hadn't stolen his spirit. For he now walked the paths of angels.

Rhett pulled away, and I lifted my head, meeting his gentle gaze. His chin dipped, slow and careful. I expected his mouth to claim mine, but instead his hand raised to caress my cheek. "I have some news. I was going to wait until later, but thought it might bring you some relief."

My brows raised.

"David went to the court of records and found Charlie's family. He has an aunt and uncle that lives two counties over."

My eyes stung with fresh tears. "Has he made contact with them?"

Rhett nodded. "They had no idea Charlie was being mistreated. His father broke contact with them after Charlie's mother passed. They want guardianship and are willing to fight for him." He stroked my hair, even as I buried my face into his chest, overcome. "The family courts aren't corrupt like all the others. It should be easy to prove Jack Davenport's negligence."

Charlie had family. Relatives that would see to it that he was safe.

"Kate?"

I angled my face toward Rhett and saw the worry marking his features, making me want to press a fingertip to smooth the creases in his brow.

His gaze flicked to the microphone then back to me. "You don't have to go through with this."

I took a stabling breath. "It's the best way." In a few minutes, I would share the truth to the world before crooked police and city officials could twist it.

KDKA would get the exclusive, and I would honor my family by exposing the real story.

Rhett's hands sunk into my hair. "Kate, by speaking out everyone will know your identity. There's no going back after this."

The secret I'd strove to conceal would be voiced over the airwaves. By me. No doubt those close to me, like Peggy, would feel betrayed. Though my family was innocent of murder, others may show contempt for their blatant crimes.

But my worth didn't come from man's approval.

My Father God loved me with a devotion that held no conditions. He didn't see me as a Chamberlin, or even as a Salvastano. He viewed me as His.

"There's concrete evidence in that ledger." Rhett had discovered what Papa and Delvina hadn't been able to decipher—that Major Ford had been using abandoned government warehouses to store alcohol and drugs. Rhett had even been able to determine the locations. "State agents have been sent out to verify. That's enough to bring them down, Kate. You don't need to speak out."

"But I do." I stood a little taller and placed my hand over Rhett's which still cupped my jaw. "I'm ready to stop hiding. I owe it to my family. To your father."

"And to yourself." His eyes were alight with tenderness. "Let them see the real you. The woman I love."

His words stitched the broken pieces of my heart.

Though I'd felt it in his touch, seen it in his gaze, I now heard from his perfect lips—he loved me. Before I could respond with a declaration of my own, his mouth met mine with an affirmation of the words he'd just spoken.

This day had been tragic and beautiful. Terrifying and peaceful. Rhett held me against him, causing thankfulness to sweep in like an ocean's tide, rhythmic and constant. I didn't deserve his affection but I'd be a fool to refuse it. Just like God's love. I could never earn such a valuable gift, but I'd cling to it with every part of my being.

I wrapped my hands around Rhett's neck and answered his devotion with a kiss of my own. A tear slid between us, and I couldn't be sure if it was mine or his. Either way, our hearts were fused with the strongest bond, the most powerful force.

A throat cleared and I jolted.

Frank Conrad stood yards away. Lips twitching as if fighting a smile, he glanced at his watch and then to me. "Studio A ends their broadcast in a couple minutes. It's not too late to cancel." He took a step farther into the room "I pushed back some segments so you can have prime airtime, but I can easily adjust." His dark brow lowered, his gaze steady as if searching for any signs of my reluctance. "As much as this is a whopper of a story for the station, your wellbeing is more important."

I pecked his cheek, grateful for the man who'd been like a second father to me, always looking out for my welfare. "Thank you. For everything. But I need to do this." This story had to go to the people first. The city of Pittsburgh deserved the truth. And standing up to the corruption might embolden others to step forward.

Robert scampered into the room and tended to the microphone. Harold Arlin joined us, and fresh nerves nipped at my resolve. Having 'The Voice of America' interview me was daunting, but the famous broadcaster gave me a wide grin of encouragement.

"I jotted a few questions down." Harold raised a single sheet of paper. "But I'm mostly going to let you talk."

Rhett grabbed my hand, lacing our fingers. While our kiss could be continued later, there were some things that shouldn't wait. I lifted on the balls of my feet, reaching his ear. "I love you, Rhett Jennings."

His eyes warmed and his gaze dipped to my lips. We had a lifetime ahead of us to share kisses and much more.

The sound director gave the signal, and Harold opened his segment with his standard verbiage.

"Now without any more delay." Harold put in. "We have breaking news on a case very important to this Steel City. To share further, let me introduce to you, KDKA's own, Kate Chamberlin.

This was it. The moment I'd avoided since arriving in Pittsburgh had come, and this time, I welcomed it. Determination shoved fear aside, and I leaned forward to that familiar microphone. "My name is Catarina Salvastano. And I'm a mobster's daughter."

The End

AUTHOR'S NOTES

I've said this before and will probably say this for every book, but I totally love writing this section. It's the place I get to nerd out and divulge all the historical truths that are threaded throughout the story.

Let's first talk about the corruption that was so rampant during this era in the Steel City. When the subject of the prohibition is brought up, most people's minds go immediately to cities like New York and Chicago. While those cities were most certainly notable during the 'Roarin' 20s', Pittsburgh was just as corrupt, being once known as "the wettest city in a dry nation". The term *speakeasy* actually originated in Pittsburgh by a saloon owner, who ran an unlicensed bar in the 1880s, reprimanding rowdy customers to "speak easy."

Because of the flood of immigrants who never parted from their alcohol, Pittsburgh was a drinking city before, during, and after the passing of the Volstead Act. The prohibition was declared a national law, but that didn't prevent the rise of speakeasies invading the city. Crime bosses and bootleggers unashamedly bribed city officials and police forces in order to run their empires. Prohibition was only acknowledged on paper because there were over 500 speakeasies threaded throughout the Pittsburgh, ranging from seedy shacks which served flavored wood ethanol to swanky establishments complete with roulette tables and slot machines.

Acquiring alcohol in Pittsburgh was easily accomplished and usually without any repercussions. Raids of speakeasies were occasionally conducted and only when enforced on a state level.

KDKA in Pittsburgh was the world's first commercial broadcasting station. The first air date was November 2, 1920 to which the broadcaster announced the presidential election results between Warren G. Harding and James Cox. (This was also the very first election where women had the right to vote!)

This station had many of the "firsts" in the history of broadcasting. It was the first to broadcast a live major league baseball game, boxing match, and college football game. The station itself was located on the eighth floor of the Westinghouse Plant in East Pittsburgh. I had so much fun including actual people in the list of side characters. Frank Conrad was the assistant chief engineer at Westinghouse. He is credited with coining the term "broadcast" and is also responsible for the initial success of KDKA. H.P Davis was the vice president of the Westinghouse corporation and was heavily involved with KDKA. Harold Arlin was referred to the "Voice of America" because his broadcasts were heard all over the nation. He did indeed interview George "Babe" Ruth and the baseball icon did have mic fright when he went "on air." So much so, that Arlin grabbed the answers to the interview questions and read them aloud. Listeners had no idea that it was Arlin speaking and not Babe Ruth.

For the actual studio, I could only find three pictures which I used as guides and employed artistic license for the rest. For acoustic reasons, cloth draped the ceiling and the walls. The microphone was cylinder shaped and therefore nicknamed a "tomato can". During

KDKA's infancy, Westinghouse employees doubled as broadcasters and musicians.

The black cable attached to a shabby shack on the roof of Building K was, indeed, where it all began. So I had to include a scene where Kate ties the birth of the dream of radio with the hopes of resurrecting her own dreams.

The earthquake that ripped apart Kate's family was an actual event. The Calabria earthquake struck on December 28, 1908 at 5:02 am. It lasted for more than twenty seconds and was a 7.7 on the Richter scale. There were more than 80,000 casualties. Through my research, I discovered there were children who miraculously survived being trapped beneath debris for days. After that, many Italians migrated to America. A famine hit Italy in 1898 which caused a nationwide hunger, and so I used this historical event as the fictional catalyst for Delvina being sent to America.

The Liberty Tunnels congestion actually happened. When the Pittsburgh Street Railway Company declared a strike, commuters were forced to utilize their own vehicles which resulted in congestion in the newly opened, unventilated Liberty Tunnels on May 10, 1924. Many had passed out due to carbon monoxide fumes, but thankfully there were no casualties.

One final issue I'd like to point out is that of child labor. Sadly, a case like Charlie's was not out of the ordinary. Pittsburgh factories, mills, and mines employed children, often giving them the most dangerous jobs. Child labor was such a problem that, in 1905, regulations were set that children had to be at least fourteen to work in plants and mills. But there were many cases where parents falsified birth certificates so their younger children could work. I'm grateful we now have laws in place to protect our children.

ACKNOWLEDGMENTS

This writing journey is by no means a solo effort. I'm so grateful for those who've walked beside me, encouraged me, finger-fed me Hershey's kisses. The last one hasn't actually happened, but I wouldn't object if my husband felt inclined.

A huge thanks to my agent, Julie Gwinn, who has been such an amazing help getting this story (and all my other stories!) to publication. I super appreciate all the ways you've bolstered my confidence and championed my work. Also, thank you for always putting up with my extreme usage of emojis and exclamation points in my texts. To the team at Ally Publishing, thank you!

Rebekah Millet, I will forever mention you in every acknowledgement section of every book. You're not only my writing person, but the co-founder of our "over-thinker and pop-tart enthusiast" club (which isn't a legit club but if it was, we'd totally rock it), and the greatest friend/sister that a person could ever ask for. Thank you for always being there. Janyre Tromp and Janine Rosche, thank you for all our chats. You ladies are amazing and I'm grateful to call you friends. Abbi Hart and Ashley Johnson, you two have been such a beautiful encouragement to me. Thank you for all you do in the world of Christian fiction! Amy Watson, Crissy Loughridge, Joy Tiffany – Proverbs 17:17. Thank you for being you. Natalie Walters your kindness will always be celebrated here in this section. Thank you.

To my family, there's just not enough words to express how grateful I am for you. You're my support system, my cheerleaders, my people. Finally, to Jesus. Your message is life to me, and I'm thankful for the opportunity to share it through story.